Berkley Prime Crime Books by Charlaine Harris

SWEET AND DEADLY
A SECRET RAGE

The Aurora Teagarden Mysteries

REAL MURDERS
A BONE TO PICK
THREE BEDROOMS, ONE
CORPSE
THE JULIUS HOUSE

DEAD OVER HEELS
A FOOL AND HIS HONEY
LAST SCENE ALIVE
POPPY DONE TO DEATH

The Harper Connelly Mysteries

GRAVE SIGHT
GRAVE SURPRISE
AN ICE COLD GRAVE
GRAVE SECRET

The Lily Bard Mysteries

SHAKESPEARE'S LANDLORD
SHAKESPEARE'S CHAMPION
SHAKESPEARE'S CHRISTMAS
SHAKESPEARE'S TROLLOP
SHAKESPEARE'S COUNSELOR

Berkley Prime Crime Anthologies Edited by Charlaine Harris

CRIMES BY MOONLIGHT

InkLit Graphic Novels by Charlaine Harris

GRAVE SIGHT

*InkLit Graphic Novels by Charlaine Harris
and Christopher Golden*

CEMETERY GIRL: BOOK ONE: THE PRETENDERS
CEMETERY GIRL: BOOK TWO: INHERITANCE

Ace Books by Charlaine Harris

The Midnight, Texas, Novels

MIDNIGHT CROSSROAD
DAY SHIFT
NIGHT SHIFT

The Sookie Stackhouse Novels

DEAD UNTIL DARK
LIVING DEAD IN DALLAS
CLUB DEAD
DEAD TO THE WORLD
DEAD AS A DOORNAIL
DEFINITELY DEAD
ALL TOGETHER DEAD

FROM DEAD TO WORSE
DEAD AND GONE
DEAD IN THE FAMILY
DEAD RECKONING
DEADLOCKED
DEAD EVER AFTER

A TOUCH OF DEAD
AFTER DEAD

Ace Books Edited by Charlaine Harris

THE SOOKIE STACKHOUSE COMPANION

*Ace Books Edited by Charlaine Harris
and Toni L. P. Kelner*

DEAD BUT NOT FORGOTTEN

*Ace Anthologies Edited by Charlaine Harris
and Toni L. P. Kelner*

MANY BLOODY RETURNS
WOLFSBANE AND MISTLETOE
DEATH'S EXCELLENT VACATION
HOME IMPROVEMENT: UNDEAD EDITION
AN APPLE FOR THE CREATURE
GAMES CREATURES PLAY

THE
AURORA
TEAGARDEN
MYSTERIES

~ VOLUME ONE ~

Includes:
Real Murders
&
A Bone to Pick

Charlaine Harris

BERKLEY PRIME CRIME, NEW YORK

THE BERKLEY PUBLISHING GROUP
Published by the Penguin Group
Penguin Group (USA) LLC
375 Hudson Street, New York, New York 10014

USA • Canada • UK • Ireland • Australia • New Zealand • India • South Africa • China

penguin.com

A Penguin Random House Company

Berkley Prime Crime Books are published by The Berkley Publishing Group.
BERKLEY® PRIME CRIME and the PRIME CRIME logo are trademarks of
Penguin Group (USA) LLC.

Harris, Charlaine.
[Novels. Selections]
The Aurora Teagarden mysteries : volume one / Charlaine Harris.
pages ; cm. — (An Aurora Teagarden mystery)
ISBN 978-0-425-28269-4 (softcover)
1. Teagarden, Aurora Roe (Fictitious character)—Fiction.   2. Women librarians—Fiction.
3. Murder—Investigation—Fiction.   I. Harris, Charlaine. Real murders
II. Harris, Charlaine. A bone to pick   III. Title.
PS3558.A6427A6 2015
813'.54—dc23
2014042714

PUBLISHING HISTORY
Berkley Prime Crime trade paperback edition / February 2015

PRINTED IN THE UNITED STATES OF AMERICA

10 9 8 7 6 5 4

Contents

REAL MURDERS

To Mother and Father

Chapter One

"Tonight I want to tell you about that most fascinating of murder mysteries, the Wallace case," I told my mirror Enthusiastically.

I tried Sincere after that; then Earnest.

My brush caught in a tangle. "Shoot!" I said, and tried again.

"I think the Wallace case can easily fill our whole program tonight," I said Firmly.

We had twelve regular members, which worked out well with twelve programs a year. Not all cases could fill up a two-hour program, of course. Then the member responsible for presenting the Murder of the Month, as we jokingly called it, would have a guest speaker—someone from the police department in the city, or a psychologist who treated criminals, or the director of the local rape crisis center. Once or twice, we'd watched a movie.

But I'd come up lucky in the draw. There was more than enough material on the Wallace case, yet not so much that I'd be compelled to hurry over it. We'd allocated two meetings for Jack the Ripper. Jane Engle had taken one for the victims and the circumstances surrounding the crimes and Arthur Smith had taken another on the police investigation and the suspects. You can't skimp Jack.

"The elements of the Wallace case are these," I continued. "A man who called himself Qualtrough, a chess tournament, an apparently inoffensive woman named Julia Wallace, and of course the accused, her husband, William Herbert Wallace himself." I gathered all my hair into a brown switch and debated whether to put it in a roll on the back of my head, braid it, or just fasten a band around it to keep it off my face. The braid. It made me feel artsy and intellectual. As I divided my hair into clumps, my eyes fell on the framed studio portrait of my mother she'd given me on my last birthday with an offhand, "You said you wanted one." My mother, who looks a lot like Lauren Bacall, is at least five-foot six, elegant to her fingertips, and has built her own small real estate empire. I am four-foot eleven, wear big round tortoise-rimmed glasses, and have fulfilled my childhood dream by becoming a librarian. And she named me Aurora, though to a woman herself baptized Aida, Aurora may not have seemed so outrageous.

Amazingly, I love my mother.

I sighed, as I often do when I think of her, and finished braiding my hair with practiced speed. I checked my reflection in the big mirror; brown hair, brown glasses, brown eyes, pink cheeks (artificial), and good skin (real). Since it was, after all, Friday night, I'd shucked my work clothes, a plain blouse and skirt, and opted for a snug white knit top and black slacks. Deciding I wasn't festive enough for William Herbert Wallace, I tied a yellow ribbon around the top of my braid and pulled on a yellow sweater.

A look at the clock told me it was finally time to go. I slapped on some lipstick, grabbed my purse, and bounded down the stairs. I glanced around the big den/dining/kitchen area that took up the back half of the ground floor of the town house. It was neat; I hate to come home to a messy place. I tracked down my notebook and located my keys, muttering facts about the Wallace case all the while. I had thought about xeroxing the indistinct old pictures of Julia Wallace's body and passing them out to show the murder scene, but I decided that would perhaps be ghoulish and certainly disrespectful to Mrs. Wallace.

A club like Real Murders seemed odd enough to people who didn't share our enthusiasms, without adding the charge of ghoulishness. We kept a low profile.

I flipped on the outside light as I shut the door. It was already dark this early in spring; we hadn't switched to daylight savings time yet. In the excellent light over the back door, my patio with its high privacy fence looked swept and clean, the rose trees in their big tubs just coming into bud.

"Heigh ho, heigh ho, it's off to crime I go," I hummed tunelessly, shutting the gate behind me. Each of the four town houses "owns" two parking spaces: there are extra ones on the other side of the lot for company. My neighbor two doors down, Bankston Waites, was getting into his car, too.

"I'll see you there," he called. "I've got to pick up Melanie first."

"Okay, Bankston. Wallace tonight!"

"I know. We've been looking forward to it."

I started up my car, courteously letting Bankston leave the lot first on his way to pick up his lady fair. It did cross my mind to feel sorry for myself that Melanie Clark had a date and I always arrived at Real Murders by myself, but I didn't want to get all gloomy. I would see my friends and have as good a Friday night as I usually had. Maybe better.

As I backed up, I noticed that the town house next to mine had bright windows and an unfamiliar car was parked in one of its assigned spaces. So that was what Mother's message taped to my back door had meant.

She'd been urging me to get an answering machine, since the town house tenants (her tenants) might need to leave me (the resident manager) messages while I was at work at the library. Actually, I believe my mother just wanted to know she could talk to me while I wasn't even home.

I'd had the town house next door cleaned after the last tenants left. It had been in perfect condition to show, I reassured myself. I'd go meet the new neighbor tomorrow, since it was my Saturday off.

I drove up Parson Road far enough to pass the library where I worked, then turned left to get to the area of small shops and filling stations where the VFW Hall was. I was mentally rehearsing all the way.

But I might as well have left my notes at home.

Chapter Two

Real Murders met in the VFW Hall and paid the Veterans a small fee for the privilege. The fee went into a fund for the annual VFW Christmas party, so everyone was pleased with our arrangement. Of course the building was much larger than a little group like Real Murders needed, but we did like the privacy.

A VFW officer would meet a club member at the building thirty minutes before the meeting and unlock it. That club member was responsible for restoring the room to the way we'd found it and returning the key after the meeting. This year the "opening" member was Mamie Wright, since she was vice president. She would arrange the chairs in a semicircle in front of the podium and set up the refreshments table. We rotated bringing the refreshments.

I got there early that evening. I get almost everywhere early.

There were already two cars in the parking lot, which was tucked behind the small building and had a land-scaped screening of crepe myrtles, still grotesquely bare in the early spring. The arc lamps in the lot had come on automatically at dusk. I parked my Chevette under the glow of the lamp nearest the back door. Murder buffs are all too aware of the dangers of this world.

As I stepped into the hall, the heavy metal door clanged shut behind me. There were only five rooms in the build-ing; the single door in the middle of the wall to my left opened into the big main room, where we held our meet-ings. The four doors to my right led into a small confer-ence room, then the men's, the ladies', and, at the end of the corridor, a small kitchen. All the doors were shut, as usual, since propping them open required more tenacity than any of us were able to summon. The VFW Hall had been constructed to withstand enemy attack, we had decided, and those heavy doors kept the little building very quiet. Even now, when I knew from the cars outside that there were at least two people here, I heard nothing.

The effect of all those shut doors in that blank corridor was also unnerving. It was like a little beige tunnel, inter-rupted only by the pay phone mounted on the wall. I recalled once telling Bankston Waites that if that phone rang, I'd expect Rod Serling to be on the other end, telling me I had now entered the "Twilight Zone." I half smiled at the idea and turned to grasp the knob of the door to the big meeting room.

The phone rang.

I swung around and took two hesitant steps toward it, my heart banging against my chest. Still nothing moved in the silent building.

The phone rang again. My hand closed around it reluctantly.

"Hello?" I said softly, and then cleared my throat and tried again. "Hello," I said firmly.

"May I speak to Julia Wallace, please?" The voice was a whisper.

My scalp crawled. "What?" I said shakily.

"Julia . . ." whispered the caller.

The other phone was hung up.

I was still standing holding the receiver when the door to the women's room opened and Sally Allison came out.

I shrieked.

"God almighty, Roe, I don't look that bad, do I?" Sally said in amazement.

"No, no, it's the phone call . . ." I was very close to crying, and I was embarrassed about that. Sally was a reporter for the Lawrenceton paper, and she was a good reporter, a tough and intelligent woman in her late forties. Sally was the veteran of a runaway teenage marriage that had ended when the resulting baby was born. I'd gone to high school with that baby, named Perry, and now I worked with him at the library. I loathed Perry; but I liked Sally a lot, even if sometimes her relentless questioning made me squirm. Sally was one of the reasons I was so well prepared for my Wallace lecture.

Now she elicited all the facts about the phone call from

me in a series of concise questions that led to a sensible con-clusion; the call was a prank perpetrated by a club member, or maybe the child of a club member, since it seemed almost juvenile when Sally put it in her framework.

I felt somehow cheated, but also relieved.

Sally retrieved a tray and a couple of boxes of cookies from the small conference room. She'd deposited them there, she explained, when she entered and suddenly felt the urgency of the two cups of coffee she'd had after supper.

"I didn't even think I could make it across the hall into the big room," she said with a roll of her tan eyes.

"How's life at the newspaper?" I asked, just to keep Sally talking while I got over my shock.

I couldn't dismiss the phone call as lightly and logically as Sally. As I trailed after her into the big meeting room, half listening to her account of a fight she'd had with the new publisher, I could still taste the metallic surge of adrenaline in my mouth. My arms had goosepimples, and I pulled my sweater tightly around me.

As she arranged the cookies on her tray, Sally began telling me about the election that would be held to select someone to fill out the term of our unexpectedly deceased mayor. "He keeled over right in his office, according to his secretary," she said casually as she realigned a row of Oreos. "And after having been mayor only a month! He'd just gotten a new desk." She shook her head, regretting the loss of the mayor or the waste of the desk, I wasn't sure which.

"Sally," I said before I knew I was going to, "where's Mamie?"

"Who cares?" Sally asked frankly. She cocked one surprised eyebrow at me.

I knew I should laugh, since Sally and I had discussed our mutual distaste of Mamie before, but I didn't bother. I was beginning to be irritated with Sally, standing there looking sensible and attractive in her curly bronze permanent, her well-worn expensive suit, and her well-worn expensive shoes.

"When I pulled in the parking lot," I said quite evenly, "there were two cars, yours and Mamie's. I recognized Mamie's, because she's got a Chevette like mine, but white instead of blue. So you are here and I am here, but where is Mamie?"

"She's set the chairs up right and made the coffee," Sally said after looking around. "But I don't see her purse. Maybe she ran home for something."

"How'd she get past us?"

"Oh, I don't know." Sally was beginning to sound irritated with me, too. "She'll show up. She always does!"

And we both laughed a little, trying to lose our displeasure with each other in our amusement at Mamie Wright's determination to go to everything her husband attended, be in every club he joined, share his life to the fullest.

Bankston Waites and his light of love, Melanie Clark, came in as I put my notebook on the podium and slid my purse underneath it. Melanie was a clerk at Mamie's husband's insurance office, and Bankston was a loan officer at Associated Second Bank. They'd been dating about a year, having become interested in each other at Real Murders meetings, though they'd gone through Lawrenceton High

School together a few years ahead of me without striking any sparks.

Bankston's mother had told me last week in the grocery store that she was expecting an interesting announcement from the couple any day. She made a particular point of telling me that, since I'd gone out with Bankston a few times over a year ago, and she wanted me to know he was going to be out of circulation. If she was waiting in suspense for that interesting announcement, she was the only one. There wasn't anyone in Lawrenceton Bankston and Melanie's age left for them to marry, except each other. Bankston was thirty-two, Melanie a year or two older. Bankston had scanty blond hair, a pleasant round face, and mild blue eyes; he was Mr. Average. Or at least he had been; I noticed for the first time that his shoulder and arm muscles were bulging underneath his shirt sleeves.

"Have you been lifting weights, Bankston?" I asked in some amazement. I might have been more interested if he'd shown that much initiative when I'd dated him.

He looked embarrassed but pleased. "Yeah, can you tell a difference?"

"I certainly can," I said with genuine admiration. It was hard to credit Melanie Clark with being the motivation for such a revolutionary change in Bankston's sedentary life, but undoubtedly she was. Perhaps her absorption in him could be all the more complete since she had no family to claim her devotion. Her parents, both "only" children, had been dead for years—her mother from cancer, her father hit by a drunk driver.

Right now Melanie the motivator was looking miffed.

"What do you think about all this, Melanie?" I asked hastily.

Melanie visibly relaxed when I acknowledged her proprietorship. I made a mental note to speak carefully around her, since Bankston lived in one of "my" town houses. Melanie must surely know Bankston and I had gone out together, and it would be too easy for her to build something incorrect out of a landlady-tenant relationship.

"Working out's done wonders for Bankston," she said neutrally. But there was an unmistakable cast to her words. Melanie wanted me to get a specific message, that she and Bankston were having sex. I was a little shocked at her wanting me to know that. There was a gleam in her eyes that made me realize Melanie had banked fires under her sedate exterior. Under the straight dark hair conservatively cut, under the plain dress, Melanie was definitely feeling her oats. Her hips and bosom were heavy, but suddenly I saw them as Bankston must, as fertility symbols instead of liabilities. And I had a further revelation; not only were Bankston and Melanie having sex, they were having it often and exotically.

I looked at Melanie with more respect. Anyone who could pull the wool over the collective eye of Lawrenceton as effectively as Melanie had earned it.

"There was a phone call before you got here," I began, and they focused on me with interest. But before I could tell them about it, I heard a luscious ripple of laughter from the opening door. My friend Lizanne Buckley came in, accompanied by a very tall red-haired man. Seeing Lizanne here was a surprise. Lizanne didn't read a book from one year to the next, and her hobbies, if she had any, did not include crime.

"What on earth is she doing here?" Melanie said. She seemed really put out, and I decided we had here another Mamie Wright in the making.

Lizanne (Elizabeth Anna) Buckley was the most beautiful woman in Lawrenceton. Without Lizanne exerting herself in the slightest (and she never did) men would throw themselves on the floor for her to saunter on; and saunter she would, calm and smiling, never looking down. She was kind, in her passive, lazy way; and she was conscientious, so long as not too much was demanded of her. Her job as receptionist and phone answerer at the Power and Light Company was just perfect for her—and for the utility company. Men paid their bills promptly and smilingly, and anyone who got huffy over the telephone was immediately passed to someone higher on the totem pole. No one ever sustained a huff in person. It was simply impossible for ninety percent of the population to remain angry in Lizanne's presence.

But she required constant entertainment from her dates, and the tall red-haired man with the beaky nose and wire-rimmed glasses seemed to be making heavy weather of it.

"Do you know who he is, the man with Lizanne?" I asked Melanie.

"You don't recognize him?" Melanie's surprise was a shade overdone.

So I was supposed to know him. I re-examined the newcomer. He was wearing slacks and a sport coat in light brown, and a plain white shirt; he had huge hands and feet, and his longish hair flew around his head in a copper nimbus. I had to shake my head.

"He's Robin Crusoe, the mystery writer," Melanie said triumphantly.

The insurance clerk beats the librarian in her own bailiwick.

"He looks different without the pipe in his mouth," John Queensland said from behind my right shoulder. John, our wealthy real-estate-rich president, was immaculate as usual; an expensive suit, a white shirt, his creamy white hair smooth and the part sharp as an arrow. John had become more interesting to me when he'd started dating my mother. I felt there must be substance below the stuffed-shirt exterior. After all, he was a Lizzie Borden expert . . . and he believed she was innocent! A true romantic, though he hid it well.

"So what's he doing here?" I asked practically. "With Lizanne."

"I'll find out," said John promptly. "I should greet him anyway, as club president. Of course visitors are welcome, though I don't believe we've ever had any before."

"Wait, I need to tell you about this phone call," I said quickly. The newcomer had distracted me. "When I came in a few minutes ago—"

But Lizanne had spotted me and was swaying over to our little group, her semi-famous escort in tow.

"Roe, I brought you all some company tonight," Lizanne said with her agreeable smile. And she introduced us all around with facility, since Lizanne knows everyone in Lawrenceton. My hand was engulfed in the writer's huge boney one, and he really shook it, too. I liked that; I hate it when people just kind of press your hand and let it drop. I looked up and up at his crinkly mouth and little hazel eyes, and I just liked him altogether.

"Roe, this is Robin Crusoe, who just moved to Lawrenceton," Lizanne said. "Robin, this is Roe Teagarden."

He gave me an appreciative smile but he was with Lizanne, so I realistically built nothing on that.

"I thought Robin Crusoe was a pseudonym," Bankston murmured in my ear.

"I did, too," I whispered, "but apparently not."

"Poor guy, his parents must have been nuts," Bankston said with a snigger, until he remembered from my raised eyebrows that he was talking to a woman named Aurora Teagarden.

"I met Robin when he came in to get his utilities turned on," Lizanne was telling John Queensland. John was saying all the proper things to Robin Crusoe, glad to have such a well-known name in our little town, hope you stay a while, ta-dah ta-dah ta-dah. John edged Robin over to meet Sally Allison, who was chatting with our newest member, a police officer named Arthur Smith. If Robin was built tall and lanky, Arthur was short and solid, with coarse curly pale hair and the flat confrontive stare of the bull who knows he has nothing to fear because he is the toughest male on the farm.

"You're lucky to have met such a well-known writer," I said enviously to Lizanne. I still wanted to tell someone about the phone call, but Lizanne was hardly the person. She sure didn't know who Julia Wallace was. And she didn't know who Robin Crusoe was either, as it turned out.

"Writer?" she said indifferently. "I'm kind of bored."

I stared at her incredulously. Bored by Robin Crusoe?

One afternoon when I'd been at the Power and Light Company paying my bill, she'd told me, "I don't know what it is, but even when I pretty much like a man, after I date him a while, he gets to seem kind of tiresome. I just can't be bothered to act interested anymore, and then finally I tell him I don't want to go out anymore. They always get upset," she'd added, with a philosophical shake of her shining dark hair. Lovely Lizanne had never been married, and lived in a tiny apartment close to her job, and went home to her parents' house for lunch every day.

Robin Crusoe, desirable writer, was striking out with Lizanne even now. She looked—sleepy.

He reappeared at her side.

"Where do you live in Lawrenceton?" I asked, because the newcomer seemed dolefully aware he wasn't making the grade with our local siren.

"Parson Road. A town house. I'm camping there until my furniture comes, which it should do tomorrow. The rent here is so much less for a nicer place than I could find anywhere in the city close to the college."

Suddenly I felt quite cheerful. I said, "I'm your landlady," but after we'd talked about the coincidence for a moment, a glance at my watch unsettled me. John Queensland was making a significant face at me over Arthur Smith's shoulder. Since he was president, he had to open the meeting, and he was ready to start.

I glanced around, counting heads. Jane Engle and Le-Master Cane had come in on each other's heels and were chatting while preparing their coffee cups. Jane was a retired school librarian who substituted at both the school and the public libraries, a surprisingly sophisticated spinster who specialized in Victorian murders. She wore her silver hair in a chignon, and never, never wore slacks. Jane looked sweet and fragile as aged lace, but after thirty years of school children she was tough as a marine sergeant. Jane's idol was Madeleine Smith, the highly sexed young Scottish poisoner, which sometimes made me wonder about Jane's past. LeMaster was our only black member, a stout middle-aged bearded man with huge brown eyes who owned a dry cleaning business. LeMaster was most interested in the racially motivated murders of the sixties and early seventies, the Zebra murders in San Francisco and the Jones-Piagentini shooting in New York, for example.

Sally's son, Perry Allison, had come in, too, and had taken a seat without speaking to anyone. Perry had not actually joined Real Murders, but he had come to the past two meetings, to my dismay. I saw quite enough of him at work. Perry showed a rather unnerving knowledge of modern serial murderers like the Hillside Stranglers and the Green River Killer, in which the motivation was clearly sexual.

Gifford Doakes was standing by himself. Unless Gifford brought his friend Reynaldo, this was a pretty common situation, since Gifford was openly interested in massacres—St. Valentine's Day, the Holocaust, it didn't make any difference to Gifford Doakes. He liked piled bodies. Most of us were involved in Real Murders for reasons that would probably bear the light of day; gosh, who doesn't read the articles about murders in the newspaper? But Gifford was another story. Maybe he'd joined our club with the idea that we swapped some sickening sort of bloody pornography, and he was only sticking with the club in the hope that soon we'd trust him enough to share with him. When he brought Reynaldo, we didn't know how to treat him. Was Reynaldo a guest, or Gifford's date? A shade of difference there, and one which had us all a little anxious, especially John Queensland, who felt it his duty as president to speak to everyone in the club.

And Mamie Wright wasn't anywhere in the room.

If Mamie had been here long enough to set up the chairs and make the coffee, and her car was still in the parking lot, then she must be here somewhere. Though I didn't like Mamie, her non-appearance was beginning to seem so strange that I felt obliged to pin down her whereabouts.

Just as I reached the door, Mamie's husband, Gerald, came in. He had his briefcase under his arm and he looked angry. Because he looked so irate, and because I felt stupid for being uneasy, I did a strange thing; though I was searching for his wife, I let him pass without speaking.

The hall seemed very quiet after the heavy door shut off the hum of conversation. The white-with-speckles linoleum and beige paint almost sparkled with cleanliness under the harsh fluorescent lights. I was praying the phone wouldn't ring again as I looked at the four doors on the other side of the hall. With a fleeting, absurd image of "The Lady or the Tiger" I went to my right to open the door to the small conference room. Sally had told me she'd already been in the room, but just to temporarily park the tray of cookies, so I checked the room carefully. Since there was practically nothing to examine except a table and chairs, that took seconds.

I opened the next door in the hall, the women's room, even though Sally had also been in there. Since there were only two stalls, she'd have been pretty sure to know of Mamie's presence. But I bent over to look under the doors. No feet. I opened both doors. Nothing.

I didn't quite have the guts to check the adjoining men's room, but since Arthur Smith entered it while I hesitated, I figured I'd hear about it soon if Mamie was in there.

I moved on, and out of all the glaring beigeness I caught a little glimpse of something different, so I looked down at the base of the door and saw a smear. It was red-brown.

The separate sources of my uneasiness suddenly coalesced into horror. I was holding my breath when my hand reached out to open that door to the last room, the little kitchen used for fixing the refreshments . . .

. . . and saw an empty turquoise shoe upright on its ridiculous high heel, right inside the door.

And then I saw the blood spattered everywhere on the shining beige enamel of the stove and refrigerator.

And the raincoat.

Finally I made myself look at Mamie. She was so dead. Her head was the wrong shape entirely. Her dyed black hair was matted with clots of her blood. I thought, the human body is supposed to be ninety percent water, not ninety percent blood. Then my ears were buzzing and I felt very weak, and though I knew I was alone in the hall, I felt the presence of something horrible in that kitchen, something to dread. And it was not poor Mamie Wright.

I heard a door swoosh shut in the hall. I heard Arthur Smith's voice say, "Miss Teagarden? Anything wrong?"

"It's Mamie," I whispered, though I'd intended a normal voice. "It's Mrs. Wright." I ruined the effect of all this formality by simply folding onto the floor. My knees seemed to have turned to faulty hinges.

He was behind me in an instant. He half bent to help me up but was frozen by what he saw over my head.

"Are you sure that's Mamie Wright?" he asked.

The working part of my brain told me Arthur Smith was quite right to ask. Perhaps coming on this unsuspicious, I would have wondered, too. Her eye—oh my God, her eye.

"She's missing from the big room, but her car is outside. And that's her shoe." I managed to say that with my fingers pressed to my mouth.

When Mamie had first worn them, I'd thought those shoes the most poisonous footwear I'd ever seen. I hate turquoise anyway. I let myself enjoy thinking about hating turquoise. It was a lot more pleasing than thinking about what was right in front of me.

The policeman stepped over me very carefully and squatted with even more care by the body. He put his fingers against her neck. I felt bile rise up in my throat—no pulse, of course. How ridiculous! Mamie was so dead.

"Can you stand up?" he asked after a moment. He dusted his fingers together as he rose.

"If you help."

Without further ado, Arthur Smith hauled me to my feet and out the doorway in one motion. He was very strong. He kept one arm around me while he shut the door. He leaned me against that door. Deep blue eyes looked at me consideringly. "You're very light," he said. "You'll be all right for a few seconds. I'm going to use the phone right here on the wall."

"Okay." My voice sounded weird; light, tinny. I'd always wondered if I could keep my head if I found a body, and here I was, keeping my head, I told myself insanely as I watched him go down the hall to the pay phone. I was glad he didn't have to leave my sight. I might not be so level if I were standing in that hall alone, with a body behind me.

While Arthur muttered into the phone I kept my eyes on the door to the large room across the hall where John Queensland must be itching to open the meeting. I thought about what I'd just seen. I wasn't thinking about Mamie being dead, about the reality and finality of her death. I was thinking about the scene that had been staged, starring Mamie Wright as *the corpse*. The casting of the corpse had been deliberate, but the role *of the finder of the body* had by chance been taken by me. The whole thing was a scene deliberately staged by someone, and suddenly I knew what had been biting at me underneath the horror.

I thought faster than I'd ever thought before. I didn't feel sick anymore.

Arthur crossed the hall to the door of the large room and pushed it open just enough to insert his head in the gap. I could hear him address the other members of the club.

"Uh, folks, folks?" The voices stilled. "There's been an accident," he said with no emphasis. "I'm going to have to ask you all to stay in this room for a little while, until we can get things under control out here."

The situation, as far as I could see, was completely under control.

"Where's Roe Teagarden?" John Queensland's voice demanded.

Good old John. I'd have to tell Mother about that, she'd be touched.

"She's fine. I'll be back with you in a minute."

Gerald Wright's thin voice. "Where's my wife, Mr. Smith?"

"I'll get back with all of you in a few minutes," repeated the policeman firmly, and shut the door behind him. He stood lost in thought. I wondered if this detective had ever been the first on the scene of a murder investigation. He seemed to be ticking steps off mentally, from the way he was waggling his fingers and staring into space.

I waited. Then my legs started trembling and I thought I might fold again. "Arthur," I said sharply. "Detective Smith."

He jumped; he'd forgotten me. He took my arm solicitously.

I whacked at him with my free hand out of sheer aggravation. "I'm not trying to get you to help me, I want to tell you something!"

He steered me into a chair in the little conference room and put on a waiting face.

"I was supposed to lecture tonight on the Wallace case, you remember? William Herbert Wallace and his wife, Julia, England, 1931?"

He nodded his curly pale head and I could see he was a

million miles away. I felt like slapping him again. I knew I sounded like an idiot, but I was coming to the point. "I don't know how much you remember about the Wallace case—if you don't know anything, I can fill you in later." I waved my hands to show that was inconsequential, here came the real meat. "What I want to tell you, what's important, is that Mamie Wright's been killed exactly like Julia Wallace. She's been *arranged*."

Bingo! That blue gaze was almost frighteningly intense now. I felt like a bug impaled on a pin. This was not a lightweight man.

"Point out a few comparisons before the lab guys get here, so I can have them photographed."

I blew out a breath of relief. "The raincoat under Mamie. It hasn't rained here in days. A raincoat was found under Julia Wallace. And Mamie's been placed by the little oven. Mrs. Wallace was found by a gas fire. She was bludgeoned to death. Like Mamie, I think. Mr. Wallace was an insurance salesman. So is Gerald Wright. I'll bet there's more I haven't thought of yet. Mamie's about the same age as Julia Wallace. . . . There are just so many parallels I don't think I could've imagined them."

Arthur stared at me thoughtfully for a few long seconds. "Are there any photographs of the Wallace murder scene?" he asked.

The xeroxed pictures would have come in handy now, I thought.

"Yes, I've seen one. There may be more."

"Was the husband, Wallace, arrested?"

"Yes, and convicted. But later the sentence was overturned somehow or other, and he was freed."

"Okay. Come with me."

"One more thing," I said urgently. "The phone rang when I got here tonight and it was someone asking for Julia Wallace."

Chapter Three

The silent hall was not silent anymore. As we left the conference room, the law came in the back door. It was represented by a heavyset man in a plaid jacket who was taller and older than Arthur, and two men in uniform. As I stood back against the wall, temporarily forgotten, Arthur led them down the hall and opened the door to the kitchen. They crowded around the door looking in. They were all silent for a moment. The youngest man in uniform winced and then wrenched his face straight. The other uniformed man shook his head once and then stared in at Mamie with a disgusted expression. What disgusted him, I wondered? The mess that had been made with the body of a human being? The waste of a life? The fact that someone living in the town he had to protect had seen fit to do this terrible thing?

I realized the man in the plaid jacket was the sergeant of detectives; I'd seen his picture in the paper when he'd arrested a drug pusher. Now he pursed his mouth briefly and said, "Damn," with little expression.

Arthur began telling them things, going swiftly and in a low voice. I could tell what point in his narrative he'd reached when their heads swung toward me simultaneously. I didn't know whether to nod or what. I just stared back at them and felt a thousand years old. Their faces turned back to Arthur and he continued his briefing.

The two men in uniform left the building while Arthur and the sergeant continued their discussion. Arthur seemed to be enumerating things, while the sergeant nodded his head in approval and occasionally interjected some comment. Arthur had a little notebook out and was jotting in it as they spoke.

Another memory about the sergeant stirred.

His name was Jack Burns. He'd bought his house from my mother. He was married to a school teacher and had two kids in college. Now Jack Burns gave Arthur a sharp nod, as clear as a starting gun. Arthur went to the door to the meeting room and pushed it open.

"Mr. Wright, could you come here for a minute, please?" Detective Arthur Smith asked, in a voice so devoid of expression that it was a warning in itself.

Gerald Wright came into the hall hesitantly. No one in the big room could fail to know by now that something was drastically wrong, and I wondered what they'd been saying. Gerald took a step toward me, but Arthur took his arm quite firmly and guided Gerald into the little conference room. I knew he was about to tell Gerald that his wife was dead, and I found myself wondering how Gerald would take it. Then I was ashamed.

At moments I understood in decent human terms what had happened to a woman I knew, and at moments I seemed to be thinking of Mamie's death as one of our club's study cases.

"Miss Teagarden," said Jack Burns's good-old-boy drawl, "you must be Aida Teagarden's child."

Well, I had a father, too, but he'd committed the dreadful sin of coming in from foreign parts (Texas) to work on our local Georgia paper, marrying my mother, begetting me, and then leaving and divorcing Lawrenceton's own Aida Brattle Teagarden. I said, "Yes."

"I'm mighty sorry you had to see something like that," Jack Burns said, shaking his heavy head mournfully.

It was almost like a burlesque of regret, it was laid on so heavily; was he being sarcastic? I looked down, and for once said nothing. I didn't need this right now; I was shaken and confused.

"It just seems so strange to me that a sweet young woman like you would come to a club like this," Jack Burns went on slowly, his tone expressing stunned bewilderment. "Could you just kind of clarify for me what the purpose of this—organization—is?"

I had to answer a direct question. But why was he asking me? His own detective belonged to the same club. I wished this middle-aged man with his plaid suit and his cowboy boots would melt through the floor. As slightly as

I knew Arthur, I wanted him back. This man was scary. I pushed my glasses back up my nose with shaking fingers.

"We meet once a month," I said in an uneven voice. "And we talk about a famous murder case, usually a pretty old one."

The sergeant apparently gave this deep thought. "Talk about it—?" he inquired gently.

"Ah . . . sometimes just learn about it, who was killed and how and why and by whom." Our members favored different *w*'s.

I was most interested in the victim.

"Or sometimes," I stumbled on, "depending on the case, we decide if the police arrested the right person. Or if the murder was unsolved, we talk about who may have been guilty. Sometimes we watch a movie."

"Movie?" Raised beetly brows, a gentle inquiring shake of the head.

"Like *The Thin Blue Line*. Or a fictionalized movie based on a real case. *In Cold Blood* . . ."

"But not ever," he asked delicately, "what you would call a—snuff movie?"

"Oh my God," I said sickly. "Oh my God, no." In my naivete, I said, "How could you think that?"

"Well, Miss Teagarden, this here is a real murder, and we have to ask real questions." And his face was not nice at all. Our club had offended something in Jack Burns. How would Arthur fare, a policeman who was actually a member? But it seemed he would be working on the investigation in some capacity.

"Now, Miss Teagarden," Jack Burns went on, his mask back in place, his voice as buttery as a waffle, "I am going to head up this investigation, and my two homicide detectives will work on this, and Arthur Smith will assist us, since he knows all you people. I know you'll cooperate to the fullest with him. He tells me you know a little more about this than the others, that you got some kind of phone call and you found the body. We may have to talk to you a few times about this, but you just have patience with us." And I knew from his face I had better be willing to turn over my every waking minute, if that was required of me.

By this time I felt that Arthur Smith was my oldest and dearest friend, so much safer did he seem than this terrifying man with his terrifying questions. And he stepped out from behind his sergeant now, his face blank and his eyes cautious. He'd heard at least some of this conversation, which would have sounded almost routine without Burns's menacing manner.

"Miss Teagarden," Arthur said brusquely, "will you go into the room with the others now? Please don't discuss with them what's happened out here. And thanks." With Gerald presumably grieving in the small conference room and Mamie dead in the kitchen, I had to join the others unless he wanted me to stand in the bathroom.

With a medley of feelings, relief predominating, I was pushing open the door when I felt a hand on my arm. "Sorry," murmured Arthur. Over his shoulder, I saw the plaid back of Sergeant Burns's jacket as he held open the back door to admit uniformed policemen loaded down with equipment. "If you don't mind, I'll come to see you tomorrow morning about this Wallace thing. Will you be at work?"

"Tomorrow's my day off," I said. "I can be at home tomorrow morning."

"Nine o'clock too early?"

"No, that's fine."

As I went in the larger room where my fellow club members were clustered anxiously, I thought about the intelligence pitted against Arthur Smith's. Someone was painstaking and artistic in a debased and imaginative way. Someone had issued a challenge to whoever cared to take it up. "Figure out who I am if you can, you amateur students of crime. I've graduated to the real thing. Here is my work."

I felt an instinctive urge to hide what I was thinking. I wiped my mind clean of my nasty thoughts and tried not to meet the eyes of any of my fellow club members, who were all waiting tensely for me in the big room. But Sally Allison was a pro at catching reluctant eyes, and I saw her mouth open when she caught mine. I knew beyond a doubt she was going to ask me if I'd found Mamie Wright. Sally was no fool. I shook my head firmly, and she came no closer.

"Are you all right, child?" John Queensland asked, advancing with the dignity that was the keystone of his character. "Your mother will be terribly upset when she hears . . ." But since John, who was after all a wee mite pompous, realized he had no idea what my mother was going to hear, he had to trail off into silence. He asked me a question with a look.

"I'm sorry," I said in a tiny squeak. I shook my head in irritation. "I'm sorry," I said more strongly, "I don't think

Detective Smith wants me to talk until he talks to you." I gave John a small smile and went to sit by myself in a chair by the coffee urn, trying to ignore the indignant looks and mutters of dissatisfaction cast in my direction. Gifford Doakes was walking back and forth as if he were pacing a cage. The policemen outside seemed to be making him extremely nervous. The novelist Robin Crusoe was looking eager and curious; Lizanne just looked bored. LeMaster Cane, Melanie and Bankston, and Jane Engle were talking together in low voices. For the first time, I realized another club member, Benjamin Greer, was missing. Benjamin's attendance was erratic, like his life in general, so I didn't put any particular weight on that. Sally was sitting by her son Perry, whose thin slash of a mouth was twisted into a very peculiar smile. Perry's elevator did not stop at every floor.

I poured myself a cup of coffee, wishing it were a shot of bourbon. I thought of Mamie getting to the meeting early, setting everything up, making this very coffee so we wouldn't have to drink Sally's dreadful brew . . . I burst into tears, and slopped coffee all down my yellow sweater.

Those awful turquoise shoes. I kept seeing that empty shoe sitting upright in the middle of the floor.

I heard a soft sweet soothing murmur and knew Lizanne Buckley had come to my aid. Lizanne generously blocked me from the view of the room with an uncomfortable hunch of her tall body. I heard the scrape of a chair and saw a pair of long thin trousered legs. Her escort, the red-headed novelist, was helping her out, and then he tactfully moved away. Lizanne lowered herself into the chair and hitched it closer to me. Her manicured hand stuffed a handkerchief into my stubby one.

"Let's just think about something else," Lizanne said in a low, even voice. She seemed quite sure I could think about something else. "Stupid ole me," said Lizanne charmingly. "I just can't get interested in the things this Robin Crusoe likes, like people getting murdered. So if you like him, you're welcome to him. I think maybe you and him would suit each other. Nothing wrong with him," she added hastily, in case I should assume she was offering me something shoddy. "He'd just be happier with you, I think. Don't you?" she asked persuasively. She just knew a man would make me feel better.

"Lizanne," I said, with a few gasps and sobs interposed here and there, "you're wonderful. I don't know anyone to top you. There aren't too many single men our age in Lawrenceton to date, are there?"

Lizanne looked puzzled. She'd obviously noticed no lack of single men to date. I wondered where all her men came from. Probably drove from as far away as two hundred miles. "Thanks, Lizanne," I said helplessly.

Sergeant Burns appeared in the doorway and scanned the room. I had no doubt he was memorizing each and every face. I could tell by his scowl when he saw her that he knew Sally Allison was a reporter. He looked even angrier when he saw Gifford Doakes, who stopped his pacing and stared back at Burns with a sneering face.

"Okay, folks," he said peremptorily, eyeing us as if we were rather degenerate strangers caught half-dressed, "we've had a death here."

That could hardly have been a bombshell—after all, the people in this group were adept at picking up clues. But there was a shocked-sounding buzz of conversation in the wake of Burns's announcement. A few reactions were marked. Perry Allison got a strange smirk on his face, and I was even more strongly reminded that in the past Perry had had what people called "nervous problems," though he did his work at the library well enough. His mother, Sally, was watching his face with obvious anxiety. The red-haired writer's face lit with excitement, though he decently tried to tone it down. None of this could touch him personally, of course. He was new in town, had barely met a soul, and this was his first visit to Real Murders.

I envied him.

He saw me watching him, observing his excitement, and he turned red.

Burns said clearly, "I'm going to take you out of the room one by one, to the smaller room across the hall, and one of our uniformed officers will take your statement. Then I'm going to let you go home, though we'll need to talk to you all again later, I imagine. I'll start with Miss Teagarden, since she's had a shock."

Lizanne pressed my hand when I got up to leave. As I crossed the hall, I saw the building was teeming with police. I hadn't known Lawrenceton had that many in uni-form. I was learning a lot tonight, one way or another.

The business of having my statement taken would have been interesting if I hadn't been so upset and tired. After all, I'd read about police procedure for years, about police questioning all available witnesses to a crime, and here I was, being questioned by a real policeman about a real crime. But the only lasting impression I carried away with me was that of thoroughness. Every question was asked twice, in different ways. The phone call, of course, came in for a great deal of attention. The pity of it was that I could say so little about it. I was faintly worried when Jack Burns stepped in and asked me very persistently about Sally Allison and her movements and demeanor; but I had to face the fact that since Sally and I were first on the scene (though we didn't know it at the time) we would be questioned most intensely.

I had my fingerprints taken, too, which would have been very interesting under other circumstances. As I left the room I glanced toward the kitchen without wanting to. Mamie Wright, housewife and wearer of high heels, was being processed as the *murder victim*. I didn't know where Gerald Wright was; since the small conference room had been free, he must have been driven home or even to the police station. Of course he would be the most suspected, and I knew chances were he'd probably done it, but I could find no relief in the thought.

I didn't believe Gerald had done it. I thought the person, man or woman, who'd called the VFW Hall had done it, and I didn't believe Gerald Wright would have resorted to such elaborate means if he'd wanted to kill Mamie. He might have buried her in his cellar, like Crippen, but he would not have killed her at the VFW and then called to alert the rest of the club members to his actions. Actually, Gerald didn't seem to have enough sense of fun, if that was what you wanted to term it. This murder had a kind of bizarre playfulness about it. Mamie'd been arranged like a doll, and the phone call was like a childish "Nyah, nyah, you can't catch me."

As I went out to my car very slowly, I was mulling over that phone call. It was a red flag, surely, to alert the club to the near certainty that this murder had been planned and executed by a club member. Mamie Wright, wife of an insurance salesman in Lawrenceton, Georgia, had been battered to death and arranged after death to copy the murder of the wife of an insurance company employee in Liverpool, England. This had been done on the premises where the club met, on the night it met to discuss that very case. It was possible someone outside the club had a grudge against us, though I couldn't imagine why. No, someone had decided to have his own kind of fun with us. And that someone was almost surely someone I knew, almost surely a member of Real Murders.

I could scarcely believe I had to walk out to my car by myself, drive it home by myself, enter my dark home—by myself. But then I realized that all the members of Real Murders, alive or dead, with the exception of Benjamin Greer, were under police scrutiny at this very moment.

I was the safest person in Lawrenceton.

I drove slowly, double-checked myself at stop signs, and used my turn signals long before I needed to. I was so completely tired I was afraid I'd look drunk to any passing patrol officers . . . if there were any left on the streets. I was so glad to turn the car into my familiar slot, put my key in my own lock, and plod into my own territory. Functioning through a woolly fog of fatigue, I dialed Mother's number.

When she answered I told her that no matter what she heard, I was just fine and nothing awful had happened to me. I cut off her questions, left the phone off the hook, and saw by the kitchen clock that it was only 9:30. Amazing.

I trudged up the stairs, pulling off my sweater and shirt as I went. I just managed to shuck the rest of my clothes, pull on my nightgown, and crawl into bed before sleep hit me.

At 3 A.M. I woke in a cold sweat. My dream had been one big close-up of Mamie Wright's head.

Someone was crazy; or someone was unbelievably vicious. Or both.

Chapter Four

I turned the water on full force, let it get good and hot, and stepped into the shower. It was 7 A.M. on a cool, crisp spring morning, and my first conscious thought was: I don't have to go to work today. The next thought was: my life has changed forever.

Not much had ever really happened to me; not big things, either wonderful or horrible. My parents getting divorced was bad, but even I had been able to see it was better for them. I had already gotten my driver's license by then, so they didn't need to shuttle me back and forth. Maybe the divorce had made me cautious, but caution is not a bad thing. I had a neat and tidy life in a messy world, and if sometimes I suspected I was trying to fulfill the stereotype of a small-town librarian, well, I had yearnings to play other roles, too. In the movies, sometimes those dry librarians with their hair in buns suddenly let their juices gush, shook their hair loose, threw off their glasses, and did a tango.

Maybe I would. But in the meantime, I could have a small pride in myself. I had done okay the night before, not great but okay. I had gotten through it.

I went through the tedious business of drying my mass of hair and pulled on some old jeans and a sweater. I padded downstairs in my moccasins and brewed some coffee, a big pot. I'd gotten my lawn chairs and table set up on the patio a week before, when I'd decided it was going to stay spring for good, so after getting my papers from the little-used front doorstep, I carried my first cup out to the patio. It was possible to feel alone there, though of course the Crandalls on one side and Robin Crusoe on the other could see my patio from their second floor back bedroom. The back bedroom was small and I knew everyone used it as a guest room, so the chances were good that no one was looking.

Sally hadn't managed to get the story in the local paper. I was sure that had been printed before the meeting even started. But the local man employed by the city paper had had better luck. "Lawrenceton Woman Murdered" ran the uninspired headline in the City and State section. A picture of Mamie accompanied the article, and I was impressed by the stringer's industry. I scanned the story quickly. It was necessarily short, and had little in it I didn't know, except that the police hadn't found Mamie's purse. I frowned at that. It didn't seem to fit somehow. There was no hint of this murder being like any other murder. I wondered if the police had requested that fact be withheld. But it would be all over Lawrenceton soon, I was sure. Lawrenceton, despite its new population of commuters to Atlanta, was still a small town at heart. My name was included: *"Ms. Teagarden, anxious at Mrs. Wright's continued absence, searched the building and found Mrs. Wright's body in the kitchen."* I shivered. It sounded so simple in print.

I'd put the phone back on the hook, and now it rang. Mother, of course, I thought, and went back into the kitchen. I picked up the receiver as I poured more coffee.

"Are you all right?" she asked immediately. "John Queensland came over last night after the police let him go, and he told me all about it."

John Queensland was certainly making a determined effort to endear himself to Mother. Well, she'd been on her own (but not always alone) for a long time.

"I'm pretty much all right," I said cautiously.

"Was it awful?"

"Yes," I said, and I meant it. It had been horrible, but exciting, and the more hours separated me from the event, the more exciting and bearable it was becoming. I didn't want to lose the horror; that was what kept you civilized.

"I'm sorry," she said helplessly. Neither of us knew what to say next. "Your father called me," she blurted out. "You must have had your phone off the hook?"

"Uh-huh."

"He was worried, too. About you. And he said you were going to keep Phillip next weekend? He wondered if you would be able; he said if you didn't feel like it, just give him a call, he'd change his plans." Mother was doing her best not to call her ex-husband a selfish bastard for mentioning such a thing at a time like this.

I had a half brother, Phillip, six, a scary and wonderful boy whom I could stand for whole weekends occasionally without my nerves completely shattering. I'd completely forgotten that Dad and his second wife, Betty Jo, (quite a reaction to an Aida Teagarden) were leaving for a convention in Chattanooga in a few days.

"No, that'll be okay, I'll give him a call later today," I said.

"Well. You will call me if you need me to do anything? I can bring you some lunch, or you can come stay with me."

"No, I'm fine." A slight exaggeration, but close enough to the truth. I suddenly wanted to say something real, something indelible, to my mother. But the only thing I could think of wouldn't bear uttering. I wanted to say I felt more alive than I had in years; that finally something bigger than myself had happened to me. Now, instead of reading about an old murder, seeing passion and desperation and evil in print on a page, I knew these things to be possessed by people around me. And I said, "Really, I'm okay. And the police are coming by this morning; I'd better go get ready."

"All right, Aurora. But call me if you get scared. And you can always stay here."

I had a sudden flood of nervous energy after I hung up. I looked around me, and decided to put it to good use picking up. First my den/dining room/kitchen right off the patio, then the formal front room that I seldom used. I checked the little downstairs bathroom for toilet paper, and ran up the stairs to make my bed and straighten up. The guest bedroom was pristine, as usual. I gathered up my dirty clothes and trotted downstairs with the bundle, tossing it unceremoniously down the basement stairs to land in front of the washer. Lawrenceton is on high enough ground for basements to be feasible.

When I looked at the clock and saw I had fifteen minutes left before Arthur Smith was due to come, I checked the coffee level and went back upstairs to put on some makeup. That was simple enough, since I wore little, and I hardly had to look in the mirror to do it. But out of habit I did, and I didn't look any more interesting or experienced than I had the day before. My face was still pale and round, my nose short and straight and suitable for holding up my glasses, my eyes magnified behind those glasses and round and brown. My hair unbound flew all around my head in a waving brown mass halfway down my back, and for once I let it be. It would get in my way and stick to the corners of my mouth and get caught in the hinges of my glasses, but what the hell! Then I heard the double ring of the front doorbell and flew downstairs.

People almost always came to the back door instead of the front, but Arthur had parked on the street instead of in the parking area behind the apartments. Under the fresh suit, shaved jaw, and curling pale hair still damp from the shower, he looked tired.

"Are you all right this morning?" he asked.

"Yes, pretty much. Come in."

He looked all around him, openly, when he passed through the living room, missing nothing. He paused at the big room where I really lived. "Nice," he said, sounding impressed. The sunny room with the big window overlooking the patio with its rose trees did look attractive. Exposed brick walls and all the books make an intelligent-looking room, anyway, I thought, and I waved him onto the tan suede love seat as I asked him if he wanted coffee.

"Yes, black," he said fervently. "I was up most of the night."

When I bent over to put his cup on the low table in front of him, I realized with some embarrassment that his eyes weren't on the coffee cup.

I settled opposite him in my favorite chair, low enough that my feet can touch the floor, wide enough to curl up inside, with a little table beside it just big enough to hold a book and a coffee cup.

Arthur took a sip of his coffee, eyed me again as he told me it was good, and got down to business.

"You were right, the body was definitely moved after death to the position it was in when you found it," he said directly. "She was killed there in the kitchen. Jack Burns is having a hard time swallowing this theory, that she was deliberately killed to mimic the Wallace murder, but I'm going to try to convince him. He's in charge though; I'm assisting on this one since I know all the people involved, but I'm really a burglary detective."

Some questions flew through my head, but I decided it wouldn't be polite to ask them. Sort of like asking a doctor about your own symptoms at a party. "Why is Jack Burns so scary?" I asked abruptly. "Why does he make an effort to intimidate you? What's the point?"

At least Arthur didn't have to ask me what I meant. He knew exactly what Jack Burns was like.

"Jack doesn't care if people like him or not," Arthur said simply. "That's a big advantage, especially to a cop. He doesn't even care if other cops like him. He just wants cases solved as soon as possible, he wants witnesses to tell him everything they know, and he wants the guilty punished. He wants the world to go his way, and he doesn't care what he has to do to make it happen."

That sounded pretty frightening to me. "At least you know where you are with him," I said weakly. Arthur nodded matter-of-factly.

"Tell me everything you know about the Wallace case," he said.

"Well, I'm up on it of course, since it was supposed to be the topic last night," I explained. "I wonder if—whoever killed Mamie—picked it for that reason?"

I was actually kind of glad I'd finally get to deliver part of my laboriously prepared lecture. And to a fellow aficionado, a professional at that.

"The ultimate murder mystery, according to several eminent crime writers," I began. "William Herbert Wallace, Liverpool insurance salesman," I raised a finger to indicate one point of similarity, "and married with no children," I raised a second finger. Then I thought Arthur could probably do without me telling him his job. "Wallace and his wife, Julia, were middle-aged and hadn't much money, but did have intellectual leanings. They played duets together in the evening. They didn't entertain much or have many friends. They weren't known to quarrel.

"Wallace had a regular schedule for collecting insurance payments from subscribers to his particular company, and he'd bring the money home with him for one night, Tuesday. Wallace played chess, too, and was entered in a tournament at a local club. There was a play-off chart establishing when he'd be playing, posted on the wall at the club. Anyone who came in could see it." I raised my eyebrows at Arthur to make sure he marked that important point. He nodded.

"Okay. Wallace didn't have a phone at home. He got a call at the chess club right before he arrived there one day. Another member took the message. The caller identified himself as 'Qualtrough.' The caller said that he wanted to take out a policy on his daughter and asked that Wallace be given a message to come around to Qualtrough's house the next evening, Tuesday.

"Now, the bad thing about this call, from Wallace's point of view," I explained, warming to my subject, "is that it came to the club when Wallace wasn't there. And there was a telephone booth Wallace could have used, close to his home, if he himself placed the 'Qualtrough' call."

Arthur scribbled in a little leather notepad he produced from somewhere.

"Now—Wallace comes in very soon after Qualtrough has called the club. Wallace talks about this message to the other chess players. Maybe he means to impress it on their memory? Either he is a murderer and is setting up his alibi, or the real murderer is making sure Wallace will be out of the house Tuesday evening. And this dual possibility, that almost hanged Wallace, runs throughout the case." Could any writer have imagined anything as interesting as this? I wanted to ask.

But instead I plunged back in. "So on the appointed night Wallace goes looking for this man Qualtrough who wants to take out some insurance. Granted, he was a man who needed all the business he could get, and granted, we know what insurance salesmen are still like today, but even so, Wallace went to extreme lengths to find this potential customer. The address Qualtrough left at the chess club was in Menlove Gardens East. There's a Menlove Gardens North, South, and West, but no Menlove Gardens East; so it was a clever false address to give. Wallace asks many people he meets—even a policeman!—if they know where he can find this address. He may be stubborn, or he may be determined to fix himself in the memories of as many people as possible.

"Since there simply was no such address, he went home." I paused to take a long drink of my tepid coffee.

"She was already dead?" Arthur asked astutely.

"Right, that's the point. If Wallace killed her, he had to have done it before he left on this wild goose chase. If so, what I'm about to tell you was all acting.

"He gets home and tries to open his front door, he later says. His key won't work. He thinks Julia has bolted the front door and for some reason can't hear him knock. Whatever was the case, a couple who live next door leave their house and see Wallace at his back door, apparently in distress. He tells them about the front door being bolted. Either his distress is genuine, or he's been hanging around in the back alley waiting for someone else to witness his entrance."

Arthur's blond head shook slowly from side to side as he

contemplated the twists and turns of this classic. I imagined the Liverpool police force in 1931 sitting and shaking their heads in exactly the same way. Or perhaps not; they'd been convinced early on that they had their man.

"Was Wallace friendly with those neighbors?" he asked.

"Not particularly. Good, but impersonal, relationship."

"So he could count on their being accepted as impartial witnesses," Arthur observed.

"If he did it. Incidentally, the upshot of all this about the front door lock, which Wallace said resisted his key, turned out to be a major point in the trial, but the testimony was pretty murky. Also iffy was the evidence of a child who knocked on the door with the day's milk, or a newspaper or something. Mrs. Wallace answered the door, alive and well; and if it could have been proved Wallace had already left, he would have been cleared. But it couldn't be." I took a deep breath. Here came the crucial scene. "Be that as it may. Wallace and the couple *do* enter the house, *do* see a few things out of place in the kitchen and another room, I think, but no major ransacking. The box where Wallace kept the insurance money had been rifled. Of course, this was a Tuesday, when there should've been a lot of money.

"The neighbors by this time are scared. Then Wallace calls them into the front room, a parlor, rarely used.

"Julia Wallace is there, lying in front of the gas fire, with a raincoat under her. The raincoat, partially burned, is not hers. She's been beaten to death, with extreme brutality, unnecessary force. She has not been raped." I stopped suddenly. "I assume Mamie wasn't?" I said finally, frightened of the answer.

"Doesn't look like it right now," Arthur said absently, still taking notes.

I blew my breath out. "Well, Wallace theorizes that 'Qualtrough,' who of course must be the murderer if Wallace is innocent, called at the house after Wallace left. He was evidently someone Julia didn't know well, or at all, because she showed him into the company parlor." Just like I would an insurance salesman, I thought. "The raincoat, an old one of Wallace's, she perhaps threw over her shoulders because the disused room was cold until the gas fire, which she apparently lit, had had a chance to heat it. The money that had been taken hadn't actually been much, since Wallace had been ill that week and hadn't been able to collect everything he was supposed to. But no one else would have known that, presumably.

"Julia certainly hadn't been having an affair, and had never personally offended anyone that the police could discover.

"And that's the Wallace case."

Arthur sat lost in thought, his blue eyes fixed intently on some internal point. "Wobbly, either way," he said finally.

"Right," I agreed. "There's no real case against Wallace, except that he was her husband, the only person who seemed to know her well enough to kill her. Everything he said could've been true . . . in which case, he was tried for killing the one person in the world he loved, while all the time the real killer went free."

"So Wallace was arrested?"

"And convicted. But after he spent some time in prison,

he was released by a unique ruling in British law. I think a higher court simply ruled that there hadn't been enough evidence for a jury to convict Wallace, no matter what the jury said. But prison and the whole experience had broken Wallace, and he died two or three years later, still saying he was innocent. He said he suspected who Qualtrough was, but he had no proof."

"I'd have gone for Wallace, too, on the basis of that evidence," Arthur said unhesitatingly. "The probability is with Wallace, as you said, because it's usually the husband who wants his wife out of the way . . . yet since there's no clear-cut evidence either way, I'm almost surprised the state chose to prosecute."

"Probably," I said without thinking, "the police were under a lot of pressure to make an arrest."

Arthur looked so tired and gloomy that I tried to change the subject. "Why'd you join Real Murders?" I asked. "Isn't that a little strange for a policeman?"

"Not this policeman," he said a little sharply. I shrank in my chair.

"Listen, Roe, I wanted to go to law school, but there wasn't enough money." Arthur's family was pretty humble, I recalled. I thought I'd gone to high school with one of his sisters. Arthur must be three or four years older than I. "I made it through two years of college before I realized I couldn't make it financially, because I just couldn't work and carry a full course load. School bored me then, too. So I decided to go into law from another angle. Policemen aren't all alike, you know."

I could tell he'd given this lecture before.

"Some cops are right out of Joseph Wambaugh's books, because he was a cop and he writes pretty good books. Loud, drinkers, macho, mostly uneducated, sometimes brutal. There are a few nuts, like there are in any line of work, and there are a few Birchers. There aren't many Liberals with a capital 'L,' and not too many college graduates. But within those rough lines, we've got all kinds of people. Some of my friends—some cops—watch every cop show on television they can catch, so they'll know how to act. Some of them—not many—read Dostoevsky." He smiled, and it looked almost strange on him. "I just like to study old crimes, figure out how the police thought on the case, pick apart their procedure—ever read about the June Anne Devaney case, Blackburn, England, oh, about late 1930s?"

"A child murder, right?"

"Right. You know the police persuaded every adult male in Blackburn to have his fingerprints taken?" Arthur's face practically shone with enthusiasm. "That's how they caught Peter Griffiths. By comparing thousands of fingerprints with the ones Griffiths left on the scene." He was lost in admiration for a moment. "That's why I joined Real Murders," he said. "But what could a woman like Mamie Wright get out of studying the Wallace case?"

"Oh, a chaperoned husband!" I said with a grin, and then felt a sharp pang of dismay as Arthur reopened his little notebook.

Almost gently, Arthur said, "Now, this murder is real. It's a new murder."

"I know," I said, and I saw Mamie again.

"Did they quarrel much, Gerald and Mamie?"

"Never, that I saw or heard," I said firmly and truthfully. I'd always believed Wallace was innocent. "She just seemed to be keeping an eye on him around other women."

"Do you think her suspicions were correct?"

"It never occurred to me they could be. Gerald is just so stuffy and . . . Arthur? Could Gerald have done this?" I didn't mean emotionally, I meant practically, and Arthur realized it.

"Do you know why Gerald says he was late to the meeting, why Mamie came on her own instead of riding with him? He got a call from a man he didn't know, asking Gerald to talk with him about some insurance for his daughter."

I know my mouth was hanging open. I slowly shut it, but feared I looked no more intelligent.

"Someone's really slapping us in the face, Arthur," I said slowly. "Maybe especially challenging you. Mamie wasn't even killed because she was *Mamie*." That was especially horrible. "It was just because she was an insurance salesman's wife."

"But you'd figured it out last night. You know that."

"But what if there are more? What if he copies the June Anne Devaney murder, and kills a three-year-old? What if he copies the Ripper murders? Or kills people like Ed Gein did, to eat?"

"Don't go imagining nightmares," Arthur said briskly. He was so matter of fact I knew he'd already thought of the possibility himself. "Now, I've got to write down everything you did yesterday, starting from when you left work."

If he meant to jolt me out of the horrors, he succeeded.

Even if only on paper, I was someone who had to account for her movements; not exactly a suspect, but a possibility. Then too, my arrival time at the meeting would help pinpoint the time of death. Though I'd gone over this all the night before, once more I carefully related my trivial doings.

"Do you have a good account of the Wallace killing I could borrow?" he asked, rising from the couch reluctantly. He looked even more worn, as if relaxing for a while hadn't helped, just made him feel his exhaustion. "And I need a list of club members, too."

"I can help you with the Wallace killing," I said. "But you'll have to get the list from Jane Engle. She's the club secretary." I had the book on hand I'd used to prepare my lecture. I checked to make sure my name was written inside, told Arthur I'd have him arrested if he didn't return it, and walked with him to the front door.

To my surprise, he put his hands on my shoulders and gripped them with no mean pressure.

"Don't look so dismal," he said. The wide blue eyes caught mine. I felt a jolt tingle up my spine. "You caught something last night most people wouldn't have. You were tough and smart and quick-thinking." He caught a loose strand of my hair and rolled it between his fingers. "I'll talk to you soon," he said. "Maybe tomorrow."

As it turned out, we spoke somewhat sooner than that.

Chapter Five

I'd noticed a moving van parked in front of Robin Crusoe's apartment when I let Arthur out. Out of sheer curiosity, when the phone began to ring, I decided to take my calls on my bedside phone, which had a long cord, so I could stare out the front windows at the unloading. And the phone was ringing nonstop, as the news about Mamie Wright's murder spread among friends and co-workers. Just when I was about to dial his number, my father called. He seemed about equally concerned with my emotional health and with whether or not I still felt I could keep Phillip.

"Are you okay?" Phillip himself said softly. He is a shrieker in person, but unaccountably soft-spoken over the telephone.

"Yes, brother, I'm okay," I answered.

"'Cause I really want to come see you. Can I?"

"Sure."

"Are you going to make pecan pie?"

"I might, if I was asked nicely."

"Please, please, please?"

"That's pretty nice. Count on the pie."

"Yahoo!"

"Do you feel I'm blackmailing you?" Father asked when Phillip relinquished the phone.

"Well, yes."

"Okay, okay, I feel guilty. But Betty Jo really wants to go to this convention. Her best friend from college married a newspaperman, too, and they're going to be there."

"Tell her I'll still keep him." I loved Phillip, though at first I'd been terrified to even hold him, having no experience whatsoever with babies. To give Betty Jo credit, she's always been all for Phillip's getting to know his big sister.

After I'd hung up, the rest of the day gaped ahead of me like a black cave. Since it was my day off I tried to do day-off things; I paid bills, did my laundry.

My best friend, Amina Day, had just moved to Houston to take such a good job that I couldn't grudge her the move; but I missed her, and I'd felt very much an unadventurous village bumpkin before I'd stepped into the VFW kitchen. Amina wasn't going to believe I'd had a bona fide shocking experience right in Lawrenceton. I decided to call her that night, and the prospect cheered me.

Now that the first shock of last night had worn off, it all seemed curiously unreal, like a book. I'd read so many books, both fiction and nonfiction, in which a young woman walked into a room (across a field, down the stairs, in an alley) and found *the body.* I could distance myself from the reality of a dead Mamie by thinking of the situation, rather than the person.

I picked out all these distinctions while eating a nutritious lunch of Cheez-its and tuna fish. All this thinking led me back to the depressing conclusion that so little had happened in my life for so long, that when something did, I had to pick at it over and over. No moment was going to sneak by *me* unobserved and unanalyzed.

Clearly, some action was called for.

With the taste of lunch in my mouth, it was easy to decide that that action should take the form of going to the grocery store. I made one of my methodical little lists and gathered up my coupons.

Of course the store was extra crowded on Saturday, and I saw several people who knew what had happened the night before. I found myself reluctant to talk about it to people who hadn't been there. I hadn't been asked to avoid mentioning the murder's connection to an old murder case, but I didn't see any sense in having to explain it to ten people in a row, either. Even the minimal responses I made slowed me down considerably, and forty minutes later I was only halfway through my list. As I stood at the meat counter debating between "lean" and "extra lean" hamburger, I heard a tapping noise. It grew more and more imperative, until I looked up. Benjamin Greer, the only member of Real Murders who hadn't been at the meeting the night before, was tapping on the clear glass that separated the butchers from the refrigerated meat counter. Behind him, gleaming steel machines were doing their job, and another butcher in a bloodstained apron like Benjamin's was packing roasts.

Benjamin was stout with wispy blond hair that he swept up and over his premature bald spot. He'd tried to grow a mustache to augment his missing scalp hair, but it had given the impression that his upper lip was dirty, and I was glad to see he'd shaved the thing off. He wasn't very tall, and he wasn't very bright, and he tried to make up for these factors with a puppylike friendliness and willingness to do whatever one asked. On the down side, if his help was not needed, no matter how tactfully you expressed it, he turned sullen and self-pitying. Benjamin was a difficult person, one of those people who make you feel ashamed of yourself if you dislike him, while making it almost impossible to like him.

I disliked him, of course. He'd asked me out three times, and every time, feeling deeply ashamed of myself, I'd told him no. Even as desperate for a date as I was, I couldn't stomach the thought of going out with Benjamin.

He'd tried a fundamentalist church, he'd tried coaching Little League, and now he was trying Real Murders.

I smiled at him falsely and damned the hamburger meat that had led me into his sight.

He hurried through the swinging door to the right of the meat. I steeled myself to be nice.

"The police came to my apartment last night," he said breathlessly. "They wanted to know why I hadn't come to the meeting."

"What did you say?" I asked bluntly. The bloodstained

apron was making me feel unwell. Suddenly hamburger seemed quite distasteful.

"Oh, I hated to miss your presentation," he assured me, as if I'd been worried, "but I had something else I had to do." Put that in your pipe and smoke it, his expression said. Benjamin's words were as mild and apologetic and his voice was as abased as usual, but his face was another matter.

I looked inquiring and waited. Definitely not the hamburger. Maybe no red meat at all.

"I'm in politics," Benjamin told me, his voice modest but his face triumphant.

"The mayoral race?" I guessed.

"Right. I'm helping out Morrison Pettigrue. I'm his campaign manager." And Benjamin's voice quivered with pride.

Whoever Morrison Pettigrue was, he was sure to lose. The name rang a faint bell, but I wasn't willing to stand there waiting to recall what I knew.

"I wish you luck," I said with as good a smile as I could scrape together.

"Would you like to go to a rally with me next week?"

My God, he *wanted* me to kick him in the face. That was the only explanation. I looked at him and thought, you pathetic person. Then I felt ashamed, of course, and that made me angry at myself, and him.

"No, Benjamin," I said with finality. I could not offer an excuse. I did not want this to happen again.

"Okay," he said, with martyrdom in his voice. "Well . . . I'll be seeing you." The hurt quivered dramatically just under his brave smile.

The old reply came to the tip of my tongue, and I bit it back. But as I wheeled my cart away, I whispered, "Not if I see you first." As I slowed down to stare at the dog food bags, just so he wouldn't look out the window and see me speeding away as fast as I could move, I realized there were a couple of funny things about our conversation.

He hadn't asked any questions about last night. He hadn't asked who had been at the meeting, he hadn't said how strange it was that the only night he'd missed was the night something extraordinary happened. He hadn't even asked how it felt to discover Mamie's body, something everyone I'd seen today had been trying to ask me in round-about ways.

I puzzled over it while I selected shampoo, and then decided not to worry about Benjamin Greer. Instead, I would get mad at the shelf stockers. Naturally, every kind of heavily sugared cereal based on a cartoon show was at my eye level, while cereal bought by grown-ups was stacked way above my head. I could reach them, but then the stockers had laid other boxes down on top of the row of upright boxes. If I pulled out the one I could reach, the others on top of it would come toppling down, making lots of noise and attracting lots of attention. You can tell I know from experience.

I turned sideways to maximize my stretch and stood on my tiptoes. No go. I was just going to have to switch brands or start eating cereal that tasted like bubble gum. That horrible thought galvanized me into another attempt.

"Here, young lady, let me get that for you," said an

unbearably patronizing voice from somewhere above me. A huge hand reached over my head, grasped the box easily, and like a crane lowered the box into my cart.

I gripped the cart handle as if it were my temper. I breathed out once deeply, and then in again. I slowly turned to face my benefactor. I looked up—and up—into a comically dismayed face topped by a thatch of longish red hair.

"Oh, gosh, I'm sorry," said Robin Crusoe. Hazel eyes blinked at me anxiously from behind his wire-rims. "I thought—from the back, you know, you look about twelve. But certainly not from the *front*."

He realized what he'd just said, and his eyes closed in horror.

I was beginning to enjoy this.

A fleeting image crossed my mind of us in an intimate situation, and I wondered if it would work at all. I couldn't help it; I began to smile.

He smiled back, relieved, and I saw his charm instantly. He had a crooked smile, a little shy.

"I don't think we should talk like this," he said, indicating the difference in our heights. "Why don't I come over after I get my groceries put up? You live right by me, I think you said last night? You make me want to pick you up so I can see you better."

That so closely matched a certain image crossing my mind that I could feel my face turning red. "Please do come over. I'm sure you have a lot of questions after last night," I said.

"That would be great. My place is in such a mess that I need a break from looking at boxes."

"Okay, then. About an hour?"

"Sure, see you then—your name's really Roe?"

"Short for Aurora," I explained. "Aurora Teagarden."

He didn't seem to think my name was unusual at all.

"Coffee? Soft drink? Orange juice?" I offered.

"Beer?" he countered.

"Wine."

"Okay. I don't usually drink at this hour, but if anything will drive you to drink, it's moving."

Feeling naughty at having a drink before five in the afternoon, I filled two glasses and joined him in the living room. I sat in the same chair I'd taken that morning when Arthur had been there, and felt incredibly female and powerful at entertaining two men in my home on the same day.

Robin, like Arthur, was impressed with the room. "I hope mine looks half this good when I've finished unpacking. I have no talent at all for making things look nice."

My friend Amina would have said I didn't either. "Are you settled in?" I asked politely.

"I got my bed put together while the moving men were unloading the rest of the van, and I've hung my clothes in the closet. At least I had a chair for the detective to sit in this morning. They carried it in right as he walked to the door."

"Arthur Smith?" I was surprised. He hadn't told me he was going to interview Robin after he left my place. I'd shut the door assuming he'd get in his car and drive off. He must have left Robin's apartment before I started spying out the front upstairs window.

"Yes, he was checking up on the way I happened to come to the club meeting—"

"How *did* you know about it?" I interrupted with intense curiosity.

"Well," he said with reddening face, "when I went to the utility company, I got to talking with Lizanne, and when she found out I write mysteries, she remembered the club. Evidently you told her about it one time." I hadn't imagined Lizanne was listening. She'd looked, as usual, bored. "So Lizanne called John Queensland, who said Real Murders was meeting that very night and visitors could come, so I asked her . . ."

"Just wondered," I said neutrally.

"That Sergeant Burns, he's a grim kind of man," Robin said thoughtfully. "And Detective Smith is no lightweight."

"You didn't even know Mamie. It's out of the question you could be suspected."

"Well, I guess I could have known her before. But I didn't, and I think Smith believes that. But I bet he'll check. That's a guy I wouldn't like to have on my trail."

"Mamie wouldn't have gotten there before 7:00," I said thoughtfully. "And I have no alibi for 7:00 to 7:30. She had to meet the VFW president at the VFW Hall to get the key. And I think after every meeting she had to run by his house to return the key."

"Nope. Yesterday she dropped by the president's house and picked up the key. She told them she needed to get in early, she had some kind of appointment to meet someone there before the meeting."

"How'd you know that?" I was agog and indignant.

"The detective asked to use the phone to call the station, and I pieced that together from listening to his end of the conversation," he said frankly. Aha, another person who was curious by nature.

"Oh. So," I said slowly, thinking as I went, "whoever killed her actually had plenty of time to fix everything up. He got her to come early somehow, so he'd have buckets of time to kill her and arrange her and go home to clean up." I drained my glass and shuddered.

Robin said hastily, "Tell me about the other club members."

I decided that question was the real purpose of his visit. I felt disappointed, but philosophical.

"Jane Engle, the white-haired older lady," I began. "She's retired but works from time to time substitute teaching or substituting at the library. She's an expert on Victorian murders." And then I ran down the list on my fingers: Gifford Doakes, Melanie Clark, Bankston Waites, John Queensland, LeMaster Cane, Arthur Smith, Mamie and Gerald Wright, Perry Allison, Sally Allison, Benjamin Greer. "But Perry's only just started coming," I explained. "I guess he's not really a member."

Robin nodded, and his red hair fell across his eyes. He brushed it back absently.

That absorption in his face and the small gesture did something to me.

"What about you?" he asked. "Give me a little biography."

"Not much to tell. I went to high school here, went to a small private college, did some graduate work at the university in library science and came home and got a job at the local library."

Robin looked disconcerted.

"All right, it never occurred to me not to come back," I said after a moment. "What about you?"

"Oh, I'm going to teach a course at the university. The writer they had lined up had a heart attack . . . Do you ever do impulsive things?" Robin asked suddenly.

One of the strongest impulses I'd ever felt urged me to put down my wineglass, walk over to Robin Crusoe, a writer I'd known only a few hours, sit on his lap, and kiss him until he fainted.

"Almost never," I said with real regret. "Why?"

"Have you ever experienced . . ."

My doorbell chimed twice.

"Excuse me," I said with even deeper regret, and answered the front door.

Mr. Windham, my mail carrier, handed me a brown-wrapped package. "I couldn't fit this in your box," he explained.

I glanced at the mailing label. "Oh, it's not to me, it's to Mother," I said, puzzled.

"Well, we have to deliver by addresses, so I had to bring it here," Mr. Windham said righteously.

Of course, he was right; my address was on the package. The return address was my father's home in the city. The label itself was typed, as usual for Father. He's gotten a new typewriter, I thought, surprised. His old Smith-Corona had been the only typewriter he'd ever used. Maybe he'd mailed it to Mother from his office and used a typewriter there? Then I noticed the date.

"Six days?" I said incredulously. "It took six days for this to travel thirty miles?"

Mr. Windham shrugged defensively.

My father hadn't said a word about mailing us anything. As I shut the front door, I reflected that Father hadn't sent Mother a package in my memory, certainly never since the divorce. I was eaten up with curiosity. I stopped at the kitchen phone on my way back to the living room. She was in her office, and said she'd stop by on her way to show a house. She was as puzzled as I was, and I hated to hear that little thread of excitement in her voice.

Robin seemed to be dozing in his chair, so I quietly picked up our wineglasses and washed them so I could put them away before Mother got there. I didn't need her arching her eyebrows at me. Actually, I was glad to have a breather. I'd almost done something radical earlier, and it was almost as much fun to think about nearly having done it as it would have been (maybe) to do it.

When Mother came through the gate, Robin woke up— if he'd really been asleep—and I introduced them.

Robin stood courteously, shook hands properly, and admired Mother as she was used to being admired, from her perfectly frosted hair to her slim elegant legs. Mother was wearing one of her very expensive suits, this one in a champagne color, and she looked like a million-dollar saleswoman. Which she was, several times over.

"So nice to see you again, Mr. Crusoe," she said in her

husky voice. "I'm sorry you had such a bad experience your first evening in our little town. Really, Lawrenceton is a lovely place, and I'm sure you won't regret living here and commuting to the city."

I handed her the box. She looked at the return address sharply, then began ripping open the wrapping while she kept up an idle conversation with Robin.

"Mrs. See's!" we exclaimed simultaneously when we saw the white and black box.

"Candy?" Robin said uncertainly. He sat back down when I did.

"Very good candy," Mother said happily. "They sell it out west, and in the midwest, too, but you can't get it down here. I used to have a cousin in St. Louis who'd send me a box every Christmas, but she passed away last year. So Roe and I were thinking we'd never get a box of Mrs. See's again!"

"I want the chocolate-almond clusters!" I reminded her.

"They're yours," Mother assured me. "You know I only like the creams . . . hum. No note. That's odd."

"I guess Dad just remembered how much you liked them," I offered, but it was a weak offering. Somehow the gesture just wasn't like my father; it was an impulse gift, since Mother's birthday was months away, and he hadn't been giving her a birthday present since they divorced, anyway. So, a nice impulse. But my father never did impulsive things; I came by my caution honestly.

Mother had offered the box to Robin, who shook his head. She settled down to the delightful task of choosing her first piece of Mrs. See's. It was one of our favorite little

Christmas rituals, and the spring weather felt all wrong suddenly.

"It's been so long," she mused. She finally sighed and lifted a piece. "Aurora, isn't this the one with caramel filling?"

I peered at the chocolate in question. I was sitting down, Mother was standing up, so I could see what she hadn't. There was a hole in the bottom of the chocolate.

It had gotten banged around in shipment?

Abruptly I leaned forward and pulled another chocolate out of its paper frill. It was a nut cluster and it was pristine. I breathed out a sigh of relief. Just in case, I picked up another cream. It had a hole in the bottom, too.

"Mom. Put the candy down."

"Is this a piece you wanted?" she asked, eyebrows raised at my tone.

"Put it *down*."

She did, and looked at me angrily.

"There's something wrong with it, Mom. Robin, look." I poked at the piece she'd relinquished with my finger.

Robin lifted the chocolate delicately with his long fingers and peered at the bottom. He put it down and looked at several more. My mother looked cross and frightened.

"Surely this is ridiculous," she said.

"I don't think so, Mrs. Teagarden," Robin answered finally. "I think someone's tried to poison you, and maybe Roe, too."

Chapter Six

So Arthur came to my apartment on official business twice in one day, and he brought another detective with him this time, or maybe she brought him. Lynn Liggett was a homicide detective, and she was as tall as Arthur, which made her tall for a woman.

I can't say I was afraid right then. I was confused at the label apparently addressed by my father, I was indignant that someone had tried to trick us into eating something unhealthy, but I was sure that with poisons being so hard to obtain, whatever was in the candy would prove to be something that might have caused us to have a few bad hours, but simply couldn't have killed Mother or me.

Arthur seemed pretty grim about the whole thing, and Lynn Liggett asked us questions. And more questions. I could see the lapel pin on Mother's jacket heave. When

Detective Liggett bagged the candy and carried it out to Arthur's car, Mother said to me in a furious whisper, "She acts like we are people who don't live decent lives!"

"She doesn't know us, Mother," I said soothingly, though to tell the truth I was a little peeved with Detective Liggett myself. Questions like, "Have you recently finished a relationship that left someone bitter with you, Mrs. Teagarden?" and "Miss Teagarden, how long have you known Mr. Crusoe?" had not left a good taste in my mouth either. I'd never before been able to understand why good citizens didn't cooperate with the police—after all, they had their job to do, they didn't know you personally, to them all citizens should be treated alike, blah blah blah, right?

Now I could understand. Jack Burns looking at me like I was a day-old catfish corpse had been one thing, an isolated incident maybe. I wanted to say, Liggett, romantic relationships don't figure in this, some maniac mailed this candy to Mother and dragged me into it by addressing it to me! But I knew Lynn Liggett was obliged to ask us these questions and I was bound to answer them. And still I resented it.

Maybe it wouldn't have bothered me if Lynn Liggett hadn't been a woman.

Not that I didn't think women should be detectives. I certainly did think women should be detectives, and I thought many women I knew would be great detectives— you should see some of my fellow librarians tracking down an overdue book, and I'm not being facetious.

But Lynn Liggett seemed to be evaluating me as a fellow woman, and she found me wanting. She looked down at me and found me smaller than her "every whichaways," as I remembered my grandmother saying. I conjectured that since being tall must have given Detective Liggett problems, she automatically assumed I felt superior to her as a woman, since I was so short and therefore more "feminine." Since she couldn't compete with me on that level, Liggett figured she'd be tougher, more suspicious, coldly professional. A strong frontier woman as opposed to me, the namby-pamby, useless stay-back-in-the-effete-east toy woman.

I know a lot about role-playing, and she couldn't pull that bull on me. I was tempted to burst into tears, pull out a lace handkerchief—if I had possessed such a useless thing—and say, "Ar-thur! Little ole me is just so scared!" Because I could see that this had little to do with me, but much to do with Arthur.

Getting right down to the nitty-gritty, Homicide Detective Liggett had the hots for Burglary Detective Smith, and as Detective Liggett saw it, Detective Smith had the hots for me.

It's taken me a long time to spell out what I sensed in a matter of minutes. I was disappointed in Lynn Liggett, because I would have liked to be her friend and listen to her stories about her job. I hoped she was a more subtle detective than she was a woman. And I had to answer the damn questions anyway, even though I knew, Mother knew, and I believe Arthur knew, that they were a waste of time.

Robin stayed the whole time, though his presence was not absolutely necessary once he'd told his simple story to the detectives. "I ran into Roe Teagarden in the grocery, and asked her if I could come over here to relax a little since my place is such a mess. When the candy came, she seemed quite surprised, yes. I also saw the hole in the bottom of the piece of candy when Mrs. Teagarden held it up. No, I didn't know either Roe or Mrs. Teagarden until the last two days. I met Mrs. Teagarden briefly when I went by her real estate office to rendezvous with the lady who was going to show me the apartment next door, and I didn't meet Roe until the Real Murders meeting last night."

"And you've been here since when?" Arthur asked quietly. He was standing in the kitchen talking to Robin, while Detective Liggett questioned Mother and me as we sat on the couch and she crouched on the love seat.

"Oh, I've been here about an hour and a half," Robin said with a slight edge.

Arthur's voice had had absolutely no overtone whatsoever (Liggett was not quite that good), but I had the distinct feeling that everyone here was following his or her own agenda, except possibly my mother. She was certainly no dummy when a sexual element entered the air, however, and in fact she suddenly gave me one of her dazzling smiles of approval, which I could have done without since Detective Liggett seemed to intercept it and interpret it as some kind of reflection on her.

My mother rose and swept up her purse and terminated the interview. "My daughter is fine and I am fine, and I cannot imagine that my former husband sent this candy or ever intended to hurt either of us," she said decisively. "He adores Aurora, and he and I have a civil relationship. Our little family habits are no secret to anyone. I don't imagine our little Christmas custom of a box of candy has gone unremarked. Probably, I've bored people many times by talking about it. We'll be interested to hear, of course, when you all find out what is actually in the candy—if anything. Maybe the holes in the bottom are just to alarm us, and this is some practical joke. Thanks for coming, and I have to be getting back to the office." I stood up too, and Lynn Liggett felt forced to walk to the door with us.

My mother got into her car first, while Arthur and Lynn conferred together on the patio. Robin was clearly undecided about what he should do. Arthur throwing out his male challenge, in however subdued a way, had struck Robin by surprise, and he was squinting thoughtfully at my stove without seeing it. He was probably wondering what he'd gotten into, and if this murder investigation was going to be as much fun as he'd anticipated.

I was abruptly sick of all of them. Maybe I hadn't been a big dating success because I was a boring person, but possibly it had been because I had limited tolerance for all this preliminary maneuvering and signal reading. My friend Amina Day loved all this stuff and was practically a professional at it. I missed Amina suddenly and desperately.

"Come have lunch with me in the city Monday," Robin suggested, having reached some internal decision.

I thought a moment. "Okay," I agreed. "I covered for another librarian when she took her kid to the orthodontist last week, so I don't have to go in Monday until two o'clock."

"Are you familiar with the university campus? Oh, sure, you went there. Well, meet me at Tarkington Hall, the English building. I'll be finishing up a writer's workshop at

Charlaine Harris

11:45 on the third floor in Room 36. We'll just leave from there, if that suits you."

"That'll be fine. See you then."

"If you need me for anything, I'll be at home all day tomorrow getting ready for my classes."

"Thanks."

The phone rang inside and I turned to get it as Robin sauntered out my gate, waving a casual hand to the two detectives. An excited male voice asked for Arthur, and I called him to the phone. Lynn Liggett had recovered her cool, and when I called, "Arthur! Phone!" her mouth only twitched a little. Oops, silly me. Should have said Detective Smith.

I watered my rose trees while Arthur talked inside. Lynn regarded me thoughtfully. The silence between us was pretty fragile, and I felt small talk was not a good idea, but I tried anyway.

"How long have you been on the force here?" I asked.

"About three years. I came here as a patrol officer, then got promoted."

Maybe Detective Liggett and I would have become bosom buddies in a few more minutes, but Arthur came out of the apartment then with electricity crackling in every step.

"The purse has been found," he said to his co-worker.

"No shit! Where?"

"Stuffed under the front seat of a car."

Well, say which one! I almost said indignantly.

But Arthur didn't, of course, and he and his confrere were out the gate with nary a word for me. And I'll give this to Lynn Liggett, she was too involved in her work to look back at me in triumph.

To keep my hands busy while my mind roamed around, I began refinishing an old wooden two-drawer chest that I'd had in my guest bedroom for months waiting for just such a moment. After I wrestled it down the stairs and out onto the patio, the sanding turned out to be just the thing I needed.

Naturally I thought about the candy incident, and wondered if the police had called my father yet. I couldn't imagine what he'd think of all this. As I scrubbed my hands under the kitchen sink after finishing, I had a new thought, one I should have had before. Did sending the candy to Mother imitate another crime? I went to my shelves and began searching through all my "true murder" books. I couldn't find anything, so this incident wasn't patterned after one of the better-known murders. Jane Engle, my fellow librarian, had a larger personal collection than I, so I called her and told her what had happened.

"That rings a faint bell . . . it's an American murder, I think," Jane said interestedly. "Isn't this bizarre, Roe? That such things could happen in Lawrenceton? To us? Because I really begin to think this is happening to us, to the members of our little club. Did you hear that Mamie's purse has been found under the seat in Melanie Clark's car?"

"Melanie! Oh, I can't believe it!"

"The police may be taking that seriously, but Roe, you

and I know that's ridiculous. I mean, Melanie Clark. It's a plant."

"Huh?"

"A club member was killed, and another club member is being used to divert suspicion."

"You think whoever killed Mamie took her purse and deliberately planted it under Melanie's car seat," I said slowly.

"Oh, yes." I could picture Jane standing in her tiny house full of her mother's furniture, Jane's silver chignon gleaming amid bookcases full of gory death.

"But Melanie and Gerald Wright could have had something going," I protested weakly. "Melanie could really have done it."

"Aurora, you know she's absolutely head over heels about Bankston Waites. The little house she rents is just down the street from mine and I can't help but notice his car is there a great deal." Jane tactfully didn't specify whether that included overnight.

"Her car is here a lot too," I admitted.

"So," Jane said persuasively, "I am sure that this candy thing is another old murder case revisited, and maybe the police will find the poison in another club member's kitchen!"

"Maybe," I said slowly. "Then none of us are safe."

"No," Jane said. "Not really."

"Who could have it in for us that bad?"

"My dear, I haven't the slightest. But you can bet I'll be thinking about it, and I'm going to start looking for a case like yours right this moment."

"Thanks, Jane," I said, and I hung up with much to think about, myself.

I had nothing special to do that night, as my Saturday nights had tended to run the past couple of years. Right after I ate my Saturday splurge of pizza and salad, I remembered my resolution to call Amina in Houston.

Miraculously, she was in. Amina hadn't been in on a Saturday night in twelve years, and she was going out later, she said immediately, but her date was a department store manager who worked late on Saturday.

"How is Houston?" I asked wistfully.

"Oh, it's great! So much to do! And everyone at work is so friendly." Amina was a first-rate legal secretary.

People almost always were friendly to Amina. She was a slender brown-eyed freckle-faced extrovert almost exactly my age, and I'd grown up with her and remained best friends with her through college. Amina had married and divorced childlessly, the only interruption in her long, exhaustive dating career. She was not really pretty, but she was irresistible—a laughing, chattering live wire, never at a loss for a word. She had a great talent for enjoying life and for maximizing every asset she'd been born with or acquired (her hair was not exactly naturally blond). My mother should have had Amina for a daughter, I thought suddenly.

After Amina finished telling me about her job, I dropped my bombshell.

"You found a body! Oh, yick! Who was it?" Amina shrieked. "Are you okay? Are you having bad dreams? Was the chocolate really poisoned?"

Amina being my best friend, I told her the truth. "I don't know yet if the chocolate was poisoned. Yes, I'm having bad dreams, but this is really exciting at the same time."

"Are you safe, do you think?" she asked anxiously. "Do you want to come stay with me until this is all over? I can't believe this is happening to you! You're so nice!"

"Well, nice or not," I retorted grimly, "it's happening. Thanks for asking me, Amina, and I will come to see you soon. But I have to stay here for now. I don't think I'm in any more danger. This was my turn to be targeted, I guess, and I came out okay." I skipped my speculation with Arthur that maybe the killer would go on killing, and Jane Engle's conjecture that maybe we would all be drawn in, and cut right to Amina's area of expertise.

"I have a situation here," I began, and at once had her undivided attention. The nuances and dosey-does between the sexes were Amina's bread and butter. I hadn't had anything like this to tell Amina since we were in high school. It was hard to credit that grown people still engaged in all this—foreplay.

"So," Amina said when I'd finished. "Arthur is a little resentful that this Robin spent the afternoon at your place, and Robin's trying to decide whether he likes you well enough to keep up the beginning of your relationship in view of Arthur's slight proprietary air. Though Arthur is not the proprietor of anything yet, right?"

"Right."

"And you haven't actually had a date with either of these bozos, right?"

"Right."

"But Robin has asked you to lunch in the city for Monday."

"Uh-huh."

"And you're supposed to meet him at the classroom."

"Yep."

"And Lizanne has definitely discarded this Robin." Amina and Lizanne had always had a curious relationship. Amina operated on personality and Lizanne on looks, but they'd both run through the male population of Lawrenceton and surrounding towns at an amazing rate.

"Lizanne formally bequeathed him to me," I told Amina.

"She's not greedy," Amina conceded. "If she doesn't want 'em, she lets 'em know, and she lets 'em go. Now, if you're going to meet him at the university, you realize he's going to be sitting in a classroom full of little chickies just panting to hop in bed with a famous writer. He's not ugly, right?"

"He's not conventionally handsome," I said. "He has charm."

"Well, don't wear one of those blouse and skirt combinations you're always wearing to work!"

"What do you suggest I wear?" I inquired coldly.

"Listen, you called me for advice," Amina reminded me. "Okay, I'm giving it to you. You've had an awful time. Nothing makes you feel better than a few new clothes, and you can afford it. So go to my mom's shop tomorrow when it opens, and get something new. Maybe a classic town 'n country type dress. Stick to little earrings, since you're so short, and maybe a few gold chains." (A few? I was lucky to have one my mother had given me for Christmas. Amina's boyfriends gave her gold chains for every occasion, in whatever length or thickness they could afford. She probably had twenty.) "That should be fine for a casual lunch in the city," Amina concluded.

"You think he'll notice me as a woman, not just a fellow murder buff?"

"If you want him to notice you as a woman, just lust after him."

"Huh?"

"I don't mean lick your lips or pant. Keep conversation normal. Don't do anything obvious. You have to keep it so you don't lose anything if he decides he's not interested." Amina was interested in saving face.

"So what do I do?"

"Just *lust*. Keep everything going like normal, but sort of concentrate on the area below your waist and above your knees, right? And send out *waves*. You can do it. It's like the Kegel exercise. You can't show anyone how to do it, but if you describe it to a woman, she can pick it up."

"I'll try," I said doubtfully.

"Don't worry, it'll come naturally," Amina told me. "I have to hang up, the doorbell is ringing. Call me again and tell me how it goes, okay? The only thing wrong with Houston is that you aren't here."

"I miss you," I said.

"Yeah, and I miss you, but you needed me to leave," Amina said, and then she did hang up.

And after a moment's disbelief, I knew she was right. Her departure had freed me from the role of the most popular woman's best friend, a role that required I not attempt to make the most of myself because even the best of me could not compete with Amina. I almost had to be the intellectual drab one.

I was sitting thinking about what Amina had said when the phone rang while my hand was still resting on it. I jumped a mile.

"It's me again," Amina said rapidly. "Listen, Franklin is waiting for me in the living room, but I ran back here to my other phone to tell you this. You said Perry Allison was in that club with you? You watch out for Perry. When he was in college with me, he and I took a lot of the same courses our freshman year. But he would have these mood swings. He'd be hyper-excited and follow me around just jabbering, then he'd be all quiet and sullen and just stare at me. Finally the college called his mother."

"Poor Sally," I said involuntarily.

"She came and got him and I think committed him, not just because of me but because he was skipping classes and no one would room with him because his habits got so strange."

"I think he's beginning to repeat that pattern, Amina. He's still holding together at the library, but I see Sally looking worried these days."

"You just watch out for him. He never hurt anyone that I know of, though he made a bunch of people nervous. But if he's involved in this murder thing, you watch out!"

"Thanks, Amina."

"Sure, 'bye now."

And she was gone again to enjoy herself with Franklin.

Chapter Seven

Sunday dawned warm and rainy. A breeze swooped over the fence and rustled my rose trees. It was not a morning to eat breakfast on the patio. I fried bacon and ate my bakery sweet roll while listening to a local radio broadcast. The mayoral candidates were answering questions on this morning's talk show. The election promised more interest than the usual Democratic shoo-in, since not only was there a Republican candidate who actually had a slim chance, there was a candidate from the—gasp—Communist Party! Of course, this was the candidate whose campaign Benjamin Greer was managing. Poor miserable Benjamin, hoping that the Communist Party and politics would be his salvation. Of course the Communist, Morrison Pettigrue, was one of the New People, one of those who'd fled the city but wanted to stay close to it.

At least this would be a unifying election for Lawrenceton. None of the candidates was black, which always made for a tense campaign and a divisive one. The Republican and Democrat were having the time of their political lives, giving sane, sober answers to banal questions, and thoroughly enjoying Pettigrue's fiery responses that sometimes bordered on the irrational.

Bless his heart, I thought sadly, not only is he a Communist but he's also very unappealing. I'd made a point of looking for Pettigrue's campaign posters on the way back from the grocery store the day before. They said nothing about the Communist Party (just "Elect Morrison Pettigrue, the People's Choice, for Mayor") and they showed him to be a grim-featured swarthy man who had obviously suffered badly from acne.

I listened while I ate breakfast, but then I switched to some country and western music for my dishwashing. Domestic chores always went faster when you could sing about drinkin' and cheatin'.

It was such a nice little morning I decided to go to church. I often did. I sometimes enjoyed it and felt better for going, but I felt no spiritual compulsion. I went because I hoped I'd "catch it," like deliberately exposing myself to the chicken pox. Sometimes I even wore a hat and gloves, though that was bordering on parody and gloves were not so easy to find anymore. It wasn't a hat-and-gloves day, today, too dark and rainy, and I wasn't in a role-playing mood, anyway.

As I pulled into the Presbyterian parking lot, I wondered if I'd see Melanie Clark, who sometimes attended. Had she been arrested? I couldn't believe stolid Melanie truly was in danger of being charged with Mamie Wright's murder. The only possible motive anyone could attribute to Melanie was an affair with Gerald Wright. Someone . . . some murderer, I reminded myself . . . was playing an awful joke on Melanie.

I drifted through the service, thinking about God and Mamie. I felt horrible when I thought of what another human being had done to Mamie; yet I had to face it, when she had been alive, the predominant feeling I'd had for her had been contempt. Now Mamie's soul, and I believe we do all have one, was facing God, as I would one day too. This was too close to the bone for me, and I buried that thought so I could dig it up later when I wasn't so vulnerable.

I made my way out of church, speaking with most of the congregation along my way. All the talk I heard was about Melanie and her predicament, and the latest information appeared to be that Melanie had had to go down to the police station for a while, but on Bankston's vehement vouching for her every move on the evening of Mamie Wright's death, she'd been allowed to go home and (the feeling went) was thus exonerated.

Melanie herself was an orphan, but Bankston's mother was a Presbyterian. Today of course she was the center of an attentive group on the church steps. Mrs. Waites was as blond and blue-eyed as her son, and ordinarily just as phlegmatic. But this Sunday she was an angry woman and didn't care who knew it. She was mad at the police for suspecting "that sweet Melanie" for one single minute. As if a girl like that was going to beat a fly to death, much less a grown woman! And those police suggesting that maybe things weren't as they should be between Melanie and Mr. Wright! As if wild horses could drag Melanie and Bankston away from each other! At least this awful thing had gone and gotten Bankston to speak his mind. He and Melanie were going to be married in two months. No, a date hadn't been set, but they were going to decide about one today, and Melanie was going to go down to Millie's Gifts this week and pick out china and silver patterns.

This was a triumphant moment for Mrs. Waites, who had been trying to marry off Bankston for years. Her other children were settled, and Bankston's apparent willingness to wait for the right woman to come to him, instead of actively searching himself, had tried Mrs. Waites to the limit.

I would have to go pick out a fork or salad plate. I'd given lots of similar gifts in a hundred different patterns. I sighed, and tried hard not to feel sorry for myself as I drove to Mother's. I always ate Sunday lunch with her, unless she was off on one of the myriad real estate conventions she attended or out showing houses.

Mother (who had spent a rare Sunday morning at home) was in fine spirits because she'd sold a $200,000 house the day before, after she'd left my apartment. Not too many women can get poisoned chocolates, be interrogated by the police, and sell expensive properties in the same day.

"I'm trying to get John to let me list his house," she told me over the pot roast.

"What? Why would he sell his house? It's beautiful."

"His wife has been dead several years now, and all the children are gone, and he doesn't need a big house to rattle around in," my mother said.

"You've been divorced for twelve years, your child is gone, and you don't need a big house to rattle around in either," I pointed out. I had been wondering why my mother didn't unload the "four br two-story brick w/frpl and 3 baths" I'd grown up in.

"Well, there's a possibility John will have somewhere else to live soon," Mother said too casually. "We may get married."

God, everyone was doing it!

I pulled myself together and looked happy for Mother's sake. I managed to say the right things, and I meant them, and she seemed pleased.

What on earth could I get them for a wedding present?

"Since John doesn't seem to want to talk about his involvement with Real Murders right now," Mother said suddenly, "why don't you just tell me about this club?"

"John's an expert on Lizzie Borden," I explained. "If you really want to know about his main interest, apart from golf and you, it's Lizzie. You ought to read Victoria Lincoln's *A Private Disgrace*. That's one of the best books about the Borden case I've read."

"Um, Aurora . . . who was Lizzie Borden?"

I gaped at my mother. "That's like asking a baseball fan who Mickey Mantle was," I said finally. "I didn't know that a person could not know who Lizzie Borden was. Just ask John. He'll talk your ear off. But if you read the book first, he'll appreciate it."

Mother actually wrote the title in her little notebook. She really meant it about John Queensland, she was really serious about getting married. I couldn't decide how I felt; I only knew how I ought to feel. At least acting that out made my mother happy.

"Really, Aurora, I want you to tell me about the club in general, though I do want to discuss John's particular interest intelligently, of course. Now that you and he are both tied in with this horrible murder, and you and I got sent that candy, I want to know what the background on these crimes is."

"Mother, I can't remember when Real Murders started . . . about three years ago, I guess. There was a book signing at Thy Sting, the mystery book store in the city. And all of us now in Real Murders turned up for the signing, which was being held for a book about a real murder. It was such a funny coincidence, all us Lawrenceton people showing up, interested in the same thing, that we sort of agreed to call each other and start something up we could all come to in our own town. So we began meeting every month, and the format for the meetings just evolved—a lecture and discussion on a real murder most months, a related topic other months." I shrugged. I was getting tired of explaining Real Murders. I expected Mother to change the subject now, as she always had before when I'd tried to talk about my interest in the club.

"You told me earlier that you believe Mamie Wright's

murder was patterned on the Wallace murder," Mother said instead. "And you said that Jane Engle believes that the candy being sent to us is also patterned like another crime—she's trying to look it up?"

I nodded.

"You're in danger," my mother said flatly. "I want you to leave Lawrenceton until this is all over. There's no way you can be implicated, like poor Melanie was with that purse hidden in her car, if you're out of town."

"Well, that would be great, Mom," I said, knowing she hated to be called "Mom," "but I happen to have a job. I'm supposed to just go to my boss and tell him my mother is scared something might happen to me, so I have to get out of town for an indefinite period of time? Just hold my job, Mr. Clerrick?"

"Aren't you scared?" she asked furiously.

"Yes, yes! If you had seen what this killer can do, if you had seen Mamie Wright's head, or what was left of it, you'd be scared too! But I can't leave! I have a life!"

My mother didn't say anything, but her unguarded response, which showed clearly in those amazing eyebrows, was "Since when?"

I went home with a plateful of leftovers for supper, as usual, and decided to have a Sunday afternoon and evening of self-pity. Sunday afternoons are good for that. I took off my pretty dress (no matter what Amina says, I do have some pretty and flattering clothes) and put on my nastiest sweats. I stopped short of washing off my makeup and messing up my hair, but I felt that way.

What I hated to do most was wash windows, so I decided

today was the day. The clouds had lightened a little and I no longer expected rain, so I collected all the window washing paraphernalia and did the downstairs, grimly spraying and wiping and then repeating the process. I carried around my step stool, even with its boost barely reaching the top panes. When they were shining clearly, I trudged upstairs with my cleaning rag and spray bottle and began on the guest bedroom. It overlooked the parking lot, so I had a great view of the elderly couple next door, the Crandalls, coming home in their Sunday best. Perhaps they'd been to a married child's for lunch . . . They had several children here in town, and I recalled Teentsy Crandall mentioning at least eight grandchildren. Teentsy and her husband, Jed, were laughing together, and he patted her on the shoulder as he held open the gate. No sooner were they inside than Bankston's blue car entered the lot and he and Melanie emerged holding hands and smoldering at each other. Even to me, and I am not really experienced, it was apparent that they could hardly wait until they got inside.

As a crowning touch to a feel-sorry-for-yourself afternoon, it could hardly be beat. What did I have to look forward to? I asked myself rhetorically. *60 Minutes* and heated-up pot roast.

I decided I'd take Amina's advice after all. I'd be there when her mom's shop opened at 10:00 the next morning. With luck and my charge card, I could be ready for my trip to the city to have lunch with Robin Crusoe.

Then I decided that there was, after all, something I could do with my evening. I picked up my personal phone book and began dialing.

Chapter Eight

By 8:00 they were all there. It was crowded in my apartment, with Jane, Gerald, and Sally given the best seats and the others perched on chairs from the dinette set or sitting on the floor, like the lovebirds, Melanie and Bankston. I hadn't called Robin, because he had only been to Real Murders one time; one disastrous time. LeMaster Cane was sitting apart from everyone else, speaking to no one, his dark face deliberately blank. Gifford had brought Reynaldo, and they were huddled together with their backs pressed against the wall, looking sullen. Gerald still looked shocked, his pouchy face white and strained. Benjamin Greer was trying to be buddies with Perry Allison, who was openly sneering. Sally was trying not to watch her son, and carrying on a sporadic conversation with Arthur, who

looked exhausted. John's creamy white head was bent toward Jane, who was talking quietly.

Even under the circumstances, I was sorely tempted to stand and say, "I guess you're wondering why I called you all here," but I didn't quite have the nerve. And after all, they knew why they were here.

I had assumed John would take the lead, since he was the president of our club. But he was looking at me expectantly, and I realized that it was up to me to start.

"Friends," I said loudly, and the little rags of conversation stopped as though they'd been trimmed off with a knife. I paused for a minute, trying to marshall my thoughts, and Gifford said, "Stand up so we can see ya."

I saw several nods, so I stood. "First," I resumed, "I want to tell Gerald we're all sorry, grieved, about Mamie." Gerald looked around listlessly, acknowledging the murmur of sympathy with a nod of his head.

"Then," I went on, "I think we need to talk about what's happening to us." I had everyone's undivided attention. "I guess you all know about the tampered-with candy sent to me and my mother. I can't say poisoned, because we don't know for sure it was; so I can't be sure the intent was to kill. But I suppose we can assume that." I looked around to see if anyone would disagree. No one did. "And of course you all also know that Mamie's purse was put in Melanie's car."

Melanie looked down in embarrassment, her straight dark hair swinging forward to hide her face. Bankston put his arm around her and held her close. "As if Melanie would do such a thing," he said hotly.

"Well, we all know that," I said.

"Of course," Jane chimed indignantly.

"I know," I went on very, very carefully, "that Sally and Arthur are in a delicate position tonight. Sally might want to report to the paper that we met, and Arthur will have to tell the police that he was here and what happened. I can see that. But I hope that Sally will agree that tonight is off the record."

Everyone looked at Sally, who threw back her bronze head and glared at us all. "The police want me not to print that the murder was a copy," she said in exasperation. "But everyone in Real Murders has been telling other people anyway. I'm losing the best story I ever had. Now you all want me to not be a reporter tonight. It's like asking Arthur not to be a policeman for a couple of hours."

"Then you won't keep this off the record?" Gifford said unexpectedly. "'Cause if this isn't off the record, I'm out the door." He stared at Sally, and smoothed back his long hair.

"Oh, all right," Sally said. Her tan eyes snapped as she glared around the room. "But I'm telling you all, this is the last time anything said to me about these murders is off the record!"

That reduced us all to speechlessness for a moment.

"Just what did you want us here for, dear?" Jane asked.

Good question. I took the plunge.

"It's probably one of us, right?" I said nervously.

No one moved. No one turned to look at the person beside him.

A presence in the room gathered power in that silence.

That presence was fear, of course. We were all afraid, or getting there.

"But it may be an enemy of someone here," said Arthur finally.

"So, who has enemies?" I inquired. "I know that sounds naive, but for God's sake, we have to think, or we'll be mired in this until someone else dies."

"I think you're overstating this," said Melanie. She actually had a little social smile on her lips.

"How, Melanie?" asked Perry suddenly. "How could Roe possibly be overstating this? We all know what's happened. We sure don't have to be geniuses to figure out that Mamie's murder was meant to be like Julia Wallace's. One of us is nuts. And we all know, from reading so much about it, that a psychotic murderer can be as nice as pie on the outside and a screaming loony inside. What about Ted Bundy?"

"I just meant—" Melanie began uncertainly, "I just meant that maybe, I don't know, someone we don't know is doing this, and it really isn't tied in to us at all. Maybe the presence of a group like ours sparked all this in someone's mind."

"Maybe pigs can fly," muttered Reynaldo, and Gifford laughed.

It wasn't a normal laugh, and the presence was bumping and flopping around the room like a blind thing, ready to grab the first person it lit on. Everyone was getting more and more nervous. I had made a mistake, and we were accomplishing nothing.

"If any one of you does have an enemy, someone who knows about your membership in Real Murders, someone who, maybe, has been reading your club handouts or reading your books, getting interested in what we study, now is the time for you to think of that person," I said. "If we can't come up with someone like that, then this is the last meeting of Real Murders."

This brought another silence, that of shocked realization.

"Of course," breathed Jane Engle. "This is the end of us."

"It may be the end, literally, of more of us if we can't figure this out," Sally said bluntly. "Whoever this is, is going to go on. Can any of you see this stopping? It isn't in the picture. Someone's having a great time, and I'd put my money on it being someone in this room."

"I for one have better things to do than sit in a room with all these accusations going around," Benjamin said. "I'm in politics now, and I would have quit Real Murders anyway. Don't anyone come trying to kill me, that's all, because I'll be waiting for him."

He left amid uneasy whispering, and before he was quite out my back door, Gifford said audibly, "Benjamin isn't worth killing. What an asshole."

We were all feeling some permutation on that theme, I imagine.

"I'm sorry," I said to everyone. "I thought I could accomplish something. I thought if we were all together, we could remember something that would help solve this horrible murder."

Everyone began to shift slightly, preparing to gather up whatever or whoever they'd come with.

John Queensland exhibited an unexpected sense of drama.

"The last meeting of Real Murders is now adjourned," he said formally.

Chapter Nine

I looked wonderful. Amina's mom had nodded thoughtfully when I told her I needed something new to wear to
lunch in the city, and it had to be something I could wear
to work too. Amina hadn't told me to add that, but Amina
wasn't paying the bill. Mrs. Day flicked the laden hangers
with a professional hand. She glanced from blouses to me
with narrowed eyes, while I tried not to look as silly (or as
hopeful) as I felt.

She extracted an ivory blouse with dark green vines
twining up it, and a dark green bow ("At your age, honey,
you don't need a bright one, too young") that nestled in the
wild waves of my hair with definite femininity. I got
khaki-colored pants with a wide belt and extravagant
pleats, and shoes, too. I slipped them on to wear away from

the store. Mrs. Day clucked over my lipstick (not dark enough), but I stuck by my guns. I hated dark lipstick.

This was not a showy outfit, but it was a definite change for me. I felt great, and as I drove the mile out of town that got me to the interstate circling the city, I felt quite confident Robin would be impressed.

I felt less certain when I peeked through the one glass pane in the classroom door. As Amina had predicted, there were lots of cute college "chickies" in Robin's creative writing workshop. I was willing to bet seven out of nine wrote poetry that dealt with world hunger and bitter endings to relationships. At least five weren't wearing bras. The four men in the workshop were of the serious and scraggly variety. They probably wrote existential plays. Or poetry about bitter endings to relationships.

When the rest rose to leave, two of the cute chickies lingered to fascinate Robin. I was smiling, thinking of Amina as I went into the classroom.

Robin naturally thought the grin was for him. He beamed back. "Glad you found the room okay," he said, and the young women—I reminded myself they were not girls—turned to stare at me. "Lisa, Kimberly, this is Aurora Teagarden." Oh, I hadn't seen that one coming. Robin and his good manners. The brunette looked incredulous, and the streaky blond sniggered before she could stop herself.

"Are you ready for lunch?" Robin asked, and their faces straightened in a jiffy.

Thanks, Robin. "Yes, let's go," I said clearly, smiling all the while.

"Sure. Well, I'll see you in class Wednesday," he told Lisa and Kimberly. They sauntered out with their armfuls of books, and Robin tossed a couple of anthologies into his briefcase. "Let me just stow this in my office," he said. His office was right across the hall and was full of books and papers, but not his, Robin explained. "James Artis was supposed to teach three writers' workshops and one class on the history of the mystery novel. But when he had a heart attack, he recommended me."

"Why'd you take it?" I asked. We strolled across campus companionably, heading for a salad and sandwich restaurant just down the street.

"I needed a change," he said. "I was tired of being shut up in a room writing all day. I'd written three books in a row with little or no break in between, I had no exciting ideas for my next book, and teaching just sounded interesting. James recommended Lawrenceton as a place where I wouldn't have to go broke paying rent, and after I'd been staying in a vacant visitor's room in one of the men's dorms for a couple of weeks, I was grateful to find the town house."

"Are you planning on staying for any length of time?" I asked delicately.

"That depends on the success of the workshops and the class," he said, "and James's health. Even if I leave the university, I might stay in the area. So far I like it here just as well as the place I was living before. I don't really have ties anywhere anymore. My parents have retired to Florida, so I don't have a reason to go back to my home town . . . St. Louis," he said in answer to my unspoken question.

He held open the door to the restaurant. It was a ferny

place, with waiters and waitresses in matching aprons and blue jeans. Our waiter's name was Don, and he was happy to serve us today. A local "mellow" rock listening station was being piped in for all us old rockers, who ranged in age from twenty-eight to forty-two. As we were looking at the menus, I decided to start lusting, as per Amina's instructions. While we ordered, I seemed to get it misdirected, for Don got pretty red in the face and kept trying to look down my blouse. Robin seemed to be receiving the brunt of it though. He rather hesitantly (high noon, public place, had to teach a class that afternoon) took my hand across the table.

I never knew how to react to that. My thoughts always ran, Wow, he took my hand, does that mean he wants to go to bed with me, or date me more, or what? And I never knew where to look. Into his eyes? Too challenging. At his hand? Pretty stupid. And was I supposed to move my hand to clasp his? Uncomfortable. I never *was* much good at this.

Our salads arrived, so we unhitched hands and picked up our forks with some relief. I was wondering whether I should try to keep on lusting while I ate, when I realized James Taylor had trailed to an end and the news was starting. The name of my town always made me pay attention. A neutral woman's voice was saying, "In other news, Lawrenceton mayoral candidate Morrison Pettigrue was found slain today. Pettigrue, thirty-five, was campaigning as the candidate of the Communist Party. His campaign manager, Benjamin Greer, found Pettigrue dead of stab wounds in the bathtub of his Lawrenceton home. Sheets of paper were floating in the water, but police would not say whether any of those sheets contained a suicide note. Police have no suspects in the slaying, and declined to speculate on whether the killing was, as Greer claims, a political assassination."

Our forks poised in midair, Robin and I stared at each other like stricken loonies, and not in lust either.

"In the tub," Robin said.

"With a knife. And the paper clinches it."

"Marat," we said in unison.

"Poor Benjamin," I said on my own. He'd rejected us, launched on his own new direction, and gotten kicked in the nuts.

"Smith would recognize it, right?" Robin asked me after some fruitless speculation on our part.

"I think so," I said confidently. "Arthur's smart and well-read."

"Did you ever find out if the chocolates fit a pattern?"

"It rang a bell with Jane Engle," I told him, and then had to explain who she was and why her memory was reliable. He'd only met the members of Real Murders once. "She's looking for the right case."

"Do you think she'll know by tomorrow night?" he asked.

"Well, I may see her today. Maybe she will have found something by then."

"Is there a nice restaurant in Lawrenceton?"

"Well, there's the Carriage House." It was a real carriage house, and required a reservation; the only place in Lawrenceton that had the pretensions to do so. I offered the names of a few more places, but the Carriage House had struck his fancy.

"This lunch is a washout, we haven't eaten half our salad," he pointed out. "Let me take you out tomorrow night, and we'll have time to talk and eat."

"Why, thanks. Okay. The Carriage House is a dressy place," I added, and wondered if the hint offended him.

"Thanks for warning me," Robin said to my relief. "I'll walk you back to your car."

When I glanced at my watch, I saw he was right. All this walking, lusting, and speculation had used up as much time as I had, and I'd just make it to work on time.

"If you don't mind making our reservation, I'll pick you up tomorrow at 7:00," Robin said as we reached my car.

Well, we had another date, though I didn't think it was strictly a social date. Robin had a professional interest in these murders, I figured, and I was the local who could interpret the scene for him. But he gave me a peck on the cheek as I eased into my car, and I drove back to Lawrenceton singing James Taylor.

That was much nicer than picturing dark, scowling, acne-scarred Morrison Pettigrue turning the bath water scarlet with his blood.

Chapter Ten

"Cordelia Botkin, 1898," Jane hissed triumphantly.

She'd come up behind me as I was reshelving books that had been checked in. I was at the end of a stack close to the wall, about to wheel my cart around the end and onto the next row. I drew in a breath down low in my chest, shut my eyes, and prayed to forgive her. Tuesday morning had been going so well.

"Roe, I'm so sorry! I thought you must have heard me coming."

I shook my head. I tried not to lean on the cart so obviously.

"Cordelia who?" I finally managed to say.

"Botkin. It's close enough. It doesn't actually fit, but it's close enough. This was so sloppy that I think it was an afterthought, or maybe this was even supposed to come off before Mamie Wright was killed."

"You're probably right, Jane. The box of candy took six days to get here, and it was mailed from the city, so whoever sent it probably thought I'd get it in two or three days."

I glanced around to see if anyone was in earshot. Lillian Schmidt, another librarian, was shelving books a few stacks away, but she wasn't actually within hearing distance.

"How does it fit, Jane?"

Jane flipped open the notebook she always seemed to have with her. "Cordelia Botkin lived in San Francisco. She became the mistress of the Associated Press bureau chief, John Dunning. He'd left a wife back in . . ." Jane scanned her notes, ". . . Dover, Delaware. Botkin mailed the wife several anonymous letters first, did your mother get any?"

I nodded. With a very stiff upper lip, Mother had told Lynn Liggett something she'd never thought significant enough to tell me: she'd gotten an incomprehensible and largely nasty anonymous letter in the mail a few days before the candy came. She'd thought the incident so ugly and meaningless that she hadn't wanted to "upset" me with it. She had thrown it away, of course, but it had been typed.

I was willing to bet it had been typed on the same machine that had typed the mailing label on the package.

"Anyway," Jane continued after checking her notes, "Cordelia finally decided Dunning was going back to his wife, so she poisoned some bonbons and mailed them to Dunning's wife. The wife and a friend of hers died."

"Died," I said slowly.

Jane nodded, tactfully keeping her eyes on her notes. "Your father is still in newspapers, isn't he, Roe?"

"Yes, he's not a reporter, but he's head of the advertising department."

"And he's living with his new wife, which could be said to represent 'another woman.'"

"Well, yes."

"So obviously the murderer saw the outline was roughly the same and seized the opportunity."

"Did you tell Arthur Smith about this?"

"I thought I had better," Jane said, with a wise nod of her head.

"What did he say?" I asked.

"He wanted to know which book I'd gotten my information from, wrote that down, thanked me, looked harassed, and told me good-bye. I got the impression he's having trouble convincing his superiors about the significance of these murders. What was in the candy, do you know yet?"

"No, they took the box to the state lab for analysis. Arthur warned us that some of the tests take quite a while."

Lillian was moving closer and looking curious, a chronic state with Lillian. But all my co-workers were regarding me with more than normal interest. A quiet librarian finds a body at the meeting of a pretty odd club on Friday night, gets a box of doctored chocolates in the mail on Saturday, turns up dressed in all new and uncharacteristic clothes on

Monday, has a whispered conference with an excited woman on Tuesday.

"I'd better go. I'm disturbing you at work," Jane whispered. She knew Lillian quite well. "But I was so excited when I tracked down the pattern, I just had to run down here and tell you. Of course, the Communist man's murder was patterned after the Marat assassination. Poor Benjamin Greer! He found the body, the newscast said."

"Jane, I appreciate your researching this for me," I hissed back. "I'll take you out to lunch next week to thank you." The last thing I wanted to talk about was Morrison Pettigrue's murder.

"Oh, my goodness, that's not necessary. You gave me something to do for a while. Substituting at the school and filling in here are interesting, but nothing has been as much fun in a long time as tracking down the right murder. However, I suspect I will have to get a new hobby. All these deaths, all this fear. This is getting too close to the bone for me." And Jane sighed, though whether over the deaths of Mamie Wright and Morrison Pettigrue, or because she had to find a new hobby, I could not tell.

I was on the second floor of the library, which is a large gallery running around three walls and overlooking the ground floor, where the children's books, periodicals, and circulation desk are located. I was watching Jane stride out the front door and thinking about Cordelia Botkin when I recognized someone else who was exiting. It was Detective Lynn Liggett. The library director, Sam Clerrick, seemed to be walking her to the door. This struck me unpleasantly. I could only suppose that Lynn Liggett had been at the library asking questions about me. Maybe she had wanted to know my work hours? More about my character? How long I had been at work that day?

Filled with uneasy speculation, I rounded the corner of the next stack. I began shelving books automatically, still brooding over Detective Liggett's visit to the library. There was nothing bad Sam Clerrick could tell her about me, I reasoned. I was a conscientious employee. I was always on time, and I almost never got sick. I had never yelled at a member of the public, no matter how I'd been tempted—especially by parents who dumped their children at the library in the summer with instructions to amuse themselves for a couple of hours while mommy and daddy went shopping.

So why was I worried? I lectured myself. I was just seeing the down side of being involved in a criminal investigation. It was practically my civic duty not to mind being the object of police scrutiny.

I wondered if I could reasonably be considered a suspect in Mamie's murder. I could have done it, of course. I'd been home unobserved for at least an hour or more before I left for the meeting. Maybe one of the other tenants could vouch for my car being in its accustomed place, though that wouldn't be conclusive proof. And I supposed if I could have found a place that sold Mrs. See's, I could have mailed myself the candy. I could have typed the label on one of the library typewriters. Maybe Detective Liggett had been getting typing samples from all the machines! Though if the samples did match the label, it wouldn't be proof that I typed it myself. And if the sample didn't match,

I could have used another machine—maybe one in my mother's office?

Now the murder of Morrison Pettigrue was another kettle of fish entirely. I had never met Mr. Pettigrue, and now never would. I hadn't known where he lived until one of the other librarians had told me, but I couldn't prove either of those things, now that I came to think about it. Ignorance is hard to prove. Besides, if he'd been killed late Sunday night after the abortive last meeting of Real Murders, I had no alibi at all. I'd been home alone feeling sorry for myself.

However, if by some miracle the killing could be proved to have occurred during the hour we were all together, we'd all be cleared! That would be too good to be true.

I was so busy trying to imagine all the pros and cons of arresting me that I bumped into Sally Allison, literally. She was looking at the books on needlework, of which the library had scores, Lawrenceton being a hell of a town for needlework.

I murmured an apology. Sally murmured back, "Don't think about it," but then she stayed glued to her spot, her eyes all too pointedly on the titles in front of her. The past couple of months, Sally has been a frequent patron of the library, even during what I supposed were her working hours. I didn't think she came to check out books, though she did leave with some every time. I was convinced she was checking on Perry. I wasn't surprised after what Amina had told me. Sometimes Sally didn't even speak to her son, I'd noticed, but eyed him from a distance, as if watching for some sign of trouble.

"How's your mother, Roe?" Sally asked.

"Just fine, thank you."

"Gotten over your scare about the candy? I didn't get to ask you last night."

Sally had called both Mother and me for an interview when she'd read the police blotter after the candy incident. Mother and I separately had been as brief as was congruent with courtesy, we discovered later when we compared notes. I thought my name had been in the paper enough recently, and Mother thought the whole incident too sordid to discuss. (Mother also, in her career-woman mode, thought an attempted poisoning would be bad for business.)

"Sally, I wasn't scared, because I didn't know then and I don't know now that someone was actually trying to hurt me or my mother. I'm going to say frankly, Sally, that you're my friend and you're a reporter, and I'm not sure recently just who I'm talking to."

Sally turned to face me. She was not angry, but she was determined. "Being a reporter on a small newspaper doesn't mean I'm not a real reporter, Roe. You're a Teagarden, so what happens to you is doubly news. Your mother is a very prominent woman in this town, and your father is a well-known man. The owner of our newspaper will not keep this police gag order agreement much longer. Does that answer your question? Lillian's coming. Have you read this book on bargello?"

I blinked and recovered. "Now, Sally, I can't sew on a button. You'd have to ask Mother if you want to know about needlework. Or Lillian," I added brilliantly, as my co-worker wheeled her own cart past the other end of the stack.

Lillian, whose ears are as fine-tuned as a bat's, heard her own name and turned in, and right away she and Sally were embroiled in an incomprehensible conversation about French knots and candlewicking. A little sadly, I returned to my shelving. When I was no longer news, I wondered whether Sally would decide she was just a friend again.

When I looked at my watch and discovered it was four o'clock and I was due to get off at six, I realized I'd better think about what I was going to wear to the Carriage House with Robin. He had mentioned picking me up at seven, which gave me a scant hour to get home, shower, redo my makeup, and dress. Reservations had been no problem; Tuesday was not a heavy night at the Carriage House, and I'd told them 7:15. Now I had to decide what to wear. My dark blue silk was back from the cleaner's. Had I ever taken the matching sandals to be repaired after I noticed the strap coming loose? Desperately I wished I had bought the black heels I'd seen at Amina's mom's shop the previous morning. They'd had bows on the back of the heel, and I'd thought they were ravishing. Would I have time to run by and get them?

Gradually I became aware that someone was humming on the other side of my stack with a droning, bee-like monotony. It could only be Lillian. Sure enough, when I pulled out a veterinarian's "humorous look at life with animals in and out of the house" which had been thrown in with the 364's, Lillian's round face was visible through the gap.

"I think we should be earning more money," Lillian said sulkily, "and I think we should be asked before being scheduled to work nights, and I think they should never have hired that new head librarian."

"Sam Clerrick? Nights?" I said foolishly, not knowing where to begin with my questions. Lillian had been a big Sam Clerrick fan before this moment, to the best of my knowledge. Mr. Clerrick seemed intelligent and tough to me, but I was reserving judgment on his ability to manage people.

"Oh, you haven't heard," Lillian said with pleasure. "What with all the excitement in your life lately, I guess you haven't had too much time to pay attention to ordinary everyday stuff."

I rolled my eyes to the ceiling. "Lillian, what?"

Lillian wriggled her heavy shoulders in anticipation. "You know, the Board of Trustees met two nights ago? Of course, Sam Clerrick was there, and he told them that in his view staying open at night hadn't been tried sufficiently four years ago, when it was such a flop—you remember? He wants to reinstate it for a time, with the present staff. So instead of being open one night a week we'll be open three, for a four-month trial."

Four years ago Lawrenceton had been a smaller town, and remaining open more than one night a week past six o'clock had only resulted in a higher electric bill and some bored librarians. Our one late night was a token bow to people who worked odd hours and couldn't get to the library any other time. Business had been picking up on that night, I thought fairly, and in view of Lawrenceton's recent population boom, another try at a night opening was reasonable. Still, I felt mildly perturbed at the change in my schedule.

On the other hand, it was hard to regard my job as the most important thing in my life lately.

"How's he going to do it without increasing staff?" I asked without much interest.

"Instead of being on two librarians at a time, we'll be on in terms of librarian and volunteer on an open night."

The volunteers were a mixed bunch. Mostly they tended to be older men and middle-aged to elderly women who really enjoyed books and felt at home in a library. Once they'd been trained, they were a godsend, except the very small percentage who'd taken the job to see their friends and gossip. That small percentage soon got bored and quit the program, anyway.

"I'm game," I told Lillian.

"We're going to find out more about it officially today," Lillian went on, looking disappointed at my mild reaction. "There's a staff meeting at 5:30, so Perry Allison's going to relieve you at the circulation desk. Hey," and Lillian looked at her watch obviously, "isn't it time for you to get down there now?"

"Yes, Lillian, I see that it is," I said with elaborate patience, "and I am going." We took turns on circulation as we did on almost every job, since the staff was too small for much specialization but definitely full of individuals who didn't hesitate to make their preferences known. I was darned if I was going to scurry downstairs because Lillian had looked at her watch, so I continued, "I'm willing to give night hours another shot. More time off during the day might be nice, too." *Since my night social calendar is not exactly crowded*, but I didn't feel it necessary to share that thought with Lillian.

I was relieved that the meeting wasn't going to be after the official library closing at 6:00. I suddenly recalled for sure that the sandals that went with the blue silk dress had a broken strap. "Crumbs," I muttered, shelving the last book on my cart with such force that one on the opposite side shot out and landed on the floor.

"My goodness," said Lillian triumphantly as she bent to retrieve it. "What's put us in such a snit, huh?"

I said something besides "crumbs," but I only moved my lips.

I usually enjoyed my tour in Circulation. I got to stand at the big desk to one side of the main entrance. I answered questions and accepted the books, taking the fines if the books were overdue, sliding their cards back in and putting them on book carts for transportation back to their shelves. Or I checked the books out. If there was a lot of traffic, I got a helper.

Today was a slow day, which was good since my mind wouldn't stay on my work but meandered down its own path. How close my mother had come to eating a piece of that candy. How Mamie's head had looked from the back. How glad I was I hadn't seen the front. Whether the importance of being the *finder of the body* had given Benjamin a new lease on life after the death of his political ambitions. How pleased I was about going out with Robin that night. How exciting I found Arthur Smith's blue eyes.

I yanked my thoughts away from this half-pleasant half-frightening stream of thought to exchange desultory conversation with the volunteer sitting with me at the check-out desk: Lizanne Buckley's father, Arnie, a 66-year-old white-haired retiree with a mind like a steel trap. Once Mr. Buckley grew interested in a subject, he read everything he could find about it, and he forgot precious little of what he read. When he was through with that subject, he was through for good, but he remained a semi-authority on it. Mr. Buckley confessed on this warmish sleepy afternoon that he was beginning to find it difficult to find a new subject to research. I asked him how he's found them before, and he said it had always happened naturally.

"For example, I see a bee on my roses. I say to myself, Gee! Isn't that bee smaller than the one over on that rose? Are they the same kind of bee? Does this kind only get pollen from roses? Why aren't there more roses growing wild if bees carry rose pollen all over? So I read up on bees, and maybe roses. But lately, I don't know, nothing seems to jump out and grab me."

I sympathized and suggested now that warmer weather would permit him to take more walks, a new subject would present itself.

"In view of what's been happening in this town recently," Mr. Buckley commented, "I thought it might be interesting to research murderers."

I looked at him sharply, but he wasn't trying to hint about the involvement of Real Murders members in the series of crimes.

"Why don't you do that?" I asked after a minute.

"The books are all checked out," he said.

"What?"

"Almost all the nonfiction books about murder and murderers are out," he elaborated patiently.

That wasn't so startling, once I had time to mull it over. All the members of Real Murders—all the former members of Real Murders—were undoubtedly boning up and preparing themselves however they could for what might happen.

But someone might be boning up to make the happening occur.

That was sickening. I looked it in the face for a second, then had to turn away. I could not visualize, did not dare to visualize, someone I knew poring over books, trying to select what old murder to imitate next, what terrible act to re-create on the body of someone he knew.

Perry came to the desk to relieve me so I could attend the meeting, which seemed so irrelevant I almost picked up my sweater and walked out the front door instead. I had a date tonight, too. Suddenly my pleasure in that date was ashes in my mouth. At least part of my bleak mood could be written up to Perry; he was definitely in the throes of one of his downswings. His lips were set in a sullen line, the parentheses from nose to mouth deeper.

I felt sorry for Perry suddenly, and said, "Hi, see you later," as warmly as I could as I passed him on my way to the conference room. I regretted the warmth as he smiled in return. I wished he had stayed sullen. His smile was as vicious and meaningless as a shark's. I could imagine Perry as the Victorian poseur Neal Cream, giving prostitutes poison pills and then hanging around, hoping to watch them swallow.

"Go along to the meeting now," he said nastily.

I gladly left as Arnie Buckley began the uphill battle of making conversation with Perry.

With no enthusiasm at all, I slumped in a dreadful metal chair in the library conference room and heard the news that was already stale. Mr. Clerrick, with his usual efficiency and lack of knowledge of the human race, had already prepared the new duty charts and he distributed them on the spot, instead of giving everyone the chance to digest and discuss the new schedule.

I was down for Thursday night from six to nine, with Mr. Buckley penciled in tentatively as my volunteer; the volunteers hadn't yet been asked individually if they were willing to work nights, though the volunteer president had agreed in principle. Mr. Clerrick was going to put an advertisement in the newspaper telling our patrons the exciting news. (He actually said that.)

"Going out with our new resident writer tonight?" Perry inquired smoothly when I returned to the check-in desk.

He took me by surprise; my mind had been firmly on work, for once.

"Yes," I said bluntly, without thought. "Why?"

I'd let my distaste show; a mistake. I should have kept the surface of things amiable.

"Oh, no reason," Perry said airily, but he began to smile, a smile so false and disagreeable that for the first time I felt a little afraid.

"I'll take the desk now," I said. "You can go back to your work." I didn't smile and my voice was flat; it was too late now to patch it up. For an awful minute I didn't think he'd go, that the terrible gloom in Perry's head made him utterly reckless of keeping the surface of his life sewn together.

"See you later," Perry said, with no smile at all.

I watched him go with goose bumps on my arms.

"Did he say something nasty to you, Roe?" asked Mr. Buckley. He looked as pugnacious as a tiny old man with white hair can look.

"Not really. It's the way he said it," I answered, wanting to be truthful but not wanting to upset Lizanne's father.

"That boy's got snakes in his head," Mr. Buckley pronounced.

"I think you must be right. Now about this new schedule . . ."

We were soon busy again, and the surface of things was restored; but I thought Perry Allison did indeed have snakes in his head, and that his mother's frequent calls at the library were monitoring visits. Sally Allison was aware of the snakes, frightened they might slither through the widening holes in Perry's mental state.

Mr. Buckley and I were kept busy until closing time, with a spate of "patrons" of all ages, coming in to do schoolwork, returning books after they'd left work. Being busy made me feel more like myself again, more like there was a point to what I was doing.

Arthur Smith was waiting by my car. I was so intent on getting home to get ready, and was so short on time, that I was more miffed than glad to see him at first.

"I hated to interrupt you at work unless I had to," he said in his serious way.

"It's all right, Arthur. Do you have any news for me?" I thought perhaps the lab had analyzed whatever was in the chocolates.

"No, the lab work hasn't come back yet. Do you have any time?"

"Um . . . well, a few minutes."

To my pleasure, he didn't look surprised at my lack of time.

"Well, come sit in my car, or walk with me down the block."

I elected to walk, not wanting Lillian Schmidt to see me in a car with a man in the parking lot, for some reason. So we strolled down the sidewalk in the cooling of the evening. I can't keep up with some men since my legs are so short that they have to slow considerably but Arthur seemed to adapt well.

"What did you expect of that meeting Sunday night?" he asked abruptly.

"I don't know what I expected. A miracle. I wanted someone to have an idea that would make the whole nightmare go away. Instead, someone went out and killed Morrison Pettigrue. My meeting really worked, huh?"

"That death was planned before the meeting. What bites me is that I sat there in the same room with whoever killed that man, hours before he did it, and I didn't feel a thing. Even knowing a murderer was in that room . . ." He stopped, shook his head violently, and kept walking.

"Do the other police believe what you do, that one person is doing all this?"

"I'm having a hard time convincing some of the other detectives about the similarities of these two cases to old murders. And since the Pettigrue murder, they're even less inclined to listen, even though when I saw the scene I told them myself it was like the assassination of Jean-Paul Marat. They almost laughed. There are so many right-wing loonies who might want to kill an avowed Communist, only one or two of the other detectives are willing to accept that all these incidents are related."

"I saw Lynn Liggett at the library today. I guess she was checking up on me."

"We're checking up on anyone remotely involved," Arthur said flatly. "Liggett's just doing her job. I'm supposed to find out where you were Sunday night."

"After the meeting?"

He nodded.

"At home. In bed. Alone. You know I didn't have anything to do with Mamie's death, or the chocolates, or Morrison Pettigrue's murder."

"I know. I saw you when you found Mrs. Wright's body."

I felt a ridiculous flood of warmth and gratitude at being believed.

It was already late, and I did have to get ready, so I ventured, "Is there anything else you wanted to see me about?"

"I'm a divorced man without any children," Arthur said abruptly.

Taken aback, I nodded. I tried to look intelligently inquiring.

"One of the reasons I got divorced . . . my wife couldn't stand the fact that in police work, sometimes things came up and I couldn't make it on time for something we'd planned. Even in Lawrenceton, which is not New York or even Atlanta, right?"

He paused for a response, so I said, "Right," uncertainly.

"So, I want to go out with you." Those hard blue eyes turned on me with devastating effect. "But things will come up, and sometimes you'll be disappointed. You'd have to understand beforehand, if you want to go out with me too. I don't know if you do, but I wanted to get this all out front."

I thought: (a) this was admirably frank, (b) did this guy have an ego, or what?, (c) since he had said, "I don't know if you do," there was hope for him, though it had probably been just a sop thrown in my direction, and (d) I did want to go out with him, but not from a position of weakness. Arthur was a strength-respecter.

It took me a few moments to work this through. A few days before, I would have said, "Okay," meekly, but since then I had weathered a few storms and it seemed to me I could manage better for myself.

I watched my feet pacing along the sidewalk as I said, "If you're saying you want to go out with me, but that anything you're doing is more important than plans we might make, I can't agree to abide by such a lopsided—understanding." I watched my feet move steadily. Arthur's shoes were shiny and black and would last maybe twenty years. "Now, if you're saying the police department has priority in a crisis, I can see that. If you're not just providing a blanket excuse in advance to cover any time you just might feel like not showing up." I took a deep breath. So far those shoes had not marched off in another direction. "Okay. Also, this is sounding very—exclusive, since we haven't even been out yet. I would like to handle this one date at a time."

I'd underestimated Arthur.

"I must have sounded too egotistical to swallow," he said. "I'm sorry. Will you go out with me one time?"

"Okay," I said. Then I didn't know what to do. I looked sideways at him and he was smiling. "What did I say 'okay' to?" I asked.

"Unless I get assigned something I have to do, you have to remember this department is in the middle of a murder investigation . . ." As if I was going to forget! ". . . Saturday night? I've got a popcorn popper and a VCR."

No first dates at a man's apartment. By God, he could take me out someplace the first time. I didn't feel like wrestling right away. My experience was limited, but I knew that much. Besides, with Arthur I might not wrestle, and I didn't want to start a relationship that way.

"I want to go roller skating," I said out of the blue.

Arthur couldn't have looked more stunned if I'd told him I wanted to jump off the library roof. Why had I said that? I hadn't gone skating in years. I'd be black and blue and make a klutz of myself in the bargain.

But maybe he would too.

"That's original," Arthur said slowly. "You really want to do that?"

Stuck with it, I nodded grimly.

"Okay," he said firmly. "I'll pick you up at six, Saturday night. If that's all right. Then after we harm ourselves enough, we can go out to eat. All this is assuming I can have an evening off in the middle of three investigations. But maybe we'll have it wrapped up by then."

"Fine," I said. I could accept that.

We'd circled the block, so we parted at our respective cars. I watched Arthur pull out of the parking lot, and saw he was shaking his head to himself. I laughed out loud.

I hated being late and I was late for my date with Robin. I had to ask him to wait downstairs while I put on the finishing touches.

I'd bought the shoes and I was enchanted with myself. Robin didn't seem surprised or put out at having to wait; but I felt rude and at a disadvantage, as if I should have something better to show as the end result of all this preparation. However, as I looked in my full-length mirror before going down, I saw I hadn't turned out badly. There hadn't been time to put up my hair, so I wore it loose with the front held back with a cloisonne butterfly comb. The blue silk dress was sober but at least did emphasize my visible assets.

I felt very unsure before I went down the stairs, very self-conscious when I saw Robin look up. But he seemed pleased, and said, "I like your dress." In his gray suit he didn't seem like the companionable person who'd drunk my wine, or the college professor I'd pelvically lusted after at the restaurant, but more like the fairly famous writer he really was.

We discussed the Pettigrue murder at our table at the Carriage House, where the hostess seemed to recognize Robin's name vaguely. Though maybe she was thinking of the book character. She pronounced it "Cur-so" and gave us a good table.

I asked him to tell me about his job at the university and how it would jibe with his writing time, both questions he seemed to have answered before. I realized this man was used to being interviewed, used to being recognized. I only felt better when I recalled that Lizanne had "bequeathed" him to me, and right on the tail of that thought, Lizanne's parents, Arnie and Elsa, were seated at the table opposite ours. The Crandalls, who had the town house to the right of mine, sat down with them.

I had a social obligation here, so I identified them to Robin and went over to their table.

Arnie Buckley jumped right up and pumped Robin's hand enthusiastically. "Our Lizanne told us all about you!" he said. "We're proud a famous writer like you has come to live in Lawrenceton. Do you like it?" Mr. Buckley had always been a Chamber of Commerce member and unashamed Lawrenceton booster.

"It's an exciting place," said Robin honestly.

"Well, well, you'll have to come by the library. Not as sophisticated as what you'll find in the city, but we like it! Elsa and I are both volunteers. Get to give our time to something now that we're retired!"

~ 122 ~

"I mostly just help with the book sale," Elsa said modestly.

Elsa was Lizanne's stepmother, but she had been as pretty as Lizanne's mother must have been. Arnie Buckley was a lucky man when it came to pretty women. Now gray-haired and wrinkled, Elsa was still pleasant to look at and be with.

I hadn't known the Buckleys were friends of the Crandalls, but I could see where the attraction would lie. Jed Crandall, like Mr. Buckley, was no chair-bound retiree, but a pepper pot of a man, easily angered and easily appeased. His wife had always been called Teentsy, and was still, though now she certainly outweighed her husband by forty pounds or more.

Teentsy and Jed now said the proper things to Robin about their being neighbors, asking him to drop in, Teentsy saying since he was a poor bachelor (and here she shot me a sly look) he might run short of food sometime, and if he did, just to knock on their door, they had a-plenty, as he could look at her and tell!

"Are you at all interested in guns?" Jed asked eagerly.

"Mr. Jed has quite a collection," I told Robin hastily, thinking he might need to be forewarned.

"Well, sometimes, from a professional standpoint. I'm a mystery writer," he explained when the Crandalls looked blank, though the Buckleys were nodding with vigor, bless their hearts.

"Come by then, don't be a stranger!" Jed Crandall urged.

"Thank you, nice meeting you," Robin said to the table

in general, and in a chorus of "see you soon's" and "nice to've met you's" we retired to our table.

The meeting nudged Robin's voracious curiosity, and in telling him about the Crandalls and the Buckleys I began to feel more comfortable. We talked about Robin's new job, and then our food came, and by the time we began eating, I was ready to talk about the murders.

"Jane Engle came by the library today with a pretty solid theory," I began, and told Robin about the likeness of "our" case to that of Cordelia Botkin. He was intrigued.

"I've never heard of anything quite like this," he said after our salad had been served. "What a book this would make! Maybe I'll write about it myself, my first nonfiction book." He had more distance from the case; new in town, he didn't know the victims personally (unless you could term Mother a victim) and probably he didn't know the perpetrator either. I was surprised that the crimes were so exciting to him, until he said after he'd swallowed a mouthful of tomato, "You know, Roe, writing about crime doesn't mean you have direct experience. This is the closest I've ever come to a real murder."

I could have said the same thing as a reader. I'd been an avid fan of both real and fictional crime for years, but this was my closest brush with violent death.

"I hope I never come any closer," I said abruptly.

He reached across the table and took my hand. "It doesn't seem too likely," he said cautiously. "I know the poisoned candy—well, we don't know yet if it was really poisoned or not, do we? That was scary. But it was impersonal, too, wasn't it? Your mother's situation vaguely fit the Botkin case, even if not as well as Mamie Wright fit Julia Wallace's profile. That was why she was picked."

"But it was sent to *my address*," I said, suddenly letting a fear overwhelm me that I thought I'd suppressed. "That was to involve me. My mother fit the pattern; though that wouldn't have been any consolation to me if she'd died," I added sharply. "But sending it to my place. That was a deliberate attempt to make me—die. Or at least a witness to my mother's dying, or getting sick, depending on what was in the chocolates. That doesn't fit any pattern. That's about as personal as you can get."

"What kind of person could *do* that?" Robin asked.

I met his eyes. "That's the core, isn't it," I said. "That's one reason we like old murders so much. At a safe remove, we can think about the kind of person who can 'do that' without remorse. Almost anyone could kill another person. I guess I could, if it came to being cornered. But I'm sure, I have to be sure, that not many people could sit back and plan other people dying as part of a game the killer decided to play. I have to believe that."

"I do too," he said.

"This really is someone who isn't acting for any of the famous motives Tennyson Jessie wrote about," I continued. "It must be someone acting out something he's always wanted to do. For some reason, now he's able to actually do it."

"A member of your club."

"A former member," I said sadly, and told Robin about the Sunday night meeting.

We had to talk about something else; didn't we have

anything to discuss besides murders? Robin, bless him, seemed to see I couldn't take any more, and began telling me about his agent and about the process of getting a book published. He kept me laughing with anecdotes about book signings he'd endured, and I responded with stories about people that came to the library and some of the wilder questions they'd asked. We actually had a cheerful evening, and we were still at our table when the Crandalls and the Buckleys paid their bill and left.

Since the Carriage House was at the south end of town, we had to pass in front of our town houses to turn into the driveway on the side. There was a man standing in front of the row of town houses, on the sidewalk. As we went by, he turned his white face to us, and by the light of the streetlamp, I thought I recognized Perry.

I was distracted though by the kiss Robin gave me at my back door. It was unexpected and delicious, and the disparity in our heights was overcome quite satisfactorily. Maybe his asking me out hadn't been quite so impersonal as I'd supposed; his side of the kiss was delivered with great enthusiasm.

I went upstairs humming to myself and feeling very attractive; and when I slipped into my dark bedroom and peered out the window, the street was empty.

That night it rained. I was wakened by the drops pelting against my window. I could see the lightning flicker through my curtains.

I crept downstairs and rechecked my locks. I listened, and heard only the rain. I looked out all the windows and saw only the rain. By the streetlamp out front, I saw the water racing down the slight slope to the storm drain at the end of the block. Nothing else stirred.

Chapter Eleven

Getting up and going to work the next morning wasn't too easy, but it was reassuring. I caught myself humming in the shower and I put on more eye shadow than usual, but my denim skirt, striped blouse, and braided hair felt like a comforting uniform. Lillian and I were mending books in a windowless back room all morning. We managed to get along by swapping recipes or discussing the academic prowess of Lillian's seven-year-old. Though my part of this discussion consisted only of saying "Oh, my goodness," or "Ooh," at the appropriate moments, that suited me. I might have children myself one day—maybe stocky blond ones? Or big-nosed giants with flaming hair? And I would certainly tell everyone I met how wonderful they were.

It was good to get up from the work table and stretch before going home for lunch. I'd been so slow getting up I'd had a scanty breakfast, so I was pretty hungry and trying to visualize what was in my refrigerator as I twisted my key in the lock. When a voice boomed out from behind me, I wasn't frightened, just aggravated that I wasn't going to get to eat.

"Roe! Teentsy said you'd be coming in about now! Listen, we got a little problem in our place," old Mr. Crandall was saying.

I turned around, resigned to postponing food. "What's the little problem, Mr. Crandall?"

Mr. Crandall was not eloquent about anything but guns, and finally I realized that if I was to understand the problem Teentsy was having with the washer, I'd better go along with him.

It wasn't right to feel put-upon; after all, this was my job. But I had been looking forward to eating without Lillian's voice droning in my ears, and since it was Wednesday, there should be a new *Time* in my mailbox. I sighed quietly, and trudged across the patio in Mr. Crandall's wake.

The Crandalls' washer and dryer were in the basement, of course, as they were in all four units. There was a straight flight of rather steep stairs down to the basement, open on one side except for a railing. I clopped down the Crandalls' stairs, Teentsy Crandall right behind me telling me about the washer catastrophe in minute detail. When I reached the bottom, I saw a spreading water stain. With a sinking feeling of doom and dismay, I knew I'd have to spend my lunch hour tracking down a plumber.

Despite all the odds against it, I struck gold with my first phone call. The Crandalls watched admiringly as I talked Ace Plumbing into paying my tenants a call in the next hour. Since Ace was one of the two plumbing firms my mother used for all her properties, perhaps it wasn't totally amazing to find them willing; but to actually get them to commit themselves to coming right away—now that was amazing! When I was off the phone and Teentsy put a plate with country fried steak, potatoes, and green beans in front of me, I suddenly saw the bright side of being a resident manager. "Oh, you don't need to do that," I said weakly, and dug in. Calories and cholesterol did not factor in Teentsy's cooking, so her food was absolutely delicious with that added spice of guilt.

Teentsy and Jed Crandall seemed delighted to have someone to talk to. They were quite a pair, Teentsy with her bountiful bosom and childish voice and gray curls, and Jed with his hard-as-a-rock seamed face.

While I ate, Teentsy frosted a cake and Mr. Crandall—I couldn't bring myself to call him Jed—talked about his farm, which he'd sold the year before, and about how convenient it was for them to live in town where all their doctors and kinfolk and grandchildren were. He sounded unconvinced though, and I could tell he was spoiling for something to do.

"That sure was a nice young man we saw you with last night," Teentsy said archly. "Did you two have a good time?"

I was willing to bet Teentsy knew exactly when Robin had brought me home. "Oh, yes, it was fine," I said in as noncommittal a voice as I could summon.

I glanced around their den and kitchen area. Mine was lined with books; Mr. Crandall's was lined with guns. I knew next to nothing about firearms, and was fervently content to keep it that way, but even I could tell these guns were of all different ages and types. I started wondering about their value, and from there it was a natural leap to being concerned about my mother's insurance coverage of these units; what would her responsibility be in case of theft, for example? Though it would take a foolhardy burglar to attempt to take anything away from Jed Crandall.

Thinking of hazards and security in general led my thoughts in another direction. I looked at the Crandalls' back door. Sure enough, they'd added two extra locks.

I laid down my fork. "Mr. Jed, I have to talk to you about those extra locks," I said gently.

Yes, he *had* read his lease agreement carefully. His tough old face went sheepish in an instant.

"Oh, Jed," chided Teentsy, "I told you you needed to speak to Roe about those locks."

"Well, Roe," her husband said, "you can see this gun collection needs more protection than one lock on the back door."

"I can appreciate how you feel, and I even agree," I said carefully, "but you know that if you do put on extra locks, you must give me a key, and you have to leave the locks in and give me all the keys if you ever decide to move. Of course I hope you never will, but you do have to give me an extra set of keys now."

While Mr. Crandall grumbled on about a man's home being his castle, and it going against the grain to give

anyone else keys to that castle—even a nice gal like me—
Teentsy was on her feet and rummaging through a drawer
in the kitchen. She came up with a handful of keys immediately, and began sorting through them with a troubled
look on her face.

"Now I've been promising myself I'd go through these
and throw away the old ones we didn't need, and since
we're retired, I should have all the time in the world, but
still I haven't done it," she told me. "Well, here are two
that I'm sure are the spares for these locks . . . here, Jed,
try them and make sure."

While her husband tested the keys in the locks, she
stirred the others around with a helpless finger. "That
looks like the key to that old trunk . . . I don't know about
this one . . . you know, Roe, now that I think about it, one
of these keys is to that apartment next door that that
Mr. Waites rents now. I know you remember Edith Warn-
stein, she had it before him. She gave us an extra key
because she said she was always locking herself out and it
was always when you were at work."

"Well, when you find it, just bring it over sometime," I
said. Mr. Crandall handed me his extra keys, which had
proved to be the right ones, and I thanked Teentsy for the
delicious lunch, feeling even more guilty that they'd fed me
and then I'd "invaded their castle." It was hell being conscientious, sometimes. I felt much better when my departure
coincided with the arrival of the plumber. Judging solely by
his appearance—two-day beard stubble, bandanna over
long ringlets of black hair, and DayGlo overalls—I wouldn't
have trusted him with *my* washer, but he hefted his tool

bag in an authoritative way and actually wrote it down when I told him to bill my mother's company for the repairs, so I left feeling I'd performed a service.

I almost literally ran into Bankston on my way out the Crandalls' patio gate. He was hefting his golf bag and looked shining clean, right out of the shower. He'd obviously been out at the country club having a few rounds. He looked surprised to see me. "The Crandalls having plumbing problems?" he asked, nodding toward the plumber's truck.

"Yes," I said distractedly, after glancing at my watch. "Your washer and dryer okay?"

"Oh, sure. Listen, how are you doing after your troubles of the past few days?"

Bankston was being nice and polite, but I didn't have the time or the inclination to chitchat.

"Pretty well, thanks. I was glad to hear that you and Melanie are getting married," I added, remembering that I did owe something to courtesy. "I didn't have the chance to say anything the other night when we met at my place. Congratulations."

"Thanks, Roe," he said, in his deliberate way. "We were lucky to finally really get to know each other." His clear eyes were glowing, and it was apparent to me that he returned Melanie's strong feelings. I was a little envious, to tell the truth, and bitchily wondered what two such stolid people could have to "really get to know." I was also late.

"Congratulations," I repeated sunnily, and pretty much meant it. "I've got to run." I rabbited away to my place to put the keys to the Crandalls' apartment on my official key ring, and though I needed to hurry back to the library, I took an extra minute to label them.

I would've been late anyway.

I drove north on Parson Road to get back to the library. The Buckleys' house was along the way, to my left.

By sheer coincidence, out of all the people who could have been driving by when Lizanne came out that front door, it was I. I just glanced to my left to admire the flowers in the Buckleys' front yard, and the front door opened, and a figure stumbled out. I knew it was Lizanne by the color of her hair and her figure and because her parents owned the house, but nothing about her posture and attitude was like Lizanne. She slumped on the front doorstep, clinging to the black iron railing that ran down the red-brick steps.

God forgive me, half of me wanted to continue on my route to the library and go back to work, in blessed ignorance; but the half that said my friend needed help seemed to control the car. I pulled over and crossed the street and then the lawn, dreading to reach Lizanne and find out why her face was so contorted and why there were stains on her hose, especially at the knees.

She didn't know I was there. Her long fingers with their beautifully manicured nails were ripping at her skirt, and her breath tore in and out of her lungs with a horrible wheeze. There were tear stains on her face, though no tears were coming now. From her smell she had vomited recently. The slow, sweet, casual beauty had vanished.

I put my arm around her and tried to forget the sour

smell, but it made my own stomach begin to lurch uneasily. The Crandalls' delicious lunch threatened to come right back up. I shut my eyes for a second. When I opened them she was looking at me and her fingers were clenched instead of restless.

"They're both dead, Roe," she said clearly and terribly. "My mama and my daddy are both dead. I knelt down to make sure, and I have my own daddy's blood on my clothes."

Then she fell silent and stared at her skirt, and knowing I was inadequate, could not rise to this ghastly situation, I let my thoughts trace what they were good at: the pattern, the terrible impersonal pattern that real people were being forced to fit. This time it was Lizanne plus dead stepmother and father plus broad daylight plus bloody demise.

I wondered where the hatchet was.

"I just walked to the back door to eat lunch with them like I do every day," she said suddenly. "And when the door was locked, and they wouldn't answer, I unlocked the front here—this is the only key I have. They were—there was blood on the walls."

"The walls?" I murmured stupidly, having no idea what I was going to say until it came out.

"Yes," she said seriously, asserting an incredible truth, "the *walls*. Daddy is on the sofa in there, Roe, the one where he sits to watch television, and he's just all . . . he's . . . and Mama is upstairs in the guest bedroom on the floor by the bed."

I held her as tightly as I could and she bent and clung to me.

"I shouldn't have had to see them like that," she whispered.

"No."

Then she lapsed into silence.

I had to call the police.

I stood up like an old woman, and I felt like one. I turned to face the door Lizanne had shut behind her, and reached out like someone in a dream and opened it.

There was blood everywhere, sprayed in trails across the wall. Lizanne was right; blood on the walls. And the ceilings. And the television set.

Arnie Buckley was visible from the front door, which opened opposite the doorway into the den. I supposed it was Arnie. It was the right size and was lying in Arnie's house, on his couch. His face had been obliterated.

I wanted to scream until someone knocked me out with a good strong shot. Nothing would get me to set one foot further into this house. More than I ever wanted anything, I wanted to walk back across the street, get in my car, and leave without looking back. It seemed I was always opening doors to look at dead people, hacked people, beaten people. I managed to shut this door, this white-painted suburban front door with the brass knocker, and as I plodded across the Buckleys' lawn to the nearest neighbors, I looked longingly at my Chevette.

I couldn't face calling myself, and I can't remember what I said to the lady next door. I only know that I plodded back to sit by Lizanne on the steps.

She spoke once, asking me in bewilderment why her folks had been killed. I told her, honestly, that they'd been killed by the same person who'd killed Mamie Wright. I hoped she wouldn't ask me why it had to be her parents. Her parents had been picked because she had been named Elizabeth, because she was unmarried, because her "Mama" was not really her mama by blood. This was the pattern of Lizanne's life that loosely fit the Fall River, Massachusetts, murders; the murders committed in 1893 in an ugly, inconvenient, atmospherically tense home in a middle-class neighborhood, almost certainly committed by Mr. Andrew Borden's younger daughter, Lizzie.

But I didn't think Lizanne ever heard anything I said, and that's just as well. I kept my arm around her so something human and warm would be there, and the smell continued to sicken me. I continued to do it because it was all I could do.

Jack Burns got out of the squad car that pulled up on the lawn. He actually had a doctor with him, a local surgeon, and I found out later that they'd been having lunch together when the call came. The doctor looked at Lizanne, at me, and hesitated, but Jack Burns stepped around us and gestured his friend into the house. The sergeant of detectives looked inside and then looked down at me with burning eyes. I was not the object of this look, just in its path. But it scorched me, the fury in those dark eyes.

"Don't touch anything! Be careful how you walk!" he ordered the doctor.

"Well, of course, he's dead," came the doctor's voice. "If you just need me to pronounce him dead, I can sure do that."

"Any more?" Burns spat at me. He could see Lizanne wouldn't answer, I suppose.

"She said her stepmother is dead, upstairs," I told him very quietly, though I don't think Lizanne would have heard me if I'd screamed it.

"Upstairs, Doc!" he ordered.

The doctor probably trotted right up, but I wouldn't have gone with him if a gun had been at my head.

"Dead up here, too," he called down the stairs.

"Then get your ass out of there and let us go over this house," Burns said violently.

The doctor trotted out the door and after thinking for a moment, simply walked down the street. He was not about to ask Jack Burns for a ride back to the restaurant. Burns went inside but I could not hear him walking over the wooden floor. He must be standing, looking. At least he pushed the door partly closed behind him so there was something between me and the horror.

Police cars were pulling up behind Burns's, the routine about to begin. Lynn Liggett got out of the first one. She immediately began giving orders to the uniformed men who spilled out of the next car.

"How did you happen to be here?" Lynn asked without any preliminaries.

"Did you call an ambulance yet for Lizanne?" I asked. I was beginning to shake off my lethargy, my odd dreaminess.

"Yes, there's one on the way."

"Okay. I was just driving to work. She came out of the front door like this. She spoke to me a little and then I opened the door and looked in. I went next door to call the police."

Lynn Liggett pushed open the door and looked in. I kept

my eyes resolutely forward. Her fair skin took on a greenish tinge and her lips pressed together so hard they whitened.

The ambulance pulled up then, and I was glad to see it, because Lizanne's face was even waxier, and her hands were losing coordination. Her breathing seemed irregular and shallow. She was leaning on me heavily by the time the stretcher came up to the front steps, and she didn't acknowledge the presence of the ambulance drivers. They loaded her on the stretcher with quick efficiency. I walked by her down to the street, holding her hand, but she didn't know I was there, and by the time the stretcher was pushed into the back of the ambulance she seemed unconscious.

I watched the orange and white ambulance pull away from the curb. I didn't suppose I could leave. I rested on the hood of Lynn's car for what seemed like a long time, staring aimlessly ahead and thinking of as little as possible. Then I became aware Lynn Liggett was beside me.

"There's no question of Lizanne being blamed, is there?" I asked finally. I fully expected the detective to tell me to get lost and it was none of my business, but something had mellowed the woman since last I'd seen her. We had shared something terrible.

"No," Detective Liggett said. "Her neighbor says she heard Lizanne hammer on the back door and then she saw her walk around to the front and unlock the house, something so unusual that the neighbor already considered calling the police. It would take more than seven minutes to do that and clean up afterward. And it's fairly easy to see that her folks had already been dead about an hour by the time she got there."

"Mr. Buckley was due to come in to work at the library today at two, and we were going to share night duty tomorrow night," I said.

"Yes, it's written on the calendar in the kitchen in the house."

For some reason that gave me the cold shudders. Her job included looking at dead people's calendars while they lay right there in their own blood. Appointments that would never be kept. I revised my attitude about Lynn Liggett right then and there.

"You know what this is just like."

"The Borden case."

I jerked my head around to look at her in surprise.

"Arthur's inside," she explained. "He told me about it."

Arthur came out of the house then, with that same whitey-green pinched look Liggett had had. He nodded at me, not questioning my presence.

"John Queensland—from Real Murders?" I said. Arthur nodded. "Well, he's a Borden expert."

"I remembered. I'll get in touch with him this afternoon."

I thought about the sweet old couple I'd seen having a good time at the restaurant the night before. I thought about having to tell the Crandalls their best friends had been hacked to death. Then I realized I should tell the detectives where I'd seen the Buckleys last night, in case for some reason it was important. After I'd explained to Arthur and Lynn, and Lynn had written down the Crandalls' names and the time I'd seen them the previous evening, I wanted to reach over to Arthur, pat or hug him, establish warm living contact with him. But I couldn't.

"It's the worst thing I hope I ever see. They really don't look much like people anymore," Arthur said suddenly. He shoved his hands in his pockets. It was up to his fellow detectives to help him over this one, I realized. I was excluded from this bad moment, and truly, I was thankful.

I thought of a lot of things to say, but they were futile things. It was time for me to go. I got in my car and without considering what I was doing, I drove to work. I went to tell Mr. Clerrick that our volunteer wouldn't be coming in that afternoon.

The rest of the afternoon just passed. Later, I couldn't remember a single thing I'd done after I returned to work. I remembered I'd felt good when I'd gotten up that morning and I couldn't believe it. I just wanted one day with nothing happening, nothing bad, nothing good. No excitement. Just a nice dull day like I'd had almost every day until recently.

Close to closing time, I saw one of the detectives whom I didn't know personally coming into the library. He went to Sam Clerrick's office on the ground floor, emerged in a matter of moments, and made a beeline to Lillian as she stood behind the circulation desk. The detective asked Lillian a couple of questions, and she answered eagerly. He wrote a few things down on his notepad, and left with a nod to her.

Lillian looked up to the second floor where I was again shelving books, and our eyes met. She looked excited, and more than that, turning quickly away. Soon when another librarian was in earshot, Lillian called her over. Their heads tilted close together, and after that the other librarian hurried to the periodicals room, where yet another librarian would be stationed. If the police kept coming here asking about me, I realized with a sick feeling, Mr. Clerrick might let me go. I could tell myself I'd done nothing, but I suddenly knew it wouldn't make any difference. This wasn't just happening to me, I reminded myself. Probably members of Real Murders all over Lawrenceton were being similarly inconvenienced, and many other people whose lives these murders had touched, no matter how tangentially.

It was the old stone-in-the-pond effect. Instead of stones, bodies were being thrown into the pool of the community, and the resulting waves of misery, fear, and suspicion would brush more and more people until the crimes came to an end.

Chapter Twelve

Though I didn't know it until I left work, that afternoon had been a busy one for the news media, as well as the police.

Mamie's death had not aroused much interest in the city, though it had been front-page news in Lawrenceton. The box of candy had rated a couple of paragraphs on an inside page locally, and had failed to register at all in the city. But the murder of Morrison Pettigrue was news; the strange and off-beat murder of a strange and off-beat man, spiced with Benjamin's charge of political assassination. Benjamin may have been a local butcher who very obviously desired attention of any kind in the worst way, but he did deserve the title "campaign manager" and he was quotable. The two local stringers for the city papers enjoyed a couple of days of unprecedented importance.

As Sally had told us so indignantly at the meeting at my place, she'd been asked by the police to keep the Julia Wallace speculations out of the paper. An account of the Julia Wallace murder would have little appeal for twentieth-century American newspaper readers, the police told Sally and her boss. And it would hinder their investigation. Sally was on an inside track with the Wright murder, no doubt about it, being a club member and actually present when the body was found, so she was furious to see her exclusive knowledge stay exclusive. But her boss, Macon Turner, agreed with the local police chief that it should be withheld for "a few days." It was from Macon Turner I pieced all this together later; he'd been wooing my mother for some months before John Queensland gained ascendancy, and we'd become friends.

Sally became frantic after the Pettigrue murder; the minute she'd learned from her police sources that there had been paper scattered on the surface of the bathwater, and that Pettigrue had been placed in the tub after death, she mentally scrolled through the assassinations of radicals and easily came up with Charlotte Corday's stabbing of Jean-Paul Marat in revolutionary France. Corday had gained entrance to Marat's house by pretending she would give him a list of traitors in her province. Then she killed Marat while he sat in the bath to alleviate a skin disease.

After Sally had thought it through, she exploded into Macon Turner's office and demanded to report the full story. She knew it would be the biggest story of her career. Turner, a friend of the police chief, hesitated a fatal couple of days. Then the Buckleys were slaughtered, and Sally, instantly drawing the obvious conclusion, prepared her story with full disclosure of the "parallel" theory, as it became called.

Turner could no longer resist the biggest, best story that had come along since he'd bought the Lawrenceton *Sentinel*. By chance, the two stringers were not acquainted with any Real Murders members, who at any rate had not been doing a lot of talking about Mamie Wright's murder especially since the Sunday night meeting at my apartment. For example, LeMaster Cane told me later he'd decided even before the meeting that the murders in Lawrenceton were too much like old murders for it to be coincidental. But as a black man, he'd been too scared of being implicated to come forward. He'd already found by that time, too, that his hammer—with initials burned into the haft—was missing. He figured it had been used to kill Mamie.

The same afternoon the Buckleys were found slaughtered, the state lab phoned the local police to say that though the report was in the mail, they wanted Arthur and Lynn to know that what was in the candy my mother had received was a product called "Ratkill." If my mother had swallowed the candy without noticing the taste in time to spit it out, she would have been very sick. If by some wild chance her tastebuds had been jaded enough for her to eat three chocolates, she might have died. But the Ratkill had a strong odor and flavor by design, to prevent just such a thing happening; so the poisoning attempt seemed half-hearted and amateurish.

Then Lynn Liggett found the open box of Ratkill in Arthur's car.

The officer who had taken the telephone message from

the state crime lab to relay to the detectives was a man named Paul Allison, and he was the brother of the man Sally'd been married to years before. He was a friend of Sally's, and he didn't care for Arthur. Paul Allison was standing in the police station parking lot when Lynn, reaching in Arthur's car to retrieve her forgotten notebook, found an open box of Ratkill under it. Lynn assumed that Arthur had gotten a sample for some reason, and lifted it up where Paul Allison could see it, before she sensed something was wrong and instinctively tried to conceal it.

After Paul Allison had seen the Ratkill, there was no possible way to conceal its finding, and Arthur had a lot of explaining to do; so did Lynn, who had been riding with Arthur off and on.

Paul Allison decided to do his own explaining—to Sally. He called her an hour later, and her full story was in print the next morning.

Sally's story created a sensation, which it fully deserved. Sally Allison, middle-aged newswoman, had finally gotten the story she'd hankered for all her life, and she went for it, no holds barred.

The stringers had not known about the "parallel theory," but they did know something strange was happening in Lawrenceton, which normally had a very low murder rate. When the Buckleys were killed, one of the stringers was listening to her police band scanner. While the police cars converged on the Buckley house, she was loading her camera. She stopped at the gas station to fill up her car, then drove slowly up Parson until she spotted the house. In front of the house was slumped a tall, lovely woman with blood on her legs, and sitting with her arm around the tall, lovely woman was a little librarian with big round glasses and a grim expression. I had been trying to ignore the heave of my stomach, because Lizanne smelled of vomit.

Her picture of us appeared on the front page of the Metro/State section of the evening city paper. Her sources in the police department had not been silent in the meantime, and the caption read: "Elizabeth Buckley sits stunned on the steps of her parents' home after she discovered their bodies. She is being comforted by Aurora Teagarden, who discovered the body of Mrs. Gerald Wright Friday night."

So that afternoon while I worked in a daze at the library, newspeople were watching my apartment and my mother's office. It didn't occur to anyone that I might just go on to work after "comforting" Lizanne. Of course, the paper was not yet out and I had not yet seen the picture, but by the time I got back to my apartment after leaving work, a television news crew was parked in my slot in the parking lot. They'd gotten early wind of the story, and since Lizanne was incommunicado in the hospital and Arthur and Lynn were embroiled in the Ratkill discovery at the police station, my mother and I were among the few remaining targets.

That is, until the news crew spotted Robin, who was arriving home from the university. The newsman was an avid mystery buff who recognized Robin, having read of his stepping in for the stricken writer who'd had the heart attack. The camera was trained on him in a flash, and the newsman came up with some hasty questions. Robin, used to being interviewed, handled it well. He was agreeable, without giving them much information. I saw him that night on the news.

Unfortunately, they weren't looking hard enough at Robin to prevent one of them spotting me when I got home. I might think it my duty to talk to the police, but I didn't have to talk to these people. One of them was holding an early copy of the paper, and as I got hesitantly out of my car, stupidly determined on going into my apartment and taking the longest, hottest bath on record, he held it out to me. He said something, I didn't know what, because I was so appalled at seeing the picture of poor Lizanne I couldn't listen. I felt surrounded, and I was, though the three men of the news team were in my mind magnified to thirty.

I was just worn out and couldn't deal with it.

"I don't want to say anything," I said nervously, and I could tell the camera was running. The newsman was a looker with a beautiful smile, and I wanted him out of my way more than I'd ever wanted anything. I felt I was teetering dangerously on the brink of hysteria.

Robin decided to rescue me. He loomed up behind them, and motioned me to just walk between them. I wondered for a moment if they'd let me, but they parted and I scuttled by straight for Robin. He wrapped his arm around me and we turned our backs on the news team and headed for the patio gate.

I knew the camera was running still (the mystery novelist and his librarian landlady have adjacent apartments) and I had a flash of sense and a jolt of guts. I swiveled to face the camera.

"This is private property. It belongs to my mother and I am her representative here," I said ominously. "You do not have my permission to be on it. This is against the law." I said that like it was a magic charm. And indeed, it seemed to be. For they did pile in their van, and leave! I was incredibly pleased with myself, and I was surprised on looking up to see Robin beaming like a fond daddy.

"Go get 'em, Aurora," he said admiringly.

"I appreciate your sheltering me out there in the parking lot, Robin," I said, "but dammit, don't you patronize me!" I did a little independent swiveling and got in my back door without bursting into tears.

That night Arthur called me, to tell me the gloomy story of the Ratkill. "Whoever this asshole is, he's playing games and he just went too far," Arthur said savagely.

I would have thought murdering the Buckleys was going too far, myself.

After I'd commiserated as much as I decently could, I told him about the media problems I was having. I'd gotten several phone calls during my wonderful hot bath, effectively ruining it. Only the chance someone I might want to hear from would call me was keeping me from taking the phone off the hook. For the first time in my life, I was wishing I had an answering machine.

"I'm getting calls, too," Arthur said gloomily. "I'm not used to being the direct subject of all this news attention."

"Neither am I," I said. "I hate it. I'm glad librarians don't have to have press conferences as part of their job. Do you think you're clear now of any suspicion?"

"Yes, I'm not on suspension or anything like that. At least I've built up enough respect here for that."

"I'm glad." And I was. I felt like I had someone on my side in the police force as long as Arthur was there. If he'd been suspended, not only would I have felt bad for his sake, I would have felt powerless.

"Go on and take the phone off the hook," Arthur advised me now. "But first call your mom and get her to put a big sign at the entrance to your parking lot that says in great big letters, 'Private Property, Trespassers will be Prosecuted.'"

"Good idea. Thanks."

We said goodnight uneasily. We were both wondering what would happen next, and who it would happen to.

M y mother woke her handyman up with a phone call that night and told him she'd pay him triple if he had the sign in the parking lot by 7:00 the next morning. She begged me to leave town, or come to stay with her, until somehow this situation ended. She'd known the Buckleys, and was horrified by the sheer terror they must have experienced before they died; the Buckleys were her age, her acquaintances.

"John had to go in to talk to the police," she said. "If he can help them, that's wonderful, but I hated for him to go. I wish you'd never joined that damn group, Aurora. But there's no point talking about it now. Won't you come stay over here?"

"Are you going to defend me, Mother?" I asked with a weary smile.

"With my last breath," she said simply.

Suddenly I felt my mother was safer if I stayed away from her.

"I'll manage," I told her. "Thanks for taking care of the sign."

Chapter Thirteen

I had a bad night.

I dreamed that men with cameras were coming into the bathroom while I was dressing and that one of them was the murderer. I swam up from a deep sleep to find rain was patting lightly against my bedroom window. I slept again.

When finally I woke up groggy, I peered out the upstairs windows from behind my curtains to make sure no one was lying in wait for me. All the cars in the parking lot belonged there. No one was parked out front. There was a large unmistakable sign at the entrance to the parking lot. I padded down the stairs to get my coffee but took it back up to my room. Mug in hand, I watched Robin leave for work in the city. I saw Bankston go out and get his papers. Teentsy's car pulled out. She must have needed something for breakfast, for she was back within ten minutes. The shower the night before had not amounted to much, not like the rain of two nights ago; the little puddles were already gone.

By the time Teentsy returned, I'd worked up enough courage to get my own papers. They were having a screaming field day. There was a picture of Arthur, a picture of Mamie and Gerald at their wedding, a picture of the Buckleys and Lizanne when the Buckleys had celebrated their twenty-fifth wedding anniversary, and a picture of Morrison Pettigrue taken when he'd announced he was running for mayor, with Benjamin beaming in the background like a proud father.

At least no one seemed to believe that Melanie and Arthur were guilty of anything but being the butt of ghastly practical jokes. I wondered where the hatchet that had killed the Buckleys would turn up, or the knife that had killed Morrison Pettigrue. How could the murderer sustain such a frenzy of activity? Surely there must be an enormous output of physical and emotional energy involved. Surely he must stop.

I managed to dab on some makeup so I wouldn't look like I was going to keel over and yanked my hair back into a ponytail. I pulled on a red turtleneck and navy blue skirt and cardigan. I looked like hell on wheels.

My only goal was to get to the library without anyone noticing me and find out if there was any chance of putting in a normal day's work. To my utter relief, there were no strange cars in the library parking lot. The interest in me seemed to have ebbed. The day began to look possible.

I found out at work that Benjamin Greer had called a press conference that morning to announce another candidate would run for the Communist Party in the Lawrenceton mayoral election. The candidate proved to be Benjamin himself, who seemed to be the only other Communist resident of Lawrenceton. I didn't believe for a minute that Benjamin had any coherent political philosophy. He was getting as much publicity as he could while the attention of the media was still on our town. I wondered what would happen to Benjamin after the election. Would butchering at the grocery store ever be enough again?

Lillian Schmidt told me about Benjamin, and altogether covered herself with unexpected glory that morning. She worked side by side with me as though nothing at all had happened, with the exception of describing his press conference. I wanted to ask her why she was being so decent, but couldn't think of a way to phrase it that wasn't offensive. (Why are you being nice to me, when we don't like each other much? Why is a tactless person like you suddenly being the soul of tact?)

I was pulling on my sweater to leave for lunch, when Lillian said, "I know you don't have anything to do with this mess, and I don't think it's fair that all this has happened to you. That policeman coming to ask me yesterday if you were really mending books with me all morning—I just decided last night that was ridiculous. Enough is enough."

For once we agreed on something. "Thanks, Lillian," I said.

I felt a little better as I drove home. I took another route so I didn't have to pass the Buckleys' house. Over lunch I watched the news and saw Benjamin having his minutes of fame.

I was off Thursday afternoon since I was scheduled to work Thursday night. I'd been wise to make the effort to go to work in the morning, I found once I was home alone. Though I liked work, usually I liked my time off even more. Today was an exception. After I'd changed into jeans and sneakers, I couldn't settle on any one project. I did a little laundry, a little reading. I tried a new hairdo, but tore it apart before I was half through. Then my hair was tangled, and I had to brush it through so much to get out the snarls that it crackled around my head in a brown cloud of electric waves. I looked like I'd been contacted by Mars.

I called the hospital to see if I could visit Lizanne, but the nurse on her wing said Lizanne was only receiving visits from family. Then I thought of ordering flowers for the funeral, and called Sally Allison at the newspaper to find out when it would be. For the first time, the receptionist at the *Sentinel* asked my name before ringing Sally. She was riding the crest of the story, that was clear.

"What can I do for you, Roe?" she asked briskly. I felt she was only talking to me because I was still semi-newsworthy at the moment. I had been hot yesterday, but I was cooling off. The lack of excitement in Sally's voice was like a shot of adrenaline to me.

"I just wanted to know when the Buckleys' funeral would be, Sally."

"Well, the bodies have gone for autopsy, and I don't

know when they'll be released. So according to Lizanne's aunt, they just haven't been able to make any firm funeral plans yet."

"Oh. Well . . ."

"Listen, while I've got you on the line . . . one of the cops said you were on the scene yesterday." I knew Sally had seen the picture of me with Lizanne in the city paper. She was getting too full of herself. "You want to tell me what happened while you were there?" she asked coaxingly. "Is it true that Arnie was dismembered?"

"I wonder if you're really the right person to have on this story, Sally," I said after a long pause during which I thought furiously.

Sally gasped as if her pet sheep had turned and bitten her.

"After all, you're in the club, and I guess we're all really involved, somehow or other, right?" And Sally had a son who was also a member, who could not exactly be called normal.

"I think I can keep my objectivity," Sally said coldly. "And I don't think being a member of Real Murders means you're automatically—involved."

At least she wasn't asking me questions anymore.

My doorbell rang.

"I've got to go, Sally," I said gently. And hung up.

I felt mildly ashamed of myself as I went to the door. Sally was doing her job. But I had a hard time accepting her switch from friend to reporter, my changing role from friend to source. It seemed like lately people "doing their jobs" meant I got my life turned around.

I did remember to check my security spy hole. My visitor was Arthur. He looked as ghastly as I had earlier. The lines in his face looked deeper, making him appear at least ten years older.

"Have you had anything to eat?" I asked.

"No," he admitted, after some thought. "Not since five this morning. That's when I got up and went down to the station." I pulled out a chair at my kitchen table and he sat down automatically.

It's hard to perform like Hannah Housewife when you've had no warning, but I microwaved a frozen ham and cheese sandwich, poured some potato chips out of a bag, and scraped together a rather depressing salad. However, Arthur seemed glad to see the plate and ate it all after a silent prayer.

"Eat in peace," I said and busied myself making coffee and wiping down the kitchen counter. It was an oddly domestic little interval. I felt more myself, less hunted, than I had since stopping to help Lizanne. It was possible work tonight would be entirely normal. And I would come home and sleep, hours and hours, in a clean nightgown.

After he ate, Arthur looked better. When I came to remove his empty plate, he took my wrist and pulled me into his lap, and kissed me. It was long, thorough, and intense. I really liked it very much. But maybe this was a little too fast for me. When by silent mutual accord we unclenched, I wiggled off his lap and tried to slow down my breathing.

"I just wanted to do something I would *enjoy*," he said.

"Quite all right," I said a little unsteadily, and poured

him a cup of coffee while gesturing him to the couch. I sat a careful but not marked distance away.

"It's not going well?" I asked tentatively.

"Oh, it's going, now that I've got the Ratkill thing behind me. Of course our fingerprint guy had to go all over my car, and now I've got to get all that stuff off. I'm sure it won't turn up anything. Melanie Clark's car was clean as a whistle. We've completed the Buckley house search, and a neighborhood canvas to see if anyone saw anything. The only thing the house search turned up was a long hair, which may just be one of Lizanne's . . . we have to get a sample from her for comparison. And that's for your ears only. The murder weapon hasn't turned up yet, but it was a hatchet or something like that, of course."

"You're really not a suspect?"

"Well, if I ever was, I'm not now. While the Buckleys were being murdered I was going door to door with another detective asking questions about the Wright murder. And come to think of it, right before the last meeting, when Mamie Wright was done in, I was booking a DWI at the station. I drove to the meeting directly from there. And Lynn was able to swear for me that the Ratkill hadn't been in the car all morning while we were riding around knocking on doors."

"Good," I said. "Someone's got to be out of the running."

"And thank God it's me, since the department needs every warm body it can get on this one. I've got to go." He heaved himself to his feet, looking tired again.

"Arthur . . . what about me? Does anyone think I did it?"

"No, honey. Not since Pettigrue, anyway. His old house

had one of those claw-footed tubs, way off the floor, and he was a tall man, maybe six-three. You couldn't have gotten him in that tub alone, no way. And around Lawrenceton enough people would know if you were steadily seeing some guy who'd help you move the body. No, I think Pettigrue definitely let you off the hook in just about everyone's mind."

It was unnerving to think that my name had been spoken by men and women I didn't know, men and women who seriously considered I might have killed people in brutal and bloody ways. But all in all, after I'd talked to Arthur, I felt much better.

I saw him off with a light squeeze of his hand, and sat down to think a little. It was about time I thought instead of felt. I had crammed more feelings into the past week than I had in a year, I estimated.

The hair the police had found was probably brown, since it might be Lizanne's and hers was a rich chestnut. Who else could have shed that hair?

Well, I was a member of Real Murders who had long brown hair. Luckily for me, I'd been repairing books with Lillian Schmidt all morning. Melanie Clark had medium-length dull brown hair, and Sally, though her hair was shorter and lighter, could also be a contender. (Wouldn't it be something if Sally had committed all these murders so she could report them? A dazzling idea. Then I told myself to get back on track.) Jane Engle's hair was definitely gray . . . then I thought of Gifford Doakes, whose hair was long and smoothly moussed into a pagebody or sometimes gathered in a ponytail, to John Queensland's disgust. Gifford was a scary person, and he was so interested in massacres . . . and his friend Reynaldo would probably do anything Gifford wanted.

But surely someone as flamboyant as Gifford would have been noticed going into the Buckleys' house?

Well, discarding the possible clue of the hair for the moment, how had the murderer gotten in and left? A neighbor had seen Lizanne enter, too soon before I'd arrived to have done everything that had been done to the Buckleys. So someone was in a position to view the front of the Buckley house at least part of the morning. I considered other approaches and tried to imagine an aerial view of the lot, but I am not good at geography at all, much less aerial geography.

I sat a while longer and thought some more, and found myself wandering to the patio gate several times to see if Robin was home yet from the university. It was going to rain later, and the day was cooling off rapidly. The sky was a dull uniform gray.

I pulled on my jacket finally and was heading out on my own when his big car pulled in. Robin unfolded from it with an armful of papers. Why doesn't he carry his briefcase? I wondered.

"Listen, change your shoes and come with me," I suggested.

He looked down his beaky nose at my feet. "Okay," he said agreeably. "Let me drop these papers inside. Someone stole my briefcase," he said over his shoulder.

I pattered after him. "Here?" I said, startled.

"Well, since I moved to Lawrenceton, and I'm fairly

sure from here in the parking lot," he said as he unlocked his back door.

I followed him in. Boxes were everywhere, and the only thing set in order was a computer table suitably laden with computer, disc drives, and printer. Robin dumped the papers and bounded upstairs, returning in a few seconds with some huge sneakers.

"What are we going to do?" he asked as he laced them up.

"I've been thinking. How did the murderer get into the Buckleys' house? It wasn't broken into, right? At least the papers this morning said not. So maybe the Buckleys left it unlocked and the killer just walked in and surprised them, or the killer rang the doorbell and the Buckleys let him— or her—in. But anyway, how did the killer approach the house? I just want to walk up that way and see. It had to be from the back, I think."

"So we're going to see if we can do it ourselves?"

"That's what I thought." But as we were leaving Robin's, I had misgivings. "Oh, maybe we better not. What if someone sees us and calls the police?"

"Then we'll just tell them what we're doing," said Robin reasonably, making it sound very simple. Of course, *his* mother wasn't the most prominent real estate dealer in town and a society leader to boot, I reflected.

But I had to go. It had been my idea.

So out of the parking lot we went, Robin striding ahead and me trailing behind, until he looked back and shortened his stride. The parking lot let out in the middle of the street that ran beside Robin's end apartment. Robin had turned right so I did, too, and at the corner we turned north to walk the two blocks up Parson to the Buckleys'. Perhaps as I'd driven past the Buckleys' on my way home to lunch the day before, the Buckleys were being slaughtered. I caught up with Robin at the next corner, shivering inside my light jacket. The house was on this next block.

Robin looked up the street, thinking. I looked down the side street; no houses faced the road. "Of course, the trash alley," I said, disgusted with myself.

"Huh?"

"This is one of the old areas, and this block hasn't been rebuilt in ages," I explained. "There's an alley between the houses facing Parson Road and the houses facing Chestnut, which runs parallel to Parson. The same with this block we're standing on. But when you get south to our block, it's been rebuilt, with our apartments for one thing, and garbage collection is on the street."

Under the gray sky we crossed the side street and came to the alley entrance. I'd felt so pursued and viewed yesterday, it was almost eerie how invisible I felt now. No houses facing this side street, little traffic. When we walked down the graveled alley, it was easy to see how the murderer had reached the house without being observed.

"And almost all these yards are fenced, which blocks the view of the alley," Robin remarked, "and of the Buckleys' back yard."

The Buckleys' yard was one of the few unfenced ones. The ones on either side had five-foot privacy fences. We stopped at the very back of the yard by the garbage cans, with a clear view of the back door of the house. The yard was planted with the camellias and roses that Mrs. Buckley had loved. In their garbage can—what an eerie thought— was probably a tissue she'd blotted her lipstick with, grounds from the coffee they'd drunk on their last morning, detritus of lives that no longer existed.

Yes, their garbage was surely still there . . . everyone on Parson Road had garbage pickup on Monday. They'd been killed on Wednesday. I shuddered. "Let's go," I said. My mood had changed. I wasn't Delilah Detective anymore.

Robin turned slowly. "So what would you do?" he said. "If you didn't want to be observed, you'd have parked your car—where? Where we came into the alley?"

"No. That's a narrow street, and someone might remember having to pull out and around to get past your car."

"What about at the north end of the alley?"

"No. There's a service station right across the street there, it's real busy."

"So," said Robin, striding ahead purposefully, "we go back this way, the way we came. If you had an ax, where would you put it?"

"Oh, Robin," I said nervously. "Let's just go." We were leaving the alley as unobserved as we had entered, as far as I could tell, and I was glad of it.

"I," continued Robin, "would drop it in one of these garbage cans waiting to be emptied."

That was why Robin was a very good mystery writer.

"I'm sure the police have searched them," I said firmly. "I am not going to stand here and go through everyone's garbage. Then someone really would call the police." Or would they? Apparently no one had spotted us so far.

We'd reached the end of the alley, at the spot we'd entered.

"If you wouldn't park here, you might just cross the street and go through the next alley," he said thoughtfully. "Park even farther away, be even less likely to be seen and connected."

So we slipped across the narrow street into the next alley. This one had been widened a little when some apartments had been built. Their parking was in the back, and in the construction process a drainage ditch had been put in the alley to keep the parking lots clear. There were culverts to provide entrances and exits to the lots. I thought, I would put the ax in one of the culverts. And I wondered if the police had searched this block.

This alley too was silent and lifeless, and I began to have the unsettling feeling that maybe Robin and I were the only people left in Lawrenceton. The sun came out briefly and Robin took my hand, so I tried hard to feel better. But when he crouched to retie his shoe, I began looking in the ditches.

Certainly the culvert right by us hadn't been disturbed. The water oak leaves that half-blocked the opening were almost smoothly aligned, pointing in the same direction, by the heavy rain of the night before last. But the next one down . . . someone had been in that ditch, no doubt about it. The leaves had been shoved up around the opening so forcefully that the mud underneath had been uncovered. Perhaps the police had searched, but of course none of them were as short as I was, so they weren't at an angle to see a little gleam from inside the culvert, a gleam sparked by the unexpected and short-lived sunshine. And their arms weren't as long as Robin's so they couldn't have reached in and pulled out . . .

"My briefcase?" Robin said in shock and amazement. "What's it doing here?" His fingers pried the gold-tone locks.

"Don't open it!" I shrieked, as Robin opened it, and out fell a bloodstained hatchet, to land with a thud on the packed leaves in the ditch.

Chapter Fourteen

While Robin stood guard over the horrible thing in the alley, I knocked on the door of one of the apartments. I could hear a baby screaming inside, so I knew someone was awake.

The exhausted young woman who answered the door was still in her nightgown. She was trusting enough to open the door to a stranger, and tired enough to accept my need to use her telephone incuriously. The baby screamed while I looked up the number of the police station, and kept it up while I dialed and talked to the desk officer, who had some trouble understanding what I was trying to tell him. When I hung up and thanked the young woman, the baby was still crying, though it had ebbed to a whimper.

"Poor baby," I said tentatively.

"It's colic," she explained. "The doctor says the worst should be over soon."

Aside from occasionally babysitting my half-brother, Phillip, when he was small, I knew nothing about babies. So I was glad to hear that the child had a specific complaint. By the time I thanked her and she shut the door behind me, I could hear the child starting to cry again.

I trudged back to the alley where Robin was sitting glumly, his back propped against the fence on the side opposite the apartments.

"Me and my great ideas," I said bitterly, plopping down beside him.

He let that pass in a gentlemanly manner.

"Cover it up," I suggested. "I can't stand it."

"How, without getting fingerprints on it? More fingerprints, that is."

We solved that problem as a mist began to dampen my hair against my cheeks. I found a stick and Robin stuck it under the edge of the briefcase, lifting it and dragging it over the hatchet with its dreadful stains. We settled back against the fence, able now to hear the sirens approaching. I felt oddly calm.

"I wonder if I'll ever get my briefcase back," Robin said. "Someone came in our parking lot and reached in my car and took my briefcase, so he could use it for hiding a murder weapon. I'd been thinking, Roe, when this case is all over, if it ever is, that I might try my hand at nonfiction. I'm here, I'm involved through knowing some of the people. I even met the Buckleys the very night before they were killed.

I was there when you and your mother opened the chocolates. Now I'm here finding a murder weapon in *my* briefcase, and I'm telling you, I don't like this much anymore. I
don't think I even want the damn briefcase as a memento,
now that I think of it." But after sitting for a moment in
silence, he murmured, "Wait till I tell my agent."

The surface of his glasses began to be speckled with tiny
drops of moisture. I took my own off and wiped them with
a Kleenex. "I've got to admire your lack of fear, Robin," I
said.

"Lack of fear?"

"You think they're not going to want to ask you a few
questions?" I said pointedly.

He had only seconds to absorb this and look dismayed
before an unmarked car pulled in the alley, with a patrol
car right behind it. For some reason, we stood up.

And God bless me, who should emerge from the
unmarked car but my friend Lynn Liggett, and she was
mad as a wet hen.

"You're everywhere!" she said to me. "I know you didn't
do these murders, but I swear every time I turn around
you're right in front of me!" She shook her head, as if trying
to shake me out of it. Then words seemed to fail her. Her
glance fell on the overturned open briefcase, with the handle of the hatchet protruding slightly from underneath.

"Who covered it up?" she said next. After we told her,
and she lifted the briefcase from the bloody hatchet with
the same stick, all her attention was on the murder weapon.

Yet another car appeared behind the patrol car. My
heart sank even deeper as Jack Burns heaved himself out

and strolled toward us. His body language said he was out for a casual amble in a pleasant neighborhood but his dark eyes snapped with anger and menace.

He stopped at the patrolmen, apparently the ones who had conducted the original alley search the day before, and blistered them up and down in language I had only seen in print. Robin and I watched with interest as they began to search the alley for anything that might have been left by the murderer. I was willing to bet that if he'd left any other trace in the alley, this time it would be found.

People began to emerge from the apartments, and the alley that had seemed so silent and deserted began to be positively crowded. I saw the curtain move at the apartment of the young mother, and hoped the baby had calmed down by now. It occurred to me that this woman was the most likely to have seen something the previous day, since she was probably up almost all the time. I started to suggest this to Detective Liggett, but I reconsidered in time to save my head from being bitten off.

The hatchet and briefcase bagged, the policewoman turned back to us.

"Did you touch the briefcase, Miss Teagarden?" she asked me directly.

I shook my head.

"So you did," she said to Robin, who nodded meekly. "You're someone else who turns up everywhere."

Finally Robin began to look worried.

"You need to go down to the station and have your fingerprints taken," Lynn said brusquely.

"I had them made the other night," Robin reminded

her. "Everyone at the Real Murders meeting had his or her prints taken."

This reminder did not endear him to the detective.

"Whose idea was this stroll through the alley?" Lynn counterattacked.

We looked at each other.

"Well," I began, "I started wondering how the Buckleys' murderer had reached their house without being seen . . ."

"But it was definitely me that wanted to go through this alley as well as the one behind the Buckley house," Robin said manfully.

"Listen, you two," Lynn said with an assumed calm, "you don't seem to understand the real world very well."

Robin and I didn't care for that accusation. I felt him stiffen beside me, and I drew myself up and narrowed my eyes.

"We are the police, and *we* are paid too damn little to investigate murders, but that's what we do. We don't sit and read about them, we solve them. We find clues, and we track down leads, and we knock on doors." She paused and took a deep breath. I had found several flaws in her speech so far, but I wasn't about to point out to her that Arthur read a lot about murders and that the police so far hadn't solved a thing and that the clue of the hatchet would still be in the damn ditch if Robin and I hadn't unearthed it.

I had enough sense of self-preservation not to say those things. When Robin cleared his throat, I stepped on his toes.

I was sorry I'd stopped him a moment later when Lynn really began questioning him. I wouldn't have stood to her questioning as well as he, and I had to admire his composure. I could see that it did look peculiar; Robin arrives in town, the murders start. But I knew that Mamie Wright's murder had been planned before Robin came to live in Lawrenceton, and the chocolates had been sent to Mother even earlier. The officer pointed out, though, that Robin had been present at the discovery of Mamie Wright's body, having invited himself to a Real Murders meeting on his first night in town. And he'd been at my house when I'd received the chocolate box.

Lynn was certainly not the only detective who thought Robin's presence at so many key scenes was fishy. And perhaps I was not as clear and free of suspicion as Arthur had assured me, because when Jack Burns took up the questioning he was looking from Robin to me with some significance. Here, he seemed to be thinking, is someone big who could have helped this woman get Pettigrue's body in the bathtub.

"I have to go to work in an hour and a half," I said quietly to him, when I'd had all I could take.

He stopped in mid-sentence.

"Sure," he said, seeming abruptly exhausted. "Sure you do." His fuel, it seemed, had been his exasperation with his own men missing the hatchet, and he'd run out of it. I liked him a lot better all of a sudden.

When Burns had taken over the role of castigator, Lynn had started knocking door to door at the apartments asking questions. Finally she reached the apartment where I'd used the phone, and the young woman, now in jeans and a sweater—she'd undoubtedly seen the police going door to door—answered in a flash. Lynn was obviously running through her list of questions, but I noticed after about the third one, she came to point like a bird dog. The young woman had said something Lynn was interested in hearing.

"Jack," Lynn yelled, "come here."

"Go home," Burns told us simply. "We know where you are if we need you." And he hurried over to Lynn.

Robin and I blew out a breath of relief simultaneously, and almost slunk out of the alley, trying as hard as we possibly could to attract no more official attention. Once we were out into the street, Robin went flying along home and dragged me with him by the hand.

When we reached our parking lot we finally stopped for breath. Robin hugged me and dropped a quick kiss on the top of my head, the most convenient spot for him. "That was really interesting," he commented, and I began laughing until my sides hurt. Robin's red eyebrows flew up, and his glasses slid down, and then he began laughing, too. I looked at my watch while I was thinking how long it had been since I'd really whooped like that, and when I saw what the time was, I told Robin I had to go change clothes. At least for a few hours, I had forgotten to be afraid about working at the library alone that night.

It had not been noticed until the last moment that no one had been scheduled to take Mr. Buckley's place on the roster. None of the other librarians would now admit to having the evening free, and all the volunteers had been scheduled for other nights.

I told Robin this hurriedly, and he said, "I'm sure the police patrols have been stepped up. But maybe I'll stop in on you tonight. If you need me, call me. I'll be here." He went in his gate and I went in mine.

As I pulled on the same blue skirt and red turtleneck I'd worn that morning, I was doing my best not to think of the hatchet. It had been unspeakable. On my drive to work I hoped that the library would be flooded with patrons so I wouldn't have time to think.

I was taking over the checkout desk from Jane Engle, who had been substituting for one of the librarians whose child had the flu. Jane looked the same, with her perfectly neat gray hair, her perfectly clean wire-rimmed glasses, and her anonymous gray suit. But inside, I could see she was no longer a sophisticated and curious witness to the Lawrenceton murders, but a terrified woman. And she was glad to get out of the library. "All the others left at five, not a single patron's come in since then," she told me in a shaky voice. "And frankly, Aurora, I've been delighted. I'm scared to be alone with anyone anymore, no matter how well I think I know them."

I patted Jane on the arm awkwardly. Though at times we'd eaten lunch together, mostly on days after club meetings when we wanted to discuss the program, Jane and I had had a friendly, but never intimate, relationship.

"Other people are interested in our little club for the first time," Jane went on, "and I've had to answer a lot of questions no one ever bothered to ask me before. People think I'm a little strange for having belonged to Real Murders." Jane was definitely a woman who would hate to be thought strange.

"Well," I said hesitantly, "just because we had a different sort of hobby—" Come to think of it, maybe we *were* a little strange, all of us Real Murderers, as we had sometimes called ourselves laughingly.

Ho-ho.

"One of us really is a murderer, you know," Jane chimed in eerily. I felt my thoughts were becoming visible in a balloon over my head. "It's gone beyond an academic interest in death and gore and psychology. I could feel it that night we met in your apartment."

"Who do you think it is, Jane?" I said impulsively, as she tied her scarf and extracted her keys from her purse.

"I am sure it's someone in our club, of course, or possibly a near connection of some sort to a club member. I don't know if this person has always been disturbed, or if he's just now decided to play a ghastly series of tricks on his fellow members. Or maybe there is more than one murderer and they're acting together."

"It doesn't have to be someone in Real Murders, Jane, just someone who doesn't like one of us, someone who wants us to be in trouble." She was standing by the front door by then, and I wanted her to stay as much as she wanted to go.

She shrugged, not willing to argue. "It's frightening to me," she said quietly, "to imagine what case I fit. I go over my books, checking out cases, to see what elderly woman living alone I resemble. What old murder victim."

I stared at her with my mouth open. I was appalled to realize what Jane had been going through, because of her active and probably accurate mind.

Then a mother trailing two reluctant toddlers came

through the door, and Jane slipped out to go home to her waiting house, to leaf through her true crime books in search of the pattern she would fit.

Thank God other people were in the library when Gifford Doakes came in, or I might have shrieked and run. Gifford, massacre enthusiast, had always sounded the warning bell in my brain that cautions me to pick and choose my conversation topics. Though I really didn't know too much about him, I'd always kept my distance from Gifford and limited my contact with him to the bare bones of courtesy.

You wanted to be polite to Gifford. You were a little scared not to be.

I had no idea what Gifford did for a living, but he dressed like a *Miami Vice* drug lord, in extremely stylish clothes and with his long brown hair carefully arranged. I wouldn't have been surprised to see a shoulder holster under his jacket.

Maybe Gifford *was* a drug lord.

And here he came now, gliding over to the checkout desk. I glanced around; that dynamic twosome, Melanie Clark and Bankston Waites, had come in a few minutes previously, their heads close together and laughing, and I could now see Bankston upstairs in the biography section, while Melanie was flipping through *Good Housekeeping* in the magazine area on the ground floor. Probably looking for a new meatloaf recipe. But bless her, she was there within call.

Gifford was right across the desk from me, and my hand closed over the nearest thing, which proved to be the stapler. A really effective deterrent, I told myself bitterly. I could see his shadow, Reynaldo, standing outside the double glass doors, pacing around in the near dark of the parking lot. He would pass through a pool of light from the arc lamps that provided safety for the lot—theoretically—and then vanish into the gloom, reappearing seconds later.

"How ya doing, Roe?" Gifford asked perfunctorily.

"Um. Okay."

"Listen, I hear you and that writer found the murder weapon in the Buckley case today."

The Buckley case? I had a sudden vision of an anthology of accounts of the decade's most notable murders, and of Lizanne's parents' slaughter being included. Other people would read about their deaths, and speculate, as I had speculated about other unsolved cases. Could it have been the Daughter? Or the Policeman who also belonged to the Real Murders Club? I realized that these murders would be made into a book . . . maybe by Joe McGuinniss or Joan Barthel or Robin, if his taste for it revived . . . and I would be in it, because of the chocolates. Maybe just "when the candy arrived at the home of Mrs. Teagarden's daughter Aurora . . ."

For a minute I was very confused. Was I in a book about old murders that I was reading, or was this all happening to me now? It would be nice to have the distance a book would give me. But Gifford's one earring was all too real, and the leopard-like pacing of Reynaldo—in the prosaic library parking lot!—was all too real, too.

"Tell me about the ax," Gifford was demanding.

"It was a hatchet, Gifford. An ax wouldn't fit in a brief-case." I was immediately furious with myself for contradicting a scary guy like Gifford; but then I consciously realized what my unconscious must have noted. Gifford Doakes was a man with a mission, and he was not interested in sidetracks.

"This long?" He held his hands apart.

"Yes, about." Standard hatchet size.

"Wood handle with black tape wrapped around the grip?"

"Yes," I agreed. I had forgotten the tape until he mentioned it.

"Damn," he hissed, and then he said a few other things, and his dark eyes blinked rapidly. Gifford Doakes was a frightened man and a furious one. I was scared as hell, too, not only of the murderer but more immediately of Gifford. Who was maybe also the murderer.

I gripped the stapler even harder and felt like a fool planning to battle a crazy man with a stapler that didn't even, I suddenly remembered, contain staples. Well, strike that line of defense.

"Now I have to go to the police station," Gifford said unexpectedly. "That's my hatchet, I'm almost positive. Reynaldo found out it was missing yesterday."

I laid down the stapler very gently on my desk, glanced upward, and saw Bankston looking over the second-floor railing. He raised his eyebrows in a silent query. I shook my head. I didn't think I needed help anymore. I thought Gifford was just as nervous as the rest of us, and for good reason. At this moment, sophisticated pageboy and sharp clothes notwithstanding, Gifford was chewing on his thumbnail like a five-year-old facing a difficult world.

"You'd better go to the police now," I said to him carefully. And he wheeled and was out the door before I could catch my breath.

Gifford's hatchet, Robin's briefcase. Those not cast as victims were being cast as murderers, to provide even more fun for the killer.

I wondered which category was scheduled for me. Surely finder-of-the-body would suffice.

I was still pondering this and other unpleasant related topics thirty minutes later when Perry Allison came in. I could hardly believe my luck at seeing Gifford and Perry in one evening. Two great guys. At least while Gifford had been here, so had a few other people, but in the intervening half hour Bankston and Melanie and the two other patrons had trickled out the door.

This time I quietly opened a drawer and slid out a pair of scissors. I checked my watch; only fifteen minutes to go till closing time.

"Roe!" he babbled. "Qué pasa?" His hands beat a manic tattoo on the desk.

I felt a stirring of dismay. This wasn't even the familiar unpleasant Perry, who had perhaps skipped some prescribed medication. Perry was on drugs no doctor had ever given him. The appeal of "recreational" drugs had completely passed me by, but I wasn't totally naive.

"Nothing much, Perry," I said cautiously.

"How can you say that? Things here are just *hopping*,"

he told me, his eyebrows flying all over his narrow face. "A murder a day, practically. Your honey, the cop, was at my place this afternoon. Asking questions. Making insinuations. About me! I couldn't hurt a fly!"

And Perry laughed and came around the desk in a few quick steps.

"Scissors?" He whooped. "Sssssscissssors?" He experimented with hissing. I was so taken aback by his quick moves and jerky head movements, so unlike the Perry I worked with, that it took me by surprise when his hand shot out to grasp the wrist of my hand that was holding the scissors. He gripped with manic pressure.

"That hurts, Perry," I said sharply. "Let go."

But Perry laughed and laughed, never relaxing his grip. I knew in a minute I would drop the scissors and I could not imagine what would happen after that.

Abruptly, he turned enraged. "You were going to stab me," he shouted furiously. "Not one of you wants me to make it! Not one of you knows what that hospital was like!"

He was right, and under other circumstances I would have listened with some sympathy. But I was in pain and terrified.

I could just barely feel the scissors still gripped in my numbing fingers.

In a day filled with strange incidents, this crazed man screaming at me, his emotional intensity spilling over me in this quiet and civilized building where people came to pick out nice quiet civilized books.

Then he began shaking me to get me to listen, his other

hand gripping my shoulder like a vise, and he never stopped talking, angry, sad, full of pain and self-pity.

I began to get angry myself, and suddenly something in me just snapped. I raised my foot and stomped on his instep with every ounce of force I could summon. With a wail of pain, he let go of me, and in that instant I turned and raced for the front door.

I ran smack into Sally Allison.

"Oh my God," she said hoarsely. "Are you all right? He didn't hurt you?" Without waiting for an answer she shouted at her son over my head, "Perry, what in God's name has gotten into you?"

"Oh, Mom," he said hopelessly and began to cry.

"He's on drugs, Sally," I said raggedly. She held me away from her and scanned me for injuries, letting loose a visible sigh of relief when she saw no blood. She saw the scissors still in my hand and looked horrified. "You weren't going to hurt him?" she asked incredulously.

"Sally, only a mother could say that," I said. "Now, you get him out of here and take him home."

"Listen to me, please, Roe," Sally pleaded. I was still frightened, but I was acutely uncomfortable, too. I had never had anybody beg me, as Sally unmistakably was begging me now. "Listen, he didn't take his medicine today. He's okay when he takes his medicine, really. You know he can come to work and perform his job, no one's complained about that, right? So please, please don't tell anyone about this."

"About what?" asked a quiet voice above my head, and I realized Robin had come in quietly. I looked up to his craggy face, his now-serious crinkly mouth, and I was so glad to see him I could have wept. "I came to check up on you," he said to me. "Mrs. Allison, I think I met you at the club meeting."

"Yes," Sally said, trying hard to pull herself together. "Perry! Come on!"

He walked over to her, his wet face blank and tired, his shoulders slumped.

"Let's go home," his mother suggested. "We have to talk about our agreement, about the promise you made me."

Without looking at me or saying a word, Perry followed his mother out the door. I collapsed against Robin and cried a little, still holding the stupid scissors. His huge hand smoothed my hair. When the worst was over, I said, "I have to lock up, I'm closing now. I don't care if Santa Claus comes to check out a book. This library is closed."

"Going to tell me what happened?"

"You bet I am, but first I want to get out of this place." I hated detaching myself from the comfortable chest and enfolding arms; it had been nice to feel protected by a big strong man for a few seconds. But I wanted to leave that building and go home more than I wanted anything else, and with luck, we could repeat the scene at my place with amenities handy.

Chapter Fifteen

"Maybe," Robin speculated between bites of a pretzel stick, "there's more than one murderer."

If we ever spent a night together, it wasn't going to be tonight. The mood had faded.

"Oh, Robin! I can't believe that for a minute. There couldn't be two people that evil in Lawrenceton at the same time, doing the same thing!" One was bad enough; two would get us in the history books for sure.

He waved the pretzel stick at me emphatically. "Why not, Roe? A copycat killer. Maybe someone, for example, wanted the Buckleys out of the way for some reason, and after Mamie got killed he saw his chance. Or maybe someone wanted to do in Pettigrue, and killed Mamie and the Buckleys to cloud the issue."

There was a certain amount of precedent for that, but more often in mystery novels than in real life, I thought.

"I guess it's possible," I conceded. "But Robin, I just don't want to believe it."

"Maybe, then, there's more than one killer. I mean, a team of murderers."

"Jane Engle said the same thing," I recalled belatedly. "Two people? How could you look at anyone who knew you had done that, Robin?" I could truly not imagine saying, "Hey, buddy, look at the way I socked Mamie!" I felt almost nauseated. That two people could agree on such a plan, and mutually carry it out . . .

"Hillside Stranglers," Robin reminded me. "Burke and Hare."

"But the Hillside Stranglers were sex murderers," I objected, "and Burke and Hare wanted to sell the bodies to medical schools."

"Well, true. These killings are apparently just for fun. Just to tease."

I thought of Gifford and his hatchet. The killer was teasing in more than one way. "Wait till you hear this!" I exclaimed.

Robin felt better when I'd told him he and Melanie and Arthur had company in the category of Implicated Innocent. "Though it would be clever of this Gifford," Robin cautioned, "to use his own ax, and then claim its use proved him innocent."

"I wonder if Gifford is that clever," I said. "Gifford is crafty, I think, but I believe he's pretty limited in imagination."

"And how well do you know him?" asked Robin, with a tiny edge to his voice.

"Not well," I admitted. "Just through seeing him at Real Murders. He's been coming about a year, I think. And he brings a *friend* named Reynaldo. Who apparently doesn't have a last name . . ."

The phone rang, and I reached out to pick it up, surprised at getting such a late call. People in Lawrenceton do not make phone calls after 10:00 P.M. At least, not the people I know. Robin tactfully took the occasion to go into the bathroom.

"Oh, God, I just looked at my watch. Were you in bed?" Arthur asked.

"No," I said, feeling ridiculously awkward with Robin in my place. Why should I? I asked myself. I could see two men at one time if I chose.

"I just finished work and got back to my place. I don't suppose there's any chance you want to come over?"

The idea sent a certain tingle down my spine, but all the conditions that had applied to Robin were still valid; plus, Robin was showing no signs of budging. In fact, he'd just gone to the refrigerator and refreshed his drink.

"I have to work tomorrow," I said neutrally.

"Oh. Okay. I get the message. Roller skating or nothing."

Ohmygosh. I had almost forgotten. Well, I had some pretty good reasons for not thinking about a Saturday night date.

"You think you will be able to get off?" I asked cautiously.

"I think so. I have some amazing news for you. You sitting down?"

Arthur sounded strange. Like someone who was trying to be excited and happy and just couldn't manage. And he hadn't mentioned the discovery of the hatchet and briefcase.

"Yes, I'm sitting. What?"

"Benjamin Greer just confessed to all the murders."

"What? He what?"

"He confessed to killing Mamie Wright, Morrison Pettigrue, and the Buckleys."

"But what about the box of candy? Why did he do that? Mother doesn't know him at all."

"He says Morrison did that, because your mother is an example of what is worst about capitalism."

"My mom—Morrison Pettigrue? I don't believe it," I sputtered disconnectedly.

"You don't want this case to be over?"

"Yes, yes! But I don't believe he did it. I wish I did."

"He's convinced a lot of the guys down here."

"Did he know where the hatchet was hidden?"

"Everyone in town knows that now."

"Did he know what it was in?"

"Pretty much everyone knows that, too."

"Okay, who'd he steal the hatchet from, that he used to kill the Buckleys?"

"He hasn't said yet."

"Gifford Doakes told me tonight that it was his hatchet."

"He did?" And for the first time Arthur's voice showed some life and enthusiasm. "Gifford hasn't been in here yet. As far as I know."

"Well, he told me tonight at the library that his hatchet

had been missing, and he asked me about that tape around the handle. I didn't bring it up, in fact I'd forgotten about it."

"I'll pass that on to the men who are questioning Greer," Arthur promised. "That can be one of our test questions. But for some reason, Roe, this guy is convincing. He believes it, I think. And we have a witness."

Robin had abandoned being polite and was beside himself to know what I was talking about. His eyebrows were winging around his face in interrogation. I kept waving my hand to keep him quiet.

"A witness to the murder."

"No, a witness who saw him leave the hatchet in the alley."

I remembered Lynn's excitement when she'd talked to the young mother in the apartments. I was willing to bet that that was the witness.

"So what did she see?" I asked sharply.

"Listen, this is police business that I can't tell you about in detail," Arthur said flatly.

"I'm sorry if I'm trespassing, but I'm deeply involved in this, up to my neck, according to Lynn Liggett and your boss Jack Burns."

"Well. You're off the hook now."

"This is hard to soak in. I can't believe it's all over."

"I'm going to sleep," Arthur said, and the exhaustion made his voice slur. "I'm going to sleep and sleep and sleep. And when I get up, we're going to talk about going roller skating."

"Okay," I said slowly. "Listen, I just remembered that my little brother, Phillip, is coming tomorrow and spending the weekend."

"Then we'll take him with us," Arthur said smoothly, scarcely missing a beat.

"Okay. Talk to you later." I was smiling as I hung up; I couldn't help it. "It may be over, Robin," I said, almost crying.

His mouth fell open. "You mean, we don't have to worry anymore?" he asked.

"So it seems. An eyewitness places Benjamin Greer, the member of Real Murders who wasn't there the night Mamie got killed, depositing the briefcase in the culvert. And he has confessed to everything, except sending the candy, which he says Morrison Pettigrue did before he killed him. I'll have to call Mother. Pettigrue thought Mother was a terrible capitalist."

We discussed this truly stunning development up and down and sideways and forwards, until I began to yawn and feel drowsy.

"Did I hear you mention that your brother is coming?" Robin asked tactfully.

"Yes, his name is Phillip, he's six. From my father's remarriage. Dad and his wife are going to a convention in Chattanooga this weekend, and I've been scheduled for a long time to keep Phillip. Things were getting so grim here I was thinking about calling Dad and canceling or going to keep Phillip at their house, but now I guess it'll be okay to have him here."

"You two get along? What do you do when he's visiting?"

"Oh, we play games. We go to the movies. He watches television. I read to him, things he can't read himself yet. One time we went bowling. That was a real disaster, but fun, too. Sometimes he brings his ball and glove and we play catch in the parking lot. I'm not very good at that, though. Phillip is a real baseball freak, he brings his cards every time he comes and we go through them, while I try not to yawn."

"I like kids," said Robin, and I could tell he was sincere. "Maybe Saturday we can all go to the state park and have a picnic and hike one of the trails."

That would be an hour drive to and from, plus allow maybe three hours for the hike and picnic, I figured rapidly. I could be back in time for roller skating, but Phillip would probably be exhausted from the park, and I might be, too. "Maybe playing—is it called goofy golf?—would be better. I noticed a new place out on the highway into the city when I drove in Monday." That felt years ago now.

"I saw that, too," Robin said. "Maybe Saturday afternoon?"

"Okay, he'll love it. Come meet him tomorrow night," I offered. "I promised to make pecan pie—that's Phillip's favorite. What about 7:00?"

"Great," said Robin agreeably. He leaned over to give me a casual kiss. "I'll see you then." He seemed preoccupied as he left.

I locked the back door after Robin left, and checked my front door, though I seldom used it. If this whole imbroglio had had one effect, it was to make me permanently security conscious.

It had been a busy day even without the constant strain of living with a murderer in close proximity. Today we'd found the hatchet in Robin's briefcase, I'd had the weird confrontation with Gifford Doakes and the eerie scene in the library with Perry. I wondered if Sally was right in her optimistic belief that no one at work besides me had noticed that Perry was unraveling. I hadn't exactly been in the current of office gossip the past week, being mostly the subject of it, I was sure.

Then Arthur had called with the bombshell about Benjamin.

Benjamin the loser. Benjamin the murderer?

As I made up the bed in the guest room for Phillip—though he usually ended up getting spooked at spending the night in a strange place and came in my room—I realized anew how abnormal the week had been. Usually, when I knew Phillip was going to make one of his four or five annual weekend visits, I spent several days preparing. I stocked all his favorite foods, planned lots of activities, checked out an armful of children's books, consulted the local movie schedules. I overdid it.

This was probably the appropriate amount of preparation for a six-year-old's visit; I made a bed for him, checked to see if I had the ingredients for his favorite dessert, and decided to take him to his favorite fast-food place for lunch on Saturday. And I looked forward to seeing him, this unexpected brother I had acquired after I'd become an adult. In the middle of the awfulness I'd seen lately, and the anxiety I'd suffered in so many unprecedented situations, having Phillip to visit seemed like a welcome return to normality.

Benjamin Greer.

I tried to believe it.

Chapter Sixteen

I woke up smiling. It took me a second to remember why, but when I remembered, I grinned all over. The murders were at an end. I had convinced myself in my sleep that Benjamin was confessing because he had done it and wanted the attention and infamy, not because he hadn't done it but wanted the attention and infamy anyway. After all, he had announced his candidacy for mayor, that should have given him enough fuel to run on for a while. It was Friday, I didn't have to work this weekend, Phillip was coming, I was interested in two men and what's more they were both interested in me. What more could a twenty-eight-year-old librarian ask for?

I made myself up with great care, had some fun with my eye shadow, and picked my brightest skirt and blouse to wear. It was a definitely springy set, white with yellow flowers scattered all over, and I let my hair hang loose with a yellow band to hold it back.

I had a large breakfast, cereal and toast and even a banana, and sang on my way out to my car.

"You're chipper this morning," said Bankston, who was dressed in a very sober suit befitting a banker. He was smiling himself, and I remembered I'd seen Melanie's car pull out of the parking lot very early this morning.

"Oh, I have reason to be! You may not have heard yet, but someone admitted to the murders."

"Who?" Bankston said after staring at me for a moment.

"Benjamin Greer." Then I wondered belatedly if I was betraying a confidence. But my assurance returned when I remembered Arthur hadn't asked me to keep it quiet, and I hadn't told him I would. Also, I'd already told Robin, who would have throttled the news out of me if I'd hung up from my conversation with Arthur and refused to tell him. Wait; I wasn't even going to say exaggerated things like that to myself anymore.

Bankston was thunderstruck. "But he was just in to see me last week to get a loan for his candidate's campaign! Sorry, I shouldn't have mentioned that. It was a private trans-action, bank business. But I'm just so—flabbergasted."

"I was too," I assured him.

"Well, well, I'll have to stop by Melanie's and tell her," he said after a moment of thought. "This will be such a relief to her. She's had a hard time since Mrs. Wright's purse was found in her car."

Right. Being pronounced a martyr at church and getting a marriage proposal was really a hard time. But I felt too cheerful to envy Melanie; I'd gone out with Bankston twice and wouldn't have him on a silver platter, as my mother always said.

Mother. That was someone who should hear the good news, too. I'd call her today. She was going to love being termed "what was worst about capitalism." That was a hard line to take after all Mother's hard work and struggle during the first few years with her business, though then she'd had my father's presence to give her renewed strength. He hadn't left until she was well on the road to success. I was trailing off into unpleasant thoughts, and snapped myself back quickly. Joy was the keynote of the day.

At work, all the librarians and volunteers seemed to have heard the good news, and I was back in the fold. Lillian went back to being her bitchy self, which was almost comforting. Sam Clerrick ventured forth from his charts and graphs and budgets to pat me on the shoulder in passing. I poked book cards in the stamper vigorously, took overdue money with a smile instead of expressionless disapproval, shelved with precision. The morning didn't just hurry by, it hopped, skipped, and jumped by.

The telephone rang twice while I was eating my microwaved egg rolls and browsing through an encyclopedia of twentieth-century murderers. I'd had that familiar irritating feeling that someone, sometime, had said something interesting that I wanted to pursue, mentioned some names I wanted to mull over, and I'd thought flipping through the book would help. But the phone destroyed even this wisp of idea.

The first caller was my father, who always opened with, "How's my doll?"

He hated calling me "Roe" and I hated him calling me "Doll." We hadn't come up with anything neutral. "I'm okay, Dad," I said.

"Is it still okay with you if Phillip comes?" he asked anxiously. "You know, if you are upset about the situation in Lawrenceton, we can stay home."

In the background I could hear Phillip piping anxiously, "Can I go, Daddy? Can I go?"

"The crisis seems to be over," I said happily.

"They arrest someone?"

"They got a confession. I'm sure everything's going to be okay now," I said. Maybe I wasn't all that sure. But I *was* pretty sure that I was going to be okay now. And I wanted to see my little brother.

"Well, I'll be bringing him about five o'clock, then," Dad said. "Betty Jo sends her love. We really appreciate this."

I wasn't so sure about Betty Jo's love, but I was sure she did appreciate having a free, reliable babysitter for a whole weekend.

The next call was from my mother, of course. She still had some sort of psychic link to Dad, and if he called me she nearly always rang within the hour. If she was like Lauren Bacall, he was like Humphrey Bogart; an ugly guy with charisma coming out his ears. And bless his heart, he seemed quite unaware of it. But that charisma was still sending out alpha waves or something to my mother.

I knew that she must already have heard of Benjamin's confession, and sure enough, she had. She'd also heard he'd said Morrison Pettigrue had mailed her the chocolates. She was skeptical.

"How would Morrison Pettigrue hear about Mrs. See's?" she asked. "How would he know I always eat the creams?"

"He didn't have to know you always eat the creams," I pointed out. "There's just no way to get rat poison in the nut-filled ones."

"That's true," she admitted. "I still have a hard time believing that one. I barely knew the man. I'd met him at some Chamber of Commerce meeting once, and if I remember correctly, we talked about the need for new sidewalks downtown. It was a cordial conversation and he certainly gave no sign then that he thought I was some kind of leech living off the masses, or whatever."

But if Benjamin was lying about the chocolates, he could also be lying about other things. And I wanted him to be telling the truth and nothing but the truth.

"Let's just shelve this until we find out more about it," I suggested. "Maybe he'll say something that'll make sense out of the whole thing."

"Is—your brother—still staying with you this weekend?" Mother asked, in one of her lightning turns of thought.

I sighed silently. "Yes, Mother. Dad's bringing Phillip by around five, and he'll be here until Sunday evening." It would have been beneath Mother's dignity to avoid the sight of Phillip, but having made a point of talking to him once or twice, she usually stayed away while he was at my place.

"Well, I'll be talking to you again," she was saying now. I could bet on that. I asked her about her business, and she chatted about that for a few minutes.

"Are you and John still thinking about getting married?" I asked.

"Well, we're discussing it." There was a smile in her voice. "I promise you'll be the first to know when we definitely decide."

"As long as I'm the first," I said. "I really am happy for you."

"I hear you have a new beau," Mother said, which was a logical progression when you think about it.

"Which one have you heard about?" I asked, because I simply couldn't resist.

In someone less grand than my mother, I would've called the sound she made a delighted cackle. We hung up with mutual warmth, and I returned to work with the distinct feeling life was on the up and up for me.

My mother's "beau," John Queensland, came into the library that afternoon while I was on the circulation desk. I realized he was practically the opposite of my father: handsome in an elder-statesman way, and overtly as dignified and reserved as Mother. He had been a widower for some time and still lived in the big two-story house he'd shared with his wife and their two children, both of whom had children of their own now. My contemporaries, I reminded myself gloomily.

As John was checking out two staid biographies of

worthy people, he mentioned that his garage had been broken into some time within the last three weeks.

"I never use it anymore. I just park behind the house. The garage is so full of the boys' old stuff—I can't seem to get them to decide what to do with all their junk." He sounded fond rather than complaining. "But anyway, I went to track down my golf clubs since I intended scheduling a game with Bankston in this warmer weather, and the darned thing had been broken into and my golf clubs were gone."

Since John was a Real Murderer, I was sure that this theft meant something. I told John about Gifford Doakes and his hatchet—amazingly, he hadn't heard—and left him to draw his own conclusions.

"I know Benjamin Greer has confessed," I told John, "but that's a bit of evidence the police might need. Just a confession isn't enough, I gather."

"I think I'll go by the police station on my way back to the office," John said thoughtfully. "Those clubs had better be reported. The whole bag was taken, and it was a pretty distinctive set. Every time my kids went somewhere, they got a bumper sticker and put it on my golf bag, just a family joke . . ." And trailing off with unheard-of abstraction, John left the library. I thought of Arthur and sighed. I wondered if he'd appreciate being handed another out-of-the-blue fact.

Golf clubs. Maybe they'd already been used. Maybe they'd been used on Mamie. The weapon in that case had never been found, that I knew of. Maybe Benjamin would tell the police where the clubs were.

I let this nag at me until I got home and saw my father's car waiting at my apartment. As I greeted my father and hugged my half-brother, I made a resolution not to think about these killings for a couple of days. I wanted to enjoy Phillip's company.

Phillip is in the first grade and he can be very funny and very exasperating. He will eat about five things with any enthusiasm—five nutritious things, that is. (Anything with no nutritional value whatsoever is always acceptable to Phillip.) Luckily for me, one of those things is spaghetti sauce and another is pecan pie, not that either is exactly a health food.

"Roe! Are we having spaghetti tonight?" he asked eagerly.

"Sure," I said, and smiled at him. I bent and kissed him before he could say, "Yuck! No kisses!" He gave me a quick kiss back, then scrambled to get his suitcase and (much more important) a plastic garbage bag full of essential toys. "I'm going to put these in my room," he told Father, who was beaming at him with unadulterated pride.

"Son, I've got to go now," Father told him. "Your mom is anxious to get where we're going. You be good for your big sister, now, and do what she says to do without giving her any trouble."

Phillip, half listened, mumbled, "Sure, Dad," and lugged his paraphernalia into my place.

"Well, Doll, this sure is nice of you," my father said to me when Phillip had vanished.

"I like Phillip," I said honestly. "I like having him stay here."

"Here are the phone numbers where we'll be staying," Father said and fumbled a sheet of notepaper out of his pocket. "If anything goes wrong, anything at all, call us straight away."

"Okay, okay," I reassured him. "Don't worry. Have a good time. I'll see you Sunday night?"

"Yes, we should be here about five or six. If we're going to be any later than that, we'll call you. Don't forget to remind him about his prayers. Oh—if he runs a fever or anything, here's a box of chewable children's aspirin. He gets three. And he needs to have a glass of water by the bed at night."

"I'll remember." We hugged, and he got in his car with a lopsided smile and half-wave that I could see a woman would have a hard time forgetting. I watched Father drive out of the parking lot, and then heard Phillip shouting from the kitchen, "Roe! You got any cookies?"

I supplied Phillip with two awful sandwich cookies that he'd told me were his favorites. Very pleased, he bounced outside with his garbage bag of toys, having dumped the "inside" ones in the middle of my den. "I bet you have to cook, so I'm going to be out here playing," he said seriously.

I could take a hint. I got busy with the spaghetti sauce.

The next time I glanced out the window to check, I saw through my open patio gate that Phillip had already commandeered Bankston into playing baseball in the parking lot. Phillip had great scorn for my baseball playing ability, but Bankston had his approval. Bankston had taken off his suit coat and his tie immediately, and seemed not nearly so stuffy as he pitched the baseball to Phillip's waiting bat.

They'd played before when Phillip had visited, and Bankston didn't seem to consider it an imposition.

Then Robin was drawn into the game when he got home, and he was acting as Phillip's catcher when I called from the patio gate that supper was ready.

"Yahoo!" Phillip shrieked, and propped his bat against the patio wall. I smiled and shrugged at his abandoned playmates and whispered to Phillip, "Thank Bankston and Robin for a good game."

"Thank you," Phillip said obediently and dashed in to scramble into his chair at my small dining table.

I glimpsed the top of Melanie's head in Bankston's open door as he went in, and Robin said, "See you later, for pecan pie. I like your little brother," as he strolled through the gate to his patio. I felt warm and flushed with pride at having such a cute brother—and a little warm, too, at Robin's smile, which had definitely been of the personal variety.

For the next twenty minutes I was occupied in seeing that Phillip used his napkin and said his prayer and ate at least a little serving of vegetables. I looked fondly at his perpetually tousled light brown hair and his startlingly blue eyes, so different from mine. Between bites of spaghetti and garlic bread, Phillip was telling me a long, involved story about a fight on the school playground, involving a boy whose brother really knew karate and another boy who really had all the G.I. Joe attack vehicles. I listened with half an ear, the other part of my mind being increasingly occupied by the niggling feeling that I was supposed to know something. Or remember something. Or had I seen something? Whatever this "something" was, I needed to call it to mind.

"My baseball!" shrieked Phillip suddenly.

He had my full attention. The shriek, which had sprung with no warning from his throat while he was telling me what the principal had done to the playground combatants, had scared the whosis out of me.

"But Phillip, it's dark," I protested, as he catapulted out of his chair and dashed to the back door. I tried to remember if I'd ever seen him walk, and decided that I had, once, when he was about twelve months old. "Here, at least take my flashlight!"

I managed to stuff it in his hand only because he was so partial to flashlights that he slowed down long enough for me to pull it from the kitchen cabinet.

"And try to remember where you last saw the ball!" I bellowed after him.

I'd finished my meal while Phillip was relating his long story, so I scraped my plate and put it in the dishwasher (Robin was due in a few minutes, and I wanted the place to look neat). The dessert plates were out, everything else was ready, so while I waited for a triumphant Phillip to return with his baseball, I idly looked at my shelves, putting a few books back in place that were out of order. I stared at the titles of all those books about bad or crazy or crazed people, men and women whose lives had crossed the faint line that demarks those who could but haven't from those who can and have.

Phillip had been gone a long time; I couldn't hear him out in the parking lot.

The phone rang.

"Yes?" I said abruptly into the receiver.

"Roe, it's Sally Allison."

"What . . ."

"Have you seen Perry?"

"What? No!"

"Has he been . . . following you anymore?"

"No . . . at least, I haven't noticed if he has."

"He . . ." Sally trailed off.

"Come on, Sally! What's the matter?" I asked roughly. I stared out through the kitchen window, hoping to see the beam of the flashlight bobbing around through the slats in the patio fence. I remembered the night Perry'd been across the street in the dark waiting for Robin to bring me home. I was terrified.

"He didn't take his medicine today. He didn't go to work. I don't know where he is. Maybe he took some more pills."

"Call the police, then. Get them looking for him, Sally! What if he's here? My little brother's out alone in the dark!" I hung up the phone with a hysterical bang. I grabbed up my huge key ring, with some idea of taking my car around the block for a search, and I pulled out the second flashlight I kept ready.

It was my fault. The thing in the dark had gotten my little brother, a six-year-old child, and it was *my fault*. Oh Lord God, heavenly King, protect the child.

I left the back door wide open, the welcome light spilling into the deep dusk. The patio gate was already open, Phillip never remembered to close it. His bat was propped beside it as he'd left it coming in to supper.

"Phillip!" I screamed. Then I thought, maybe I should

be quiet and creep. In a frenzy of indecision, I swung the flashlight to and fro. A few yards away, a car started up and pulled out of its space. As it went by, I saw it was Melanie in Bankston's car. She smiled and waved. I gaped after her. How could she not have heard me yell?

But I couldn't reason, I just kept walking and sweeping the ground with that beam of light, seeing nothing, nothing.

"Roe, what's wrong? I was just on my way over to your place!" Robin loomed above me in the dark.

"Phillip's gone, someone's got him! He left to get his baseball, he ran out the back door, he didn't come back!"

"I'll get a flashlight," Robin said instantly. He turned to go to his telephone. "Listen—" he half turned back but kept moving, "he wouldn't think it was funny to hide, would he?"

"I don't think so," I said. I would have loved to have thought Phillip was giggling behind a bush somewhere, but I knew he wasn't. He couldn't have stayed hidden this long in the dark. He'd have jumped out long before, screaming "boo," his grin of triumph making his face shine. "Listen, Robin, go ask the Crandalls if they've seen Phillip, and call the police. Perry Allison's mom just called and he's loose somewhere. She may not call the police. I'm going to work my way around to search the front yard."

"Right," Robin said briefly, and vanished into his place.

I walked quickly through the dark (and it was full dark now), the beam of the flashlight on the sidewalk before me. I'd pause, and swing the flashlight, and step on. I passed the Crandalls' gate, and had found nothing. I opened

Bankston's gate. The flashlight beam caught something on Bankston's patio.

Phillip's baseball.

Oh, God, it had been here all the time, no wonder Phillip couldn't find it. Bankston had probably picked it up out of the parking lot to keep it to give Phillip tomorrow morning.

I lifted my hand to knock on Bankston's back door and my hand froze in midair. I thought about Melanie pulling out of the parking lot so strangely—she must have heard me scream.

And I'd told Phillip to think of where he'd seen it last. He'd seen it last in Bankston's hands.

Had Bankston been lying down in that car? Had he been lying on top of Phillip, to keep him quiet?

A long brown hair had been found in the Buckleys' house. Benjamin didn't have long brown hair. He had thinning blond hair. Like Bankston. He was medium height, like Bankston, and he had a round face. Like Bankston. It was Bankston the young mother had seen in the alley, not Benjamin Greer.

Melanie had long brown hair. *Together.* They had done the killings together.

And then I remembered that niggly little thing that had been bothering me. When John Queensland had described his golf bag, he'd said it had stickers all over it. That had been the golf bag Bankston was carrying into his place on Wednesday, so long after my lunch hour he hadn't expected me to be around at all, much less popping out of the Crandalls' gate. Bankston had stolen them from John Queensland.

Had Phillip been in Bankston's town house? I turned my flashlight on my key ring. You couldn't call it breaking and entering, I told myself hysterically. I had a key. I was the landlady. I turned it in the keyhole, opened the door as quietly as I could, and stepped inside.

I didn't call out. I left the back door open.

The kitchen light was on, and the kitchen/living room was a mess, but an ordinary mess. A library book was lying open on the counter, a book I had in my own personal library, Emlyn Williams's *Beyond Belief.* I felt sick and had to bend over.

This time they were patterning themselves after Myra Hindley and Ian Brady, the "Moors Murderers." They were going to kill a child. They were going to kill my brother. The monster was not sitting in a jail cell in the Lawrenceton City Jail. The monsters lived here.

Hindley and Brady had tortured the children for a few hours first, so Phillip might be alive. If he'd been in the car, if they'd taken him to Melanie's place, wherever that was— right, the same street where Jane Engle lived—he might have left some trace.

Abandoning silence, I raced up the stairs. No one. In the larger bedroom there was a king-sized bed with a coil of rope beside it, and a camera was on the dresser.

Hindley and Brady, two low-level office workers who'd met on the job, had tape-recorded and photographed their victims.

The extra bedroom was full of exercise equipment: the source of Bankston's newly bulging muscles. There was a file box with its lid hanging back, key still in the lock.

Anything he locked up, I wanted to see. I knocked it over and the magazines inside spilled out like a trail of slime. I looked at an open one in horror. I did not know it was possible to buy pictures of women being treated like that. When I had heard of the anti-pornography movement, I'd thought of the usual pictures of women who at least were apparently willing, being paid, and still healthy when the photo session was over.

I ran back downstairs, glanced into the living room, opened the closets. Nothing. I opened the door to the basement. The light was off, so the steps were dark from halfway down to the bottom. But something white was on one of the lower steps, just visible in the light spilling down from the kitchen.

I went down the stairs and crouched to pick it up. It was a baseball card.

I heard a muffled noise, and had time to think, Phillip! But then I felt a terrible pain across my shoulder and neck, and I was falling forward, my arms and legs tangled, my face scraping the edge of the steps. The next thing I knew I was on the floor of the basement and looking up at Bankston's face, stolid no more in the dim light but grinning like a gargoyle, and he had a golf club in his hand.

There was another switch at the bottom of the steps, and he turned it on. I heard the noise again, and with great pain turned my head to see Phillip, gagged and with his hands tied, sitting on a straight chair by the dryer. His face was wet with tears and his whole little body was curled into as tight a ball as he could manage in that chair. His feet could not touch the floor.

My heart broke.

I'd heard people say that all my life; their heart had broken because their love had deserted them, their heart had broken because their cat had died, their heart had broken because they'd dropped Grandma's vase.

I was going to die and I had cost my little brother his life, and my heart broke for what he would endure before they finally tired of him and killed him.

"We heard you come in," Bankston said, smiling. "We were down here waiting for you, weren't we, Phillip?"

Incredible, Bankston the banker. Bankston with the matching almond-tone washer and dryer. Bankston arranging a loan for a businessman in the afternoon and smashing Mamie Wright's face in the evening. Melanie the secretary, filling up her idle time while her boss was out of town by slaughtering the Buckleys with a hatchet. The perfect couple.

Phillip was crying hopelessly. "Shut up, Phillip," said the man who'd played baseball with him that afternoon. "Every time you cry, I'll hit your sister. Won't I, sis?" And the golf club whistled through the air and Bankston broke my collarbone. My shriek must have covered Melanie's steps, because suddenly she was there looking down at me with pleasure.

"When I pulled in, the Scarecrow was searching the parking lot," she said to Bankston. "Here's the tape recorder. I can't believe we forgot it!"

Gee, what a madcap couple. She sounded for all the world like a housewife who'd remembered the potato salad in the fridge just as the family was leaving on its picnic.

I decided, when the pain had ebbed enough for me to

think, that "the Scarecrow" was Robin. I managed to look at Phillip again. God bless him, he was trying so hard not to make sounds, so Bankston wouldn't hit me again. I tried to push the pain away so I could look reassuring, but I could only stare at him and try not to scream myself. If I screamed, Bankston would hit me quite a lot.

Or maybe he would hit Phillip.

"What do you think?" Bankston asked her.

"No way we can get them out of here now," Melanie said matter-of-factly. "He said he'd called the police. One of us better go up soon and offer to help search. If we don't, the police will want to look in here, I guess, get suspicious. We can't have that, can we?" and she smiled archly, and poked my leg with her foot, as if I were a piece of naughtiness that they had to conceal for convention's sake. She saw me looking at her. "Get up and get over there by the kid," she said, and then she kicked me. I moaned. "I've always wanted to do that," she said to Bankston with a smile.

It was not only the fall and the blows that made it hard to move, but the shock. I was in this most prosaic basement with these most prosaic people, and they were monsters that were going to kill me, me and my brother. I had read and marveled for years at people living cheek by jowl with psychopaths and not suspecting. And here I was, trying desperately to crawl across a concrete floor in a building my mother owned while friends looked for my brother outside, because I had never, never thought it could happen to me. I got to Phillip's side in a few moments, though the young woman I'd known all my life and gone to church with did kick me a few times on the journey. I grabbed the edge of the seat and dragged myself to my knees, and clumsily draped my good arm around Phillip. I wished Phillip would faint. His face was more than I could stand, and I had no consolation for him. We were looking at the faces of demons, and all the rules of kindness and courtesy that Phillip and I had been taught so carefully did not apply. No reward for good behavior.

"I got the tape recorder, but now we can't use it," Melanie was pouting. "I think that's when she got suspicious, when she saw me pull out of the parking lot. I didn't want to have to help her look, so I had to act like I didn't hear her. I don't guess we'll get to have any fun tonight."

"I didn't think this through," Bankston agreed. "Now they'll be out there looking for the boy and her all night, and we'll have to go volunteer, too. At least now we've got her keys, they can't use the master set to come in here." He held them up. I must have dropped them when I fell.

"You think they might insist on searching all the apartments?" Melanie asked anxiously. "We can't turn them down if they ask."

Bankston pondered. They were at the foot of the steps still. I could not get by them. I could not see any weapons besides the golf club, but even if I did attack them with my one good arm and my little remaining energy, the two of them could easily overcome me and the noise would not be heard by anyone . . . unless the Crandalls had decided to spend the evening in their basement. "We'll just have to wing it," Bankston said finally.

The baseball! Maybe Robin would see it, like I had.

"Did you talk to anyone when you pulled in?" Bankston was asking.

"Just what I told you before. Robin asked me if I had seen the boy, and I said no, but that I'd be glad to help look," Melanie said with no irony whatsoever. "Roe left the back door open, so I closed and relocked it. And I picked up the kid's baseball, it was still out on the patio."

That was our death warrant, I reckoned.

Bankston cursed. "How did it end up out there? I was sure I'd brought it in."

"Don't worry about it," Melanie said. "Even if they did find it, you could just have said you'd been keeping it for him but he didn't ever show up looking for it."

"You're right," Bankston said fondly. "What shall we do with those two? If we leave them tied up down here while we go help to search, they might somehow get loose. If we kill them right now, we lose our fun with the boy." He strolled over to us and Melanie followed.

"You acted on impulse when you grabbed him," Melanie observed. "We should just go on and take care of them now, and hide them down here good. Then when the search dies down, we'll see if we can get them out to the car and dump them. Next time, no impulses, we'll do what we planned and nothing extra."

"Are you criticizing me?" Bankston asked sharply. His voice was low and dangerous.

Her posture changed. I had never seen anything like it. She cringed and folded and became another person. "No, never," she whimpered, and she bent and licked his hand. I saw her eyes, and she was role-playing and it excited her immensely.

I was nauseated. I hoped I was blocking Phillip's view sufficiently. I huddled closer to him, though the pain from my collarbone was becoming more insistent. Phillip was shaking and he had wet himself. His breath was getting more and more ragged, and muffled sobs and whimpers broke out from time to time.

Melanie and Bankston were giving each other a kiss, and Bankston bent and bit her shoulder. She held him to her as though they would use each other right there, but then they unclenched and she said, "We'd better do it now. Why run any more risks?"

"You're right," Bankston agreed. He gave her the golf club, and she swung it through the air experimentally while he searched his pockets. In her black slacks and green sweater and knotted scarf she looked ready to tee off at the country club. In that small area the club whistled past me with no room to spare, and I started to protest, when I realized yet again that Melanie absolutely could not care less. Old assumptions die hard.

I saw a foot on the stairs behind them.

"Give me your scarf, Mel," Bankston said suddenly. Melanie unknotted it instantly. "This would be less messy, and I've never done it before," he observed cheerfully. They never looked at me or at Phillip, except in passing, and I could tell to them we were not people like they were.

The foot was joined by a matching foot, and silently took another step down.

"Maybe I should tape this," Melanie said brightly. "It won't be what we had planned, but it might be interesting."

The next step squeaked, and I screamed, "God damn you to hell! How can you do this to me? How can you do this to a little boy?"

They were as shocked as though a chair had spoken. Melanie swung the club instantly with both hands. My body was covering Phillip's on the chair, but the blow was so strong the chair was rocked. It was easy to shriek as loud as a freight train. I saw the feet descend all the way in a rush.

"Shut up, bitch!" Melanie said furiously.

"Naw, you shut up," a flat voice advised her.

It was old Mr. Crandall, and he was carrying a very large gun.

The only sound in the basement was the sobbing coming from me, as I struggled to control myself. Phillip raised his bound wrists to loop his arms over my head. I wished more than ever that he'd faint.

"You're not going to shoot," Bankston said. "You old idiot. With this concrete floor, it'll ricochet and hit them."

"I'd rather shoot them directly than leave them to you," Mr. Crandall said simply.

"Which one of us will you shoot first?" Melanie asked furiously. She'd been sidling away from Bankston a little at a time. "You can't get us both, old man."

"But I can," said Robin from higher on the stairs, and he wasn't nearly as calm as Mr. Crandall. I managed to look up. I saw Robin descending with a shotgun. "Now I don't know as much about guns as Mr. Crandall, but he loaded this for me, and if I point it and fire, I am real sure I will hit something."

If they tried anything desperate it would be now. I could feel the turmoil pouring from them. They looked at each other. I could only stare through a haze of pain at the green silk scarf in Bankston's hand. Oh, surely they must see it was over, over.

Suddenly the fight oozed out of them. They looked like what they used to be, for a moment: a bank loan officer and a secretary, who could not remember where they were or how they had come to be there. The scarf fell from Bankston's hand. Melanie lay down the golf club. They did not look at each other anymore.

There was a gust of people noise, and Arthur and Lynn Liggett came pelting down the stairs to be stopped short by the tableau.

Phillip's breath came out from behind the gag in a deep sigh, and he fainted. It seemed like such a good idea that I did it, too.

Chapter Seventeen

"If I'd had my Dynamite Man Particle Blaster they wouldn't have hurt us," Phillip whispered. He simply would not be parted from me while I was being patched up. He held on to my hand or my leg or my torso; though many kind people offered to take him and rock him, or buy him an ice cream cone, or color with him, my little brother would not be separated from me. This definitely made it harder on me, but I tried to have so much sympathy for Phillip that the pain would not seem important. I'm afraid I found that to me, pain is very important, no matter who else has been hurt.

Now he was actually in the hospital bed with me, huddling as close to me as he could get, his eyes still wide and staring, but beginning to glaze over. I thought he'd had some kind of mild tranquilizer; I thought I remembered saying that was okay. My father and stepmother were driving back from Chattanooga; Robin, bless him, had found their phone number and called, miraculously catching them in their motel room.

"Phillip, if I hadn't had you to hold on to, I would have gone nuts," I assured him. "You were so brave. I know you were scared inside, like I was, but you were brave as a lion to hold yourself together."

"I was thinking about escaping all the time. I was just waiting for a chance," he informed me. There, he was beginning to sound more like Phillip. Then, less certainly, "Roe, would they really have killed us?"

What was I supposed to say? I glanced over at Robin, who shrugged in an it's-up-to-you gesture. Why was I asking Robin what I should say to my little brother?

"Yes," I said, and took a deep breath. "Yes, they were really bad people. They were rotten apples. They were nice on the outside but full of worms on the inside."

"But they're locked up in jail now?"

"You bet." I thought about lawyers and bail and I shivered. Surely not. "They can't ever get you again. They can't ever hurt anybody again. They're far away and all locked up, and your mom and dad will carry you home even farther away from them."

"When are they gonna get here?" he asked desolately.

"Soon, soon, as fast as their car can come," I said as soothingly as I could, perhaps for the fiftieth time, and thank God at that moment my father did come in, Betty Jo right behind him and under rigid control.

"Mama!" said Phillip, and all his hard-held toughness left him. He became an instant soggy puddle of little boy.

Betty Jo swept him out of the hospital bed and into her arms and held him as tightly as he held her. "Where can I take him?" she asked the nurse who'd followed them in. The nurse told her about an empty waiting room two doors down, and Betty Jo vanished with her precious armful. I was so glad to see Betty Jo take him I could have cried. There is no substitute for a real mother. At least I am no substitute for a real mother. The past few hours had certainly taught me that, if I'd ever doubted it.

My father bent and kissed me. "I hear you saved his life," he said, and tears trickled down his face. I had never seen my father cry. "I am so thankful you are both safe. I prayed in the car all the way here. I could have lost both of you in one night." Overwhelmed, he sank into the guest chair Robin had quietly vacated. Robin stood back in the shadows, the dim room light glinted off his red hair. I would never forget how he'd looked with the shotgun in his hands.

I was just too tired to appreciate my father's emotion. It was late, so late. I had almost been strangled by a bank loan officer with a green silk scarf. I had been hit by a secretary with a golf club. I had been terrified out of my mind for myself and my little brother. I had looked into the face of evil. Strong words, I told myself hazily, but true. The face of evil.

Finally, my dear father dried his eyes, told me he'd see me very soon, and said they were taking Phillip home that very night. "We'll have to see about treatment for him," he said apprehensively. "I don't know how to help him."

"I'll see you," I mumbled.

"Thanks, Aurora," he said. "If you need help yourself, you know how to reach us." But they were dying to get Phillip away, and his voice verged on perfunctory. I was a grown-up, right? I could take care of myself. Or my mother would take care of me. I let myself have a flash of bitterness and made myself swallow it. He was not being careful of me, but he was right.

I drifted off to sleep for a second. Robin was holding my hand when I woke up. I think he had kissed me.

"That felt good," I said. So he did it again. It felt even better.

"They were stupid really," I said a little later.

"When you think about it, yes," Robin agreed. "I don't think they ever realized it wasn't a game when they began patterning the deaths after old murders. Bankston snatched Phillip on impulse when they should have waited and picked a victim from at least across town. . . . If he'd really been intelligent, he would have known taking Phillip from the same place he himself lived, then keeping him in the town house instead of getting him out to Melanie's place . . . Well, maybe they would've smuggled him out, but you started looking too soon, and they didn't even consider you having keys."

"How did you know where we were?" I asked. It had never occurred to me to question our last-minute rescue.

"When I saw Melanie pull back in, she acted strange," he began. "I had started to wonder where you'd disappeared, too, and her coming back after she'd just left a few minutes before seemed peculiar. She'd gone home to get her tape recorder, you know," he said, and looked away into the shadows of the room. "I ran around front, saw you weren't there searching, and decided there was only one place you could be. Really, I was just guessing," he said frankly. "You had disappeared as suddenly as Phillip, there were no strange cars around, Melanie tried to act concerned about Phillip being missing but she wasn't, and she had that damn tape recorder. Perry Allison is very strange and maybe dangerous, but he's also obvious." Robin reached down to take my hand. "I had to persuade Mr. Crandall in a hurry that we had to raid Bankston's place, but he was game. Even if I had made a mistake, he said, if Bankston was any kind of a man he would realize when a child and woman are missing, anything goes. Jed's a frontier kind of guy."

"How'd you get in? Didn't Melanie lock the door behind her?"

"Yes, but Mrs. Crandall had a key, the key she'd been meaning to bring over to you—I think she kept it because the former tenant used to lock herself out a lot."

I would have laughed if my side hadn't hurt so much. The emergency room doctor said I'd be able to go home in the next day or two, but my collarbone and two ribs were broken, and I was bruised all over from tumbling down the stairs. There was a spectacularly ugly combination of bruise and scrape covering one cheek.

My mother wanted me to come home with her, but I was going to tell her I'd rather be in my own place, I decided, depending on how sore I was in the morning. Mother had flown into the hospital with every eyelash in place but a wild look in those fine eyes. We had hugged and talked for a while, and she had even shed a few tears (certainly atypical), but when she learned that as far as I knew my apartment was sitting wide open and, for that matter, Bankston's as well since the police were still searching it, she decided I was well enough to leave and flew off to see to safeguarding my property and the disposition of Bankston's.

My mother was a friend of Bankston's mother, and she was terrified of seeing Mrs. Waites again. "That poor woman," Mother said. "How can she live with having raised a monster like that? The other Waites children are fine people. What happened? He's known you all your life, Aurora! How could he hurt you? How could he think of hurting a child?"

"Who knows?" I said wearily. "He was having a great time, the time of his life." I had no sympathy to spare for Bankston's mother, right now. I had no extra emotion of any kind to throw around. I was drained, exhausted, and in pain. I had bruises and bandages galore. Even Robin's kiss didn't make me feel lecherous, just raised the possibility that someday I might feel that way. He was picking up his jacket now, getting ready to go.

"Robin," I murmured. I seemed to be drifting down into sleep. He turned, and I realized that he was spent, too. His tall shoulders were stooped, the crinkly mouth drooping down at the corners. Even his flaming hair looked limp.

"You saved me," I said.

"Nah, Jed Crandall saved you," he said with an attempt at being off-hand. "I was just back-up muscle."

"You saved me. Thank you." And then I drifted down a long spiral into sleep.

When I woke up again, the clock said 3:30 A.M. Someone else was sitting in the guest chair, someone short and stocky and blond and fast asleep. Arthur's head was slumped forward on his chest and he was snoring a little. I'd have to remember that.

My mouth was dry and my throat sore, so I reached for the cup of water on the bedside table. Naturally, it was just out of reach. I wiggled painfully sideways, still stretching, but then Arthur handed it to me.

"I didn't want to wake you up," I told him.

"I was just dozing," he said quietly.

"What happened?"

"Well, we found a box of—mementoes—at Melanie Clark's little rented house."

"Mementoes?" I asked with dread.

"Yes. Pictures."

I shook my head. I didn't want to hear more.

He nodded. "Pretty awful. They photographed Mamie and the Buckleys after they died. And Morrison Pettigrue. Melanie made advances to him, it turns out, and she got him to get undressed that way. Then she killed him, and let Bankston in, and they arranged him."

"So they confessed?"

"Well, Bankston did. He was proud."

"So they weren't like Hindley and Brady in the end."

"No. Melanie tried to kill herself."

"Oh," I said after a moment. "Oh, no."

"We had a watch on them both, so we caught her fairly quickly. She had taken off her bra and was trying to hang herself with it."

So grotesque, but at least it showed human feeling.

"She was sorry," I said softly.

"No," Arthur said definitely. Sharply. "She didn't want to be separated from Bankston."

There seemed to be nothing to say. I handed my cup back to Arthur, who put it on the beside table and automatically refilled it.

"They were mad we hadn't found the weapon Bankston used to kill Mamie Wright. They were sure they'd planted it where we couldn't help but find it. It was a hammer they'd stolen from LeMaster Cane's garage, and it had his initials on it. But as it turns out, some kids had picked it up the same night they killed her, and the kids only got scared and turned it in tonight. Evidently Melanie and Bankston were going to use the golf clubs in the future. After you saw Bankston carrying them into his place—he'd just showered over at Melanie's after killing the Buckleys, and he was going to get the clubs out of his car at a time when he thought no one would be out and about at the apartments— he got scared and ditched the bag, the only distinctive thing about the set, the next dark night. But he kept one or two of the clubs on the off chance he might need a weapon. Then you and Crusoe found the briefcase. . . . We fell down on that one. I don't mind telling you, we wondered about Crusoe for a while after that. Tonight I was ready to shoot him when I saw him charging into Waites's place with a shotgun, but Jed Crandall's wife was running out of her gate saying, 'My husband and Mr. Crusoe have gone down in Bankston Waites's basement to catch the murderer!' I was half expecting to see Perry Allison down in that basement, standing over Waites's body, and yours, and Phillip's."

"Where is Perry? Does anyone know?" It was Sally's call that had sent me running out in the dark soon enough to raise the alarm so Bankston and Melanie hadn't a chance to get Phillip away.

"He's checked himself into a mental hospital in the city," Arthur said.

That was undoubtedly the place for him, but it would be hard on Sally.

"Benjamin?"

"We're sending him to State Psychiatric for evaluation. He also confessed to several other murders we'd definitely solved. Somehow finding Pettigrue's body unhinged him."

"Oh, Arthur," I said wearily, and began to cry for so many different reasons I couldn't count them. Arthur stuffed tissues in my hand, and after a while brought over a wet washrag and wiped my face very carefully.

"I guess roller skating tomorrow night is off?" Arthur asked seriously.

I gaped at him in shock until I realized that Arthur—of all people!—was making a joke. I couldn't help smiling. It slid all around my face, but it was a smile.

"I've got to go back to the station, Roe. They're still sorting through the stuff they found in the search, and there's a lot we don't know yet. How Bankston got Mamie Wright to come to the meeting early. Why he let Melanie mail you that candy. He'd bought it for her and brought it back from some convention in St. Louis. But she had it in for you in a big way, and she thought you were the one who liked chocolate creams. That was the stupidest crime, since the typewriter's sitting in Gerald Wright's insurance office. We need to ask more questions, so we can back up these confessions with some solid evidence. Bankston has waived his right to have a lawyer present, but sooner or later he's gonna regret it and that'll be the end of the confession. Back to work for me."

"Okay, Arthur. I was glad to see you come down the stairs tonight."

"I was glad to see you alive."

"It was close."

"I know." Then he bent over and kissed me, and I thought I was getting to be quite a hussy.

"I'll be back tomorrow," he promised, and then he was gone, and for the first time in forever I was alone. I was exhausted to the bone, but I could not sleep. I was afraid to close my eyes.

I turned on the television to CNN, to find that I was on it. They were using a picture I'd had made when I joined the library staff. I looked impossibly sweet and young.

I was on the news. I'd be in the books when this case joined others in accounts of true murder cases. I had seen real murderers and I had almost been really murdered. That was something to ponder. I flicked the remote control to off.

I thought of Bankston and Melanie coming into the VFW Hall that night, disappointed to see me, maybe, since they expected I would have received and eaten the chocolate by that time. And I could see them waiting, waiting, for someone there to go looking for Mamie Wright. I remembered how fresh from the shower Bankston had looked when he was carrying in the stolen golf bag the day the Buckleys had been slaughtered. He'd been so shiny and clean . . . I had never, never suspected him. I heard Melanie's voice as she'd said, "I've always wanted to do this," and kicked me.

It was too close, too recent, I'd been frightened too deeply.

Of course, this hadn't turned out to be a real puzzler, like the 1928 intrafamilial poisonings in Croyden, England, unsolved to this day. Was Mrs. Duff guilty? . . . Or could it have been . . . I drifted away in sleep.

A BONE TO PICK

For Patrick, Timothy, and Julia

Chapter One

In less than a year, I went to three weddings and one funeral. By late May (at the second wedding but before the funeral) I had decided it was going to be the worst year of my life.

The second wedding was actually a happy one from my point of view, but my smile muscles ached all the next day from the anxious grin I'd forced to my lips. Being the daughter of the bride felt pretty peculiar.

My mother and her fiancé strolled between the folding chairs arranged in her living room, ended up before the handsome Episcopalian priest, and Aida Brattle Teagarden became Mrs. John Queensland.

In the oddest way, I felt my parents had left home while I had stayed. My father and his second wife, with my half brother, Phillip, had moved across the country to California in the past year. Now my mother, though she'd still be living in the same town, would definitely have new priorities.

That would be a relief.

So I beamed at John Queensland's married sons and their spouses. One of the wives was pregnant—my mother would be a stepgrandmother! I smiled graciously at Lawrenceton's new Episcopal priest, Aubrey Scott. I oozed goodwill at the real estate salespeople from my mother's business. I grinned at my best friend, Amina Day, until she told me to relax.

"You don't have to smile every second," she whispered from one corner of her mouth, while the rest of her face paid respectful attention to the cake-cutting ceremony. I instantly rearranged my face into more sober lines, thankful beyond expression that Amina had been able to get a few days off from her job in Houston as a legal secretary. But later, at the reception, she told me my mother's wedding wasn't her only reason for coming back to Lawrenceton for the weekend.

"I'm getting married," she said shyly, when we found a corner to ourselves. "I told Mamma and Daddy last night."

"To—which one?" I said, stunned.

"You haven't been listening to a word I said when I called you!"

Maybe I *had* let the specifics roll over me like a river. Amina had dated so many men. Since she'd reached fourteen, her incredible dating career had only been interrupted by one brief marriage.

"The department store manager?" I pushed my glasses back up on my nose the better to peer up at Amina, who is a very nice five feet, five inches. On good days I say I am five feet.

"No, Roe," Amina said with a sigh. "It's the lawyer from the firm across the hall from the place I work. Hugh Price." Her face went all gooey.

So I asked the obligatory questions: how he'd asked her, how long they'd dated, if his mother was tolerable . . . and the date and location of the ceremony. Amina, a traditionalist, would finally be married in Lawrenceton, and they were going to wait a few months, which I thought was an excellent idea. Her first wedding had been an elopement with myself and the groom's best friend as incompatible attendants.

I was going to be a bridesmaid again. Amina was not the only friend I'd "stood up" for, but she was the only one I'd stood up for twice. How many times could you be bridesmaid to the same bride? I wondered if the last time I came down the aisle ahead of Amina I would have to use a walker.

Then my mother and John made their dignified exit, John's white hair and white teeth gleaming, and my mother looking as glamorous as usual. They were going to honeymoon for three weeks in the Bahamas.

My mother's wedding day.

I got dressed for the first wedding, the January one, as though I was putting on armor to go into battle. I braided my bushy, wavy brown hair into a sophisticated (I hoped) pattern on the back of my head, put on the bra that maximized my most visible assets, and slid a brand-new gold-and-blue dress with padded shoulders over my head. The heels I was going to wear were ones I'd gotten to go with a dress I'd worn on a date with Robin Crusoe, and I sighed heavily as I slid my feet into them. It had been months since I'd seen Robin, and the day was depressing enough without thinking of him. At least the heels probably hiked me up to five foot two. I put on my makeup with my face as close to the illuminated mirror as I could manage, since without my glasses I can't make out my reflection very well. I put on as much makeup as I felt comfortable with, and then a little more. My round brown eyes got rounder, my lashes got longer, and then I covered them up with my big, round tortoiseshell glasses.

Sliding a precautionary handkerchief into my purse, I eyed myself in the mirror, hoped I looked dignified and unconcerned, and went down the stairs to the kitchen of my town house apartment to gather up my keys and good coat before sallying forth to that most wretched of obligatory events, the Wedding of a Recent Former Boyfriend.

Arthur Smith and I had met through a club we both attended, Real Murders. He'd helped on the homicide investigation that had followed the murder of one of the club members, and the string of deaths that followed this initial murder. I'd dated Arthur for months after the investigation was over, and our relationship had been my only experience of a red-hot romance. We sizzled together, we became something more than a nearly thirty librarian and a divorced policeman.

And then, as suddenly as the fire had flared, it died out,

but on his side of the hearth first. I had finally gotten the message—"I'm continuing this relationship until I can figure out a way to get out without a scene"—and with an immense effort I'd gathered my dignity together and ended our relationship without causing that scene. But it had taken all my emotional energy and willpower, and for maybe six months I'd been crying into my pillow.

Just when I was feeling better and hadn't driven past the police station in a week, I saw the engagement announcement in the *Sentinel*.

I saw green for envy, I saw red for rage, I saw blue for depression. I would never get married, I decided, I would just go to other people's weddings the rest of my life. Maybe I could arrange to be out of town the weekend of the wedding so I wouldn't be tempted to drive past the church.

Then the invitation came in the mail.

Lynn Liggett, Arthur's fiancée and fellow detective, had thrown down the gauntlet. Or at least that's how I interpreted the invitation.

Now, in my blue-and-gold and my fancy hairdo, I had grasped it. I'd picked out an impersonal and expensive plate in Lynn's pattern at the department store and left my card on it, and now I was going to the wedding.

The usher was a policeman I knew from the time I dated Arthur.

"Good to see you," he said doubtfully. "You look great, Roe." He looked stiff and uncomfortable in his tux, but he offered his arm properly. "Friend of the bride, or friend of the groom?" he asked automatically, and then flushed as red as a beet.

"Let's say friend of the groom," I suggested gently, and gave myself high marks. Poor Detective Henske marched me down the aisle to an empty seat and dumped me with obvious relief.

I glanced around as little as possible, putting all my energy into looking relaxed and nonchalant, sort of as if I'd just happened to be appropriately dressed and just happened to see the wedding invitation on my way out the door, and decided I'd just drop in. It was all right to look at Arthur when he entered, everyone else was. His pale blond hair was crisp and curly and short, his blue eyes as direct and engaging as ever. He was wearing a gray tux and he looked great. It didn't hurt *quite* as much as I'd thought it would.

When the "Wedding March" began, everyone rose for the entrance of the bride, and I gritted my teeth in anticipation. I was pretty sure my fixed smile looked more like a snarl. I turned reluctantly to watch Lynn make her entrance. Here she came, swathed in white, veiled, as tall as Arthur, her straight, short hair curled for the occasion. Lynn was almost a foot taller than I, something that had obviously bothered her, but I guessed it wasn't going to bother her anymore.

Then Lynn passed me, and when I saw her in profile I gasped. Lynn was clearly pregnant.

It would be hard to say why this was such a blow; I certainly hadn't wanted to become pregnant while I was dating Arthur, and would have been horrified if I'd been faced with the situation. But I had often thought of marrying him, and I had occasionally thought about babies; most women my age, if they do want to get married, do think about babies. Somehow, just for a little while, it seemed to me that I had been robbed of something.

I spoke to enough people on the way out of the church to be sure my attendance registered and would be reported to the happy couple, and then I skipped the reception. There was no point in putting myself through that. I thought it was pretty stupid of me to have come at all; not gallant, not brave, just dumb.

The funeral came third, a few days after my mother's wedding, and, as funerals go, it was pretty decent. Though it was in early June, the day Jane Engle was buried was not insufferably hot, and it was not raining. The little Episcopal church held a reasonable number of people—I won't say mourners, because Jane's passing was more a time to be marked than a tragic occasion. Jane had been old, and, as it turned out, very ill, though she had told no one. The people in the pews had gone to church with Jane, or remembered her from her years working in the high school library, but she had no family besides one aging cousin, Parnell Engle, who was himself too ill that day to come. Aubrey Scott, the Episcopal priest, whom I hadn't seen since my mother's wedding, was eloquent about Jane's inoffensive life and her charm and intelligence; Jane had certainly had her tart side, too, but the Reverend Mr. Scott tactfully included that under "colorful." It was not an adjective I would have chosen for silver-haired Jane, never married—like me, I reminded myself miserably, and wondered if this many people would come to my funeral. My eyes wandered over the faces in the pews, all more or less familiar. Besides me, there was one other attendee from Real Murders, the disbanded club in which Jane and I had become friends—LeMaster Cane, a black businessman. He was sitting at the back in a pew by himself.

I made a point of standing by LeMaster at the graveside, so he wouldn't look so lonely. When I murmured that it was good to see him, he replied, "Jane was the only white person who ever looked at me like she couldn't tell what color I am." Which effectively shut me up.

I realized that I hadn't known Jane as well as I thought I had. For the first time, I really felt I would miss her.

I thought of her little, neat house, crammed with her mother's furniture and Jane's own books. I remembered Jane had liked cats, and I wondered if anyone had taken over the care of her gold tabby, Madeleine. (The cat had been named for the nineteenth-century Scottish poisoner Madeleine Smith, a favorite murderer of Jane's. Maybe Jane had been more "colorful" than I'd realized. Not many little old ladies I knew had favorite murderers. Maybe I was "colorful," too.)

As I walked slowly to my car, leaving Jane Engle forever in Shady Rest Cemetery—I thought—I heard someone calling my name behind me.

"Miss Teagarden!" panted the man who was hurrying to catch up. I waited, wondering what on earth he could want. His round, red face topped by thinning light brown hair was familiar, but I couldn't recall his name.

"Bubba Sewell," he introduced himself, giving my hand a quick shake. He had the thickest southern accent I'd heard in a long time. "I was Miss Engle's lawyer. You are Aurora Teagarden, right?"

"Yes, excuse me," I said. "I was just so surprised." I remembered now that I'd seen Bubba Sewell at the hospital during Jane's last illness.

"Well, it's fortunate you came today," Bubba Sewell said. He'd caught his breath, and I saw him now as he undoubtedly wanted to present himself: an expensively suited, sophisticated but down-home man in the know. A college-educated good ole boy. His small brown eyes watched me sharply and curiously. "Miss Engle had a clause in her will that is significant to you," he said significantly.

"Oh?" I could feel my heels sinking into the soft turf and wondered if I'd have to step out of my shoes and pull them up by hand. It was warm enough for my face to feel damp; of course, my glasses began to slide down my nose. I poked them back up with my forefinger.

"Maybe you have a minute now to come by my office and talk about it?"

I glanced automatically at my watch. "Yes, I have time," I said judiciously after a moment's pause. This was pure bluff, so Mr. Sewell wouldn't think I was a woman with nothing to do.

Actually, I very nearly was. A cutback in funding meant that, for the library to stay open the same number of hours, some staff had to go part-time. I hoped it was because I was the most recently hired that the first one to feel the ax was me. I was only working eighteen to twenty hours a week now. If I hadn't been living rent free and receiving a small salary as resident manager of one of Mother's apartment buildings (actually a row of four town houses), my situation would have been bleak in the extreme.

Mr. Sewell gave me such elaborate directions to his office that I couldn't have gotten lost if I'd tried, and he furthermore insisted I follow him there. The whole way he gave turn signals so far in advance that I almost made the wrong left once. In addition he would wave and point into his rearview mirror, waiting to see me nod every time in acknowledgment. Since I'd lived in Lawrenceton my whole life, this was unnecessary and intensely irritating. Only my curiosity about what he was going to tell me kept me from ramming his rear, and then apologizing picturesquely with tears and a handkerchief.

"Wasn't too hard to find, was it!" he said encouragingly when I got out of my car in the parking lot of the Jasper Building, one of the oldest office buildings in our town and a familiar landmark to me from childhood.

"No," I said briefly, not trusting myself to speak further.

"I'm up on the third floor," Lawyer Sewell announced, I guess in case I got lost between the parking lot and the front door. I bit the inside of my lip and boarded the elevator in silence, while Sewell kept up a patter of small talk about the attendance at the funeral, how Jane's loss would affect many, many people, the weather, and why he liked having an office in the Jasper Building (atmosphere . . . much better than one of those prefabricated buildings).

By the time he opened his office door, I was wondering how sharp-tongued Jane could have endured Bubba Sewell. When I saw that he had three employees in his smallish office, I realized he must be more intelligent than he seemed, and there were other unmistakable signs of prosperity—

knickknacks from the Sharper Image catalog, superior prints on the walls and leather upholstery on the chairs, and so on. I looked around Sewell's office while he gave some rapid instructions to the well-dressed red-haired secretary who was his first line of defense. She didn't seem like a fool, and she treated him with a kind of friendly respect.

"Well, well, now, let's see about you, Miss Teagarden," the lawyer said jovially when we were alone. "Where's that file? Gosh-a-Moses, it's somewhere in this mess here!"

Much rummaging among the papers on his desk. By now I was not deceived. Bubba Sewell for some reason found this Lord Peter Wimsey–like pretense of foolishness useful, but he was not foolish, not a bit.

"Here we are, it was right there all the time!" He flourished the file as though its existence had been in doubt.

I folded my hands in my lap and tried not to sigh obviously. I might have lots of time, but that didn't mean I wanted to spend it as an unwilling audience to a one-man performance.

"Hoo-wee, I'm sure glad you managed to turn it up," I said.

Bubba Sewell's hands stilled, and he shot me an extremely sharp look from under his bushy eyebrows.

"Miss Teagarden," he said, dropping his previous good-ole-boy manner completely, "Miss Engle left you everything."

Those are certainly some of the most thrilling words in the English language, but I wasn't going to let my jaw hit the floor. My hands, which had been clasped loosely in my lap, gripped convulsively for a minute, and I let out a long, silent breath.

"What's everything?" I asked.

Bubba Sewell told me that everything was Jane's house, its contents, and most of her bank account. She'd left her car and five thousand dollars to her cousin Parnell and his wife, Leah, on condition they took Madeleine the cat to live with them. I was relieved. I had never had a pet, and wouldn't have known what to do with the creature.

I had no idea what I should be saying or doing. I was so stunned I couldn't think what would be most seemly. I had done my mild grieving for Jane when I'd heard she'd gone, and at the graveside. I could tell that in a few minutes I was going to feel raw jubilation, since money problems had been troubling me. But at the moment mostly I was stunned.

"Why on earth did she do this?" I asked Bubba Sewell. "Do you know?"

"When she came in to make her will, last year when there was all that trouble with the club you two were in, she said that this was the best way she knew to make sure someone never forgot her. She didn't want her name up on a building somewhere. She wasn't a"—the lawyer searched for the right words—"philanthropist. Not a public person. She wanted to leave her money to an individual, not a cause, and I don't think she ever got along well with Parnell and Leah—do you know them?"

As a matter of fact, I am something rare in the South—a church hopper. I had met Jane's cousin and his wife at one of the churches I attended, I couldn't remember which one, though I thought it was one of Lawrenceton's more fundamentalist houses of worship. When they'd introduced themselves I'd asked if they were related to Jane, and Parnell had admitted he was a cousin, though with no great warmth. Leah had stared at me and said perhaps three words during the whole conversation.

"I've met them," I told Sewell.

"They're old and they haven't had any children," Sewell told me. "Jane felt they wouldn't outlast her long and would probably leave all her money to their church, which she didn't want. So she thought and thought and settled on you."

I thought and thought myself for a little bit. I looked up to find the lawyer eyeing me with speculation and some slight, impersonal disapproval. I figured he thought Jane should have left her money to cancer research or the SPCA or the orphanage.

"How much is in the account?" I asked briskly.

"Oh, in the checking account, maybe three thousand," he said. "I have the latest statements in this file. Of course, there are a few bills yet to come from Jane's last stay in the hospital, but her insurance will pick up most of that."

Three thousand! That was nice. I could finish paying for my car, which would help my monthly bill situation a lot.

"You said 'checking account,'" I said, after I'd thought for a moment. "Is there another account?"

"Oh, you bet," said Sewell, with a return of his former bonhomie. "Yes, ma'am! Miss Jane had a savings account she hardly ever touched. I tried a couple of times to interest her in investing it or at least buying a CD or a bond, but she said no, she liked her cash in her bank." Sewell shook his receding hairline several times over this and tilted back in his chair.

I had a vicious moment of hoping it would go all the way over with him in it.

"Could you please tell me how much is in the savings account?" I asked through teeth that were not quite clenched.

Bubba Sewell lit up. I had finally asked the right question. He catapulted forward in his chair to a mighty squeal of springs, pounced on the file, and extracted another bank statement.

"Wel-l-l-l," he drawled, puffing on the slit envelope and pulling out the paper inside, "as of last month, that account had in it—let's see—right, about five hundred and fifty thousand dollars."

Maybe this wasn't the worst year of my life after all.

Chapter Two

I floated out of Bubba Sewell's office, trying not to look as gleeful as I felt. He walked with me to the elevator, looking down at me as if he couldn't figure me out. Well, it was mutual, but I wasn't caring right now, no sirree.

"She inherited it from her mother," Sewell said. "Most of it. Also, when her mother died, Miss Engle sold her mother's house, which was very large and brought a great price, and she split the money from that with her brother. Then her brother died and left her his nearly intact share of the house money, plus his estate, which she turned into cash. He was a banker in Atlanta."

I had money. I had a *lot* of money.

"I'll meet you at Jane's house tomorrow, and we'll have a look around at the contents, and I'll have a few things for you to sign. Would nine-thirty be convenient?"

I nodded with my lips pressed together so I wouldn't grin at him.

"And you know where it is?"

"Yes," I breathed, thankful the elevator had come at last and the doors were opening.

"Well, I'll see you tomorrow morning, Miss Teagarden," the lawyer said, setting his black glasses back on his nose and turning away as the doors closed with me inside.

I thought a scream of joy would echo up the elevator shaft, so I quietly but ecstatically said, "Heeheeheehee-hee," all the way down and did a little jig before the doors opened on the marble lobby.

I managed to get home to the town house on Parson Road without hitting another car, and pulled into my parking place planning how I could celebrate. The young married couple who'd taken Robin's town house, to the left of mine, waved back hesitantly in answer to my beaming hello. The Crandalls' parking space to the right was empty; they were visiting a married son in another town. The woman who'd finally rented Bankston Waite's town house was at work, as always. There was a strange car parked in the second space allotted to my apartment, but since I didn't see anyone I assumed it was a guest of one of the other tenants who didn't know how to read.

I opened my patio gate singing to myself and hopping around happily (I am not much of a dancer) and surprised a strange man in black sticking a note to my back door.

It was a toss-up as to which of us was the more startled.

It took me a moment of staring to figure out who the man was. I finally recognized him as the Episcopal priest who'd performed Mother's wedding and Jane Engle's funeral. I'd talked to him at the wedding reception, but not at this morning's funeral. He was a couple of inches over six feet, probably in his late thirties, with dark hair beginning to gray to the color of his eyes, a neat mustache, and a clerical collar.

"Miss Teagarden, I was just leaving you a note," he said, recovering neatly from his surprise at my singing, dancing entrance.

"Father Scott," I said firmly, his name popping into my head at the last second. "Good to see you."

"You seem happy today," he said, showing excellent teeth in a cautious smile. Maybe he thought I was drunk.

"Well, you know I was at Jane's funeral," I began, but when his eyebrows flew up I realized I'd started at the wrong end.

"Please come in, Father, and I'll tell you why I'm so cheerful when it might seem . . . inappropriate."

"Well, if you have a minute, I'll come in. Maybe I caught you at a bad time? And please call me Aubrey."

"No, this is fine. And call me Aurora. Or Roe, most people just call me Roe." Actually, I'd wanted a little alone time to get used to the idea of being rich, but telling someone would be fun, too. I tried to remember how messy the place was. "Please come in, I'll make some coffee." And I just laughed.

He surely thought I was crazy as a loon, but he had to come in now.

"I haven't seen you to talk to since my mother got married," I babbled, as I twisted my key in the lock and flung open the door into the kitchen and living area. Good, it was quite neat.

"John's a wonderful man and a staunch member of the congregation," he said, having to look down at me quite sharply now that I was close. Why didn't I ever meet short men? I was doomed to go through life with a crick in my neck. "John and your mother are still on their honeymoon?"

"Yes, they're having such a good time I wouldn't be surprised if they stayed longer. My mother hasn't taken a vacation in at least six years. You know she owns a real estate business."

"That's what John told me," Aubrey Scott said politely. He was still standing right inside the door.

"Oh, I forgot my manners! Please come have a seat!" I tossed my purse on the counter and waved at the matching tan suede love seat and chair in the "living area," which lay beyond the "kitchen area."

The chair was clearly my special chair, from the brass lamp behind it for reading light to the small table loaded with my current book, a stained coffee mug, and a few magazines. Aubrey Scott wisely chose one end of the love seat.

"Listen," I said, perching opposite him on the edge of my chair, "I've got to tell you why I'm so giddy today. Normally I'm not like this at all." Which was true, more's the pity. "Jane Engle just left me a bunch of money, and, even though it may sound greedy, I've got to tell you I'm happy as a clam about it."

"I don't blame you," he said sincerely. I have noticed that, if there is one thing ministers are good at projecting, it is sincerity. "If someone had left me a bunch of money, I'd be dancing, too. I had no idea Jane was a—that Jane had a lot to leave anyone."

"Me either. She never lived like she had money. Let me get you a drink. Coffee? Or maybe a real drink?" I figured I could ask that, him being Episcopal. If he'd been, say, Parnell and Leah Engle's pastor, that question would have earned me a stiff lecture.

"If by real drink you mean one with alcohol, I wouldn't turn one down. It's after five o'clock, and conducting a funeral always drains me. What do you have? Any Seagram's, by any chance?"

"As a matter of fact, yes. What about a seven and seven?"

"Sounds great."

As I mixed the Seagram's 7 with the 7UP, added ice, and even produced cocktail napkins and nuts, it finally struck me as odd that the Episcopal priest would come to call. I couldn't exactly say, "What are you doing here?" but I was curious. Well, he'd get around to it. Most of the preachers in Lawrenceton had had a go at roping me in at one time or another. I am a fairly regular churchgoer, but I seldom go to the same church twice in a row.

It would have been nice to run upstairs to change from my hot black funeral dress to something less formal, but I figured he would run out the back door if I proposed to slip into something comfortable.

I did take off my heels, caked with mud from the cemetery, after I sat down.

"So tell me about your inheritance," he suggested after an awkward pause.

I couldn't recapture my initial excitement, but I could feel a grin turning up my lips as I told him about my friendship with Jane Engle and Bubba Sewell's approach after the service was over.

"That's amazing," he murmured. "You've been blessed."

"Yes, I have," I agreed wholeheartedly.

"And you say you weren't a particular friend of Jane's?"

"No. We were friends, but at times a month would go by without our seeing each other. And not thinking anything about it, either."

"I don't suppose you've had enough time to plan anything to do with this unexpected legacy."

"No." And if he suggested some worthy cause, I would really resent it. I just wanted to be in proud ownership of a little house and a big (to me, anyway) fortune, at least for a while.

"I'm glad for you," he said, and there was another awkward pause.

"Was there anything I could do to help you, did your note say . . . ?" I trailed off. I tried to manage a look of intelligent expectancy.

"Well," he said with an embarrassed laugh, "actually, I . . . This is so stupid, I'm acting like I am in high school again. Actually . . . I just wanted to ask you out. On a date."

"A date," I repeated blankly.

I saw instantly that my astonishment was hurting him.

"No, it's not that that's peculiar," I said hastily. "I just wasn't expecting it."

"Because I'm a minister."

"Well—yes."

He heaved a sigh and opened his mouth with a resigned expression.

"No, no!" I said, throwing my hands up. "Don't make an 'I'm only human' speech, if you were going to! I was gauche, I admit it! Of course I'll go out with you!"

I felt like I owed it to him now.

"You're not involved in another relationship at the moment?" he asked carefully.

I wondered if he had to wear the collar on dates.

"No, not for a while. In fact, I went to the wedding of my last relationship a few months ago."

Suddenly Aubrey Scott smiled, and his big gray eyes crinkled up at the corners, and he looked good enough to eat.

"What would you like to do? The movies?"

I hadn't had a date since Arthur and I had split. Anything sounded good to me.

"Okay," I said.

"Maybe we can go to the early show and go out to eat afterward."

"Fine. When?"

"Tomorrow night?"

"Okay. The early show usually starts at five if we go to the triplex. Anything special you want to see?"

"Let's get there and decide."

There could easily be three movies I did not want to see showing at one time, but the chances were at least one of them would be tolerable.

"Okay," I said again. "But if you're taking me out to supper, I want to treat you to the movie."

He looked doubtful. "I'm kind of a traditional guy," he said. "But if you want to do it that way, that'll be a new experience for me." He sounded rather courageous about it.

After he left, I slowly finished my drink. I wondered if the rules for dating clergymen were different from the rules for dating regular guys. I told myself sternly that clergymen *are* regular guys, just regular guys who professionally relate to God. I knew I was being naive in thinking I had to act differently with Aubrey Scott than I would with another date. If I was so malicious or off-color or just plain wrongheaded that I had to constantly censor my conversation with a minister, then I needed the experience anyway. Perhaps it would be like dating a psychiatrist; you would always worry about what he spotted about you that you didn't know. Well, this date would be a "learning experience" for me.

What a day! I shook my head as I plodded up the stairs to my bedroom. From being a poor, worried, spurned librarian I'd become a wealthy, secure, datable heiress.

The impulse to share my new status was almost irresistible. But Amina was back in Houston and preoccupied by her upcoming marriage, my mother was on her honeymoon (boy, would I enjoy telling *her*), my co-worker Lillian Schmidt would find some way to make me feel guilty about it, and my sort-of-friend Sally Allison would want to put it in the paper. I'd really like to tell Robin Crusoe, my mystery writer friend, but he was in the big city of Atlanta, having decided the commute from Lawrenceton to his teaching position there was too much to handle—or at least that was the reason he'd given me. Unless I could tell him face-to-face, I wouldn't enjoy it. His face was one of my favorites.

Maybe some celebrations are just meant to be private. A big wahoo would have been out of line anyway, since Jane had had to die in order for this celebration to be held. I took off the black dress and put on a bathrobe and went downstairs to watch an old movie and eat half a bag of pretzels and then half a quart of chocolate fudge ripple ice cream.

Heiresses can do anything.

It was raining the next morning, a short summer shower that promised a steamy afternoon. The thunderclaps were sharp and scary, and I found myself jumping at each one as I drank my coffee. After I retrieved the paper (only a little wet) from the otherwise unused front doorstep that faced Parson Road, it began to slow down. By the time I'd had my shower and was dressed and ready for my appointment with Bubba Sewell, the sun had come out and mist began to rise from the puddles in the parking lot beyond the patio. I watched CNN for a while—heiresses need to be well informed—fidgeted with my makeup, ate a banana, and scrubbed the kitchen sink, and then finally it was time to go.

I couldn't figure out why I was so excited. The money wasn't going to be piled in the middle of the floor. I'd have to wait roughly two months to actually be able to spend it, Sewell had said. I'd been in Jane's little house before, and there was nothing so special about it.

Of course, now I owned it. I'd never owned something that big before.

I was independent of my mother, too. I could've made it by myself on my librarian's salary, though it would have been hard, but having the resident manager's job and therefore a free place to live and a little extra salary had certainly made a big difference.

I'd woken several times during the night and thought about living in Jane's house. My house. Or after probate I could sell it and buy elsewhere.

That morning, starting up my car to drive to Honor Street, the world was so full of possibilities it was just plain terrifying, in a happy roller-coaster way.

Jane's house was in one of the older residential neighborhoods. The streets were named for virtues. One reached Honor by way of Faith. Honor was a dead end, and Jane's house was the second from the corner on the right side. The houses in this neighborhood tended to be small—two or three bedrooms—with meticulously kept little yards dominated by large trees circled with flower beds. Jane's front yard was half filled by a live oak on the right side that shaded the bay window in the living room. The driveway ran in on the left, and there was a deep single-car carport attached to the house. A door in the rear of the carport told me there was some kind of storage room there. The kitchen door opened onto the carport, or you could (as I'd done as a visitor) park in the driveway and take the curving sidewalk to the front door. The house was white, like all the others on the street, and there were azalea bushes planted all around the foundation; it would be lovely in spring.

The marigolds Jane had planted around her mailbox had died from lack of water, I saw as I got out of the car. Somehow that little detail sobered me up completely. The hands that had planted those withered yellow flowers were now six feet underground and idle forever.

I was a bit early, so I took the time to look around at my new neighborhood. The corner house, to the right of Jane's as I faced it, had beautiful big climbing rosebushes around the front porch. The one to the left had had a lot added on, so that the original simple lines of the house were obscured. It had been bricked in, a garage with an apartment on top had been connected to the house by a roofed walk, a deck had been tacked on the back. The result was not happy. The last house on the street was next to that, and I remembered that the newspaper editor, Macon Turner, who had once dated my mother, lived there. The house directly across the street from Jane's, a pretty little house with canary yellow shutters, had a Realtor's sign up with a big red SOLD slapped across it. The corner house on that side of the street was the one Melanie Clark, another member of the defunct Real Murders club, had rented for a while: now a Big Wheel parked in the driveway indicated children on the premises. One house took up the last two lots on that side, a rather dilapidated place with only one tree in a large yard. It sat blank-faced, the yellowing shades pulled down. A wheelchair ramp had been built on.

At this hour on a summer morning, the quiet was peaceful. But, behind the houses on Jane's side of the street, there was the large parking lot for the junior high school, with the school's own high fence keeping trash from being pitched in Jane's yard and students from using it as a short-cut. I was sure there would be more noise during the school year, but now that parking lot sat empty. By and by, a woman from the corner house on the other side of the street started up a lawn mower and that wonderful summer sound made me feel relaxed.

You planned for this, Jane, I thought. You wanted me to go in your house. You knew me and you picked me for this.

Bubba Sewell's BMW pulled up to the curb, and I took a deep breath and walked toward it.

He handed me the keys. My hand closed over them. It felt like a formal investiture. "There's no problem with you going on and working in this house now, clearing it out or preparing it for sale or whatever you want to do, it belongs to you and no one says different. I've advertised for anyone with claims on the estate to come forward, and so far no one has. But of course we can't spend any of the money," he admonished me with a wagging finger. "The house bills are still coming to me as executor, and they will until probate is settled."

This was like being a week away from your birthday when you were six.

"This one," he said, pointing to one key, "opens the dead bolt on the front door. This one opens the punch lock on the front door. This little one is to Jane's safe deposit box at Eastern National, there's a little jewelry and a few papers in it, nothing much."

I unlocked the door and we stepped in.

"Shit," said Bubba Sewell in an unlawyerly way.

There was a heap of cushions from the living room chairs thrown around. I could look through the living room into the kitchen and see similar disorder there.

Someone had broken in.

One of the rear windows, the one in the back bedroom, had been broken. It had been a pristine little room with chaste twin beds covered in white chenille. The wallpaper was floral and unobtrusive, and the glass was easy to sweep up on the hardwood floor. The first things I found in my new house were the dustpan and the broom, lying on the floor by the tall broom closet in the kitchen.

"I don't think anything's gone," Sewell said with a good deal of surprise, "but I'll call the police anyway. These people, they read the obituaries in the paper and go around breaking into the houses that are empty."

I stood holding a dustpan full of glass. "So why isn't anything missing?" I asked. "The TV is still in the living room. The clock radio is still in here, and there's a microwave in the kitchen."

"Maybe you're just plain lucky," Sewell said, his eyes resting on me thoughtfully. He polished his glasses on a gleaming white handkerchief. "Or maybe the kids were so young that just breaking in was enough thrill. Maybe they got scared halfway through. Who knows."

"Tell me a few things." I sat on one of the white beds and he sat down opposite me. The broken window (the storm this morning had soaked the curtains) made the room anything but intimate. I propped the broom against my knee and put the dustpan on the floor. "What happened with this house after Jane died? Who came in here? Who has keys?"

"Jane died in the hospital, of course," Sewell began. "When she first went in, she still thought she might come home, so she had me hire a maid to come in and clean . . . empty the garbage, clear the perishables out of the refrigerator, and so on. Jane's neighbor to the side, Torrance Rideout—you know him?—he offered to keep her yard mowed for her, so he has a key to the tool and storage room, that's the door at the back of the carport."

I nodded.

"But that's the only key he had," the lawyer said, getting back on target. "Then a few days later, when Jane learned—she wasn't coming home . . ."

"I visited her in the hospital, and she never said a word to me," I murmured.

"She didn't like to talk about it. What was there to say? she asked me. I think she was right. But anyway . . . I kept the electricity and gas—the heat is gas, everything else is electric—hooked up, but I came over here and unplugged everything but the freezer—it's in the toolroom and it has food in it—and I stopped the papers and started having

Jane's mail kept at the post office, then I'd pick it up and take it to her, it wasn't any trouble to me, my mail goes to the post office, too . . ."

Sewell had taken care of everything for Jane. Was this the care of a lawyer for a good client or the devotion of a friend?

"So," he was saying briskly, "the little bitty operating expenses for this house will come out of the estate, but I trust you won't mind, we kept it at a minimum. You know when you completely turn off the air or heat into a house, the house just seems to go downhill almost immediately, and there was always the slight chance Jane might make it and come home."

"No, of course I don't mind paying the electric bill. Do Parnell and Leah have a key?"

"No, Jane was firm about that. Parnell came to me and offered to go through and get Jane's clothes and things packed away, but of course I told him no."

"Oh?"

"They're yours," he said simply. "Everything"—and he gave that some emphasis, or was it only my imagination—"everything in this house is yours. Parnell and Leah know about their five thousand, and Jane herself handed him the keys to her car two days before she died and let him take it from this carport, but, other than that, *whatever* is in this house"—and suddenly I was alert and very nearly scared—"is yours to deal with however you see fit."

My eyes narrowed with concentration. What was he saying that he wasn't really saying?

Somewhere, somewhere in this house, lurked a problem. For some reason, Jane's legacy wasn't entirely benevolent.

After calling the police about the break-in and calling the glass people to come to fix the window, Bubba Sewell took his departure.

"I don't think the police will even show up here since I couldn't tell them anything was missing. I'll stop by the station on my way back to the office, though," he said on his way out the door.

I was relieved to hear that. I'd met most of the local policemen when I'd dated Arthur; policemen really stick together. "There's no point in turning on the air conditioner until that back bedroom window is fixed," Sewell added, "but the thermostat is in the hall, when you need it."

He was being mighty chary with my money. Now that I was so rich, I could fling open the windows and doors and set the thermostat on forty, if I wanted to do something so foolish and wasteful.

"If you have any problems, run into anything you can't handle, you just call me," Sewell said again. He'd expressed that sentiment several times, in several different ways. But just once he had said, "Miss Jane had a high opinion of you, that you could tackle any problem that came your way and make a success of it."

I got the picture. By now I was so apprehensive, I heartily wanted Sewell to leave. Finally he was out the front door, and I knelt on the window seat in the bay window and partially opened the sectioned blinds surrounding it to watch his car pull away. When I was sure he was gone, I opened all the blinds and turned around to survey my new territory. The living room was carpeted, the only room in the house that was, and when Jane had had this done she'd run the carpet right up onto the window seat so that it was seamlessly covered, side, top, and all. There were some hand-embroidered pillows arranged on it, and the effect was very pretty. The carpet Jane had been so partial to was a muted rose with a tiny blue pattern, and her living room furniture (a sofa and two armchairs) picked up that shade of blue, while the lamp shades were white or rose. There was a small color television arranged for easy viewing from Jane's favorite chair. The antique table beside that chair was still stacked with magazines, a strange assortment that summed up Jane—*Southern Living*, *Mystery Scene*, *Lear's*, and a publication from the church.

The walls of this small room were lined with freestanding shelves overflowing with books. My mouth watered when I looked at them. One thing I knew Jane and I had shared: we loved books, we especially loved mysteries, and more than anything we loved books about real murders. Jane's collection had always been my envy.

At the rear of the living room was a dining area, with a beautiful table and chairs I believed Jane had inherited from her mother. I knew nothing about antiques and cared less, but the table and chairs were gleaming under a light coating of dust, and, as I straightened the cushions and pushed the couch back to its place against the wall (why would anyone move a couch when he broke into a house?), I was already worried about caring for the set.

At least all the books hadn't been thrown on the floor. Straightening this room actually took only a few moments.

I moved into the kitchen. I was avoiding Jane's bedroom. It could wait.

The kitchen had a large double window that looked onto the backyard, and a tiny table with two chairs was set right in front of the window. Here was where Jane and I had had coffee when I'd visited her, if she hadn't taken me into the living room.

The disorder in the kitchen was just as puzzling. The shallow upper cabinets were fine, had not been touched, but the deeper bottom cabinets had been emptied carelessly. Nothing had been poured out of its container or wantonly vandalized, but the contents had been moved as though the cabinet itself were the object of the search, not possible loot that could be taken away. And the broom closet, tall and thin, had received special attention. I flipped on the kitchen light and stared at the wall in the back of the closet. It was marred with ". . . knife gouges, sure as shooting," I mumbled. While I stooped to reload the cabinet shelves with pots and pans, I thought about those gouges. The breaker-in had wanted to see if there was something fake about the back of the closet; that was the only interpretation I could put on the holes. And only the large bottom cabinets had been disturbed; only the large pieces of furniture in the living room.

So, Miss Genius, he was looking for something large. Okay, "he" could be a woman, but I wasn't going to the trouble of thinking "he or she." "He" would do very well for now. What large thing could Jane Engle have concealed in her house that anyone could possibly want enough to break in for? Unanswerable until I knew more, and I definitely had the feeling I would know more.

I finished picking up the kitchen and returned to the guest bedroom. The only disturbance there, now I'd cleared up the glass, was to the two single closets, which had been opened and emptied. There again, no attempt had been made to destroy or mutilate the items that had been taken from the closets; they'd just been emptied swiftly and thoroughly. Jane had stored her luggage in one closet, and the larger suitcases had been opened. Out-of-season clothes, boxes of pictures and mementos, a portable sewing machine, two boxes of Christmas decorations . . . all things I had to check through and decide on, but for now it was enough to shovel them all back in. As I hung up a heavy coat, I noticed the walls in these closets had been treated the same way as the broom closet in the kitchen.

The attic stairs pulled down in the little hall that had a bedroom door at each end and the bathroom door in the middle. A broad archway led from this hall back into the living room. This house actually was smaller than my town house by quite a few square feet, I realized. If I moved I would have less room but more independence.

It was going to be hot up in the attic, but it would certainly be much hotter by the afternoon. I gripped the cord and pulled down. I unfolded the stairs and stared at them doubtfully. They didn't look any too sturdy.

Jane hadn't liked to use them either, I found, after I'd eased my way up the creaking wooden stairs. There was very little in the attic but dust and disturbed insulation; the searcher had been up here, too, and an itchy time he must have had of it. A leftover strip of the living room carpet had been unrolled, a chest had its drawers halfway pulled out. I closed up the attic with some relief and washed my dusty hands and face in the bathroom sink. The bathroom was a good size, with a large linen cabinet below which was a half door that opened onto a wide space suitable for a laundry basket to hold dirty clothes. This half closet had received the same attention as the ones in the kitchen and guest bedroom.

The searcher was trying to find a secret hiding place for something that could be put in a drawer but not hidden behind books . . . something that couldn't be hidden between sheets and towels but could be hidden in a large pot. I tried to imagine Jane hiding—a suitcase full of money? What else? A box of—documents revealing a terrible secret? I opened the top half of the closet to look at Jane's neatly folded sheets and towels without actually seeing them. I should be grateful those hadn't been dumped out, too, I mused with half of my brain, since Jane had been a champion folder; the towels were neater than I'd ever get them, and the sheets appeared to have been ironed, something I hadn't seen since I was a child.

Not money or documents; those could have been divided to fit into the spaces that the searcher had ignored.

The doorbell rang, making me jump a foot.

It was only the glass repair people, a husband and wife team I'd called when window problems arose at my mother's apartments. They accepted me being at this address without any questions, and the woman commented when she saw the back window that lots of houses were getting broken into these days, though it had been a rarity when she'd been "a kid."

"Those people coming out from the city," she told me seriously, raising her heavily penciled eyebrows.

"Reckon so?" I asked, to establish my goodwill.

"Oh sure, honey. They come out here to get away from the city, but they bring their city habits with 'em."

Lawrenceton loved the commuters' money without actually trusting or loving the commuters.

While they tackled removing the broken glass and replacing it, I went into Jane's front bedroom. Somehow entering it was easier with someone else in the house. I am not superstitious, at least not consciously, but it seemed to me that Jane's presence was strongest in her bedroom, and having people busy in another room in the house made my entering her room less . . . personal.

It was a large bedroom, and Jane had a queen-sized four-poster with one bed table, a substantial chest of drawers, and a vanity table with a large mirror comfortably arranged. In the now-familiar way, the double closet was open and the contents tossed out simply to get them out of the way. There were built-in shelves on either side of the closet, and the shoes and purses had been swept from these, too.

There's not much as depressing as someone else's old shoes, when you have the job of disposing of them. Jane had not cared to put her money into her clothes and personal accessories. I could not ever recall Jane wearing anything I noticed particularly, or even anything I could definitely say was brand new. Her shoes were not expensive and were all well worn. It seemed to me Jane had not enjoyed her money at all; she'd lived in her little house with her Penney's and Sears wardrobe, buying books as her only extravagance. And she'd always struck me as content; she'd worked until she'd had to retire, and then come back to substitute at the library. Somehow this all seemed melancholy, and I had to shake myself to pull out of the blues.

What I needed, I told myself briskly, was to return with some large cartons, pack all Jane's clothing away, and haul the cartons over to the Goodwill. Jane had been a little taller than I, and thicker, too; nothing would fit or be suitable. I piled all the flung-down clothes and tossed the shoes on the bed; no point in loading them back into the closet when I knew I didn't need or want them. When that was done, I spent a few minutes pressing and poking and tapping in the closet myself.

It just sounded and felt like a closet to me.

I gave up and perched on the end of the bed, thinking of all the pots and pans, towels and sheets, magazines and books, sewing kits and Christmas ornaments, bobby pins and hair nets, handkerchiefs, that were now mine and my responsibility to do something with. Just thinking of it was tiring. I listened idly to the voices of the couple working in the back bedroom. You would have thought that since they lived together twenty-four hours a day they would've said all they could think of to say, but I could hear one offer the other a comment every now and then. This calm, intermittent dialogue seemed companionable, and I went into kind of a trance sitting on the end of that bed.

I had to be at work that afternoon for three hours, from one to four. I'd just have time to get home and get ready for my date with Aubrey Scott . . . did I really need to shower and change before we went to the movies? After going up in the attic, it would be a good idea. Today was much hotter than yesterday. Cartons . . . where to get some sturdy ones? Maybe the Dumpster behind Wal-Mart? The liquor store had good cartons, but they were too small for clothes packing. Would Jane's bookshelves look okay standing by my bookshelves? Should I move my books here? I could make the guest bedroom into a study. The only person I'd ever had as an overnight guest who didn't actually sleep with me, my half brother Phillip, lived out in California now.

"We're through, Miss Teagarden," called the husband half of the team.

I shook myself out of my stupor.

"Send the bill to Bubba Sewell in the Jasper Building. Here's the address," and I ripped a piece of paper off a tablet Jane had left by the telephone. The telephone! Was it hooked up? No, I found after the repair team had left. Sewell had deemed it an unnecessary expense. Should I have it hooked back up? Under what name? Would I have two phone numbers, one here and one at the town house?

I'd had my fill of my inheritance for one day. Just as I locked the front door, I heard footsteps rustling through the grass and turned to see a barrel-chested man of about forty-five coming from the house to my left.

"Hi," he said quickly. "You're our new neighbor, I take it."

"You must be Torrance Rideout. Thanks for taking such good care of the lawn."

"Well, that's what I wanted to ask about." Close up, Torrance Rideout looked like a man who'd once been handsome and still wasn't without the old sex appeal. His hair was muddy brown with only a few flecks of gray, and he looked like his beard would be heavy enough to shave twice a day. He had a craggy face, brown eyes surrounded by what I thought of as sun wrinkles, a dark tan, and he was wearing a green golf shirt and navy shorts. "My wife, Marcia, and I were real sorry about Jane. She was a real good neighbor and we were sure sorry about her passing."

I didn't feel like I was the right person to accept condolences, but I wasn't about to explain I'd inherited Jane's house not because we were the best of friends but because Jane wanted someone who could remember her for a good long while. So I just nodded, and hoped that would do.

Torrance Rideout seemed to accept that. "Well, I've been mowing the yard, and I was wondering if you wanted me to do it one more week until you get your own yardman or mow it yourself, or just whatever you want to do. I'll be glad to do it."

"You've already been to so much trouble . . ."

"Nope, no trouble. I told Jane when she went in the hospital not to worry about the yard, I'd take care of it. I've got a riding mower, I just ride it on over when I do my yard, and there ain't that much weed eating to do, just around a couple of flower beds. I did get Jane's mower out to do the tight places the riding mower can't get. But what I did want to tell you, someone dug a little in the backyard."

We'd walked over to my car while Torrance talked, and I'd pulled out my keys. Now I stopped with my fingers on the car door handle. "Dug up the backyard?" I echoed incredulously. Come to think of it, that wasn't so surprising. I thought about it for a moment. Okay, something that could be kept in a hole in the ground as well as hidden in a house.

"I filled the holes back in," Torrance went on, "and Marcia's been keeping a special lookout since she's home during the day."

I told Torrance someone had entered the house, and he expressed the expected astonishment and disgust. He hadn't seen the broken window when he'd last mowed the backyard two days before, he told me.

"I do thank you," I said again. "You've done so much."

"No, no," he protested quickly. "We were kind of wondering if you were going to put the house on the market, or live in it yourself . . . Jane was our neighbor for so long, we kind of worry about breaking in a new one!"

"I haven't made up my mind," I said, and left it at that, which seemed to stump Torrance Rideout.

"Well, see, we rent out that room over our garage," he explained, "and we have for a good long while. This area is not exactly zoned for rental units, but Jane never minded and our neighbor on the other side, Macon Turner, runs the paper, you know him? Macon never has cared. But new people in Jane's house, well, we didn't know . . ."

"I'll tell you the minute I make up my mind," I said in as agreeable a way as I could.

"Well, well. We appreciate it, and if you need anything, just come ask me or Marcia. I'm out of town off and on most weeks, selling office supplies believe it or not, but then I'm home every weekend and some afternoons, and, like I said, Marcia's home and she'd love to help if she could."

"Thank you for offering," I said. "And I'm sure I'll be talking to you soon. Thanks for all you've done with the yard."

And finally I got to leave. I stopped at Burger King for lunch, regretting that I hadn't grabbed one of Jane's books to read while I ate. But I had plenty to think about: the emptied closets, the holes in the backyard, the hint Bubba Sewell had given me that Jane had left me a problem to solve. The sheer physical task of clearing the house of what I didn't want, and then the decision about what to do with the house itself. At least all these thoughts were preferable to thinking of myself yet again as the jilted lover, brooding over the upcoming Smith baby . . . feeling somehow cheated by Lynn's pregnancy. It was much nicer to have decisions within my power to make, instead of having them made for me.

Now! I told myself briskly, to ward off the melancholy, as I dumped my cup and wrapper in the trash bin and left the restaurant. Now to work, then home, then out on a real date, and tomorrow get out early in the morning to find those boxes!

I should have remembered that my plans seldom work out.

Chapter Three

Work that afternoon more or less drifted by. I was on the checkout/check-in desk for three hours, making idle conversation with the patrons. I knew most of them by name, and had known them all my life. I could have made their day by telling each and every one of them, including my fellow librarians, about my good fortune, but somehow it seemed immodest. And it wasn't like my mother had died, which would have been an understandable transfer of fortune. Jane's legacy, which was beginning to make me (almost) more anxious than glad, was so inexplicable that it embarrassed me to talk about it. Everyone would find out about it sooner or later . . . mentioning it now would be much more understandable than keeping silent. The other librarians were talking about Jane anyway; she had substituted here after her retirement from the school system and had been a great reader for years. I'd seen several of my co-workers at the funeral.

But I couldn't think of any casual way to drop Jane's legacy into the conversation. I could already picture the eyebrows flying up, the looks that would pass when my back was turned. In ways not yet realized, Jane had made my life much easier. In ways I was just beginning to perceive, Jane had made my life extremely complicated. I decided, in the end, just to keep my mouth shut and take what the local gossip mill had to dish out.

Lillian Schmidt almost shook my resolution when she observed that she'd seen Bubba Sewell, the lawyer, call to me at the cemetery.

"What did he want?" Lillian asked directly, as she pulled the front of her blouse together to make the gap between the buttons temporarily disappear.

I just smiled.

"Oh! Well, he is single—*now*—but you know Bubba's been married twice," she told me with relish. The buttons were already straining again.

"Who to?" I asked ungrammatically, to steer her off my own conversation with the lawyer.

"First to Carey Osland. I don't know if you know her, she lives right by Jane . . . you remember what happened to Carey later on, her second husband? Mike Osland? Went out for diapers one night right after Carey'd had that little girl, and never came back? Carey had them search everywhere for that man, she just could not believe he would walk out on her like that, but he must have."

"But before Mike Osland, Carey was married to Bubba Sewell?"

"Oh, right. Yes, for a little while, no children. Then after a year, Bubba married some girl from Atlanta, her daddy was some big lawyer, everyone thought it would be a good thing for his career." Lillian did not bother to remember the name since the girl was not a Lawrenceton native and the marriage had not lasted. "But that didn't work out, she cheated on him."

I made vague regretful noises so that Lillian would continue.

"Then—hope you enjoy these, Miz Darwell, have a nice day—he started dating your friend Lizanne Buckley."

"He's dating Lizanne?" I said in some surprise. "I haven't seen her in quite a while. I've been mailing in my bill instead of taking it by, like I used to."

Lizanne was the receptionist at the utility company. Lizanne was beautiful and agreeable, slow-witted but sure, like honey making its inexorable progress across a buttered pancake. Her parents had died the year before, and for a while that had put a crease across the perfect forehead and tear marks down the magnolia white cheeks, but gradually Lizanne's precious routine had encompassed this terrible change in her life and she had willed herself to forget the awfulness of it. She had sold her parents' house, bought herself one just like it with the proceeds, and resumed breaking hearts. Bubba Sewell must have been an optimist and a man who worshiped beauty to date the notoriously untouchable Lizanne. I wouldn't have thought it of him.

"So maybe he and Lizanne have broken up, and he wants to take you out?" Lillian always got back on the track eventually.

"No, I'm going out with Aubrey Scott tonight," I said, having thought of this evasion during her recital of Bubba Sewell's marital woes. "The Episcopal priest. We met at my mother's wedding."

It worked, and Lillian's high pleasure at knowing this exclusive fact put her in a good humor the rest of the afternoon.

I didn't realize how many Episcopalians there were in Lawrenceton until I went out with their priest.

Waiting in line for the movies I met at least five members of Aubrey's congregation. I tried to radiate respectability and wholesomeness, and kept wishing my wavy bunch of hair had been more cooperative when I'd tried to tame it before he picked me up. It flew in a warm cloud around my head, and for the hundredth time I thought of having it all cut off. At least my navy slacks and bright yellow shirt were neat and new, and my plain gold chain and earrings were good but—plain. Aubrey was in mufti, which definitely helped me to relax. He was disconcertingly attractive in his jeans and shirt; I had some definitely secular thoughts.

The movie we picked was a comedy, and we laughed at the same places, which was heartening. Our compatibility extended through dinner, where a mention of my mother's wedding prompted some reminiscences from Aubrey about weddings that had gone disastrously wrong. "And the flower girl threw up at my own wedding," he concluded.

"You've been married?" I said brilliantly. But he'd brought it up on purpose, of course, so I was doing the right thing.

"I'm a widower. She died three years ago of cancer," he said simply.

I looked at my plate real hard.

"I haven't dated too much since then," he went on. "I feel like I'm pretty—inept at it."

"You're doing fine so far," I told him.

He smiled, and it was a very attractive smile.

"From what the teenagers in my congregation tell me, dating's changed a lot in the last twenty years, since last I went out on a date. I don't want—I just want to clear the air. You seem a little nervous from time to time about being out with a minister."

"Well—yes."

"Okay. I'm not perfect, and I don't expect you to be perfect. Everyone has attitudes and opinions that are not exactly toeing the line spiritually; we're all trying, and it'll take our whole lives to get there. That's what I believe. I also don't believe in premarital sex; I'm waiting for something to change my mind on that issue, but so far it hasn't happened. Did you want to know any of that?"

"As a matter of fact, yes. That's just about exactly what I did want to know." What surprised me was the amount of relief I felt at the certainty that Aubrey would not try to get me to go to bed with him. Most dates I'd had in the past ten years, I'd spent half the time worried about what would happen when the guy took me home. Especially now, after my passionate involvement with Arthur, it was a load off my mind that Aubrey wouldn't expect me to make a decision about whether or not to go to bed with him. I brightened up and really began to enjoy myself. He didn't discuss his wife again, and I knew I would not introduce the subject.

Aubrey's ban on premarital sex did not include a ban on premarital kissing, I discovered when he walked me to my back door.

"Maybe we can go out again?"

"Give me a call," I said with a smile.

"Thanks for this evening."

"Thank *you*."

We parted with mutual goodwill, and as I scrubbed my face and pulled on my nightgown, the next day didn't seem so daunting. I wasn't scheduled to work at the library, so I could work at Jane's house. My house. I couldn't get used to the ownership.

But thinking of the house led to worrying about the break-in, about the holes in the backyard I hadn't yet seen, about the object of this strange search. It must be an object too big to be in the safe deposit box Bubba Sewell had mentioned; besides, he had told me there was nothing much in the box, implying he had seen the contents already.

I drifted off to sleep thinking, Something that couldn't be divided, something that couldn't be flattened . . .

When I woke up in the morning, I knew where that something must be hidden.

I felt like I was on a secret mission. After I scrambled into some jeans and a T-shirt and ate some toast, I checked the sketchy contents of my tool drawer. I wasn't sure what

I would need. Probably Jane had these same basic things, but I didn't feel like rummaging around until I found them. I ended up with a claw hammer and two screwdrivers, and after a little thought I added a broad-bladed putty knife. I managed to stuff all these in my purse except the hammer, and finally I managed that; but the haft stuck up from the drawstringed gather. That wouldn't be too obvious, I told myself. I brushed my teeth hastily but didn't bother with makeup, so before eight o'clock I was pulling into the driveway on Honor.

I brought the car right up into the carport and entered through the kitchen door. The house was silent and stuffy. I found the thermostat in the little hall and pushed the switch to "cool." The central air hummed into life. I glanced through the rooms hastily; nothing seemed to have been disturbed during the night. I was sweating a little, and my hair kept sticking to my face, so I did track down a rubber band and pull it all back on my neck. I blew out a deep breath, braced my shoulders, and marched into the living room. I raised the blinds around the window seat to get as much light as possible, took out my tools, and began.

Whatever it was, it was in the window seat.

Jane had had it carpeted over, so no one would think of it as a container, but only as a feature of the room, a nice place to put a plant or some pretty pillows or a flower arrangement. The installer had done a good job, and I had a hell of a time prizing up the carpet. I saw Torrance Rideout pull out of his driveway, glance at the house, and drive away to work. A pretty, plump woman walked a fat dachshund down to the end of the street and back, letting the dog perform on my yard, I noticed indignantly. I recognized her, after I thought of it awhile, as I pried and pulled at the rose-colored carpet with its little blue figure. She was Carey Osland, once married to Bubba Sewell, once married to Mike Osland, the man who had decamped in such a spectacularly callous way. Carey Osland must live in the corner house with the big climbing roses by the front porch.

I plugged away, trying not to speculate about what was in the window seat, and finally I loosened enough carpet to grab an edge with both hands and yank.

The bay window really did contain a window seat with a hinged lid. I had been right. So why didn't I feel triumphant?

Whatever was in the house was my problem, Bubba Sewell had said.

Taking a deep breath, I raised the lid and peered into the window seat. The sun streamed down into the seat, bathing its contents with a gentle morning glow. There was a rather yellow pillowcase inside, a pillowcase with something round in it.

I reached in and pulled at the corner of the pillowcase, gingerly working it back and forth, trying not to disturb its contents. But finally I had to pull it off altogether, and the thing that had been in the pillowcase rolled onto its side.

A skull grinned up at me.

"Oh my God," I said, slamming the lid down and sitting on the seat, covering my face with both trembling hands. The next minute I was in frantic action, lowering those blinds and shutting them, checking to make sure the front door was locked, finding the light switch, and flipping on the overhead light in the suddenly darkened room.

I opened the window seat again, hoping its contents had miraculously changed.

The skull still lay there with its slack-jawed grin.

Then the doorbell rang.

I jumped and squeaked. For a moment I stood indecisively. Then I tossed the tools into the seat with the thing, shut the lid, and yanked the loose carpet back up. It wouldn't settle back into place very well, having been removed so inexpertly, but I did the best I could and then heaped the fancy pillows around the edges to conceal the damage. But the carpet still sagged out a little. I pushed it into place, weighted it down with my purse. It still pouched. I grabbed some books from the shelves and stacked them on the window seat, too. Much better. The carpet stayed in place. The doorbell rang again. I stood for a moment composing my face.

Carey Osland, minus the dachshund, smiled at me in a friendly way when I finally opened the door. Her dark chestnut hair was lightly threaded with gray, but her round, pretty face was unlined. She was wearing a dress that was one step up from a bathrobe, and scuffed loafers.

"Hi, neighbor," she said cheerfully. "Aurora Teagarden, isn't it?"

"Yes," I said, making a huge effort to sound casual and calm.

"I'm Carey Osland, I live in the house with the roses, on the corner," and she pointed.

"I remember meeting you before, Carey, at a bridal shower, I think."

"That's right—a long time ago. Whose was it?"

"Come in, come on in . . . Wasn't it Amina's shower, after she eloped?"

"Well, it must have been, 'cause that was when I was working at her mother's dress shop, that's why I got invited. I work at Marcus Hatfield now."

Marcus Hatfield was the Lord & Taylor of Lawrenceton.

"That's why I'm such a slob now," Carey went on smilingly. "I get so tired of being dressed up."

"Your nails look great," I said admiringly. I am always impressed by someone who can wear long nails and keep them polished. I was also trying very hard not to think about the window seat, not to even glance in that direction. I had waved Carey to the couch so she'd have her back partially to it when she half-turned to talk to me as I sat in the armchair.

"Oh, honey, they're not real," Carey said warmly. "I never could keep my nails from chipping and getting broken . . . So, you and Jane must have been good friends?"

The unexpected change of subject and Carey's very understandable curiosity took me by surprise. My neighbors were definitely not of the big city impersonal variety.

"She left me the house," I stated, figuring that settled that.

And it did. Carey couldn't think of a single way to get around that one to inquire as to our exact relationship.

I was beginning to wonder about our relationship, myself. Considering the little problem Jane had left me to deal with.

"So, do you plan on living here?" Carey had rallied and was counterattacking with even more directness.

"I don't know." And I didn't add or explain. I liked Carey Osland, but I needed to be by myself with the thing in the window seat.

"Well"—Carey took a deep breath and released it—"I guess I'd better be getting ready for work."

"Thanks for coming by," I said as warmly as I could. "I'm sure I'll be seeing you again when I have things more settled here."

"Like I said, I'm right next door, so if you need me, come on over. My little girl is away at summer camp till this weekend, so I'm all on my own."

"Thanks so much, I may be taking you up on that," I said, trying to beam goodwill and neighborliness enough to soften the fact that I did not want a prolonged conversation and I wanted her gone, things I was afraid I'd made offensively obvious.

My sigh of relief was so loud after I'd shut and locked the door behind her that I hoped she wouldn't hear it.

I sank down into the chair again and covered my face with my hands, preparing to think.

Sweet, fragile, silver-haired Jane Engle, school librarian and churchgoer, had murdered someone and put the victim's skull in her window seat. Then she'd had the window seat carpeted over so no one would think to look there for anything. The carpet was in excellent condition, but not new. Jane had lived in that house with a skull in her living room for some years.

That alone would take some hard getting used to.

I should call the police. My hand actually picked up the receiver before I remembered that the phone was disconnected and that I owed Jane Engle. I owed her big-time.

Jane had left me the house and the money and the skull.

I could not call the police and expose Jane to the world as a murderess. She had counted on that.

Drawn irresistibly, I went to the window seat and opened it again.

"Who the hell are you?" I asked the skull. With considerable squeamishness, I lifted it out with both hands. It wasn't white like bones looked in the movies, but brownish. I didn't know if it was a man's or a woman's skull, but the cause of death seemed apparent; there was a hole in the back of the skull, a hole with jagged edges.

How on earth had elderly Jane managed to deliver such a blow? Who could this be? Perhaps a visitor had fallen and bashed the back of his head on something, and Jane had been afraid she'd be accused of killing the person? That was a familiar and almost comforting plot to a regular mystery reader. Then I thought in a muddled way of *Arsenic and Old Lace*. Perhaps this was a homeless person, or a solitary old man with no family? But Lawrenceton was not large enough for a missing person to go unnoticed, I thought. At least I couldn't recall such a case for years.

Not since Carey Osland's husband had left to pick up diapers and had never returned.

I almost dropped the skull. Oh my Lord! Was this Mike Osland? I put the skull down on Jane's coffee table carefully, as if I might hurt it if I wasn't gentle. And what would

I do with it now? I couldn't put it back in the window seat, now that I'd loosened the carpet and made the place conspicuous, and there was no way I could get the carpet to look as smooth as it had been. Maybe now that the house had been burgled, I could hide the skull in one of the places the searcher had already looked?

That raised a whole new slew of questions. Was this skull the thing the searcher had been looking for? If Jane had killed someone, how did anyone else know about it? Why come looking now? Why not just go to the police and say, "Jane Engle has a skull in her house somewhere, I'm certain." No matter how crazy they'd sound, that was what most people would do. Why had this person done otherwise?

This added up to more questions than I answered at the library in a month. Plus, those questions were a lot easier to answer. "Can you recommend a good mystery without any, you know, sex, for my mother?" was a lot easier to answer than "Whose skull is sitting on my coffee table?"

Okay, first things first. Hide the skull. I felt removing it from the house would be safest. (I say "felt" because I was pretty much beyond reasoning.)

I got a brown Kroger bag from the kitchen and eased the skull into it. I put a can of coffee in another bag, figuring two bags were less conspicuous than one. After rearranging the window seat as best I could, I looked at my watch. It was ten o'clock, and Carey Osland should be at work. I'd seen Torrance Rideout leaving, but, according to what he'd told me the day before, his wife should be at home unless she was running errands.

I peeked through the blinds. The house across from Torrance Rideout's was as still as it had been the day before. The one across from Carey Osland's had two small children playing in the side yard next to Faith Street, a good distance away. All clear. But, even as I watched, a you-do-it moving van pulled up in front of the house across the street.

"Oh, great," I muttered. "Just great." After a moment, though, I decided that the moving van would be far more interesting than my departure if anyone was watching. So, before I could worry about it, I grabbed up my purse and my two paper bags and went out the kitchen door into the carport.

"Aurora?" called a voice incredulously.

With a strong feeling that fate was dealing harshly with me, I turned to the people climbing out of the moving van, to see that my former lover, Burglary Detective Arthur Smith, and his bride, Homicide Detective Lynn Liggett, were moving in across the street.

Chapter Four

From being bizarre and upsetting, my day had moved into surrealistic. I walked on legs that didn't feel like my own toward two police detectives, my purse slung on my shoulder, a can of coffee in the bag in my right hand, a perforated skull in the bag in my left. My hands began sweating. I tried to force a pleasant expression on my face, but had no idea what I had achieved.

Next they're going to say, I thought, they're going to say—*What's in the bag?*

The only plus to meeting up with the very pregnant Mrs. Smith at this moment was that I was so worried about the skull I was not concerned about the awkward personal situation I'd landed in. But I *was* aware—acutely—that I had on no makeup and my hair was restrained with a rubber band.

Arthur's fair skin flushed red, which it did when he was

embarrassed, or angry, or—well, no, don't think about that. Arthur was too tough to embarrass easily, but he was embarrassed now.

"Are you visiting here?" Lynn asked hopefully.

"Jane Engle died," I began to explain. "Arthur, you remember Jane?"

He nodded. "The Madeleine Smith expert."

"Jane left me her house," I said, and a childish part of me wanted to add, "and lots and lots of money." But a more mature part of my mind vetoed it, not only because I was carrying a skull in a bag and didn't want to prolong this encounter, but because money was not a legitimate score over Lynn acquiring Arthur. My modern brain told me that a married woman had no edge over an unmarried woman, but my primitive heart knew I would never be "even" with Lynn until I married, myself.

It was a fragmented day in Chez Teagarden.

The Smiths looked dismayed, as well they might. Moving into their little dream home, baby on the way—baby very much on the way—and then the Old Girlfriend appears right across the street.

"I'm not sure whether or not I'll live here," I said before they could ask me. "But I'll be in and out the next week or two getting things straightened out." Could I ever possibly straighten this out?

Lynn sighed. I looked up at her, really seeing her for the first time. Lynn's short brown hair looked lifeless, and, far from glowing with pregnancy, as I'd heard women did, Lynn's skin looked blotchy. But when she turned and looked back at the house, she looked very happy.

"How are you feeling, Lynn?" I asked politely.

"Pretty good. The ultrasound showed the baby is a lot further along than we thought, maybe by seven weeks, so we kind of rushed through buying the house to be sure we got in here and got everything settled before the baby comes."

Just then, thank goodness, a car pulled up behind the van and some men piled out. I recognized them as police pals of Arthur's and Lynn's; they'd come to help unload the van.

Then I realized the man driving the car, the burly man about ten years older than Arthur, was Jack Burns, a detective sergeant, and one of the few people in the world I truly feared.

Here were at least seven policemen, including Jack Burns, and here I was with . . . I was scared to even think it with Jack Burns around. His zeal for dealing out punishment to wrongdoers was so sharp, his inner rage burned with such a flame, I felt he could smell concealment and falsehood. My legs began shaking. I was afraid someone would notice. How on earth did his two teenagers manage a private life?

"Good to have seen you," I said abruptly. "I hope your moving day goes as well as they ever do."

They were relieved the encounter was over, too. Arthur gave me a casual wave as a shout from one of his buddies who had opened the back of the van summoned him to work.

"Come see us when we get settled in," Lynn told me insincerely as I said good-bye and turned to leave.

"Take it easy, Lynn," I called over my shoulder, as I crossed the street to my car on rubbery legs.

I put the bags carefully in the front seat and slid in myself. I wanted to sit and shake for a while, but I also wanted to get the hell out of there, so I turned the key in the ignition, turned on the air-conditioning full blast, and occupied a few moments buckling my seat belt, patting my face (which was streaming with sweat) with my handkerchief, anything to give me a little time to calm down before I had to drive. I backed out with great care, the unfamiliar driveway, the moving van parked right across the street, and the people milling around it making the process even more hazardous.

I managed to throw a casual wave in the direction of the moving crew, and some of them waved back. Jack Burns just stared; I wondered again about his wife and children, living with that burning stare that seemed to see all your secrets. Maybe he could switch it off at home? Sometimes even the men under his command seemed leery of him, I'd learned while I was dating Arthur.

I drove around aimlessly for a while, wondering what to do with the skull. I hated to take it to my own home; there was no good hiding place. I couldn't throw it away until I'd decided what to do with it. My safe deposit box at the bank wasn't big enough, and probably Jane's wasn't either: otherwise, surely she would have put the skull there originally. Anyway, the thought of carrying the paper bag into the bank was enough to make me giggle hysterically. I sure couldn't keep it in the trunk of my car. I checked with a glance to make sure my inspection sticker was up-to-date; yes, thank God. But I could be stopped for some traffic violation at any time; I never had been before, but, the way things were going today, it seemed likely.

I had a key to my mother's house, and she was gone.

No sooner had the thought crossed my mind than I turned at the next corner to head there. I wasn't happy about using Mother's house for such a purpose, but it seemed the best thing to do at the time.

The air was dead and hot inside Mother's big home on Plantation Drive. I dashed up the stairs to my old room without thinking, then stood panting in the doorway trying to think of a good hiding place. I kept almost nothing here anymore, and this was really another guest bedroom now, but there might be something up in the closet.

There was: a zippered, pink plastic blanket bag in which Mother always stored the blue blankets for the twin beds in this room. No one would need to get blankets down in this weather. I pulled over the stool from the vanity table, climbed up on it, and unzipped the plastic bag. I took my Kroger bag, with its gruesome contents, and inserted it between the blankets. The bag would no longer zip with the extra bulk.

This was getting grotesque. Well, more grotesque.

I took out one of the blankets and doubled up the other one in half the blanket bag, leaving the other half for the skull. The bag zipped, and it didn't look too lumpy, I decided. I pushed it to the back of the shelf.

Now all I had to dispose of was a blanket. The chest of drawers was only partially full of odds and ends; Mother kept two drawers empty for guests. I stuffed the blanket in one, slammed it shut, then pulled it right back open. She might need the drawer. John was moving all his stuff in when they got back from their honeymoon. I felt like sitting on the floor and bursting into tears. I stood holding the damn blanket indecisively, thinking wildly of burning it or taking it home with me. I'd rather have the blanket than the skull.

The bed, of course. The best place to hide a blanket is on a bed.

I stripped the bedspread off, pitched the pillow on the floor, and fitted the blanket smoothly on the mattress. In a few more minutes, the bed looked exactly like it had before.

I dragged myself out of Mother's house and drove over to my own place. It seemed as though I'd gone two days without sleep, when in fact it was only now getting close to lunchtime. At least I didn't have to go to work this afternoon.

I poured myself a glass of iced tea and for once loaded it with sugar. I sat in my favorite chair and sipped it slowly. It was time to think.

Fact One. Jane Engle had left a skull concealed in her house. She might not have told Bubba Sewell what she'd done, but she'd hinted to him that all was not well—but that I would handle it.

Question: How had the skull gotten in Jane's house? Had she murdered its—owner? occupant?

Question: Where was the rest of the skeleton?

Question: How long ago had the head been placed in the window seat?

Fact Two. Someone else knew or suspected that the skull was in Jane's house. I could infer that this someone else was basically law-abiding since the searcher hadn't taken the chance to steal anything or vandalize the house to any degree. The broken window was small potatoes compared with what could have been wreaked on Jane's unoccupied house. So the skull was almost certainly the sole object of the search. Unless Jane had—horrible thought—something else hidden in her house?

Question: Would the searcher try again, or was he perhaps persuaded that the skull was no longer there? The yard had been searched, too, according to Torrance Rideout. I reminded myself to go in the backyard the next time I went to the house and see what had been done there.

Fact Three. I was in a jam. I could keep silent forever, throw the skull in a river, and try to forget I ever saw it; that approach had lots of appeal right now. Or I could take it to the police and tell them what I'd done. I could already feel myself shiver at the thought of Jack Burns's face, to say nothing of the incredulity on Arthur's. I heard myself stammer, "Well, I hid it at my mother's house." What kind of excuse could I offer for my strange actions? Even I could not understand exactly why I'd done what I'd done, except that I'd acted out of some kind of loyalty to Jane, influenced to some extent by all the money she'd left me.

Then and there, I pretty much ruled out going to the police unless something else turned up. I had no idea what my legal position was, but I couldn't imagine what I'd done so far was so very bad legally. Morally was another question.

But I definitely had a problem on my hands.

At this inopportune moment the doorbell rang. It was a day of unwelcome interruptions. I sighed and went to answer it, hoping it was someone I wanted to see. Aubrey?

But the day continued its apparently inexorable downhill slide. Parnell Engle and his wife, Leah, were at my front door, the door no one ever uses because they'd have to park in the back—ten feet from my back door—and then walk all the way around the whole row of town houses to the front to ring the bell. Of course, that was what Parnell and Leah had done.

"Mr. Engle, Mrs. Engle," I said. "Please come in."

Parnell opened fire immediately. "What did we do to Jane, Miss Teagarden? Did she tell you what we did to her that offended her so much she left everything to you?"

I didn't need this.

"Don't you start, Mr. Engle," I said sharply. "Just don't you start. This is *not a good day.* You got a car, you got some money, you got Madeleine the cat. Just be glad of it and leave me alone."

"We were Jane's own blood kin—"

"Don't start that with me," I snapped. I was simply beyond trying to be polite. "I don't know why she left everything to me, but it doesn't make me feel very lucky right now, believe me."

"We realize," he said with less whine and more dignity, "that Jane did express her true wishes in her will. We know that she was in her good senses up until the end and that she made her choice knowing what she was doing. We're not going to contest the will. We just don't understand it."

"Well, Mr. Engle, neither do I." Parnell would have had that skull at the police station in less time than it takes to talk about it. But it was good news that they weren't small-minded enough to contest the will and thereby cause me endless trouble and heartache. I knew Lawrenceton. Pretty soon people would start saying, "Well, why *did* Jane Engle leave everything to a young woman she didn't even know very well?" And speculation would run rampant; I couldn't even imagine the things people would make up to explain Jane's inexplicable legacy. People were going to talk anyway, but any dispute about the will would put a nasty twist on that speculation.

Looking at Parnell Engle and his silent wife, with their dowdy clothes and grievances, I suddenly wondered if I'd gotten the money to pay me for the inconvenience of the skull. What Jane had told Bubba Sewell might have been just a smoke screen. She may have read my character thoroughly, almost supernaturally thoroughly, and known I would keep her secret.

"Good-bye," I said to them gently, and closed my front door slowly, so they couldn't say I'd slammed it on them. I locked it carefully, and marched to my telephone. I looked up Bubba Sewell's number and dialed. He was in and available, to my surprise.

"How's things going, Miss Teagarden?" he drawled.

"Kind of bumpy, Mr. Sewell."

"Sorry to hear that. How can I be of assistance?"

"Did Jane leave me a letter?"

"What?"

"A letter, Mr. Sewell. Did she leave me a letter, something I'm supposed to get after I've had the house a month, or something?"

"No, Miss Teagarden."

"Not a cassette? No tape of any kind?"

"No, ma'am."

"Did you see anything like that in the safe deposit box?"

"No, no, can't say as I did. Actually, I just rented that box after Jane became so ill, to put her good jewelry in."

"And she didn't tell you what was in the house?" I asked carefully.

"Miss Teagarden, I have no idea what's in Miss Engle's house," he said definitely. Very definitely.

I stopped, baffled. Bubba Sewell didn't want to know. If I told him, he might have to do something about it, and I hadn't yet decided what should be done.

"Thanks," I said hopelessly. "Oh, by the way . . ." And I told him about Parnell and Leah's visit.

"He said for sure they weren't going to contest?"

"He said they knew that Jane was in her right mind when she made her will, that they just wanted to know why she left everything the way she did."

"But he didn't talk about going to court or getting his own lawyer?"

"No."

"Let's just hope he meant it when he said he knew Jane was in her right mind when she made her will."

On that happy note we told each other good-bye.

I returned to my chair and tried to pick up the thread of my reasoning. Soon I realized I'd gone as far as I could go.

It seemed to me that if I could find out who the skull had belonged to, I'd have a clearer course to follow. I could start by finding out how long the skull had been in the window seat. If Jane had kept the bill from the carpet layers, that would give me a definite date, because the skull had for sure been in the window seat when the carpet was installed over it. And it hadn't been disturbed since.

That meant I had to go back to Jane's house.

I sighed deeply.

I might as well have some lunch, collect some boxes, and go to work at the house this afternoon as I'd planned originally.

This time yesterday I'd been a woman with a happy future; now I was a woman with a secret, and it was such a strange, macabre secret that I felt I had GUILTY KNOWLEDGE written on my forehead.

The unloading across the street was still going on. I saw a large carton labeled with a picture of a baby crib being carried in, and almost wept. But I had other things to do today than beat myself over the head with losing Arthur. That grief had a stale, preoccupied feel to it.

The disorder in Jane's bedroom had to be cleared away before I could think about finding her papers. I carried in my boxes, found the coffeepot, and started the coffee (which I'd brought back, since I had carried it away in the morning) to perking. The house was so cool and so quiet that it almost made me drowsy. I turned on Jane's bedside radio; yuck, it was on the easy listening station. I found the public radio station after a second's search, and began to pack clothes to Beethoven. I searched each garment as I packed, just on the off chance I would find something that would explain the hidden skull. I just could not believe Jane would leave me this problem with no explanation.

Maybe she'd thought I'd never find it?

No, Jane had thought I'd find it sooner or later. Maybe not this soon. But sometime. Perhaps, if it hadn't been for the break-in and the holes in the backyard (and here I reminded myself again to check them), I wouldn't have worried about a thing, no matter how mysterious some of Bubba Sewell's statements had been.

Suddenly I thought of the old saw "You don't look a gift horse in the mouth." I recalled the skull's grin all too clearly, and I began laughing.

I had to laugh at something.

It didn't take quite as long as I expected to pack Jane's clothes. If something had struck my fancy, it wouldn't have bothered me to keep it; Jane had been a down-to-earth woman, and in some ways I supposed I was, too. But I saw nothing I wanted to keep except a cardigan or two, so anonymous that I wouldn't be constantly thinking, I am wearing Jane's clothes. So all the dresses and blouses, coats and shoes and skirts that had been in the closet were neatly boxed and ready to go to the Goodwill, with the vexing exception of a robe that slipped from its hanger to the floor. Every box was full to the brim, so I just left it where it fell. I loaded the boxes into my car trunk, then decided to take a break by strolling into the backyard and seeing what damage had been done there.

Jane's backyard was laid out neatly. There were two concrete benches, too hot to sit on in the June sun, placed on either side of a concrete birdbath surrounded by monkey grass. The monkey grass was getting out of hand, I noticed. Someone else had thought so, too; a big chunk of it had been uprooted. I'd dealt with monkey grass before and admired the unknown gardener's persistence. Then it came to me that this was one of the "dug up" spots that Torrance Rideout had filled in for me. Looking around me more carefully, I saw a few more; all were around bushes, or under the two benches. None were out in the middle of the grass, which was a relief. I had to just shake my head over this; someone had seriously thought Jane had dug a hole out in her yard and stuck the skull in it? A pretty futile search after all this time Jane had had the skull.

That was a sobering thought. Desperate people are not gentle.

As I mooched around the neat little yard, counting the holes around the bushes that had screened the unattractive school fence from Jane's view, I became aware of movement in the Rideouts' backyard. Minimal movement. A woman was sunbathing on the huge sun deck in a lounge chair, a woman with a long, slim body already deeply browned and semiclad in a fire engine red bikini. Her chin-length, dyed, pale blond hair was held back by a matching band, and even her fingernails seemed to be the same shade of red. She was awfully turned out for sunbathing on her own deck, presuming this was Marcia Rideout.

"How are you, new neighbor?" she called languidly, a slim brown arm raising a glass of iced tea to her lips. This was the movement I'd glimpsed.

"Fine," I lied automatically. "And you?"

"Getting along, getting by." She beckoned with a lazy wave. "Come talk for a minute."

When I was settled in a chair beside her, she extended a thin hand and said, "Marcia Rideout."

"Aurora Teagarden," I murmured as I shook her hand, and the amusement flitted across her face and vanished. She pulled off her opaque sunglasses and gave me a direct look. Her eyes were dark blue, and she was drunk, or at least on her way there. Maybe she saw something in my face, because she popped the sunglasses right back on. I tried not to peer at her drink; I suspected it was not tea at all, but bourbon.

"Would you like something to drink?" Marcia Rideout offered.

"No thanks," I said hastily.

"So you inherited the house. Think you'll like living there?"

"I don't know if I will live there," I told her, watching her fingers run up and down the dripping glass. She took another sip.

"I drink sometimes," she told me frankly.

I really couldn't think of anything to say.

"But only when Torrance isn't coming home. He has to spend the night on the road sometimes, maybe once every two weeks or so. And those days he's not coming home to spend the night, I drink. Very slowly."

"I expect you get lonely," I offered uncertainly.

She nodded. "I expect I do. Now, Carey Osland on the other side of you, and Macon Turner on the other side of me, *they* don't get lonely. Macon sneaks over there through the backyards, some nights."

"He must be an old-fashioned guy." There was nothing to

prevent Macon and Carey from enjoying each other's company. Macon was divorced and Carey was, too, presumably, unless Mike Osland was dead . . . and that reminded me of the skull, which I had enjoyed forgetting for a moment.

My comment struck Marcia Rideout as funny. As I watched her laugh, I saw she had more wrinkles than I'd figured, and I upped her age by maybe seven years. But from her body you sure couldn't tell it.

"I didn't used to have such a problem with being lonely," Marcia said slowly, her amusement over. "We used to have people renting this apartment." She waved in the direction of the garage with its little room on top. "One time it was a high school teacher. I liked her. Then she got another job and moved. Then it was Ben Greer, that jerk that works at the grocery chopping meat—you know him?"

"Yeah. He is a jerk."

"So I was glad when he moved. Then we had a housepainter, Mark Kaplan . . ." She seemed to be drifting off, and I thought her eyes closed behind the dark glasses.

"What happened to him?" I asked politely.

"Oh. He was the only one who ever left in the night without paying the rent."

"Gosh. Just skipped out? Bag and baggage?" Maybe another candidate for the skull?

"Yep. Well, he took some of his stuff. He never came back for the rest. You sure you don't want a drink? I have some real tea, you know."

Unexpectedly, Marcia smiled, and I smiled back.

"No, thanks. You were saying about your tenant?"

"He ran out. And we haven't had anyone since. Torrance

just doesn't want to fool with it. The past couple of years, he's gotten like that. I tell him he must be middle-aged. He and Jane and their big fight over that tree!"

I followed Marcia's pointing red-tipped finger. There was a tree just about midway between the houses. It had a curiously lopsided appearance, viewed from the Rideouts' deck.

"It's just about straddling the property line," Marcia said. She had a slow, deep voice, very attractive. "You won't believe, if you've got any sense, that people could fight about a tree."

"People can fight about anything. I've been managing some apartments, and the tizzy people get into if someone uses their parking space!"

"Really, I can believe it. Well, as you can see, the tree is a little closer to Jane's house . . . your house." Marcia took another sip from her drink. "But Torrance didn't like those leaves, he got sick of raking them. So he talked to Jane about taking the tree down. It wasn't shading either house, really. Well, Jane had a fit. She really got hot. So Torrance just cut the branches that were over our property line. Ooo, Jane stomped over here the next day, and she said, 'Now, Torrance Rideout, that was petty. I have a bone to pick with you.' I wonder what the origin of that saying is? You happen to know?"

I shook my head, fascinated with the little story and Marcia's digression.

"There wasn't any putting the branches back, they were cut to hell," said Marcia flatly, her southern accent roughening. "And somehow Torrance got Jane calmed down. But things never were the same after that between Torrance and Jane. But Jane and I still spoke, and we were on the board of the orphans' home together. I liked her."

I had a hard time picturing Jane that angry. Jane had been a pleasant person, even sweet occasionally, always polite; but she was also extremely conscious of personal property, rather like my mother. Jane didn't have or want much in the way of things, but what she had was hers absolutely, not to be touched by other hands without proper permission being asked and granted. I saw from Marcia's little story how far that sense of property went. I was learning a lot about Jane now that it was too late. I hadn't known she'd been on the board of the orphans' home, actually and less bluntly named Mortimer House.

"Well," Marcia continued slowly, "at least the past couple of years they'd been getting along fine, Jane and Torrance . . . she forgave him, I guess. I'm sleepy now."

"I'm sorry you had the trouble with Jane," I said, feeling that somehow I should apologize for my benefactress. "She was always such an intelligent, interesting person." I stood to leave; Marcia's eyes were closed behind her sunglasses, I thought.

"Shoot, the fight she had with Torrance was nothin', you should have heard her and Carey go to it."

"When was that?" I asked, trying to sound indifferent.

But Marcia Rideout was asleep, her hand still wrapped around her drink.

I trudged back to my task, sweating in the sun, worried about Marcia burning since she'd fallen asleep on the lounge. But she'd been slathered with oil. I made a mental note to look out the back from time to time to see if she was still there.

It was hard for me to picture Jane being furious with anyone and marching over to tell him about it. Of course, I'd never owned property. Maybe I would be the same way now. Neighbors could get very upset over things uninvolved people would laugh about. I remembered my mother, a cool and elegant Lauren Bacall type, telling me she was going to buy a rifle and shoot her neighbor's dog if it woke her up with its barking again. She had gone to the police instead and gotten a court order against the dog's owner after the police chief, an old friend, had come to her house and sat in the dark listening to the dog yapping one night. The dog's owner hadn't spoken to Mother since, and in fact had been transferred to another city, without the slightest sign of their mutual disgust slackening.

I wondered what Jane had fought with Carey about. It was hard to see how this could relate to my immediate problem, the skull; it sure wasn't the skull of Carey Osland or Torrance Rideout. I couldn't imagine Jane killing the Rideouts' tenant, Mark whatever-his-name-was, but at least I had the name of another person who might be the skull.

Back in my house once again—I was practicing saying "my house"—I began to search for Jane's papers. Everyone has some cache of canceled checks, old receipts, car papers, and tax stuff. I found Jane's in the guest bedroom, sorted into floral-patterned cardboard boxes by year. Jane kept everything, and she kept all those papers for seven years, I discovered. I sighed, swore, and opened the first box.

Chapter Five

I plugged in Jane's television and listened to the news with one ear while I went through Jane's papers. Apparently all the papers to do with the car had already been handed over to Parnell Engle, for there were no old inspection receipts or anything like that. It would have helped if Jane had kept all these papers in some kind of category, I told myself grumpily, trying not to think of my own jumble of papers in shoe boxes in my closet.

I'd started with the earliest box, dated seven years ago. Jane had kept receipts that surely could be thrown away now: dresses she'd bought, visits by the bug-spray man, the purchase of a telephone. I began sorting as I looked, the pile of definite discards getting higher and higher.

There's a certain pleasure in throwing things away. I was concentrating contentedly, so it took me a while to realize I was hearing some kind of sound from outside. Someone seemed to be doing something to the screen door in the kitchen. I sat hunched on the living room floor, listening with every molecule. I reached over and switched off the television. Gradually I relaxed. Whatever was being done, it wasn't being done surreptitiously. Whatever the sound was, it escalated.

I stiffened my spine and went to investigate. I opened the wooden door cautiously, just as the noise repeated. Hanging spread-eagled on the screen door was a very large, very fat orange cat. This seemed to explain the funny snags I'd noticed on the screen when I went in the backyard earlier.

"Madeleine?" I said in amazement.

The cat gave a dismal yowl and dropped from the screen to the top step. Unthinkingly, I opened the door, and Madeleine was in in a flash.

"You wouldn't think a cat so fat could move so fast," I said.

Madeleine was busy stalking through her house, sniffing and rubbing her side against the door frames.

To say I was in a snit would be putting it mildly. This cat was now Parnell and Leah's. Jane knew I was not partial to pets, not at all. My mother had never let me have one, and gradually her convictions about pet hygiene and inconvenience had influenced me. Now I would have to call Parnell, talk with him again, either take the cat to him or get him to come get the cat . . . she would probably scratch me if I tried to put her in my car . . . another complication in my life. I sank into one of the kitchen chairs and rested my head on my hands dismally.

Madeleine completed her house tour and came and sat in front of me, her front paws neatly covered by her plumy tail. She looked up at me expectantly. Her eyes were round and gold and had a kind of stare that reminded me of Arthur Smith's. That stare said, "I am the toughest and the baddest, don't mess with me." I found myself giving a halfhearted chuckle at Madeleine's machisma. Suddenly she crouched, and in one fluid movement shifted her bulk from the floor to the table—where Jane *ate*! I thought, horrified.

She could stare at me more effectively there. Growing impatient at my stupidity, Madeleine butted her golden head against my hand. I patted her uncertainly. She still seemed to be waiting for something. I tried to picture Jane with the cat, and I seemed to recall she'd scratched the animal behind the ears. I tried that. A deep rumble percolated somewhere in Madeleine's insides. The cat's eyes halfclosed with pleasure. Encouraged by this response, I kept scratching her gently behind the ears, then switched to the area under her chin. This, too, was popular.

I grew tired of this after a while and stopped. Madeleine stretched, yawned, and jumped heavily down from the table. She walked over to one of the cabinets and sat in front of it, casting a significant look over her shoulder at me. Fool that I am, it took me a few minutes to get the message. Madeleine gave a soprano yowl. I opened the bottom cabinet, and saw only the pots and pans I'd reloaded the day before. Madeleine kept her stare steady. She seemed to feel I was a slow learner. I looked in the cabinets above the counter and found some canned cat food. I looked down at Madeleine and said brightly, "This what you wanted?" She yowled again and began to pace back and forth, her eyes never leaving the black and green can. I hunted down the electric can opener, plugged it in, and used it. With a flourish, I set the can down on the floor. After a moment's dubious pause—she clearly wasn't used to eating from a can—Madeleine dived in. After a little more searching, I filled a plastic bowl with water and put it down by the can. This, too, met with the cat's approval.

I went to the phone to call Parnell, my feet dragging reluctantly. But of course I hadn't had the phone hooked up. I reminded myself again I'd have to do something about that, and looked at the cat, now grooming herself with great concentration. "What am I going to do with you?" I muttered. I decided I'd leave her here for the night and call Parnell from my place. He could come get her in the morning. Somehow I hated to put her outside; she was an inside cat for the most part, I seemed to remember Jane telling me . . . though frankly I'd often tuned out when Jane chatted about the cat. Pet owners could be such bores. Madeleine would need a litter box; Jane had had one tucked away beside the refrigerator. It wasn't there now. Maybe it had been taken to the vet's where Madeleine had been boarded during Jane's illness. It was probably sitting uselessly at the Engles' house now.

I poked around in the trash left in Jane's room from my cleaning out the closet. Sure enough, there was a box of the appropriate size and shape. I put it in the corner by the refrigerator in the kitchen, and as Madeleine watched with keen attention, I opened cabinets until I found a half-full bag of cat litter.

I felt rather proud of myself at handling the little problem the cat presented so quickly; though, when I considered, it seemed Madeleine had done all the handling. She had gotten back to her old home, gained entrance, been fed and watered, and had a toilet provided her, and now she jumped up on Jane's armchair in the living room, curled into a striped orange ball, and went to sleep. I watched her for a moment enviously, then I sighed and began sorting papers again.

In the fourth box I found what I wanted. The carpet had been installed three years ago. So the skull had become a skull sometime before that. Suddenly I realized what should have been obvious. Of course Jane had not killed someone and put his head in the window seat fresh, so to speak. The skull had already been a skull, not a head, before Jane had sealed it up. I was willing to concede that Jane obviously had a side unknown to me, or to anyone, though whoever had searched the house must at least suspect it. But I could not believe that Jane would live in a house with a decomposing head in the window seat. Jane had not been a monster.

What had Jane been? I pulled up my knees and wrapped my arms around them. Behind me, Madeleine, who had observed Jane longer than anyone, yawned and rearranged herself.

Jane had been a woman in her late seventies with silver hair almost always done up in a regal chignon. She had never worn slacks, always dresses. She had had a lively mind—an intelligent mind—and good manners. She had been interested in true crime, at a safe distance; her favorite cases were all Victorian or earlier. She had had a mother who was wealthy and who had held a prominent place in Lawrenceton society, and Jane had behaved as though she herself had neither. She had inherited from somewhere, though, a strong sense of property. But as far as the liberation of women went—well, Jane and I had had some discussions on that. Jane was a traditionalist, and though as a working woman she had believed in equal pay for equal work, some of the other tenets of the women's movement were lost on her. "Women don't have to confront men, honey," she'd told me one time. "Women can always think their way around them." Jane had not been a forgiving person, either; if she got really angry and did not receive an adequate apology, she held a grudge a good long while. She was not even aware of grudge holding, I'd observed; if she had been, she would have fought it, like she'd fought other traits in herself she didn't think were Christian. What else had Jane been? Conventionally moral, dependable, and she'd had an unexpectedly sly sense of humor.

In fact, wherever Jane was now, I was willing to bet she was looking at me and laughing. Me, with Jane's money and Jane's house and Jane's cat and Jane's skull.

After sorting more papers (I might as well finish what I've begun, I thought), I got up to stretch. It was raining outside, I discovered to my surprise. As I sat on the window seat and looked out the blinds, the rain got heavier and heavier and the thunder started to boom. The lights came on across the street in the little white house with yellow shutters, and through the front window I could see Lynn unpacking boxes, moving slowly and awkwardly. I wondered how having a baby felt, wondered if I would ever know. Finally, for no reason that I could discern, my feelings for Arthur ended, and the pain drained away. Tired of poring over receipts left from a life that was over, I thought about my own life. Living by myself was sometimes fun, but I didn't want to do it forever, as Jane had. I thought of Robin Crusoe, the mystery writer, who had left town when my romance with Arthur had heated up. I thought of Aubrey Scott. I was tired of being alone with my bizarre problem. I was tired of being alone, period.

I told myself to switch mental tracks in a hurry. There was something undeniably pleasant about being in my own house watching the rain come down outside, knowing I didn't have to go anywhere if I didn't want to. I was surrounded by books in a pretty room. I could occupy myself however I chose. Come on, I asked myself bravely, what do you choose to do? I almost chose to start crying, but instead I jumped up, found Jane's Soft Scrub, and cleaned the bathroom. A place isn't really yours until you clean it. Jane's place became mine, however temporarily, that afternoon. I cleaned and sorted and threw away and inventoried. I opened a can of soup and heated it in my saucepan on my stove. I ate it with my spoon. Madeleine came into the kitchen when she heard me bustling around and jumped up to watch me eat. This time I was not horrified. I looked over the book I'd pulled from Jane's shelves and addressed a few remarks to Madeleine while I ate.

It was still raining after I'd washed the pot and the spoon

and the bowl, so I sat in Jane's chair in the living room, watching the rain and wondering what to do next. After a moment, the cat heaved herself up onto my lap. I wasn't quite sure how I felt about this liberty on the cat's part, but I decided I'd give it a try. I stroked the smooth fur tentatively and heard the deep percolation start up. What I needed, I decided, was to talk to someone who knew Lawrenceton in depth, someone who knew about Carey Osland's husband and the Rideouts' tenant. I'd been assuming the skull came from someone who lived close by, and suddenly I realized I'd better challenge that assumption.

Why had I thought that? There had to be a reason. Okay—Jane couldn't transport a body any distance. I just didn't think she'd been strong enough. But I remembered the hole in the skull and shuddered, feeling distinctly queasy for a moment. She'd been strong enough to do that. Had Jane herself cut off the head? I couldn't even picture it. Granted, Jane's bookshelves, like mine, were full of accounts about people who had done horrible things and gone unsuspected for long periods of time, but I just couldn't admit Jane might be like that. Something wasn't adding up.

It just might be my own dearly held assumptions and preconceptions. Jane, after all, was a Little Old Lady.

I was worn out physically and mentally. It was time to go back to my place. I unseated the cat, to her disgust, and filled her water dish, while making a mental note to call Parnell. I stuffed my car full of things to throw or give away, locked up, and left.

For Christmas, my mother had given me an answering machine, and its light was blinking when I let myself into my kitchen. I leaned against the counter while I punched the button to hear my messages.

"Roe, this is Aubrey. Sorry I didn't catch you in. I'll talk to you later. See you at church tomorrow?"

Ah oh. Tomorrow was Sunday. Maybe I should go to the Episcopal church. But since I didn't always go there, wouldn't it look a little pointed to show up right after I'd had a date with the pastor? On the other hand, here he was inviting me personally, and I'd hurt his feelings if I didn't show . . . oh hell.

"Hi, honey! We're having such a good time John and I decided to stay for a few more days! Stop by the office and make sure everyone's busy, okay? I'll be calling Eileen, but I think it would impress everyone if you went yourself. Talk to you later! Wait till you see my tan!"

Everyone at Mother's office knew that I was strictly an underling, and that I didn't know jack about the real estate business, though it wasn't uninteresting. I just didn't want to work full-time for Mother. Well, I was glad she was having a great time on her second (literally) honeymoon, and I was glad she'd finally taken a vacation of any sort. Eileen Norris, her second-in-command, was probably ready for Mother to come back. Mother's force of character and charm really smoothed things over.

"Roe, this is Robin." I caught my breath and practically hugged the answering machine so I wouldn't miss a word. "I'm leaving tonight for maybe three weeks in Europe, traveling cheap and with no reservations, so I don't know where I'll be when. I won't be working at the university next year. James Artis is over his heart attack. So I'm not sure what I'll be doing. I'll get in touch when I come back. Are you doing okay? How's Arthur?"

"He's married," I said to the machine. "He married someone else."

I rummaged in my junk drawer frantically. "Where's the address book? Where's the damn book?" I muttered. My scrabbling fingers finally found it, I searched through it, got the right page, punched in numbers frantically.

Ring. Ring. "Hello?" a man said.

"Robin?"

"No, this is Phil. I'm subleasing Robin's apartment. He's left for Europe."

"Oh, no," I wailed.

"Can I take a message?" the voice asked, tactfully ignoring my distress.

"So he's going to be coming back to that apartment when he returns? For sure?"

"Yep, his stuff is all here."

"Are you reliable? Can you give him a message in three weeks, or whenever he comes back?"

"I'll try," the voice said with some amusement.

"This is important," I warned him. "To me, anyway."

"Okay, shoot. I've got a pencil and paper right here."

"Tell Robin," I said, thinking as I spoke, "that Roe, R-O-E, is fine."

"Roe is fine," repeated the voice obediently.

"Also say," I continued, "that Arthur married Lynn."

"Okay, got it . . . anything else?"

"No, no thank you. That's all. Just as long as he knows that."

"Well, this is a fresh legal pad, and I've labeled it 'Robin's Messages,' and I'll keep it here by the phone until he comes back," said Phil's voice reassuringly.

"I'm sorry to sound so—well, like I think you'll throw it in the wastebasket—but this is the only way I have to get in touch with him."

"Oh, I understand," said Phil politely. "And really, he will get this."

"Thanks," I said weakly. "I appreciate it."

"Good-bye," said Phil.

"Parnell? This is Aurora Teagarden."

"Oh. Well, what can I do for you?"

"Madeleine showed up at Jane's house today."

"That dang cat! We've been looking for her high and low. We missed her two days ago, and we were feeling real bad, since Jane was so crazy about that durn animal."

"Well, she came home."

"We sure got a problem. She won't stay here, Aurora. We've caught up with her twice when she started off, but we can't keep chasing after her. As a matter of fact, we're leaving town tomorrow for two weeks, going to our summer place at Beaufort, South Carolina, and we were going to check her back in the vet's, just to make sure everything went okay. Though animals mostly take care of themselves."

Take care of themselves? The Engles expected pampered Madeleine to catch her own fish and mice for two weeks?

"Is that right?" I said, letting incredulity drip from my

voice. "No, I expect she can stay at the house for that two weeks. I can feed her when I go over there and empty her litter box."

"Well," said Parnell doubtfully, "her time's almost up."

The cat was dying? Oh my Lord. "That's what the vet said?" I asked in amazement.

"Yes, ma'am," Parnell said, sounding equally amazed.

"She sure looks fat for a cat that sick," I said doubtfully.

I could not understand why Parnell Engle suddenly began laughing. His laugh was a little hoarse and rusty, but it was from the belly.

"Yes, ma'am," he agreed with a little wheeze of joy, "Madeleine is fat for a cat that's so sick."

"I'll keep her then," I said uncertainly.

"Oh, yes, Miss Teagarden, thanks. We'll see you when we come back."

He was still barely controlling his chuckles when he hung up. I put down the receiver and shook my head. There was just no accounting for some people.

Chapter Six

As I retrieved my Sunday paper from my seldom-used front doorstep, I could tell it was already at least 83 degrees. The paper predicted 98 for the day, and I thought its forecast was modest. My central air was already humming. I showered and reluctantly put my hair up in hot curlers, trying to bring order to chaos. I poured my coffee and ate breakfast (a microwaved sweet roll) while I burrowed through the news. I love Sunday mornings, if I get up early enough to really enjoy my paper. Though I have my limits: I will only read the society section if I think my mother will be in it, and I will not read anything about next season's fashions. Amina Day's mom owned a women's clothing shop she had named Great Day, and I pretty much let her tell me what to buy. Under Mrs. Day's influence I'd begun to weed out my librarian clothes, my solid-color interchangeable blouses and skirts. My wardrobe was a bit more diverse now.

The paper exhausted, I padded up the stairs and washed my glasses in the sink. While they dried, I squinted myopically into my closet. What was suitable for the girlfriend of the minister? Long sleeves sounded mandatory, but it was just too hot. I scooted hangers along the bar, humming tunelessly to myself. Shouldn't the girlfriend of the minister be perky but modest? Though perhaps, at nearly thirty, I was a bit old to be perky.

For a dizzying moment I imagined all the clothes I could buy with my inheritance. I had to give myself a little shake to come back to reality and review my wardrobe of the here and now. Here we go! A sleeveless navy blue shirtwaist with big white flowers printed on it. It had a full skirt and a white collar and belt. Just the thing, with my white purse and sandals.

All dressed, with my makeup on, I popped on my glasses and surveyed the result. My hair had calmed down enough to be conventional, and the sandals made my legs look longer. They were hell to walk in, though, and my tolerance time for the high heels would expire right after church.

I walked as quickly as I safely could from my back door across the patio, out the gate in the fence around it, to the car under the long roof that sheltered all tenants' cars. I unlocked the driver's door and flung it open to let the heat blast escape. After a minute I climbed in, and the air conditioner came on one second after the motor. I had worked too hard on my appearance to arrive at the Episcopal church with sweat running down my face.

I accepted a bulletin from an usher and seated myself a carefully calculated distance from the pulpit. The middle-aged couple on the other end of the pew eyed me with open interest and gave me welcoming smiles. I smiled back before becoming immersed in figuring out the hymn and prayer book directions. A loud chord signaled the entrance of the priest, acolyte, lay reader, and choir, and I rose with the rest of the congregation.

Aubrey was just beautiful in his vestments. I drifted into an intoxicating daydream of myself as a minister's wife. It felt very odd to have kissed the man conducting the service. Then I got too involved in managing the prayer book to think about Aubrey for a while. One thing about the Episcopalians, they can't go to sleep during the service unless they're catnappers. You have to get up and down too often, and shake people's hands, and respond, and go up to the altar rail for communion. It's a busy service, not a spectator sport like in some churches. And I believed I had been to every church in Lawrenceton, except maybe one or two of the black ones.

I tried to listen with great attention to Aubrey's sermon, since I would surely have to make an intelligent comment later. To my pleasure, it was an excellent sermon, with some solid points about people's business relationships and how they should conform to religious teachings, too, just as much as personal relationships. And he didn't use a single sports simile! I kept my eyes carefully downcast when I went up to take communion, and tried to think about God rather than Aubrey when he pressed the wafer into my hand.

As we were folding up our kneelers, I saw one of the couples who had spoken to Aubrey while he and I were in line at the movies. They gave me a smile and wave, and huddled to talk to the man and woman with whom I'd been sharing a pew. After that, I was beamed on even more radiantly, and the movie couple introduced me to the pew couple, who asked me about twenty questions as rapidly as they could so they'd have the whole scoop on the pastor's honey.

I felt like I was flying under false colors—we'd only had one date. I began to wish I hadn't come, but Aubrey'd asked me, and I had enjoyed the service. It seemed now I had to pay for it, since there was no quick exit. The crowd had bottlenecked around the church door, shaking hands and exchanging small talk with Aubrey.

"What a good sermon," I told him warmly, when it was finally my turn. My hand was taken in both of his for a moment, pressed and released. A smooth gesture, in one quick turn showing me I was special, yet not presuming too much.

"Thanks, and thanks for coming," he said. "If you're going to be home this afternoon, I'll give you a call."

"If I'm not there, just leave a message on my machine and I'll call you back. I may have to go over to the house."

He understood I meant Jane's house, and nodded, turning to the old lady behind me in line with a happy "Hi, Laura! How's the arthritis?"

Leaving the church parking lot, I felt a distinct letdown. I guess I had hoped Aubrey would ask me to Sunday lunch, a big social event in Lawrenceton. My mother always had me over to lunch when she was home, and I wondered, not for the first time, if she'd still want me to come over when she and John Queensland got back from their honeymoon. John belonged to the country club. He might want to take Mother out there.

I was so dismal by the time I unlocked my back door that I was actually glad to see the message light blinking on the answering machine.

"Hi, Roe. It's Sally Allison. Long time no see, kiddo! Listen, what's this I hear about you inheriting a fortune? Come have lunch with me today if this catches you in time, or give me a call when you can, we'll set up a time."

I opened the phone book to the *A*'s, looked up Sally's number, and punched the right buttons.

"Hello!"

"Sally, I just got your message."

"Great! You free for lunch since your mom is still out of town?"

Sally knew *everything*.

"Well, yes, I am. What do you have in mind?"

"Oh, come on over here. Out of sheer boredom, I have cooked a roast and baked potatoes and made a salad. I want to share it with someone."

Sally was a woman on her own, like me. But she was divorced, and a good fifteen years older.

"Be there in twenty minutes, I need to change. My feet are killing me."

"Well, wear whatever you see when you open your closet. I have on my oldest shorts."

"Okay, bye."

I shucked off the blue-and-white dress and those painful sandals. I pulled on olive drab shorts and a jungle print blouse and my huaraches and pounded back down the stairs. I made it to Sally's in the twenty minutes.

Sally is a newspaper reporter, the veteran of an early runaway marriage that left her with a son to raise and a reputation to make. She was a good reporter, and she'd hoped (a little over a year ago) that reporting the multiple murders in Lawrenceton would net her a better job offer from Atlanta; but it hadn't happened. Sally was insatiably curious and knew everyone in town, and everyone knew that, to get the straight story on anything, Sally was the person to see. We'd had our ups and downs as friends, the ups having been when we were both members of Real Murders, the downs having mostly been at the same time Sally was trying to make a national, or at least regional, name for herself. She'd sacrificed a lot in that bid for a life in the bigger picture, and, when the bid hadn't been taken up, she'd had a hard time. But now Sally was mending her fences locally, and was as plugged in to the Lawrenceton power system as she ever had been. If her stories being picked up by the wire services hadn't gotten her out of the town, it had certainly added to her power in it.

I had always seen Sally very well dressed, in expensive suits and shoes that lasted her a very long time. When I reached her house, I saw Sally was a woman who put her money on her back, as the saying goes. She had a little place not quite as nice as Jane's, in a neighborhood where the lawns weren't kept as well. Her car, which hadn't been washed in weeks, sat in dusty splendor uncovered by carport or garage. Getting in it would be like climbing in an oven. But the house itself was cool enough, no central air but several window air conditioners sending out an icy stream that almost froze the sweat on my forehead.

Sally's hair was as perfect as ever. It looked like it could be taken off and put on without one bronze curl being dislodged. But instead of her usual classic suits, Sally was wearing a pair of cutoffs and an old work shirt.

"Girl, it's hot!" she exclaimed as she let me in. "I'm glad I don't have to work today."

"It's a good day to stay inside," I agreed, looking around me curiously. I'd never been in Sally's house before. It was obvious she didn't give a damn about decor. The couch and armchairs were covered by throws that looked very unfortunate, and the cheap coffee table had rings on top. My resident manager's eye told me that the whole place needed painting. But the bookcase was wonderfully stuffed with Sally's favorite Organized Crime books, and the smell coming from the kitchen was delicious. My mouth watered.

Of course I was going to have to pay for my dinner with information, but it just might be worth it.

"Boy, that smells good! When's it going to be on the table?"

"I'm making the gravy now. Come on back and talk to me while I stir. Want a beer? I've got some ice cold."

"Sure, I'll take one. It's the 'ice cold' that does it."

"Here, drink some ice water first for your thirst. Then sip the beer for your pleasure."

I gulped down the glass of ice water and twisted the cap off the beer. Sally had put out one of those round plastic grippers without my even having to ask. I closed my eyes to appreciate the beer going down my throat. I don't drink beer any other time of the year, but summer in the South is what beer was made for. Very cold beer. "Ooo," I murmured blissfully.

"I know. If I didn't watch out, I could drink a whole sixpack while I cooked."

"Can I set the table or anything?"

"No, I already got everything done, I think. Soon as this gravy is ready—whoa, let me look at the biscuits—yep, they're nice and brown—we'll be ready to eat. Did I get the butter out?"

I scanned the table, which at least was a few feet from the stove. Sally must have been burning up over there.

"It's here," I reassured her.

"Okay, here we go. Roast, biscuits, baked potatoes, a salad, and for dessert"—Sally took off a cake cover with a flourish—"red velvet cake!"

"Sally, you're inspired. I haven't had red velvet cake in ten years."

"My mama's recipe."

"Those are always the best. You're so smart." A good southern compliment that could mean almost anything, but this time I meant it quite sincerely. I am not a person who often cooks whole meals for herself. I know single people are supposed to cook full meals, lay the table, and act like they had company, really—but how many single people actually do it? Like Sally, when I cook a big meal, I want someone else to appreciate it and enjoy it.

"So, what's this about you and the man of the cloth?"

Closing in for the kill already. "Sally, you need to wait till I've eaten something," I said. Was the roast worth it?

"What?"

"Oh Sally, it's really nothing. I've had one date with Aubrey Scott, we went to the movies. We had a nice time, and he asked me to come to the church today, which I did."

"Did you now? How was the sermon?"

"Real good. He's got brains, no doubt about it."

"You like him?"

"Yes, I like him, but that's it. What about you, Sally, are you dating anyone in particular?"

Sally was always so busy asking other people questions, she hardly ever got asked any herself. She looked quite pleased.

"Well, since you ask, I am."

"Do tell."

"This is gonna sound funny, but I'm dating Paul Allison."

"Your husband's brother?"

"Yes, that Paul Allison," she said, shaking her head in amazement at her own folly.

"You take my breath away." Paul Allison was a policeman, a detective about ten years older than Arthur—not much liked by Arthur or Lynn, if I remembered correctly. Paul was a loner, a man never married who did not join in the police force camaraderie with much gusto. He had thinning brown hair, broad shoulders, sharp blue eyes, and a suggestion of a gut. I had seen him at many parties I'd attended while I dated Arthur, but I'd never seen him with Sally.

"How long has this been going on?" I asked.

"About five months. We were at Arthur and Lynn's wedding, I tried to catch you then, but you left the church before I could. I didn't see you at the reception?"

"I had the worst headache. I thought I was starting the flu. I just went on home."

"Oh, it was just another wedding reception. Jack Burns had too much to drink and wanted to arrest one of the waiters he remembered having brought in before on drug charges."

I was even more glad I'd missed it now.

"How's Perry?" I asked reluctantly, after a pause. I was sorry to bring poor, sick Perry up, but courtesy demanded it.

"Thanks for asking," she said. "So many people don't even want to, because he's mentally sick instead of having cancer or something. But I do want people to ask, and I go see him every week. I don't want people to forget he's alive. Really, Roe, people act like Perry's dead because he's mentally ill."

"I'm sorry, Sally."

"Well, I do appreciate your asking. He's better, but he's not ready to get out yet. Maybe in two more months. Paul's been going with me to see Perry the past three or four times."

"He must really love you, Sally," I said from my heart.

"You know," she said, and her face brightened, "I really

think he does! Bring your plate over, I think everything's ready."

We served ourselves from the stove, which was fine with me. Back at the table, we buttered our biscuits and said our little prayer, and dug in like we were starving.

"I guess," I began after I had told Sally how good everything was, "that you want to hear about Jane's house."

"Am I as transparent as all that? Well, I did hear something, you know how gossip gets around, and I thought you would rather me ask you and get it straight than let all this talk around town get out of hand."

"You know, you're right. I would rather you get it right and get it out on the gossip circuits. I wonder who's started the talk?"

"Uh, well. . . ."

"Parnell and Leah Engle," I guessed suddenly.

"Right the first time."

"Okay, Sally. I am going to give you a gossip exclusive. There's no way this could be a story in the paper, but you see everyone in town, and you can give them the straight scoop from the horse's mouth."

"I am all ears," Sally said with a perfectly straight face.

So I told her an amended and edited account. Leaving out the cash amount, of course.

"Her savings, too?" Sally said enviously. "Oh, you lucky duck. And it's a lot?"

Glee rolled over me suddenly as it did every now and then when I forgot the skull and remembered the money. I nodded with a canary-full grin.

Sally closed her eyes in contemplation of the joy of having a lot of money all of a sudden.

"That's great," she said dreamily. "I feel good just knowing someone that's *happened* to. Like winning the lottery."

"Yeah, except Jane had to die for me to get it."

"My God, girl, she was old as the hills anyway."

"Oh, Sally, Jane wasn't so old as people go nowadays. She was in her seventies."

"That is plenty old. I won't last so long."

"I hope you do," I said mildly. "I want you to make me some more biscuits sometime."

We talked some more about Paul Allison, which seemed to make Sally quite happy. Then I asked her about Macon Turner, her boss.

"I understand he's seeing my new maybe-neighbor, Carey Osland," I said casually.

"They are hot and heavy and have been," Sally said, with a wise nod. "That Carey is really appealing to the opposite sex. She has had quite a dating—and marriage—history."

I understood Sally exactly. "Really?"

"Oh, yes. First she was married to Bubba Sewell, back when he was nothing, just a little lawyer right out of school. Then that fell through, and she married Mike Osland, and by golly one night he goes out to get diapers and never comes home. Everyone felt so sorry for her when her husband left, and, having been in something of the same position, I did feel for her. But at the same time, I think he might have had some reason to take off."

My attention sharpened. A number of instant scenarios

ran through my head. Carey's husband kills Carey's lover, then flees. The lover could have been Mark Kaplan, the Rideouts' vanished tenant, or some unknown. Or maybe Mike Osland could be the skull, reduced to that state by Carey's lover or Carey.

"But she has a little girl at home," I said in the interest of fairness.

"Wonder what she tells that little girl when she has overnight company?" Sally helped herself to more roast.

I disliked this turn of the conversation. "Well, she was very nice to me when she came over to welcome me to the neighborhood," I stated, flatly enough to end that line of conversation. Sally shot me a look and asked if I wanted more roast.

"No thanks," I said, giving a sigh of repletion. "That was so good."

"Macon really has been more agreeable at the office since he began dating Carey," Sally said abruptly. "He started seeing her after his son went away, and it just helped him deal with it a lot. Maybe Carey having some-body leave her, she was able to help Macon out."

"What son?" I didn't remember Mother mentioning any son during the time she'd dated Macon.

"He has a boy in his late teens or early twenties by now, I guess. Macon moved here after he got divorced, and the boy moved here with him, maybe seven years ago now. After a few months, the boy—his name was Edward, I think—anyway, he decided he was just going to take some savings his mother had given him and take off. He told Macon he was going to India or some such place, to contemplate or buy drugs or something. Some crazy thing. Of course, Macon was real depressed, but he couldn't stop him. The boy wrote for a while, or called, once a month . . . but then he stopped. And Macon hasn't seen hide nor hair of that child since then."

"That's terrible," I said, horrified. "Wonder what happened to the boy?"

Sally shook her head pessimistically. "No telling what could happen to him wandering by himself in a country where he didn't even speak the language."

Poor Macon. "Did he go over there?"

"He talked about it for a while, but when he wrote the State Department they advised him against it. He didn't even know where Edward had been when he disappeared . . . Edward could have wandered anywhere after he wrote the last letter Macon got. I remember someone from the embassy there went to the last place Edward wrote from and, according to what they told Macon, it was sort of a dive with lots of Europeans coming and going, and no one there remembered Edward, or at least that's what they were saying."

"That's awful, Sally."

"Sure is. I think Perry being in the mental hospital is better than that, I really do. At least I know where he is!"

Incontrovertible truth.

I stared into my beer bottle. Now I'd heard of one more missing person. Was a part of Edward Turner's last remains in my mother's pink blanket bag? Since Macon told everyone he'd heard from the boy since Edward had left, Macon would have to be the guilty one. That sounded like the end of a soap opera. "Tune in tomorrow for the next install-ment," I murmured.

"It is like a soap," Sally agreed. "But tragic."

I began my going-away noises. The food had been great, the company at least interesting and sometimes actually fun. Sally and I parted this time fairly pleased with each other.

After I left Sally's I remembered I had to check on Madeleine. I stopped at a grocery and got some cat food and another bag of cat litter. Then I realized this looked like permanency, rather than a two-week stay while the Engles vacationed in South Carolina.

I seemed to have a pet.

I was actually looking forward to seeing the animal.

I unlocked the kitchen door at Jane's with my free hand, the other one being occupied in holding the bags from the grocery. "Madeleine?" I called. No golden purring dictator came to meet me. "Madeleine?" I said less certainly.

Could she have gotten out? The backyard door was locked, the windows still shut. I looked in the guest bed-room, since the break-in had occurred there, but the new window was still intact.

"Kitty?" I said forlornly. And then it seemed to me I heard a noise. Dreading I don't know what, I inched into Jane's bedroom. I heard the strange mew again. Had some-one hurt the cat? I began shaking, I was so sure I would find a horror. I'd left the door to Jane's closet ajar, and I could tell the sound was coming from there. I pulled the door open wide, with my breath sucked in and my teeth clenched tight.

Madeleine, apparently intact, was curled up on Jane's old bathrobe, which had fallen to the bottom of the closet when I was packing clothes. She was lying on her side, her muscles rippling as she strained.

Madeleine was having kittens.

"Oh *hell*," I said. "Oh—hell hell hell." I slumped on the bed despondently. Madeleine spared me a golden glare and went back to work. "Why me, Lord?" I asked self-pityingly. Though I had to concede it looked like Madeleine would be saying the same thing if she could. Actually, this was rather interesting. Would Madeleine mind if I watched? Apparently not, because she didn't hiss or claw at me when I sat on the floor just outside the closet and kept her company.

Of course Parnell Engle had been fully aware of Madeleine's impending motherhood, hence his merriment when I'd told him Madeleine could stay with me.

I pondered that for a few seconds, trying to decide if Parnell and I were even now. Maybe so, for Madeleine had had three kittens already, and there seemed to be more on the way.

I kept telling myself this was the miracle of birth. It sure was messy. Madeleine had my complete sympathy. She gave a final heave, and out popped another tiny, slimy kitten. I hoped two things: that this was the last kitten and that Madeleine didn't run into any difficulties, because I was the last person in the world who could offer her any help. After a few minutes, I began to think both my hopes had been fulfilled. Madeleine cleaned the little things, and all four lay there, occasionally making tiny movements, eyes shut, about as defenseless as anything could be.

Madeleine looked at me with the weary superiority of someone who has bravely undergone a major milestone. I wondered if she were thirsty; I got her water bowl and put it near her, and her food bowl, too. She got up after a moment and took a drink but didn't seem too interested in her food. She settled back down with her babies and looked perfectly all right, so I left her and went to sit in the living room. I stared at the bookshelves and wondered what in hell I would do with four kittens. On a shelf separate from those holding all the fictional and nonfictional murders, I saw several books about cats. Maybe that was what I should dip into next.

Right above the cat shelf was Jane's collection of books about Madeleine Smith, the Scottish poisoner, Jane's favorite. All of us former members of Real Murders had a favorite or two. My mother's new husband was a Lizzie Borden expert. I tended to favor Jack the Ripper, though I had by no means attained the status of Ripperologist.

But Jane Engle had always been a Madeleine Smith buff. Madeleine had been released after her trial after receiving the Scottish verdict "Not Proven," wonderfully accurate. She had almost certainly poisoned her perfidious former lover, a clerk, so she could marry into her own respectable upper-middle-class milieu without the clerk's revealing their physical intimacy. Poison was a curiously secret kind of revenge; the hapless L'Angelier had deceived himself that he was dealing with an average girl of the time, though the ardency of her physical expressions of love should have proved to him that Madeleine had a deep vein of passion. That passion extended to keeping her name clean and her reputation intact. L'Angelier threatened to send Madeleine's explicit love letters to her father. Madeleine pretended to effect a reconciliation, then slipped arsenic into L'Angelier's cup of chocolate.

For lack of anything better to do, I pulled out one of the Smith books and began to flip through it. It fell open right away. There was a yellow Post-it note stuck to the top of the page.

It said, in Jane's handwriting, *I didn't do it.*

Chapter Seven

I didn't do it.

The first thing I felt was overwhelming relief. Jane, who had left me so much, had not left me holding the bag, so to speak, on a murder she herself had committed.

She *had* left me in the position of concealing the murder someone else had committed, a murder Jane also had concealed, for reasons I could not fathom.

I had believed the only question I had to answer was whose skull? Now I had also to find out who put the hole in that skull.

Was my situation really any better? No, I decided after some consideration. My conscience weighed perhaps an ounce less. The question of going to the police took on a different slant now that I would not be accusing Jane of murder by taking in the skull. But she'd had something to do with it. Oh, what a mess!

Not for the first (or the last) time, I wished I could have five minutes' conversation with Jane Engle, my benefactress and my burden. I tried to think of the money, to cheer myself up; I reminded myself that the will was a little closer to probate now, I'd be able to actually spend some without consulting Bubba Sewell beforehand.

And, to tell you the truth, I still felt excellent about that money. I had read so many mysteries in which the private detective had sent back his retainer check because the payer was immoral or the job he was hired to do turned out to be against his code of honor. Jane wanted me to have that money to have fun with, and she wanted me to remember her. Well, here I was remembering her every single day, by golly, and I certainly intended to have fun. In the meantime, I had a problem to solve.

It seemed to me that Bubba knew something about this. Could I retain him as my lawyer and ask him what to do? Wouldn't attorney-client privilege cover my admission I'd located and rehidden the skull? Or would Bubba, as an officer of the court, be obliged to disclose my little lapse? I'd read a lot of mysteries that had probably contained this information, but now they all ran together in my head. The laws probably varied from state to state, too.

I could tell Aubrey, surely? Would he be obligated to tell the police? Would he have any practical advice to offer? I was pretty confident I knew what his moral advice would be; the skull should go into the police station now, today, pronto. I was concealing the death of someone who had been dead and missing for over three years, at a minimum. Someone, somewhere, needed to know this person had died. What if this was Macon Turner's son? Macon had been wanting to know the whereabouts of his son for a long time, had been searching for him; if there was even a faint chance his son's letters to him had been forged, it was inhumane to keep this knowledge from Macon.

Unless Macon had caused the hole in the skull.

Carey Osland had believed all these years her husband had walked out on her. She should know he had been prevented from returning home with those diapers.

Unless Carey herself had prevented him.

Marcia and Torrance Rideout needed to know their tenant had not voluntarily skipped out on his rent.

Unless they themselves had canceled his lease.

I jumped to my feet and went into the kitchen to fix myself—something. Anything. Of course, all that was there was canned stuff and unopened packages. I ended up with a jar of peanut butter and a spoon. I stuck the spoon in the jar and stood at the counter licking the peanut butter off.

Murderers needed to be exposed, truth needed to see the light of day. Et cetera. Then I had another thought: whoever had broken into this house, searching for the skull, had been the murderer.

I shivered. Not nice to think.

And even now, that little thought trickled onward, that murderer was wondering if I'd found the skull yet, what I'd do with it.

"This is bad," I muttered. "Really, really bad."

That was constructive thinking.

Start at ground zero.

Okay. Jane had seen a murder, or maybe someone burying a body. For her to get the skull, she had to know the body was there, right? Jane literally knew where the bodies were buried. I actually caught myself smiling at my little joke.

Why would she not tell the police immediately?

No *answer.*

Why would she take the skull?

No *answer.*

Why would anyone pick Jane's demise as the time to look for the skull, when she'd obviously had it for years?

Possible answer: the murderer did not know for sure that Jane was the person who had the skull.

I imagined someone who had committed a terrible crime in the throes of who knew what passion or pressure. After hiding the body somewhere, suddenly this murderer finds that the skull is gone, the skull with its telltale hole, the skull with its identifiable teeth. Someone has taken the trouble to dig it up and take it away, and the killer doesn't know who.

How horrible. I could almost pity the murderer. What fear, what terror, what dreadful uncertainty.

I shook myself. I should be feeling sorry for the skull, as I thought of it.

Where could Jane have seen a murder?

Her own backyard. She had had to know where the body was buried exactly; she had had to have leisure to dig without interruption or discovery, presumably; she could not have carted a skull any distance. My reasoning of a few days before was still valid, whether or not Jane was the murderer. The murder had happened on this street, in one of these houses, somewhere where Jane could see it.

So I went out in the backyard and looked.

I found myself staring at the two cement benches flanking the birdbath. Jane had been fond of sitting there in the evenings, I recalled her saying. Sometimes the birds had perched on the bath while she sat there, she could sit so still, she had told me proudly. I did wonder if Madeleine had been outside with Jane enjoying this, and dismissed the thought as unworthy. Jane had been many things—I seemed to be finding more and more things she'd been every day—but she hadn't been an out-and-out sadist.

I sat on one of the cement benches with my back to Carey Osland's house. I could see almost all the Rideouts' sun deck clearly, of course: no Marcia in red there today. I could see their old garden plot and some clear lawn. The very rear of their yard was obscured by the bushes in my own yard. Beyond the Rideouts' I could discern one little section of Macon Turner's, which had lots of large bushes and rather high grass. I would have to come out here at night, I thought, to find if I could see through the windows of any of these houses.

It was hot, and I was full of roast beef and peanut butter. I slid into a trance, mentally moving people around their backyards, in various murderous postures.

"What you doing?" asked a voice behind me curiously.

I gasped and jumped.

A little girl stood behind me. She was maybe seven or eight or even a little older, and she was wearing shorts and a pink T-shirt. She had chin-length, wavy, dark hair and big dark eyes and glasses.

"I'm sitting," I said tensely. "What are you doing?"

"My mom sent me over to ask you if you could come drink some coffee with her."

"Who's your mom?"

Now that was funny, someone not knowing who her mom was.

"Carey Osland." She giggled. "In that house right there," she pointed, obviously believing she was dealing with a mentally deficient person.

The Osland backyard was almost bare of bushes or any concealment at all. There was a swing set and a sandbox; I could see the street to the other side of the house easily.

This was the child who had needed diapers the night her father left the house and never returned.

"Yes, I'll come," I said. "What's your name?"

"Linda. Well, come on."

So I followed Linda Osland over to her mother's house, wondering what Carey had to say.

Carey, I decided after a while, had just been being hospitable.

She'd gone the afternoon before to pick up Linda from camp, had spent Sunday morning washing Linda's shorts and shirts, which had been indescribably filthy, had listened to all Linda's camp stories, and now was ready for some adult companionship. Macon, she told me, was out playing golf at the country club. She said it like she had a right to know his whereabouts at all times and like other people should realize that. So, if their relationship had had its clandestine moments, it was moving out into the open. I noticed that she didn't say anything about their getting married, and didn't hint that was in the future.

Maybe they were happy just like they were.

It would be a great thing, not to want to get married. I sighed, I hoped imperceptibly, and asked Carey about Jane.

"I feel myself wanting to get to know her better now," I said, with a what-can-you-do? shrug.

"Well, Jane was a different kettle of fish," Carey said, with a lift of her dark brows.

"She was an old meanie," Linda said suddenly. She'd been sitting at the table cutting out paper doll clothes.

"Linda," her mother admonished, without any real scolding in her voice.

"Well, remember, Mama, how mad she got at Burger King!"

I tried to look politely baffled.

Carey's pretty, round face looked a little peeved for just a second. "More coffee?" she asked.

"Yes, thanks," I said, to gain more time before I had to go.

Carey poured and showed no sign of explaining Linda's little remark.

"Jane was a difficult neighbor?" I asked tentatively.

"Oh." Carey sighed with pursed lips. "I wish Linda hadn't brought that up. Honey, you got to learn to forget unpleasant things and old fights, it doesn't pay to remember stuff like that."

Linda nodded obediently and went back to her scissors.

"Burger King was our dog; Linda named him of course," Carey explained reluctantly. "We didn't keep him on a leash, I know we should have, and of course our backyard isn't fenced in . . ."

I nodded encouragingly.

"Naturally, he eventually got run over. I'm ashamed of us even having an outside dog without having a fence," Carey confessed, shaking her head at her own negligence. "But Linda did want a pet, and she's allergic to cats."

"I sneeze and my eyes get red," Linda explained.

"Yes, honey. Of course, we had the dog when Jane had just gotten her cat, and of course Burger King chased Madeleine every time Jane let her out, which wasn't too often, but every now and then . . ." Carey lost her thread.

"The dog treed the cat?" I suggested helpfully.

"Oh yes, and barked and barked," Carey said ruefully. "It was a mess. And Jane got so mad about it."

"She said she would call the pound," Linda chimed in. "Because there's a leash law and we were breaking it."

"Well, honey, she was right," Carey said. "We were."

"She didn't have to be so mean about it," Linda insisted.

"She was a little shirty," Carey said confidentially to me. "I mean, I know I was at fault, but she really went off the deep end."

"Oh dear," I murmured.

"I'm surprised Linda remembers any of this because it was a long time ago. Years, I guess."

"So did Jane end up calling the animal control people?"

"No, no. Poor Burger got hit by a car over on Faith, right

here to the side of the house, very soon after that. So now we have Waldo here"—and the tip of her slipper poked the dachshund affectionately—"and we walk him three or four times a day. It's not much of a life for him, but it's the best we can do."

Waldo snored contentedly.

"Speaking of Madeleine, she came home," I told Carey.

"She did! I thought Parnell and Leah picked her up from the vet's where she'd been boarded while Jane was sick?"

"Well, they did, but Madeleine wanted to be at her own house. As it turns out, she was expecting."

Linda and Carey both exclaimed over that, and I regretted telling them after a moment, because of course Linda wanted to see the little kitties and her mother did not want the child to cough and weep all afternoon.

"I'm sorry, Carey," I said as I took my leave.

"Don't worry about it," Carey insisted, though I was sure she wished I had kept my mouth shut. "It's just one of those things Linda has to learn to live with. I sure hope someday I can afford to fence the backyard; I'll get her a Scottie puppie, I swear I will. A friend of mine raises them, and those are the cutest puppies in the world. Like little walking shoe brushes."

I considered the cute factor of walking shoe brushes as I went through Carey's backyard to my own. Carey's yard was so open to view it was hard to imagine where a body could have been buried on her property, but I couldn't exclude Carey either; her yard might not have been so bare a few years before.

I could be rid of all this by getting in my car and driving

to the police station, I reminded myself. And for a moment I was powerfully tempted.

And I'll tell you what stopped me: not loyalty to Jane, not keeping faith with the dead; nothing so noble. It was my fear of Sergeant Jack Burns, the terrifying head of the detectives. The sergeant, I had observed in my previous contacts with him, burned for truth the way other men burn for a promotion or a night with Michelle Pfeiffer.

He wouldn't be happy with me.

He would want to nail me to the wall.

I would keep the skull a secret a little longer.

Maybe somehow I could wriggle out of this with a clear conscience. That didn't seem possible at this moment, but then it hadn't seemed possible someone would die and leave me a fortune, either.

I went in to check on Madeleine. She was nursing her kittens and looking smug and tired at the same time. I refilled her water bowl. I started to move her litter box into the room with her, but then I reconsidered. Best to leave it in the place she was used to going.

"Just think," I told the cat, "a week ago, I had no idea that soon I'd have a cat, four kittens, a house, five hundred and fifty thousand dollars, and a skull. I didn't know what I was missing."

The doorbell rang.

I jumped maybe a mile. Thanks to Jane's cryptic note, I now knew I had something to fear.

"Be back in a minute, Madeleine," I said, to reassure myself rather than the cat.

This time, instead of opening the door, I looked through

Jane's spyhole. When I saw lots of black, I knew my caller was Aubrey. I was smiling as I opened the door.

"Come in."

"I just thought I'd drop by and see the new house," he said hesitantly. "Is that okay?"

"Sure. I just found out today I have kittens. Come see them."

And I led Aubrey into the bedroom, telling him Madeleine's saga as we went.

The proximity of the bed startled him a little, but the kittens entranced him.

"Want one?" I asked. "It occurs to me I'll have to find homes for all of them in a few weeks. I'll have to call a vet and find out when they can be separated from her. And when I can have her neutered."

"You're not going to take her back to Jane's cousin?" Aubrey asked, looking a little amused.

"No," I said without even thinking about it. "I'll see how I like living with a pet. She seems pretty attached to this house."

"Maybe I will take one," Aubrey said thoughtfully. "My little house can get lonely. Having a cat to come home to might be pretty nice. I do get asked out a lot. That's where I've been since church, as a matter of fact; a family in the church asked me to their home for lunch."

"I bet it wasn't as good as my lunch." I told him about Sally's roast beef, and he said he'd had turkey, and we ended up sitting by the kittens talking about food for a while. He didn't cook for himself much, either.

And the doorbell rang.

We had been getting along so cozily, I had to resist an impulse to say something very nasty.

I left him in the bedroom staring at the kittens, all asleep and tiny, while I scrambled into the living room and opened the door.

Marcia Rideout, wide awake and gorgeous in white cotton shorts and a bright red camp shirt, smiled back at me. She certainly wasn't drunk now; she was alert and cheerful.

"Good to see you again," she said with a smile.

I marveled again at her perfect grooming. Her lipstick was almost professionally applied, her eye shadow subtle but noticeable, her hair evenly golden and smoothly combed into a page boy. Her legs were hairless and beautifully brown. Even her white tennis shoes were spotless.

"Hi, Marcia," I said quickly, having become aware I was staring at her like a guppy.

"I'll just take a minute of your time," she promised. She handed me a little envelope. "Torrance and I just want to give a little party on our sun deck this Wednesday to welcome you into the neighborhood."

"Oh, but I—" I began to protest.

"No no, now. We wanted to have a little cookout anyway, but your inheriting the house just makes a good excuse. And we have new neighbors across the street, too, they're going to come. We'll all get to know each other. I know this is short notice, but Torrance has to travel this Friday and won't be back until late on Saturday." Marcia seemed like a different person from the indolent drunk I'd met a few days before. The prospect of entertaining seemed to bring her to life.

How could I refuse? The idea of being honored at the same party with Lynn and Arthur was less than thrilling, but refusal would be unthinkable, too.

"Do bring a date if you want, or just come on your own," Marcia said.

"You really won't mind if I bring someone?"

"Please do! One more won't make a bit of difference. Got anyone in mind?" Marcia asked, her brows arched coyly.

"Yes," I said with a smile, and said no more. I was just hoping with all my might that Aubrey would not choose this moment to emerge from the bedroom. I could picture Marcia's eyebrows flying clean off her face.

"Oh," Marcia said, obviously a little taken aback by my marked lack of explanation. "Yes, that'll be fine. Just come as you are, we won't be fancy, that's not Torrance and me!"

Marcia seemed very fancy indeed to me.

"Can I bring anything?"

"Just yourself," Marcia responded, as I'd expected. I realized that the party preparations would keep her excited and happy for the next three days.

"I'll see you then," she called as she bounced down the steps and started back over to her house.

I took the little invitation with me when I went back to Aubrey.

"Could you go to this with me?" I asked, handing it to him. I thought if he turned me down I was going to be horribly embarrassed, but I had no one else to ask, and if I was going to a party with Arthur and Lynn present, I was damn sure going to have a date.

He pulled the invitation out and read it. It had a chef on

the front wearing a barbecue apron and holding a long fork. "Something good is on the grill!" exclaimed the print. When you opened it, it said, ". . . and you can share it with us on *Wednesday, 7:00* at *Marcia and Torrance's* house. See you then!"

"A little on the hearty side," I said, as neutrally as I could. I didn't want to seem uncharitable.

"I'm sure I can, but let me check." Aubrey pulled a little black notebook out of his pocket. "The liturgical calendar," he explained. "I think every Episcopalian priest carries one of these." He flipped through the pages, then beamed up at me. "Sure, I can go." I blew out a sigh of sheer relief. Aubrey produced a little pencil in disgraceful shape and wrote in the time and address, and, to my amusement, "Pick up Aurora." Would he forget me otherwise?

Stuffing the book back into his pocket, he got to his feet and told me he'd better be going. "I have youth group in an hour," he said, checking his watch.

"What do you do with them?" I asked as I walked him to the door.

"Try to make them feel okay about not being Baptists and having a big recreation center to go to, mostly. We go in with the Lutherans and the Presbyterians, taking turns to have the young people on Sunday evening. And it's my church's turn."

At least it was too early in our relationship for me to feel at all obliged to take part in that.

Aubrey opened the door to leave, then seemed to remember something he'd forgotten. He bent over to give me a kiss, his arm loosely around my shoulders. There was no doubt this time about the jolt I felt clear down to the soles of my feet. When he straightened up, he looked a little energized himself.

"Well!" he said breathlessly. "I'll give you a call this week, and I look forward to Wednesday night."

"Me, too," I said with a smile, and saw past his shoulder the curtains in the house across the way stir.

Ha! I thought maturely, as I shut the door behind Aubrey.

Chapter Eight

M onday turned out to be a much busier day than I'd
expected. When I went in to work to put in what I
thought would be four hours, I found that one of the other
librarians had caught a summer cold ("The worst kind," all
the other librarians said wisely, shaking their heads. I thought
any cold was the worst kind). The head of the library, Sam
Clerrick, asked if I'd put in eight hours instead, and after a
little hesitation I agreed. I felt very gracious, because now I
had it within my financial power (well, almost within my
financial power) to quit my job completely. There's nothing
like patting yourself on the back to give you energy; I worked
happily all morning, reading to a circle of preschoolers and
answering questions.

I did feel justified in taking a few extra minutes on my

coffee break to call the phone company and ask them if the number I had at the town house could also be the number for Jane's house, at least for a while. Even if that wasn't possible, I wanted Jane's phone hooked back up. To my pleasure, it was possible to get my number to ring at Jane's, and I was assured it would be operational within the next couple of days.

As I was hanging up, Lillian Schmidt lumbered in. Lillian is one of those disagreeable people who yet have some redeeming qualities, so that you can't write them off entirely—but you sure wish you could. Furthermore, I worked with Lillian, so it was in my interest to keep peace with her. Lillian was narrow-minded and gossipy, but fair; she was a devoted wife and mother, but talked about her husband and daughter until you wanted them to be swallowed up in an earthquake; she knew her job and did it competently, but with so much groaning and complaining about minute details that you wanted to smack her. Reacting to Lillian, I sounded like a wild-eyed Communist, an incurable Polyanna, and a free-sex advocate.

"It's so hot outside, I feel like I need another shower," she said by way of greeting. Her forehead was beaded with perspiration. She pulled a tissue from the box on the coffee table and dabbed at her face.

"I hear you had a windfall," she continued, tossing the tissue into the trash and missing. With a deep sigh, Lillian laboriously bent over to retrieve it. But her eyes flicked up to take in my reaction.

"Yes," I said with a bright smile.

Lillian waited for me to elaborate. She eyed me wryly when I didn't say anything. "I didn't know you and Jane Engle were such good friends."

I considered several possible responses, smiling all the while. "We were friends."

Lillian shook her head slowly. "I was a friend of Jane's, too, but she didn't leave me any house."

What could I say to that? I shrugged. If Jane and Lillian had had any special personal relationship, I certainly couldn't recall it.

"Did you know," Lillian continued, switching to another track, "that Bubba Sewell is going to run for state representative in the fall?"

"Is he really." It wasn't a question.

Lillian saw that she'd made an impression. "Yes, his secretary is my sister-in-law, so she told me even before the announcement, which is tomorrow. I knew you'd be interested since I saw you talking to him at Jane's funeral. He's trying to get his house in order, so to speak, so he doesn't want even a whiff of anything funny that might be dug up during the campaign. He's going to be running against Carl Underwood, and Carl's had that seat for three terms."

Lillian had gotten to give me information I hadn't possessed, and that had made her happy. After a couple more complaints about the school system's insensitivity to her daughter's allergies, she stumped off to actually do some work.

I remained seated on the hard chair in the tiny coffee-break room, thinking hard about Bubba Sewell. No wonder he hadn't wanted to know what was fishy in Jane's house! No wonder he had catered to her so extensively. It was good word of mouth for him, that he would go to such lengths for his elderly client, especially since he wasn't gaining anything from her will—except a fat fee for handling it.

If I told Bubba Sewell about the skull he'd hate me for the rest of his life. And he was Carey Osland's first husband; maybe somehow he was involved in the disappearance of Carey's second husband?

As I washed my mug in the little sink and set it in the drainer, I dismissed any urge I'd ever felt to confide in the lawyer. He was running for office; he was ambitious; he couldn't be trusted. A pretty grim summation for someone who might be my elected representative in the statehouse. I sighed, and started for the check-in desk to shelve the returned books.

On my lunch hour, I ran over to the house on Honor to let the cat out and check on the kittens. I picked up a hamburger and drink at a drive-through.

When I turned off Faith I saw a city work crew cleaning the honeysuckle and poison ivy from around the DEAD END sign at the end of the street. It would take them hours. Vines and weeds had taken over the little area and had obviously been thriving for years, twining around the sign itself and then attaching to the rear fence of the house backing onto the end of our street. The city truck was parked right in the middle of the road down by Macon Turner's house.

For the first time since I'd inherited Jane's house, I saw the newspaper editor himself, perhaps also returning to his home for lunch. Macon's thinning, brownish-gray hair was long and combed across the top of his head to give his scalp some coverage. He had an intelligent face, thin lipped and sharp, and wore suits that always seemed to need to go to the cleaners; in fact, Macon always gave the impression that he did not know how to take care of himself. His hair always needed trimming, his clothes needed ironing, he usually seemed tired, and he was always one step behind his schedule. He called to me now as he pulled letters out of his mailbox, giving me a smile that held a heavy dose of charm. Macon was the only man my mother had ever dated that I personally found attractive.

I waited, standing in the driveway with my little paper bag of lunch in one hand and my house keys in the other, while Macon walked over. His tie was crooked, and he was carrying his suit coat, a lightweight khaki, almost dragging the ground. I wondered if Carey Osland, whose house was not exactly a model of neatness, realized what she was taking on.

"Good to see you, Roe! How's your mother and her new husband?" Macon called before he was quite close enough. The cleanup crew, two young black men being watched by an older one, turned their heads to cast us a glance.

It was one of those moments that you always remember for no apparent reason. It was dreadfully hot, the sun brilliant in a cloudless sky. The three workmen had huge, dark stains on their shirts, and one of the younger men had a red bandanna over his head. The ancient city dump truck was painted dark orange. Condensation from the cup containing my soft drink was making a wet blotch on the paper bag; I worried that the bag would break. I was feeling glad to see Macon, but also impatient to get inside the cool house and eat lunch and check on Madeleine's brood. I felt a trickle of sweat start up under my green-and-white-striped dress, felt it roll its ticklish way down under my belt to my hips. I looped my purse strap over my shoulder so I could have a free hand to hold up my hair in the vain hope of catching a breeze across my neck; I hadn't had time to braid my hair that morning. I looked down at a crack in the driveway and wondered how to get it repaired. Weeds were growing through in unattractive abundance.

I was just thinking that I was glad Mother had married John Queensland, whom I found worthy but often boring, rather than Macon, whose face was made disturbingly attractive by his intelligence, when one of the workmen let out a yell. It hung in the thick, hot air; all three men froze. Macon's head turned in midstride, and he paused as his foot hit the ground. All movement seemed to become deliberate. I was acutely aware of turning my head slightly, the better to see what the man with the red bandanna was lifting off the ground. The contrast of his black hand against the white bone was riveting.

"God almighty! It's a dead man!" bellowed the other worker, and the slow motion speeded up into a sequence too swift for me to replay afterward.

I decided that day that the dead person could not be Macon Turner's son; or, at least if it was, Edward had not been killed by Macon. Macon's face never showed the slightest hint that this find might have a personal slant. He was excited and interested and almost broke his door down to get in to call the police.

Lynn came out of her house when the police car appeared. She looked pale and miserable. Her belly preceded her like a tugboat pulling her along.

"What's the fuss?" she asked, nodding toward the workmen, who were reliving their find complete with quotes and gestures while the patrolman peered down into the thick weeds and vines choking the base of the sign.

"A skeleton, I think." I said cautiously. Though I was sure it was not a *complete* skeleton.

Lynn looked unmoved. "I bet it turns out to be a Great Dane or some other big dog. Maybe even some cow bones or deer bones left over from some home butchering."

"Could be," I said. I looked up at Lynn, whose hand was absently massaging her bulging belly. "How are you doing?"

"I feel like . . ." She paused to think. "I feel like if I bent over, the baby's so low I could shake hands with it."

"Oo," I said. I squinched up my face trying to imagine it.

"You've never been pregnant," Lynn said, a member of a club I'd never belonged to. "It's not as easy as you might think, considering women have done it for millions of years." Right now, Lynn was a lot more interested in her own body than in the body at the end of the road.

"So you're not working now?" I asked, keeping one eye cocked at the patrolman, who was now using his radio. The workmen had calmed down and moved into the shade of a tree in Macon's front yard. Macon disappeared into his house, popping back out with a camera and notepad.

"No. My doctor told me I had to take off work and keep my feet up for as long each day as I can. Since we got most of the boxes unpacked and the nursery is ready, I just do house things about two hours each day, and the rest of the time," she told me gloomily, "I just wait."

This was so—un-Lynn.

"Are you excited?" I asked hesitantly.

"I'm too uncomfortable to be excited. Besides, Arthur is excited enough for both of us."

I found that hard to picture.

"You don't mind anymore, do you?" Lynn asked suddenly.

"No."

"You dating anyone else?"

"Sort of. But I just stopped minding."

Luckily Lynn stopped there, because I simply would not say anything more about it.

"Do you think you'll keep the house?"

"I have no idea." I almost asked Lynn if it would bother her if I did, then I realized I didn't want to know the answer.

"Are you going to that party?" Lynn asked after a moment.

"Yes."

"We will too, I guess, though I'm not much in partying shape. That Marcia Rideout looked at me like she'd never seen a pregnant woman when she came over to meet me and leave the invitation. She made me feel like the Good-year blimp and an unmade bed all at once."

I could see how that would be, given Marcia's aggres-sively good grooming.

"I better go check on the kittens," I told Lynn. The situation down at the end of the street was static. The patrolman leaned against his car, waiting for someone else to show up, apparently. Macon was standing at the end of the pavement looking down at the bones. The workmen were smoking and drinking RC Colas.

"Oh, you have kittens? Can I see?" For the first time, Lynn looked animated.

"Sure," I said with some surprise. Then I realized Lynn was in the mood to see baby anything.

The kittens were more active today. They tumbled over one another, their eyes still not open, and Madeleine surveyed them with queenly pride. One was coal black, the others marmalade and white like their mother. Soon their energy ran out and they began to nurse, dropping off into sleep directly after. Lynn had carefully lowered herself to the floor and watched silently, her face unreadable. I went into the kitchen to replenish Madeleine's water and food, and I changed the litter box while I was at it. After I washed my hands and had a gulp of my drink and most of my hamburger, I went back to the bedroom to find Lynn still staring.

"Did you watch them being born?" she asked.

"Yep."

"Did it look like she hurt?"

"It looked like it was work," I said carefully.

She sighed heavily. "Well, I expect that," she said, trying to sound philosophical.

"Have you gone to Lamaze?"

"Oh, yeah. We do our breathing exercises every night," she said unenthusiastically.

"You don't think they're going to work?"

"I have no idea. You know what's really scary?"

"What?"

"No one will tell you."

"Like who?"

"*Anyone.* It's the damnedest thing. I really want to know what I'm up against. So I ask my best friend, she's had two. She says, 'Oh, when you see what you get it's worth it.' That's no answer, right? So I ask someone else who didn't use any anesthesia. She says, 'Oh, you'll forget all about it when you see the baby.' That's not an answer either. And my mom was knocked out, old-style, when she had me. So she can't tell me, and she probably wouldn't. It's some kind of mom conspiracy."

I thought it over. "Well, I sure can't answer any questions, but I'd tell you the truth if I could."

"I expect," Lynn said, "that I'll be telling you, and pretty soon."

When I left the house to return to the library, I saw two police cars parked in Macon Turner's driveway, and the city truck was gone. The rest of the skeleton having been found was a great relief to me. Now the police would be working on finding out who it was. Perhaps the remaining bones would be enough? If they could find out from the bones, I mentally promised the skull I would give it a decent burial.

I was guiltily aware I was not taking any morally firm position.

That evening the doorbell rang just as I had eased off my shoes and rolled my panty hose down. I hastily yanked them off, pushed them under my chair, and stuck my bare feet into my shoes. I was a hot, wrinkled mess with a headache and a bad conscience.

Sergeant Jack Burns filled my doorway from side to side. His clothes were always heavy on polyester, and he had long Elvis sideburns, but nothing could detract from the air of menace that emanated from him in a steady stream. He was so used to projecting it that I think he might have been surprised if you had told him about it.

"May I come in?" he asked gently.

"Oh, of course," I said, backing to one side.

"I come to ask you about the bones found today on Honor Street," he said formally.

"Please come have a seat."

"Thank you, I will. I been on my old feet all day," he said in a courtly way. He let himself down on my couch, and I sat opposite him in my favorite chair.

"You just come in from work?"

"Yes, yes I did."

"But you were at Jane Engle's house on Honor Street today when the road crew found the skeleton."

"Yes, I had come there on my lunch hour to feed the cat."

He stared and waited. He was better at this than I was.

"Jane's cat. Uh—she ran away from Parnell and Leah Engle and came back home; she had kittens in the closet. In Jane's bedroom."

"You know, you sure turn up a lot for a law-abiding

citizen, Miss Teagarden. We hardly seem to have any homicides in Lawrenceton without you showing up. Seems mighty strange."

"I would hardly call having inherited a house on the same street 'mighty strange,' Sergeant Burns," I said bravely.

"Well, now you think about it," he suggested in a reasonable voice. "Last year when we had those deaths, there you were. When we caught them that did it, there you were."

About to get killed myself, I said, but only in my head, because you didn't interrupt Sergeant Jack Burns.

"Then Miss Engle dies, and here you are on the street with a skeleton in the weeds, a street with a suspicious number of reported break-ins, including one in this house you just inherited."

"A suspicious number of break-ins? Are you saying other people on Honor besides me have reported their house being entered?"

"That's what I'm saying, Miss Teagarden."

"And nothing taken?"

"Nothing the owner would admit to missing. Maybe the thief took some pornographic books or some other thing the homeowner would be embarrassed to report."

"There certainly wasn't anything like that in Jane's house, I'm sure," I said indignantly. Just an old skull with some holes in it. "It may be that something was missing. I wouldn't know. I only saw the house after the burglary. Ah—who else reported their houses had been broken into?"

Jack Burns actually looked surprised before he looked suspicious.

"Everyone, now. Except that old couple in the end house on the other side of the street. Now, do you know anything about the bones found today?"

"Oh, no. I just happened along when they were discovered. You know, I've only been in the house a few times, and I've never stayed there. I only visited Jane over the past couple of years. Before she went into the hospital."

"I think," Jack Burns said heavily and unfairly, "this is one mystery the police department can handle, Miss Teagarden. You keep your little bitty nose out of it."

"Oh," I said furiously, "I will, Sergeant." And as I rose to show him out, my heel caught on the balled-up panty hose under my chair and dragged them out for Jack Burns's viewing.

He gave them a look of scorn, as if they'd been sleazy sexual aids, and departed with his awful majesty intact. If he had laughed, he would've been human.

Chapter Nine

I'd only had half a cup of coffee the next morning when the phone rang. I'd gotten up late after an uneasy sleep. I'd dreamed the skull was under my bed and Jack Burns was sitting in a chair by the bed interrogating me while I was in my nightgown. I was sure somehow he would read my mind and bend over to look under the bed; and if he did that I was doomed. I woke up just as he was lifting the bedspread.

After I'd poured my coffee, made my toast, and retrieved my Lawrenceton *Sentinel* from the front doorstep, I settled at the kitchen table for my morning read. I'd gotten the page one lead story (SEWELL CHALLENGES INCUMBENT) skimmed and was just searching for the comics when I was interrupted.

I picked up the phone, convinced the call was bad news, so I was pleasantly surprised to here Amina's mom on the other end. As it turned out, my original premise was correct.

"Good morning, Aurora! It's Joe Nell Day."

"Hi, Miss Joe Nell. How you doing?" Amina bravely called my mother "Miss Aida."

"Just fine, thanks, honey. Listen, Amina called me last night to tell me they've moved the wedding day up."

I felt a chill of sheer dismay. Here we go again, I thought gloomily. But this was Amina's mother. I stretched my mouth into a smile so my voice would match. "Well, Miss Joe Nell, they're both old enough to know what they're doing," I said heartily.

"I sure hope so," she said from the heart. "I'd sure hate Amina to go through another divorce."

"No, not going to happen," I said, offering reassurance I didn't feel. "This is going to be the one."

"We'll pray about it," Miss Joe Nell said earnestly. "Amina's daddy is fit to be tied. We haven't even met this young man yet."

"You liked her first husband," I said. Amina would always marry someone nice. It was staying that way that was the problem. What was this guy's name? Hugh Price. "She had so many positive things to tell me about Hugh." He was positively good-looking, he was positively rich, he was positively good in bed. I hoped he wasn't positively shallow. I hoped Amina really loved him. I wasn't too concerned about him loving Amina; I took that as an easy accomplishment since I loved her.

"Well, they're both veterans of the divorce wars, so they should know what they want and don't want. Anyway, why I called you, Aurora, moving up the wedding day means you need to come in and get fitted for your bridesmaid's dress."

"Am I the only one?" I hoped desperately I could wear something personally becoming rather than something that was supposed to look good on five or six different females of varying builds and complexions.

"Yes," said Miss Joe Nell with open relief. "Amina wants you to come down and pick what you want as long as it will look good with her dress, which is a mint green."

Not white. I was kind of surprised. Since Amina had decided to send out invitations and have a larger wedding because her first one was so hole-in-the-wall, I'd felt she'd do the whole kit and caboodle. I was relieved to hear she was moderating her impulse.

"Sure, I can come in this morning," I said obligingly. "I don't have to work today."

"Oh, that's just great! I'll see you then."

This was when your mother owning a dress shop was really convenient. There was sure to be something at Great Day that would suit me. If not, Miss Joe Nell would find something.

When I went upstairs to get dressed, on impulse I turned into the back bedroom, the guest room. The only guest who'd ever slept in it had been my little half brother Phillip when he used to come spend an occasional weekend with me. Now he was all the way in California; our father and his mother had wanted to get him as far away from me and Lawrenceton as possible, so he wouldn't have to remember what had happened to him here. While he was staying with me.

I fought off drearily familiar feelings of guilt and pain, and flung open the closet door. In this closet I kept the things I wasn't wearing currently, heavy winter coats, my few cocktail and evening dresses . . . and my bridesmaid dresses. There were four of them: a lavender ruffled horror from Sally Saxby's wedding, Linda Erhardt's floral chiffon, a red velvet with white "fur" trim from my college roommate's Christmas "nuptials," and a somewhat better pink sheath from Franny Vargas's spring marriage. The lavender had made me look as if I'd been bushwhacked by a Barbie doll, the floral chiffon was not bad but in blonds' colors, the red velvet had made me look like Dolly Parton in the chest but otherwise we'd all looked like Santa's helpers, and the pink sheath I'd had cut to knee length and had actually worn to some parties over the years.

I'd worn jeans to Amina's first, runaway wedding.

That had been the most useful bridesmaid's outfit of all.

Now that I had worked myself into an absolutely great mood, what with thinking of Phillip and reviewing my history as a bridesmaid, I decided I'd better get myself in gear and go do things.

What did I need to do besides go by Great Day?

I had to go check on Madeleine and the kittens. I had to go by Mother's office; she'd asked me to on the message left on my machine, and I hadn't done it yet. I felt an urge to go check on the skull, but I decided I could be pretty sure it hadn't gone anywhere.

"Stupid," I muttered at my mirror as I braided my hair. I slapped on a little makeup and pulled on my oldest jeans and a sleeveless T-shirt. I might have to go by Mother's office, but I wasn't going to look like a junior executive. All her salespeople were sure I would go to work for Mother someday, completely disrupting their food chain. Actually, showing houses seemed like an attractive way to pass the time, and now that I had my own money—almost—I really might think about looking into it seriously.

But of course I didn't have to work for Mother. I gave the mirror a wicked grin, picturing the furor for a happy second, before I lapsed back to reality. Wrapping the band around the end of the braid to secure it, I admitted to myself that of course I would work for Mother if I did decide to take the plunge and switch jobs. But I'd miss the library, I told myself as I checked my purse to make sure I had everything. No I wouldn't, I realized suddenly. I'd miss the books. Not the job or the people.

The prospect of possibly resigning kept me entertained until I got to Great Day.

Amina's father was a bookkeeper, and of course he did the books for his wife's business. He was there when I came in, the bell over the door tinkling to announce my arrival. Miss Joe Nell was using some kind of hand-held steamer to get the wrinkles out of a newly arrived dress. She was a very attractive, fair woman in her middle forties. She'd been young when she had Amina, her only daughter. Amina's younger brother was still in graduate school. Miss Joe Nell was very religious, and, when my mother and father had gotten divorced when I was a teenager, one of my many fears was that Miss Joe Nell would disapprove of the divorce so much she wouldn't let me stay with Amina anymore. But Miss Joe Nell was a loving woman and sympathetic, too; my worry had been banished quickly.

Now she put down the steamer and gave me a hug.

"I just hope Amina's doing the right thing," she whispered.

"Well, I'm sure she is," I said with a confidence I was far from feeling. "I'm sure he's a good man."

"Oh, it's not him I worry about so much," Miss Joe Nell said, to my surprise. "It's Amina."

"We just hope she's really ready to settle this time," rumbled Mr. Day. He sang bass in the church choir, had for twenty years, and would until he could sing no more.

"I hope so, too," I admitted. And we all three looked at one another rather dolefully for a long second.

"Now, what kind of dress does Amina want me to try on?" I asked briskly.

Miss Joe Nell shook herself visibly and led me over to the formal dresses. "Let's see," she said. "Her dress, like I said, is mint green, with some white beading. I have it here, she tried on several things when she was home for your mother's wedding. I thought she was just sort of dreaming and planning, but I bet she had a little idea back then that they would move the date up."

The dress was beautiful. Amina would look like an American dream in it.

"So we can coordinate my dress easily," I said in an optimistic tone.

"Well, I looked at what we have in your size, and I found a few things that would look lovely with this shade of green. Even if you pick a solid in a different color, your bouquet could have green ribbons that would sort of tie it together . . ."

And we were off and running, deep in wedding talk.

I was glad I'd braided my hair that morning, because by the time I'd finished hauling dresses off and on it would have been a crow's nest otherwise. As it was, loose hairs crackling with electricity were floating around my face by the time I was done. One of the dresses became me and would coordinate, and, though I doubted I would ever have occasion to wear it again, I bought it. Mrs. Day tried to tell me she would pay for it, but I knew my bridesmaid's duty. Finally she let me have it at cost, and we both were satisfied. Amina's dress had long, see-through sleeves and solid cuffs, a simple neckline, beaded bodice, and a full skirt, plain enough to set off the bridal bouquet but fancy enough to be festive. My dress had short sleeves but the same neckline, and it was peach with a mint green cummerbund. I could get some heels dyed to match—in fact, I thought the heels I'd had dyed to match Linda Erhardt's bridesmaid's dress might do. I promised Miss Joe Nell I'd bring them by the store to check, since my dress had to remain at Great Day to have its hem raised.

And it had only taken an hour and a half, I discovered when I got back in my car. I remembered when I'd gone dress hunting with Sally Saxby and her mother, and four other bridesmaids. The expedition had consumed a whole very long day. It had taken me awhile to feel as fond of Sally as I had before we went dress hunting in Atlanta.

Of course, now Sally had been Mrs. Hunter for ten

years and had a son almost as tall as me, and a daughter who took piano lessons.

No, I would *not* be depressed. The dress had been found, that was a good thing. I was going by the office, that was another good thing. Then I would go see the cats at the new house, as I was trying to think of it. Then I would treat myself to lunch somewhere good.

When I turned into the rear parking lot of my mother's office, I noticed no one dared to park in her space though she was actually out of the country. I pulled into it neatly, making a mental note to tell Mother this little fact. Mother, thinking "Teagarden Homes" was too long to fit on a Sold sign, had instead named her business Select Realty. Of course this was a blatant attempt to appeal to the "up" side of the market, and it seemed to have worked. Mother was a go get 'em Realtor who never let business call her if she could get out there and beat the bushes for it first. She wanted every Realtor she hired to be just as aggressive, and she didn't care what the applicant looked like as long as the right attitude came across. An injudicious rival had compared Select Realtors to a school of sharks, in my hearing. Marching up the sidewalk to the old home Mother had bought and renovated beautifully, I found myself wondering if my mother would consider me a suitable employee.

Everyone who worked at Select Realty dressed to the nines, so I was fairly conspicuous, and I realized my choice of jeans and T-shirt had been a mistake. I had wanted to look as unlike a Realtor as I could, and I had succeeded in looking like an outdated hippie.

Patty Cloud, at the front desk, was wearing a suit that

cost as much as a week's salary from the library. And this was the *receptionist*.

"Aurora, how good to see you!" she said with a practiced smile. Patty was at least four years younger than me, but the suit and the artificial ease made her seem as much older.

Eileen Norris passed through the reception area to drop some papers labeled with a Post-it Note on Patty's desk, and stopped in her tracks when she recognized me.

"My God, child, you look like something the cat dragged in!" Eileen bellowed. She was a suspiciously dark-haired woman about forty-five, with expensive clothes from the very best big women's store. Her makeup was heavy but well done, her perfume was intrusive but attractive, and she was one of the most overwhelming women I'd ever met. Eileen was something of a town character in Lawrenceton, and she could talk you into buying a house quicker then you could take an aspirin.

I wasn't exactly pleased with her greeting, but I'd made an error in judgment, and Eileen was not one to let that go by.

"I'm just dropping in to deliver a message. Mother is extending her honeymoon a little."

"I'm so glad she is," Eileen boomed. "That woman hadn't taken a vacation in a coon's age. I bet she's having a real good time."

"No doubt about it."

"And you're checking up on the children while their mama's away?"

There was also no doubt Eileen wasn't happy with the idea of the boss's daughter "checking up."

"Just wanted to see that the building was still standing," I said lightly. "But I do have a realty question to ask."

Mackie Knight, a young black Realtor Mother had just taken on, came in just then with clients, a pair of newly-weds I recognized since their picture had been in the paper the same day Mother and John's had been. The couple looked a little dazed, and were arguing in a weary way between a house on Macree and a house on Littleton. Safely ahead of them, Mackie rolled his eyes at us as they passed through.

"He's working out good," Eileen said absently. "The younger couples don't mind having a black Realtor, and the black clients love it. Now, you said you had a realty question?"

"Yes, I do. What are houses in the area right around the junior high selling for?"

Patty and Eileen snapped to attention. This was Business.

"How many bedrooms?"

"Ah—two."

"Square footage?"

"Maybe fourteen hundred."

"A house on Honor in that area just sold," Eileen said promptly. "Just a minute and I'll look that up."

She marched back to her desk, her high heels making little thumps on the carpet. I followed her through the unobtrusively attractive gray and blue halls to her office, second in size only to Mother's. It had probably been the second best bedroom. Mother had what had been the master bedroom, and the kitchen had the copying machine and a little snack area. The other rooms were much smaller

and occupied by Mother's lesser minions. Eileen's desk
was aggressively busy, papers everywhere, but they were in
separate stacks, and she doubtless was capable of juggling
many balls at a time.

"Honor, Honor," she muttered. She must have been looking up the price of the little house Arthur and Lynn had
bought. Her ringed fingers flipped expertly through a stack
of listings. "Here we go," she murmured. "Fifty-three," she
said more loudly. "Are you interested in buying or selling?"
I could tell Eileen was no longer concerned with my blue
jeans and messy braid.

"Maybe selling. I inherited the house right across the
street from that house you're looking at now." I nodded at
the listing sheet.

"Really," Eileen said, staring. "You? Inherited?"

"Yes."

"And you may want to sell the house instead of living
in it?"

"Yes."

"Is the house paid for by the previous owner? The owner doesn't owe any money on it, I mean?"

"No, it's paid for." I thought I remembered Bubba
Sewell telling me that. Yes, I did. Jane had been paying on
the house until her mother died, when she'd had the cash
to complete buying it in one whack.

"You have a completely free house and you don't want
it? I would've thought a two bedroom was just the right
size for you. Not that I wouldn't love to list it for you,"
Eileen said, recalled to her senses.

A frail, pretty woman in her late thirties stuck her head

in. "Eileen, I'm off to show the Youngman house, if you've got the key handy," she said with a teasing smile.

"Idella! I can't believe I did it again!" Eileen hit her forehead with the heel of her hand, but very lightly so as not to smear her makeup.

"I'm sorry, I didn't know you had company," the woman continued.

"Idella, this is Aurora Teagarden, Aida's daughter," Eileen said, rummaging through her purse. "Aurora, you may not know Idella Yates yet? She came in with us earlier this year."

While Idella and I exchanged nice-to-meet-you's, Eileen kept up with her search. Finally she unearthed a key with a large label attached. "Idella, I'm sorry," Eileen boomed. "I don't know why I don't remember to put the keys back on the keyboard. That seems to be one thing I cannot remember. We're supposed to put them back on the main keyboard, that Patty watches, every time we use a key to show a house," Eileen explained to me. "But for some reason, I just cannot get it through my head."

"Don't worry about it," Idella said sweetly, and with a nod to me she left to go show the house. She did glance at her watch rather pointedly as she left, letting Eileen know that, if she was late to meet her client, Eileen was the one to blame.

Eileen sat staring after Idella with a curiously uneasy look on her face. Eileen's face was only used to positive emotions, emerging full-blown. Something like "uneasy" sat very oddly on her strong features.

"There's something funny about that woman," Eileen

said abruptly and dismissively. Her face fell back into more familiar lines. "Now, about that house—do you know things like how old the roof is, whether it's on city water, how old the house itself is? Though I think all the houses in that area were built about nineteen fifty-five or so. Maybe some in the early sixties."

"If I make up my mind definitely, I'll get all that information," I promised, wondering how on earth I'd find out about the roof. I might have to go through every one of Jane's receipts, unless perhaps one of her neighbors might remember the roofing crew. Roofing crews usually made their presence felt. A vagrant thought crossed my mind. What if one of the houses was older than it appeared, or had been built on the site of a much older home? Maybe there was a basement or a tunnel under one of the houses where the body had been until it had been tossed into the weeds at the end of the street?

Admittedly this was a pretty stupid idea, and when I asked Eileen about it she dismissed it as it deserved. "Oh, no," she said briskly, beginning to shake her head before I even finished my sentence. "What a strange notion, Roe. That area is much too low for basements, and there wasn't anything there before the junior high was built. It was timberland."

Eileen insisted on walking me out of the office. I decided it was because I was a potential client, rather than because I was Aurora Teagarden. Eileen was not a toady.

"Now, when is your mother coming back?" she asked.

"Oh, soon, sometime this week. She wasn't definite. She just didn't want to call in to the office; maybe she was scared if she talked to one of you she'd just get to talking about work. She was just using me as a messenger to you all." All of the other offices that I passed were busy or showed signs of work in progress. Phones were ringing, papers were being copied, briefcases were being packed with paperwork.

For the first time in my life, I wondered how much money my mother had. Now that I didn't need it anymore, I was finally curious. Money was something we never talked about. She had enough for her, and did her kind of thing—expensive clothes, a very luxurious car (she said it impressed clients), and some good jewelry. She didn't play any sport; for exercise she had installed a treadmill in one of the bedrooms of her house. But she sold a lot of real estate, and I assumed she got a percentage from the sales of the Realtors she employed. I was very fuzzy on how that worked, because I'd just never thought it was my business. In a moment I was not too proud of, I wondered if she'd made a new will now that John and she had married. I frowned at myself in the rearview mirror as I sat at a stoplight.

Of course, John already had plenty of money of his own, and he had two sons . . .

I shook my head impatiently, trying to shake those bad thoughts loose. I tried to excuse myself by reasoning that it was really no wonder that I was will- and death-conscious lately, or for that matter that I was more than usually interested in money matters. But I wasn't happy with myself, so I was quicker to be displeased when I pulled into the driveway of the house on Honor to find Bubba Sewell waiting for me.

It was as if I'd conjured him up by thinking about him.

"Hello," I said cautiously as I got out of the car. He got out of his and strode over to me.

"I took a chance on finding you here. I called the library and found out you were off today."

"Yes, I don't work every day," I said unnecessarily. "I came to check on the kittens."

"Kittens." His heavy eyebrows flew up behind his glasses.

"Madeleine came back. She had kittens in the closet in Jane's room."

"Have Parnell and Leah been over here?" he asked. "Have they given you much trouble?"

"I think Parnell feels we're even now that I have four kittens to find homes for," I said.

Bubba laughed, but he didn't sound like he meant it.

"Listen," he began, "the county bar association dinner-dance is next weekend and I wondered if you would go with me?"

I was so surprised I almost gaped at him. Not only was he reportedly dating my beautiful friend Lizanne, but also I could have sworn that Bubba Sewell was not the least bit interested in me as a woman. And though my dating schedule was certainly not heavy, I had learned long ago that it was better to be home alone with a good book and a bag of potato chips than it was to be out on a date with someone who left you cold.

"I'm sorry, Bubba," I said. I was not accustomed enough to turning down dates to be good at it. "I'm just very busy right now. But thank you for asking me."

He looked away, embarrassed. "Okay. Maybe some other time."

I smiled as noncommittally as I could.

"Is everything going—all right?" he asked suddenly.

How much did he know?

"You read about the bones found around the dead end sign?" It had been below the report about Bubba's run for representative: CITY WORKERS FIND BONES. It had been a very short story; I expected a much fuller account in the next morning's paper. Maybe, I suddenly thought, now that the law had the bones, there would be more information on the sex and age of the skeleton included in the next story. The few paragraphs this morning had stated that the bones were going to a pathologist for examination. I swam out of my thoughts to find Bubba Sewell eyeing me with some apprehension.

"The bones?" he prompted. "A skeleton?"

"Well, there wasn't a skull," I murmured.

"Was that in the paper?" he asked sharply. I'd made a mistake; as a matter of fact, the skeleton's skull-lessness had not been mentioned in the story.

"Gosh, Bubba," I said coolly. "I just don't know."

We stared at each other for a minute.

"Gotta be going," I said finally. "The cats are waiting."

"Oh, sure." He tucked his mouth in and then relaxed it. "Well . . . if you really need me, you know where I am. By the way, had you heard I'm running for office?"

"Yes. I'd heard that, sure had." And we looked at each other for a second more. Then I marched up the sidewalk and unlocked the front door. Madeleine slithered out instantly and headed for the soft dirt around the bushes. Her litter box was only a backup system: she preferred to go out-of-doors. Bubba Sewell was gone by the time I locked the front door behind me.

Chapter Ten

I rattled around restlessly in the "new" house for a few hours. It was mine, all mine, but somehow I didn't feel too cheerful about that anymore. Actually, I preferred my town house, a soulless rental. It had more room, I was used to it, I liked having an upstairs I didn't have to clean if company was coming. Could I stand living across the street from Arthur and Lynn? Next door to the unpredictable Marcia Rideout? Jane's books were already cramming the bookcases. Where would I put mine? But if I sold this house and bought a bigger one, probably the yard would be bigger, and I hadn't ever taken care of one . . . If Torrance hadn't mowed the yard for me, I wouldn't know how to cope. Maybe the yard crew that did the lawn at the town houses?

I maundered on in my head, opening the kitchen cabinets and shutting them, trying to decide which pots and pans were duplicates of mine so I could take them to the local Baptist church, which kept a room of household goods for families who got burned out or suffered some equal disaster. I finally chose some in a lackadaisical way and carried them out to the car loose; I was out of boxes. I was treading water emotionally, unable to settle on any one task or course of action.

I wanted to quit my job.

I was scared to. Jane's money seemed too good to be true. Somehow, I feared it might be taken away from me.

I wanted to throw the skull in the lake. I was also scared of whoever had reduced the skull to its present state.

I wanted to sell Jane's house because I didn't particularly care for it. I wanted to live in it because it was safely mine.

I wanted Aubrey Scott to adore me; surely a minister would have a specially beautiful wedding? I did not want to marry Aubrey Scott because being a minister's wife took a lot more internal fortitude than I had. A proper minister's wife would have marched out of the house with that skull and gone straight to the police station without a second thought. But Aubrey seemed too serious a man to date without the prospect of the relationship evolving in that direction.

I did run the pots and pans to the Baptist church, where I was thanked so earnestly that it was soothing, and made me think better of my poor character.

On the way back to the new house, I stopped at Jane's bank on impulse. I had the key with me, surely? Yes, here it was in my purse. I went in hesitantly, suddenly thinking that the bank might present difficulties about letting me see the safe deposit box. But it wasn't too difficult. I had to explain to three people, but then one of them remembered Bubba Sewell coming by, and that made everything all right. Accompanied by a woman in a sober business suit, I got Jane's safe deposit box. Something about those vaults where they're kept makes me feel that there's going to be a dreadful secret inside. All those locked boxes, the heavy door, the attendant! I went into the little room that held only a table and a single chair, shut the door. Then I opened the box, telling myself firmly that nothing dreadful could be in a box so small. Nothing dreadful, but a good deal that was beautiful. When I saw the contents of the long metal box, I let my breath out in a single sigh. Who would ever have imagined that Jane would want these things?

There was a pin shaped like a bow, made out of garnets with the center knot done in diamonds. There were garnet and diamond earrings to match. There was a slim gold chain with a single emerald on it, and a pearl necklace and bracelet. There were a few rings, none of them spectacular or probably extremely valuable, but all of them expensive and very pretty. I felt I had opened the treasure chest in the pirate's cave. And these were mine now! I could not attach any sentiment to them, because I'd never seen Jane wear them—perhaps the pearls, yes; she'd worn the pearls to a wedding we'd both attended. Nothing else rang any bells. I tried on the rings. They were only a little loose. Jane and I both had small fingers. I was trying to imagine what I could wear the bow pin and earrings to; they'd look great on a winter white suit, I decided. But as I held the pieces and touched them, I knew that despite Bubba Sewell's saying there was nothing else in the safe deposit box, I was disappointed that there was no letter from Jane.

After I'd driven back to the house, despite an hour spent watching Madeleine and her kittens, I still could not ground myself. I ended up throwing myself on the couch and turning on CNN, while reading some of my favorite passages from Jane's copy of Donald Rumbelow's book on Jack the Ripper. She had marked her place with a slip of paper, and for a moment my heart pounded, thinking Jane had left me another message, something more explicit than *I didn't do it*. But it was only an old grocery list: eggs, nutmeg, tomatoes, butter . . .

I sat up on the couch. Just because this piece of paper had been a false alarm didn't mean there weren't any other notes! Jane would put them where she would think I'd find them. She had known no one but me would go through her books. The first one had been in a book about Madeleine Smith, Jane's main field of study. I riffled through Jane's other books about the Smith case. I shook them.

Nothing.

Then maybe she'd hidden something in one of the books about the case that most intrigued me—well, which one would that be? Either Jack the Ripper or the murder of Julia Wallace. I was already reading Jane's only Ripper book. I flipped through it but found no other notes. Jane also had only one book on Julia Wallace, and there again I found no message. Theodore Durrant, Thompson-Bywater, Sam Sheppard, Reginald Christie, Crippen . . . I shook Jane's entire true-crime library with no results.

I went through her fictional crime, heavy on women writers: Margery Allingham, Mary Roberts Rinehart, Agatha Christie . . . the older school of mysteries. And Jane had an unexpected shelf of sword-and-sorcery science fiction, too. I didn't bother with those, at least initially; Jane would not have expected me to look there.

But in the end I went through those as well. After two hours, I had shaken, riffled, and otherwise disturbed every volume on the shelves, only a trace of common sense preventing me from flinging them on the floor as I finished. I'd even read all the envelopes in the letter rack on the kitchen wall, the kind you buy at a handcraft fair; all the letters seemed to be from charities or old friends, and I stuffed them irritably back in the rack to go through at a later date.

Jane had left me no other message. I had the money, the house, the cat (plus kittens), the skull, and the note that said I *didn't do it.*

A peremptory knock on the front door made me jump. I'd been sitting on the floor so lost in the doldrums I hadn't heard anyone approach. I scrambled up and looked through the peephole, then flung the door open. The woman outside was as well-groomed as Marcia Rideout, as cool as a cucumber; she was not sweating in the heat. She was five inches taller than me. She looked like Lauren Bacall.

"Mother!" I said happily, and gave her a brief hug.

She undoubtedly loved me, but she didn't like her clothes wrinkled.

"Aurora," she murmured, and gave my hair a stroke.

"When did you get back? Come in!"

"I got in really late last night," she explained, coming into the room and staring around her. "I tried to call you this morning after we got up, but you weren't home. You weren't at the library. So after a while, I decided I'd phone in to the office, and Eileen told me about the house. Who is this woman who left you the house?"

"How's John?"

"No, don't put me off. You know I'll tell you all about the trip later."

"Jane Engle. John knows—John knew her, too. She was in Real Murders with us."

"At least that's disbanded now," Mother said with some relief. It would have been hard for Mother to send John off to a monthly meeting of a club she considered only just on the good side of obscenity.

"Yes. Well, Jane and I were friends through the club, and she never married, so when she died, she left me—her estate."

"Her estate," my mother repeated. Her voice was beginning to get a decided edge. "And just what, if you don't mind my asking, does that estate consist of?"

I could tell her or I could stonewall her. If I didn't tell her, she'd just pull strings until she found out, and she had a bunch of strings to pull.

"This Jane Engle was the daughter of Mrs. John Elgar Engle," I said.

"The Mrs. Engle who lived in that gorgeous mansion on Ridgemont? The one that sold for eight hundred and fifty thousand because it needed renovation?"

Trust Mother to know her real estate.

"Yes, Jane was the daughter of that Mrs. Engle."

"There was a son, wasn't there?"

"Yes, but he died."

"That was only ten or fifteen years ago. She couldn't have spent all that money, living here." Mother had sized up the house instantly.

"I think this house was almost paid for when old Mrs. Engle died," I said.

"So you got this house," Mother said, "and . . . ?"

"And five hundred and fifty thousand dollars," I said baldly. "Thereabouts. And some jewelry."

Mother's mouth dropped open. It was the first time in my life I think I'd ever astonished my mother. She's not a moneygrubbing person, but she has a great respect for cash and property, and it is the way she measures her own success as a professional. She sat down rather abruptly on the couch and automatically crossed her elegant legs in their designer sportswear. She will go so far as to wear slacks on vacation, to pool parties, and on days she doesn't work; she would rather be mugged than wear shorts.

"And of course I now have the cat and her kittens," I continued maliciously.

"The cat," Mother repeated in a dazed way.

Just then the feline in question made her appearance, followed by a chorus of forlorn mews from the kittens in Jane's closet. Mother uncrossed her legs and leaned forward to

look at Madeleine as if she had never seen a cat before. Madeleine walked right up to Mother's feet, stared up at her for a moment, then leaped onto the couch in one flowing motion and curled up on Mother's lap. Mother was so horrified she didn't move.

"This," she said, "is a cat you inherited?"

I explained about Parnell Engle, and Madeleine's odyssey to have her kittens in "her" house.

Mother neither touched Madeleine nor heaved her legs to remove her.

"What breed is she?" Mother asked stiffly.

"She's a mutt cat," I said, surprised. Then I realized Mother was evaluating the cat. Or valuing her. "Want me to move her?"

"Please," my mother said, still in that stiff voice.

Finally I understood. My mother was scared of the cat. In fact, she was terrified. But, being Mother, she would never admit it. That was why we'd never had cats when I was growing up. All her arguments about animal hair on everything, having to empty a litter tray, were just so much smoke screen.

"Are you scared of dogs, too?" I asked, fascinated. I carefully scooped Madeleine off Mother's lap, and scratched her behind the ears as I held her. She obviously preferred Mother's lap, but put up with me a few seconds, then indicated she wanted down. She padded into the kitchen to use her litter box, followed by Mother's horrified gaze. I pushed my glasses up on my nose so I could have a clear view of this unprecedented sight.

"Yes," Mother admitted. Then she took her eyes off Madeleine and saw my face. Her guard snapped up immediately.

"I've just never cared for pets. For God's sake, go get yourself some contact lenses so you'll stop fiddling with those glasses," she said very firmly. "So. Now you have a lot of money?"

"Yes," I admitted, still enthralled by my new knowledge of my mother.

"What are you going to do?"

"I don't know. I haven't made any plans yet. Of course, the estate has to go through probate, but that shouldn't take too long, Bubba Sewell says."

"He's the lawyer who's handling the estate?"

"Yes, he's the executor."

"He's sharp."

"Yes, I know."

"He's ambitious."

"He's running for office."

"Then he'll do everything right. Running for office has become just like running under a microscope."

"He asked me out, but I turned him down."

"Good idea," my mother said, to my surprise. "It's never wise to have a social relationship mixed up with money transactions or financial arrangements."

I wondered what she would say about a social relationship mixed up with religion.

"So you had a good time?" I asked.

"Yes, we did. But John came down with something like the flu, so we had to come home. He's over the worst, and I expect he'll be out and about tomorrow."

"He didn't want to stay there until he got over it?" I couldn't imagine traveling with the flu.

"I suggested it, but he said when he was sick, he didn't want to be in a resort where everyone else was having fun, he wanted to be home in his own bed. He was quite stubborn about it. But, up until that time, we really had a great honeymoon." Mother's face looked almost soft as she said that, and it was borne in on me for the first time that my mother was in love, maybe not in as gooey a way as Amina, but she was definitely feeling the big rush.

It occurred to me that John had come back to Lawrenceton and gotten in Mother's bed, not his own. "Has John sold his house yet?" I asked.

"One of his sons wanted it," Mother said in as noncommittal a voice as she could manage. "Avery, the one that's expecting the baby. It's a big old house, as you know."

"How did John David feel about that? Not that it's any of my business." John David was John's second son.

"I wouldn't have presumed to advise John about his family business," Mother began answering indirectly, "because John and I signed a prenuptial agreement about our financial affairs."

This was news to me, and I felt a distinct wave of relief. I'd never considered it before, but all the complications that could arise when both parties had grown children suddenly occurred to me. I'd only thought of what Mother might leave when she died, this very day. I should have known, as property conscious as she was, she would have taken care of everything.

"So I didn't advise him," Mother was continuing, "but he thought out loud when he was trying to figure out what was fair to do."

"You're the obvious person for input when it comes to real estate questions."

"Well, he did ask me the value of the house on the current market."

"And?"

"I had it appraised, and I think—now I don't know, but I think—he gave John David the cash value of the house, and deeded over the house to Avery."

"So John David didn't want the house at all?"

"No, his work requires that he transfer every few years, and it didn't make sense for him to own a house in Lawrenceton."

"That worked out well."

"Now I'm going to tell you what I did about my house."

"Oh, Mom!" I protested.

"No," she said firmly. "You need to know this."

"Okay," I said reluctantly.

"I think a man needs to know he has a home that's his," she said. "And since John gave up his house, I have left him mine for his lifetime. So if I die before John, he gets to stay in the house until he dies. I thought that was only right. But, after John passes away, it's yours to do with as you will, of course."

This was just my season for having things willed to me. Suddenly I realized that Mother would leave me her business and her money, as well as the house; with Jane's money, and her little house, too, I need never work another day in my life.

What a startling prospect.

"Whatever you do is fine with me," I said hastily, aware

that Mother was looking at me in a funny way. "I don't want to talk about it."

"We'll have to sometime," Mother warned.

What was with her today? Had getting remarried somehow awakened or reinforced her feelings of her own mortality? Was it signing the prenuptial agreement with all these arrangements for what would happen after her death? She was just back from her honeymoon. She should be feeling pretty frisky.

"Why are you talking about all this now?" I asked bluntly.

She considered this. "I don't know," she said in a puzzled way. "I certainly didn't come here expecting to talk about it. I was going to tell you about the hotel and the beach and the tour we took, but somehow I got sidetracked. Maybe when we talked about what Jane Engle left you, I started thinking about what I was going to leave you. Though, of course, now you won't need it as badly. It does seem strange to me that Jane left all her money and property to someone who isn't even a member of the family, someone who wasn't even that close a friend."

"It seems strange to me, too, Mom," I admitted. I didn't want to tell my mother that Jane had left everything to me because she saw me starting out like her, single and bookish, and maybe Jane had seen something else in me that struck a chord with her; we were both fascinated by death between the pages of a book. "And it's going to seem strange to a lot of other people."

She thought about that for a little. She waited delicately to see if I would enlighten her about Jane's motives.

"I'm glad for you," Mother said after a minute, seeing I

wasn't going to offer any more information about my relationship with Jane. "And I don't expect we have to worry about what people say."

"Thanks."

"I'd better get back to my sick husband," Mother said fondly.

How strange it was to hear that. I smiled at her without thinking about it. "I'm glad for you, too," I told her honestly.

"I know that." She gathered her purse and keys, and I rose to walk her to her car.

She was discussing a dinner party an old friend was planning to give for her and John, and I was wondering if I should ask to bring Aubrey, when Marcia Rideout came out of her front door. She was wearing another matched and beautifully ironed shorts set, and her hair was a little blonder, it seemed to me.

"Is that your momma I see with you?" she called when she was halfway down her drive. "Do you just have a minute?"

We both waited with polite, expectant smiles.

"Aida, you may not remember me," Marcia said, with her head tilted coyly to one side, "but you and I were on the Fallfest committee together a couple of years ago."

"Oh, of course," Mother said, professional warmth in her voice. "The festival turned out very well that year, didn't it?"

"Yes, but it was sure a lot of work, more than I ever bargained for! Listen, we're all just so thrilled Roe is moving on our street. I don't know if she told you yet or not, I understand you've been away on your honeymoon, but Torrance and I are giving Aurora and our other new neighbors"—and Marcia nodded her smooth head at the little yellow-shuttered house across the street—"a little get-together tomorrow night. We would just love it if you and your new husband could come."

Nothing nonpluses Mother. "We'd love to, but I'm afraid John came back from the Bahamas with just a touch of flu," she explained. "I tell you what, I may just drop in by myself for a few minutes, just to meet Aurora's new neighbors. If my husband is feeling better, maybe he'll come, too. Can I leave it that indefinite?"

"Oh, of course, that poor man, the flu in this pretty weather! And on his honeymoon! Bless his heart!"

"Who are the other new people on the street?" Mother inquired, to stem Marcia's pity.

"A police detective and his brand-new wife, who is also a police detective! And she's going to have a baby just any time now. Isn't that exciting? I don't think I'd ever met a real detective until they moved in, and now we have two of them on the street. We should all be real safe now! We've had a lot of break-ins on this street the past few years—but I'm sure your daughter is as safe as can be, now," Marcia tacked on hastily.

"Would that detective be Arthur Smith?" Mother asked. I heard the permafrost under her words. I could feel my face begin to tighten. I had never known how much Mother knew or guessed about my relationship with Arthur, but I had a feeling she'd gotten a pretty accurate picture. I turned my face away a little under pretext of pushing up my glasses.

"Yes. He's such a solemn young man, and handsome,

too. Of course, not as handsome as the man Roe is dating." Marcia actually winked.

"You don't think so?" my mother said agreeably. I bit my upper lip.

"Oh, no. That minister is so tall and dark. You can tell from my marrying Torrance, I like tall, dark men. And that mustache! It may not be nice to say this about a man in the ministry, but it's just plain sexy."

My mother had been totting up this description. "Well, I'll sure try to come, thanks so much for inviting me," she said in a perfectly polite but unmistakably conclusive way.

"I'll just go back to cleaning the house," Marcia said brightly, and, after a chorus of good-byes, off she trotted.

"Dating Father Scott?" Mother asked when she was sure Marcia was out of earshot. "And you're over that lousy policeman?"

"Yes to both."

Mother looked quite unsettled for a minute. "You turned down a date with Bubba Sewell, you're over that Arthur Smith, and you're dating a minister," she said wonderingly. "There's hope for your love life after all."

As I waved to her as she drove down the street, it was a positive satisfaction for me to think of the skull in her blanket bag.

Chapter Eleven

In a burst of morning energy, I was singing in the shower when the telephone rang. Blessing answering machines, I barely paused in my rendition of "The Star-Spangled Banner." The shower is probably the only place our national anthem should be sung, especially by people with a limited vocal range, a category that definitely includes me. As I rinsed the shampoo out of my hair, I did a medley of my favorite ads. For my finale, as I toweled I warbled "Three Little Ducks."

There is something to be said for living by oneself when one wants to sing unheard.

It would be hard to say why I was in such a festive mood. I had to go in to work for five hours, then come back to the town house to prepare for the party. I was pleased at the prospect of seeing Aubrey, but not goo-goo eyed. I was more or less getting used to being rich by now (though the word still gave me a thrill up my spine), and I was on standby regarding action on the skull. I squinted into my makeup mirror as I put on a little eye shadow.

"I'm going to quit my job," I told my reflection, smiling.

The *pleasure* of being able to say that! To decide, just like that! Money was wonderful.

I remembered the phone message and pressed the play button, beaming at my reflection in the mirror like an idiot, my drying hair beginning to fly around my head in a dark, wavy nimbus.

"Roe?" began the voice, faint and uncertain. "This is Robin Crusoe, calling from Italy. I called in and got your message from Phil . . . the guy subletting my apartment. Are you all right? He said Arthur married someone else. Can I come see you when I get back from Europe? If that's not a good idea, send a note to my old address. Well, write me either way, and I'll get it when I get back. That should be in a few weeks, probably late next month. Or earlier. I'm running out of money. Good-bye."

I had frozen when I first heard the voice begin. Now I sat breathing shallowly for a few seconds, my brush in my hand, my teeth biting my lower lip gently. My heart was beating fast, I'll admit. Robin had been my tenant and my friend and almost my lover. I really wanted to see him again. Now I would have the pleasure of composing a note that would say very delicately that I *definitely* wanted him to come calling when he got back. I didn't want him to get the impression I was sitting in Lawrenceton with my tongue hanging out while I panted, but I did want him to come, if he was of the same mind in a few weeks. And if I was. I could take my time composing that note.

I brushed my hair, which began to crackle and fly around even more wildly. I gathered it all together and put a band on it about halfway down its length, not as stodgy as a "real" ponytail. And I tied a frivolous bow around the band. However, I did wear one of my old "librarian" outfits that so disgusted Amina: a solid navy skirt of neutral length with a navy-and-white-striped blouse, plain support hose, and unattractive but very comfortable shoes. I cleaned my glasses, pushed them up on my nose, nodded at my reflection in the full-length mirror, and went downstairs.

If I'd known how to cha-cha, I think I would have done it going up the ramp from the employees' parking lot into the library.

"Aren't we happy today?" Lillian said sourly, sipping from her cup of coffee at the worktable in the book-mending room.

"Yes, ma'am, we are," I said, depositing my purse in my little locker and snapping the padlock shut. My only claim to fame in my history as a librarian in Lawrenceton was that I had never once lost my padlock key. I kept it on a safety pin and pinned it to my skirt or my slip or my blouse. Today I pinned it to my collar and marched off to Mr. Clerrick's office, humming a military tune. Or what I imagined was a military tune.

I tapped on the half-open door and stuck my head in. Mr. Clerrick was already at work on a heap of papers, a steaming cup of coffee at his elbow and a smoldering cigarette in the ashtray.

"Good morning, Roe," he said, looking up from his desk. Sam Clerrick was married with four daughters, and, since he worked in a library, that meant he was surrounded by women from the moment he got up to the moment he went to bed. You would think he would have learned how to treat them. But his greatest and most conspicuous failure was in people management. No one would ever accuse Sam Clerrick of coddling anyone, or of favoritism; he didn't care for any of us, had no idea what our home lives were like, and made no allowances for any individual's personality or work preferences. No one would ever like him; he would never be accused of being unfair.

I had always been a little nervous around someone who played his emotional cards as close to his chest as Sam Clerrick. Suddenly leaving did not seem so simple.

"I'm going to quit my job," I said quietly, while I still had some nerve. As he stared, that little bit of nerve began to trickle away. "I'm on part-time anyway. I don't feel like you really need me anymore."

He kept peering at me over his half-glasses. "Are you giving me notice, or quitting, no more work as of today?" he asked finally.

"I don't know," I said foolishly. After I considered a moment, I said, "Since you have at least three substitute librarians on your call list, and I know at least two of them would love to go regular part-time, I'm quitting, no more work as of five hours from now."

"Is there something wrong that we can talk about?"

I came all the way into the room. "Working here is

okay," I told him. "I just don't have to anymore, financially, and I feel like a change."

"You don't need the money," he said in amazement.

He was probably the only person working at the library, or perhaps the only person in Lawrenceton, who didn't know by now about the money.

"I inherited."

"My goodness, your mother didn't die, I hope?" He actually put his pencil down, so great was his concern.

"No, no relative."

"Oh—good. Well. I'm sorry to see you go, even though you were certainly our most notorious employee for a while last year. Well, it's been longer than that now, I suppose."

"Did you think about firing me then?"

"Actually, I was holding off until you killed Lillian."

I stared at him blankly until I accepted the amazing fact that Sam Clerrick had made a joke. I began laughing, and he began laughing, and suddenly he looked like a human being.

"It's been a pleasure," I said, meaning it for the first time, and turned and left his office.

"Your insurance will last for thirty days," he called after me, running a little truer to form.

As luck would have it, that morning at the library business was excruciatingly slow. I didn't want to tell anyone I'd quit until I was actually leaving, so I hid among the books all morning, reading the shelves, dusting, and piddling along. I didn't get a lunch break, since I was just working five hours; I was supposed to bring it with me or get one of the librarians going out to bring back something from a fast-food place, and eat it very quickly. But that would mean eating in the break room, and there was sure to be someone else in there, and having a conversation without revealing my intention would be seen as fraudulent, in a way. So I dodged from here to there, making myself scarce, and by two o'clock I was very hungry. Then I had to go through the ritual of saying good-bye, I enjoyed working with you, I'll be in often to get books so we'll be seeing each other.

It made me sadder than I thought it would. Even saying good-bye to Lillian was not the unmitigated pleasure I had expected. I would miss having her around because she made me feel so virtuous and smart by contrast, I realized with shame. (*I* didn't moan and groan about every little change in work routine, *I* didn't bore people to tears with detailed accounts of boring events, *I* knew who Benvenuto Cellini was.) And I remembered Lillian finally standing by me when things had been so bad during the murders months before.

"Maybe you can hunt for a husband full-time now," Lillian said in parting, and my shame vanished completely. Then I read in Lillian's face the knowledge that the only thing she had that I could possibly want was a husband.

"We'll see," I told her, and held my hands behind my back so I wouldn't choke her.

I retrieved my purse and turned in my locker key, and I walked out the back door for the last time.

I went straight to the grocery store. I wanted something for lunch, I wanted something to put in the refrigerator at the house on Honor for snacks while I was there. I zoomed through the grocery store tossing boxes and produce bags in my cart with abandon. I celebrated quitting my job by getting one of the really expensive microwave meals, the kind with a neat reusable plate. This was getting fancy for me, for lunch anyway. Maybe now I would have time to cook. Did I want to learn to cook in any more detail? I could make spaghetti, and I could make pecan pie. Did I need to know anything else? I debated it as I stood in front of the microwave at the town house.

I could decide at my leisure. I was now a woman of leisure.

I liked the sound of it.

The woman of leisure decided to celebrate by buying a new outfit to wear to the Rideouts' party. I would not go to Great Day, I decided; I'd share the wealth and go to Marcus Hatfield instead. Usually Marcus Hatfield made me nervous; though it was a mere satellite of the big Atlanta store, the selection was just too great, the saleswomen too aggressively groomed. Maybe my contact with Marcia was inuring me to immaculate grooming; I felt I could face even the cosmetics-counter woman without flinching.

I pulled my skirt straight and stiffened my spine before I entered. I can buy anything in this store, I reminded myself. I marched through the doors in my hopeless librarian's outfit. I was almost immediately confronted by a curvy vision in bright flowers, perfect nails, and subtle makeup.

"Hey, neighbor," exclaimed the vision. It was Carey Osland in her working getup. I could see why she preferred loafers and housedresses. She looked marvelous, almost edible, but definitely not comfortable. "I'm glad to see you," Carey was saying warmly while I was decoding her identity.

"Good to see you, too," I managed.

"Can I help you today?"

"I need something new to wear tonight."

"To the sun-deck party."

"Yes. It's so nice of the Rideouts to be giving it."

"Marcia loves to entertain. There's nothing she likes better than to have a bunch of people over."

"She said she didn't like it when her husband had to be away overnight."

"No. I expect you noticed she drinks a little then. She's been like that as long as I've known her, I guess . . . though I don't know her very well. She knows a lot of people around town, but she never seems to be close friends with anyone. Were you thinking of a sports outfit or did you want a sundress, something like that?"

"What?"

"For the party."

"Oh, sorry, I was off in the clouds somewhere. Um . . . what are you going to wear?"

"Oh, I'm too fat to wear a sundress," Carey said cheerfully. "But you'd look real pretty in one; and, so it wouldn't be too dressy, you could wear flat sandals and go real plain on your jewelry."

I looked dubiously at the dress Carey had pulled out. Mrs. Day would never have suggested it for me. But, then, Mrs. Day didn't carry too much like this at her shop. It was white and orange, very pretty but very casual, and there wasn't a back to it.

"I couldn't wear a bra with that," I pointed out.

"Oh, no," Carey agreed calmly.

"I would jiggle," I said doubtfully.

"Go try it on," Carey said with a wink. "If you don't like it, we have all kinds of cute shorts sets and lightweight pants, and any of them would be just fine, but just put this dress on."

I had never had to almost completely undress to try on clothes before. I pulled on the dress and bounced up and down on the balls of my feet, my eyes on the dressing-room mirror. I was trying to gauge the amount of jiggle. I am chesty for such a small person, and there was enough jiggle to give me pause.

"How is it?" Carey called from outside my cubicle.

"Oh . . . I don't know," I said doubtfully. I bounced again. "After all, I'm going with a minister."

"He's human," Carey observed. "God made bosoms, too."

"True." I turned around and observed my back. It looked very bare. "I can't carry this off, Carey," I told her.

"Let me see."

I reluctantly opened the door of the cubicle.

"Wow," said Carey. "You really look *good*," she said with squinted eyes. "Very sexy," she added in a conspiratorial whisper.

"I just feel too conspicuous. My back feels cold."

"He'd love it."

"I don't know about that."

I looked in a bigger mirror at the end of the row of dressing rooms. I considered. No, I decided finally. I could not go out in that dress with someone I hadn't slept with.

"I'm not going to wear it tonight, so I still need to find something else for that," I told Carey. "But I think I'll buy it anyway."

Carey became the complete saleswoman. The orange-and-white dress was whisked away to be put on a hanger, and she brought several more things for me to try on. Carey seemed to be determined that I wanted to present a sexy, sophisticated image, and I became sorry I hadn't gone to Great Day. Finally we found a cotton knit shorts and shirt that represented a compromise. The shirt was scoop-necked and white with red polka dots, and the red shorts were cut very full, like a little skirt, with a long tie belt that matched the shirt. I certainly had a lot of exposed skin, but at least it wasn't on my back. Carey talked me into red sandals and red bracelet and earrings to match before I called a halt to my shopping.

When I carried my purchases back to the town house, I called Aubrey at his church. "Who's calling?" the church secretary asked, when I wanted to be connected to Aubrey.

"Roe Teagarden."

"Oh!" she said breathlessly. "Sure, Roe, I'll tell him. He's such a nice man, we just love him here at St. John."

I stared at the phone for a second before I realized I was being given a boost in my assumed effort to win the heart of their priest. The congregation of St. John's must think it was time their leader married again, and I must be respectable enough at first glance to qualify as a suitable mate.

"Roe?"

"Hi, Aubrey," I said, shaking myself out of my thoughts. "Listen, would you meet me tonight at the house on Honor instead of picking me up here at the town house? I want to feed the cat before the party."

"Sure. Are we supposed to bring anything? A bottle of wine?"

"She didn't want me to bring anything to eat, but if you want to bring a bottle of wine, I imagine they'd be glad." A nice thought on Aubrey's part.

"This is casual, right?"

"It's going to be on their sun deck, so I'm sure it is."

"Good. I'll see you at your new house at seven, then."

"That's just fine."

"I look forward to it," he said quietly.

"Me, too."

I got there early, and pulled my car all the way inside the carport so there'd be room for Aubrey's. After tending to Madeleine's needs, I thought of the clothes still in Jane's drawers. I'd cleaned out the closet, but not the chest of drawers. I pulled one open idly to see what I had to contend with. It turned out to be Jane's sleepwear drawer. Jane had had an unexpected taste in nightgowns. These certainly weren't what I'd call little-old-lady gowns, though they weren't naughty or anything like that. I pulled out the prettiest, a rose pink nylon, and decided I might actually keep it. Then I thought, Maybe I'll just spend the night here. Somehow the idea struck me as fun. The sheets on the bed were clean, changed by the maid hired to straighten everything out after Jane had gone into the hospital. Here was a gown. I'd just put a little food in the refrigerator. The air conditioner was running. There was a toothbrush in a sealed container in the bathroom, and an unopened tube of toothpaste. I would see what waking up in my new house was like.

The doorbell rang, announcing Aubrey's arrival. I answered it feeling a little self-conscious because of the scoop neckline. Sure enough, Aubrey's eyes went instantly to my cleavage. "You should have seen the one I didn't wear," I said defensively.

"Was I that obvious?" he said, a little embarrassed.

"Carey Osland says God made bosoms, too," I told him, and then closed my eyes and wished the ground would swallow me up.

"Carey Osland says truly," he said fervently. "You look great."

Aubrey had a knack for taking the embarrassment out of situations.

"You look nice yourself," I told him. He was wearing what would be a safe outfit at ninety percent of Lawrenceton's social occasions: a navy knit shirt and khaki slacks, with loafers.

"Well, now that we've admired each other, isn't it time to go?"

I glanced at my watch. "Right on the dot."

He offered his arm like the usher at a wedding, and I laughed and took it. "I'm going to be a bridesmaid again," I told him. "And you know what they say about women who are bridesmaids so often." Then I felt furious with myself all over again, for even introducing the subject of weddings.

"They say, 'What a beautiful bridesmaid,'" Aubrey offered tactfully.

"That's right," I said, relieved. If I couldn't do better than this, I'd have to keep my mouth shut all evening.

From my first glimpse of Marcia it was apparent to me that she lived to entertain. The food even had little mesh tents over it to keep flies off, a practical touch in Lawrenceton in the summer. The cloths covering the tables erected on the sun deck for the occasion were starched and bright. Marcia was her usual well-turned-out self, as starched and bright as the tablecloths in blue cotton shorts and blouse. She had dangly earrings and painted nails, top and bottom. She exclaimed over the wine and asked if we wanted a glass now. We refused politely and she went in to put it in the refrigerator, while Torrance, looking exceptionally tan in his white shorts and striped shirt, took our drink orders. We both took gin and tonics with lots of ice, and went to sit on the built-in bench that ran all the way around the huge deck. My feet could barely touch the deck. Aubrey sat very close when he sat next to me.

Carey and Macon came in right on our heels, and I introduced them to Aubrey. Macon had met him before at a ministerial council meeting Macon had covered for the paper, and they immediately plunged into an earnest conversation about what the council hoped to accomplish in the next few months. Carey eyed my outfit and winked at me, and we talked over the men about how good Marcia and the party food looked. Then the couple who lived in the house across from Carey, the McMans, came up to be introduced, and they assumed that Aubrey and I owned Jane's house together, that we were cohabiting. As we were straightening that out, Lynn and Arthur came in. Lynn was elephantine and obviously very uncomfortable in a maternity shorts outfit. Arthur was looking a little worried and doubtful. When I saw him I felt—nothing.

When Arthur and Lynn worked their way around to us, he seemed to have shaken off whatever had been troubling him. Lynn looked a little more cheerful, too. "I wasn't feeling too well earlier," she confided as Arthur and Aubrey tried to find something to talk about. "But it seems to have stopped for the moment."

"Not good—how?"

"Like gas pains," she said, her mouth a wry twist at this confession. "Honestly, I've never been so miserable in my life. Everything I eat gives me heartburn, and my back is killing me."

"And you're due very soon?"

"Not for a couple more weeks."

"When's your next doctor's appointment?"

"In your last month, you go every week," Lynn said knowledgeably. "I'm due to go back in tomorrow. Maybe he'll tell me something."

I decided I might as well admit wholesale ignorance. Lynn certainly needed something to feel superior about. She had looked sourly on my red and white shorts outfit. "So what could he tell you?" I asked.

"Oh. Well, for example, he could tell me I've started

dilating—you know, getting bigger to have the baby. Or he could tell me I'm effacing."

I nodded hastily, so Lynn wouldn't explain what that meant.

"Or how much the baby has dropped, if its head is really far down."

I was sorry I'd asked. But Lynn was looking in better spirits, and she went on to tell Aubrey how they'd decorated the nursery, segueing neatly from that domestic subject to a discussion of the break-ins on the street, which were being generally discussed. The McMans complained about the police inaction on the crimes, unaware that they were about to become very embarrassed.

"You're going to have to understand," Arthur said, his pale blue eyes open wide, which meant he was very irritated, "that if nothing is stolen and no fingerprints are found, and no one sees anything, the burglar is going to be almost impossible to find unless an informant turns in something."

The McMans, small and mousy and shy, turned identical shades of mortification when they realized that the new couple next door were both police detectives. After an embarrassing bumble of apologies and retractions, Ca talked about her break-in—which had occurred and her daughter were at Carey's folks' ho giving two years ago—and Marcia r which had "scared her to death

"I came back from shopp Torrance was out of town; Torrance is out of town"—an glance—"and I saw the back window of the kitchen was broken out, oh you should have seen me make tracks over to Jane's house."

"When was that?" I asked. "Around the time Carey's house was broken into?"

"You know, it was. It was maybe a month later. I remember it was cold and we had to get the glass fixed in a hurry."

"When was your house broken into?' I asked Macon, who was holding Carey's hand and enjoying it.

"After the Laverys," he said, after a moment's thought. "They're the people who owned the house you bought," he said to Arthur. "They got transferred five months ago, so I know they're relieved not to have to make two house payments. My break-in, and the Laverys', was like the others . . . back window, house searched and messed up, but nothing apparently taken."

"When was that?" I persisted. Arthur shot me a sharp look, but Lynn seemed more interested in her stomach, which she was massaging slowly.

"Oh, sometime about a year and a half ago, maybe longer."

"So Jane's house was the only one that hadn't been broken into until very recently?"

Carey, Macon, the McMans, and Marcia and Torrance exchanged glances.

"I think that's right," Macon said. "Come to think of it. d it's been quite a while since the last one. I know I 't thought about it in ages until Carey told me about house."

"So everyone's been broken into—everyone on the street?" Was that what Jack Burns had told me?

"Well," Marcia said, as she poured dressing on the salad and tossed it, "everyone but the Inces, whose house is on the two lots across from Macon and us. They're very, very old and they never go out anymore. Their daughter-in-law does everything for them, shopping and taking them to doctor appointments and so on. They haven't been bothered, or I'm sure Margie—that's the daughter-in-law—would've come over and told me about it. Every now and then she comes over and has a cup of coffee after she's been to see them."

"I wonder what it means?" I asked no one in particular.

An uncomfortable silence fell.

"Come on, you all, the food's all ready and waiting!" Marcia said cheerfully.

Everyone rose with alacrity except Lynn. I heard Arthur murmur, "You want me to bring you something, hon?"

"Just a little bit," she said wearily. "I'm just not very hungry."

It didn't seem to me that Lynn would have any room left for food, the baby was taking up so much.

Torrance went through the house to answer the front doorbell. The rest of us shuffled through the line, oohing and ahhing appropriately at the gorgeous food. It was presented in a beautiful way, all the dishes decorated and arranged as if far more important people than we were coming to taste it. Unless Marcia had had help, this table represented hours of work. But the food itself was comfortingly homely.

"Barbecued ribs!" exclaimed Aubrey happily. "Oh boy. Roe, you're just going to have to put up with me. I make a mess when I eat them."

"There's not a neat way to eat ribs," I observed. "And Marcia has put out extra large napkins, I see."

"I'd better take two."

Just then I heard a familiar voice rising above the general chatter. I turned to peer around Aubrey, my mouth falling a little open in a foolish way.

"Mother!" I said, in blank surprise.

It was indeed Mother, in elegant cream slacks and midnight blue blouse, impressive but casual gold necklace and earrings, and her new husband in tow.

"I'm so sorry we were late," she was apologizing in her Lauren Bacall–gracious-woman mode, the one that always made people accept her apology. "John wasn't sure until the last minute whether he felt like coming or not. But I did so want to meet Aurora's new neighbors, and it was so kind of you to invite us . . ."

The Rideouts gushed back, there was a round of introductions, and suddenly the party seemed livelier and more sophisticated.

Despite his tired eyes, John looked well after their honeymoon, and I told him so. For a few minutes, John seemed a little puzzled as to what exactly Aubrey was doing at the party, but when it sunk in that his minister was my date, John took a deep breath and rose to the occasion, discussing church affairs very briefly with Aubrey, just enough to make them comfortable with each other without boring the non-Episcopalians. Mother and John joined in the food line behind us, Mother sparing a cold glance for Arthur, who was sitting beside his wife and eating while giving her a solicitous look or laying his hand on her shoulder every few seconds.

"She's about to pop. I thought they just got married a few months ago," Mother hissed in my ear.

"Mom, hush," I hissed back.

"I need to talk to you, young lady," Mother responded in a low voice so packed with meaning that I began to wonder what I could have done that she'd heard of. I was almost as nervous as I'd been at six when she used that voice with me.

We sat back down at the picnic tables set with their bright tablecloths and napkins, and Marcia rolled around a cart with drinks and ice on it. She was glowing at all the compliments. Torrance was beaming, too, proud of his wife. I wondered, looking at Lynn and Arthur, why the Rideouts hadn't had children. I wondered if Carey Osland and Macon would try to have another one if they married. Carey was probably forty-two, but women were having them later and later, it seemed. Macon must have been at least six to ten years older than Carey—of course, he had a son who was at least a young adult . . . the missing son.

"While I was in the Bahamas," John said quietly into my ear, "I tried to get a minute to see if the house of Sir Harry Oakes was still standing."

I had to think for a minute. The Oakes case . . . okay, I remembered.

"Alfred de Marigny, acquitted, right?"

"Yes," said John happily. It was always nice to talk to someone who shared your hobby.

"Is this a historical site in the Bahamas?" Aubrey asked from my right.

"Well, in a way," I told him. "The Oakes house was the site of a famous murder." I swung back around to John. "The feathers were the strangest feature of that case, I thought."

"Oh, I think there's an easy explanation," John said dismissively. "I think a fan blew the feathers from a pillow that had been broken open."

"After the fire?"

"Yes, had to have been," John said, wagging his head from side to side. "The feathers looked white in the picture, and otherwise they would've been blackened."

"Feathers?" Aubrey inquired.

"See," I explained patiently, "the body—Sir Harry Oakes—was found partially burned, on a bed, with feathers stuck all over it. The body, I mean, not the bed. Alfred de Marigny, his son-in-law, was charged. But he was acquitted, mostly because of the deplorable investigation by the local police."

Aubrey looked a little—what? I couldn't identify it.

John and I went on happily hashing over the murder of Sir Harry, my mother to John's left carrying on a sporadic conversation with the mousy McMans across from her.

I turned halfway back to Aubrey to make sure he was appreciating a point I was making about the bloody handprint on the screen in the bedroom and noticed he had dropped his ribs on his plate and was looking under the weather.

"What's the matter?" I asked, concerned.

"Would you mind not talking about this particular

topic while I eat my ribs, which looked so good until a few minutes ago?" Aubrey was trying to sound jocular, but I could tell he was seriously unhappy with me.

Of course I was at fault. That had the unfortunate result of making me exasperated with Aubrey, as well as myself. I took a few seconds to work myself into a truly penitent frame of mind.

"I'm sorry, Aubrey," I said quietly. I stole a peek at John out of the corner of my eye. He was looking abashed, and my mother had her eyes closed and was silently shaking her head as if her children had tried her beyond her belief, and in public at that. But she quickly rallied and smoothly introduced that neutral and lively subject, the rivalry of the phone companies in the area.

I was so gloomy over my breach of taste that I didn't even chip in my discovery that my phone company could make my phone ring at two houses at the same time. Arthur said he was glad that he had been able to keep his old phone number. I wondered how Lynn felt about giving up her own, but she didn't look as if she gave a damn one way or another. Right after Arthur finished eating and they had thanked Marcia and Torrance in a polite murmur for the party, the good food, and the fellowship, they quietly left to go home.

"That young lady looks uncomfortable," Torrance commented in a lull in the telephone wars. Of course, that led to a discussion of Arthur and Lynn and their police careers, and since I was also a newcomer on the street the discussion moved logically to my career, which I was obliged to tell them—including my mother—had come to an end.

I thought if my mother's face held its mildly interested smile any longer, it would crack.

Aubrey had finished his supper finally and joined in the conversation, but in a subdued way. I thought we were going to have to talk sometime soon about my interest in murder cases and the fact that he found them nauseating. I was trying not to think about how much fun it had been to talk to John about the fascinating Oakes case . . . and it had occurred while the duke and duchess of Windsor were governing the islands! I'd have to catch my new stepfather alone sometime and we could really hash it over.

I was recalled to the here and now by my mother's voice in my ear. "Come to the bathroom for a moment!"

I excused myself and went in the house with her. I'd never been in the Rideouts' before, and I could only gather an impression of spotless maintenance and bright colors before I was whisked into the hall bathroom. It seemed like a teenager sort of thing to do, going into the bathroom together, and just as I opened my mouth to ask my mother if she had a date to the prom, she turned to me after locking the door and said—

"What, young woman, is a skull doing in my blanket bag?"

For what felt like the tenth time in one day I was left with my mouth hanging open. Then I rallied.

"What on earth were you doing getting a blanket out in this weather?"

"Getting a blanket for my husband while he was having chills with the flu," she told me through clenched teeth. "Don't you dare try to sidetrack me!"

"I found it," I said.

"Great. So you found a human skull, and you decided to put it in a blanket bag in your mother's house while she was out of town. That makes perfect sense. A very rational procedure."

I was going to have to level with her. But locked in Marcia Rideout's bathroom was not the situation.

"Mom, I swear that tomorrow I'll come to your house and tell you all about it."

"I'm sure any time would be okay with you because you have no job to go to," my mother said very politely. "However, I have to earn my living, and I am going to work. I will expect you to be at my house tomorrow night at seven o'clock, when I had better hear a good explanation for what you have done. And while I'm saying drastic things, I might as well tell you something else, though since you have been an adult I have tried not to give you any advice on your affairs of the heart—or whatever. Do *not* sleep with my husband's minister. It would be very embarrassing for John."

"For John? It would be embarrassing for *John*?" Get a hold, I told myself. I took a deep breath, looked in the gleaming mirror, and pushed my glasses up on my nose. "Mother, I can't tell you how glad I am that you have restrained yourself, all these years, from commenting on my social life, other than telling me you wished I had more of one."

We looked at each other in the mirror with stormy eyes.

Then I tried smiling at her. She tried smiling at me. The smiles were tiny, but they held.

"All right," she said finally, in a more moderate voice. "We'll see you tomorrow night."

"It's a date," I agreed.

When we came back to the sun deck, the party talk had swung around to the bones found at the end of the street. Carey was saying the police had been to ask her if there was anything she remembered that might help to identify the bones as her husband's. "I told them," she was saying, "that that rascal had run off and left me, not been killed. For weeks after he didn't come back, I thought he might walk back through that door with those diapers. You know," she told Aubrey parenthetically, "he left to get diapers for the baby and never came back." Aubrey nodded, perhaps to indicate understanding or perhaps because he'd already heard this bit of Lawrenceton folklore. "When the police found the car at the Amtrak station," Carey continued, "I knew he'd just run off. He's been dead to me ever since, but I definitely don't believe those bones are his." Macon put his arm around her. The mousy McMans were enthralled at this real-life drama. My mother stared at me in sudden consternation. I pretended I didn't see it.

"So I told them he'd broken his leg once, the year before we got married, if that would tell them anything, and they thanked me and said they'd let me know. But after the first day he was gone, when I was so distraught; well, after the police told me they'd found his car, I didn't worry about him anymore. I just felt mad."

Carey had gotten upset, and was trying very hard not to let a tear roll down her cheeks. Marcia Rideout was staring at her, hoping her party was not going to be ruined by a guest weeping openly.

Torrance said soothingly, "Now, Carey, it's not Mike, it's some old tramp. That's sad, but it's nothing for us to worry about." He stood, holding his drink, his sturdy body and calm voice somehow immensely reassuring.

Everyone seemed to relax a little. But then Marcia said, "But where's the skull? On this evening's television news they said there wasn't a skull." Her hand was shaking as she put the lid on a casserole. "Why wasn't the head there?"

It was a tense moment. I couldn't help clenching my drink tighter and looking down at the deck. My mother's eyes were on me; I could feel her glare.

"It sounds macabre," Aubrey said gently, "but perhaps a dog or some other animal carried off the skull. There's no reason it couldn't have been with the rest of the body for some time."

"That's true," Macon said after a moment's consideration.

The tension eased again. After a little more talk, my mother and John rose to leave. No one is immune to my mother's graciousness; Marcia and Torrance were beaming by the time she made her progress out the front door, John right behind her basking in the glow. The McMans soon said they had to pay off their babysitter and take her home, since it was a school night. Carey Osland, too, said she had to relieve her sitter. "Though my daughter is beginning to think she can stay by herself," she told us proudly. "But for now she definitely needs someone there, even when I'm just two houses away."

"She's an independent girl," Macon said with a smile. He seemed quite taken with Carey's daughter. "I'd only been around boys before, and girls are so different to raise. I hope I can do a better job helping Carey than I did raising my son."

Since the Rideouts were childless, and so was I, and so was Aubrey, we had no response that would have made sense.

I thanked Marcia for the party, and complimented her and Torrance on the decorations and food.

"Well, I did barbecue the ribs," Torrance admitted, running his hand over his already bristly chin, "but all the rest of the fixing is Marcia's work."

I told Marcia she should be a caterer, and she flushed with pleasure. She looked just like a department store mannequin with a little pink painted on the cheeks for realism, so pretty and so perfect.

"Every hair is in place," I told Aubrey wonderingly as we walked over to his car parked in my driveway. "She wouldn't ever let her hair do this," and I sunk my hands into my own flyaway mop.

"That's what I want to do," Aubrey said promptly, and, stopping and facing me, he ran his hands through my hair. "It's beautiful," he said in an unministerly voice.

Woo-woo. The kiss that followed was long and thorough enough to remind me of exactly how long it had been since I had biblically known anyone. I could tell Aubrey felt the same.

We mutually disengaged. "I shouldn't have done that," Aubrey said. "It makes me . . ."

"Me, too," I agreed, and he laughed, and the mood was broken. I was very glad I hadn't worn the orange-and-white dress. Then his hands would have been on my bare back . . . I started to chatter to distract myself. We leaned against his car, talking about the party, my new stepfather's flu, my quitting my job, his retreat for priests he'd be attending that Friday and Saturday at a nearby state park.

"Shall I follow you home?" he asked, as he slid into his car.

"I might spend the night here," I said. I bent in and gave him a light kiss on the lips and a smile, and then he left.

I walked to the kitchen door and went in. The moon through the open kitchen curtains gave me plenty of light, so I went to the bedroom in darkness. The contrast of quiet and dark with the talk, talk, talk I'd done that day made me sleepier than a pill would have. I switched on the bathroom light briefly to brush my teeth and shuck my clothes. Then I pulled the rose pink nightgown over my head, switched off the bathroom light, and made my way to the bed in darkness. To the quiet hum of the air-conditioning and the occasional tiny mew from the kittens in the closet, I fell fast asleep.

Chapter Twelve

I woke up. I knew where I was instantly—in Jane's house. I swung my legs over the side of the bed automatically, preparing to trek to the bathroom. But I realized in a slow, middle-of-the-night way that I didn't need to go.

The cats were quiet.

So why was I awake?

Then I heard movement somewhere else in the house, and saw a beam of light flash through the hall. Someone was in the house with me. I bit the insides of my mouth together to keep from screaming.

Jane's clock radio on the bedside table had a glowing face that illuminated the outline of the bedside phone. With fingers that were almost useless, I lifted the receiver, taking such care, such care . . . no noise. Thank God it was a push-button. From instinct I dialed the number I knew so well, the number that would bring help even faster than 911.

"Hello?" said a voice in my ear, groggy with sleep.

"Arthur," I breathed. "Wake up."

"Who is this?"

"It's Roe. I'm across the street in Jane's house. There is someone in the house."

"I'll be there in a minute. Stay quiet. Hide."

I hung up the phone so gently, so delicately, trying to control my hands, oh Lord, let me not make a sound.

I knew what had given me away: it was my downward glance when the skull was mentioned at the party. Someone had been watching for just such a reaction.

I slid my glasses on while I was thinking. I had two options on hiding: under the bed or in the closet with the cats. The intruder was in the guest bedroom, just a short hall length away. I could see the flashlight beam bobbing here and there; searching, searching again, for the damn *skull*! The best place to hide would be the big dirty-clothes closet in the bathroom; I was small enough to double up in there, since it was almost square to match the linen closet on top of it. If I hid in the bedroom closet, the intruder might hear the cat noises and investigate. But I couldn't risk slipping into the bathroom now, with the light flashing in the hallway unpredictably.

In response to my thoughts, it seemed, the light bobbed out of the guest bedroom, into the little hall, through the big archway into the living room. When it was well within the living room, I slid off the bed onto my feet with the tiniest of thumps . . .

. . . and landed right on Madeleine's tail. The cat yowled, I screamed, a startled exclamation came from the living room. I heard thumping footsteps and, when a blob was in the doorway, pausing, maybe fumbling for a light switch, I leaped. I hit someone right in the chest, wrapped my right arm around a beefy neck, and with my left hand grabbed a handful of short hair and pulled as hard as I could. Something from a self-defense course I'd taken popped into my mind and I began shrieking at the top of my lungs.

Something hit me a terrible blow on the back, but I tightened my grip on the short hair and my stranglehold on the neck. "Stop," wheezed a heavy voice, "stop, stop!" And blows began raining on my back and legs. I was being shaken loose by all the staggering and my own weight, and I had to stop screaming to catch my breath. But I sucked it in and had opened my mouth to shriek again when the lights came on.

My attacker whirled to face the person who'd turned on the light, and in that whirl I was slung off onto the floor, landing not quite on my feet and staggering into the bedpost to collect a few more bruises.

Lynn Liggett Smith stood leaning against the wall in the hall, breathing heavily, the gun in her hand pointing at Torrance Rideout, who had only a flashlight dangling from his hand. If the flashlight had been a knife, I'd have been bleeding from a dozen wounds; as it was, I felt like Lee's Army had marched over me. I held on to the bedpost and panted. Where was Arthur?

Torrance took in Lynn's weak stance and huge belly and turned back to me.

"You have to tell me," he said desperately, as if she wasn't even there, "you have to tell me where the skull is."

"Put your hands against the wall," Lynn said steadily but weakly. "I'm a police officer and I will shoot."

"You're nine months pregnant and about to fall down," Torrance said over his shoulder. He turned to me again. "*Where is the skull?*" His broad, open face was crossed with seams I'd never noticed before, and there was blood trickling down from his scalp onto his white shirt. I seemed to have removed a square inch of hair.

Lynn fired into the ceiling.

"Put your hands against the wall, you bastard," she said coldly.

And he did.

He hadn't realized that if Lynn really shot at him she stood an excellent chance of hitting me. Before he got the idea, I moved to the other side of the bed. But then I couldn't see Lynn. This bedroom was too tight. I didn't like Torrance being between me and the door.

"Roe," Lynn said from the hall, slowly. "Pat him down and see if he's got a gun. Or knife." She sounded like she was in pain.

I hated getting so close to Torrance. Did he respect the gun enough? Had he picked up on the strain in Lynn's voice? I wished, for a moment, that she had gone on and shot him.

My only ideas about patting a suspect down came from

television. I had a shrinking distaste for touching Torrance's body, but I pursed my lips and ran my hands over him.

"Just change in his pocket," I said hoarsely. My screaming had hurt more than Torrance's ears.

"Okay," said Lynn slowly. "Here are the cuffs."

When I looked right in her face, I was shocked. Her eyes were wide and frightened, she was biting her lower lip. The gun was steady in her hand, but it was taking all her will to keep it so. The carpet looked dark around her feet, which were wearing slippers that were dark and light pink. I looked more closely. The darkness on her slippers was wetness. She had fluid trickling down her legs. There was a funny smell in the air. Lynn's water had broken.

Where was Arthur?

I closed my eyes for a second in sheer consternation. When I opened them, Lynn and I were staring at each other in panic. Then Lynn hardened her glare and said, "Take the cuffs, Roe."

I reached through the narrow doorway and took them. Arthur had shown me how to use his one day, so I did know how to close them on Torrance's wrists.

"Hold out your hands behind you," I said as viciously as I could. Lynn and I were going to lose control any minute. I'd gotten one cuff on when Torrance erupted. He swung the arm with the cuff on it around, and the flying loose cuff caught me on the side of the head. But he mustn't get the gun! I gripped whatever of him I could grab, blinded by pain, and hobbled him enough to land us both on the floor, rolling around in the limited space, me hanging on for my own dear life, him desperately trying to be rid of me.

"Torrance, stop!" shrieked yet another voice, and we were still, him on top of me panting and me underneath barely breathing at all. Past his shoulder I could see Marcia, her hair still smooth, her blue shorts and shirt obviously hastily pulled on.

"Honey, it doesn't make any difference anymore, we have to stop," she said gently. He got off me to swing around and look at her heavily. Then Lynn moaned, a terrible sound.

Torrance seemed mesmerized by his wife. I crawled past him and past her, actually brushing her leg as I went by. They both ignored me in the eeriest way.

Lynn had slid down the wall. She was making a valiant attempt to hold the gun up but couldn't manage anymore. When she saw me, her eyes made an appeal and her hand fell to the floor and released the gun. I took it and swung around, fully intending to somehow shoot both the Rideouts, our recent hosts. But they were still wrapped up in each other, and I could have riddled them both for all they paid attention to me. With the affronted feeling of being a child whose anger adults won't take seriously, I turned back to Lynn.

Her eyes were closed, and her breathing was funny. Then I realized she was breathing in a pattern.

"You're having the baby," I said sadly.

She nodded, still with her eyes closed, and kept her breathing going.

"You called some backup, right?"

She nodded again.

"Arthur must have been out on a call; that was you on

the phone," I observed, and I went into the bathroom right at my back to wash my hands and get some towels.

"I don't know nothin' 'bout birthin' no babies," I told my reflection, pushed my glasses up on my nose, had the fleeting thought that it was nothing short of amazing they hadn't been cracked, and went to squat by Lynn's side. I gingerly pulled up her nightgown and lay towels on the floor beneath her drawn-up knees.

"Where is the skull?" Torrance asked me. His voice sounded defeated.

"At my mom's house in a closet," I said briefly, my attention absorbed by Lynn.

"So Jane had it all the time," he said, in a wooden voice from which all the wonder was leached. "That old woman had it all the time. She was furious after the tree thing, you know. I couldn't believe it, all those years we were good neighbors, then there was this trouble about the damn tree. Next thing I know, there was a hole in the yard and the head was gone. But I never connected the two things. I even left Jane's house for last because I thought she was least likely to have it."

"Oh, Torrance," Marcia said pitifully. "I wish you had told me. Was it you who broke into all the houses?"

"Looking for the head," he said. "I knew someone around here had to have it, but it never occurred to me it could be Jane. It had to be someone who could have seen me burying him, but not Jane, not that sweet little old lady. I just knew that if she'd seen me burying him, she'd have called the police. And I had to wait," Torrance meandered on, "so long between each house, because after each break-in, people would be so cautious for a long time . . ."

"You even pretended to break into our house," marveled his wife.

Gingerly I stole a peek under the nightgown. I was instantly sorry.

"Lynn," I told her hesitantly, "I see what I think is the baby's head, I guess."

Lynn nodded emphatically. Her eyes flew open, and she focused on a point on the wall opposite. Her breathing became ragged for a few moments. "Get yourself together!" I said earnestly. Lynn was the only person who knew what was happening. Lynn seemed to take that as advice offered from compassion, and squeezed my hand till I thought of screaming again.

Suddenly she caught her breath, and her whole body tensed.

I peeked again.

"Oh dear," I breathed. This was really quite a lot worse than watching Madeleine the cat. I followed my own advice and pulled myself together, despite my desire to run screaming out of this house and never come back. I let go of Lynn's hand and moved between her legs. There was barely room. It was lucky I was a small person.

Lynn strained again.

"Okay, Lynn," I said bracingly. "It's coming. I'll catch it."

Lynn seemed to rest for a moment.

"Whose skull?" I asked Torrance. Marcia had sunk to the floor, and they were sitting knee to knee holding hands.

"Oh," he said as if he'd lost interest. "The skull is Mark. Mark Kaplan. The boy who rented our apartment."

Lynn gathered herself and pushed again. Her eyes were glazed, and I was scared to death. I hesitantly put my hands where they might do some good.

"Lynn, I see more of the head," I told her.

Amazingly, Lynn smiled. And she gathered herself. And pushed.

"I've got the head, Lynn," I told her in a shaky voice. I was trying to sound confident, but I failed. Would the baby's neck break if I let its head flop? Oh dear Jesus, I needed help. I was so inadequate.

Lynn did it again.

"That's the shoulders," I whispered, holding this tiny, bloody, vulnerable thing. "One more push should do it," I said bracingly, having no idea at all what I was talking about. But it seemed to hearten Lynn, and she started pulling herself together again. I wished that she could take a break, so I could, but I had told her the truth out of sheer ignorance. Lynn pushed like she was in the Olympics of baby extrusion, and the slippery thing shot out of her like a hurtling football, or so it seemed to me. And I caught it.

"What?" asked Lynn weakly.

It took me a second of sheer stupidity to understand her. I should be doing something! I should make it cry! Wasn't that important?

"Hold it upside down and whack it on its back," Marcia said. "That's what they do on TV."

Full of terror, I did so. The baby let out a wail. So it was breathing, it was alive! So far so good. Though still hooked up to Lynn, this child was okay for now. Should I do something to the umbilical cord? What? And I heard sirens coming, thank the Lord.

"What?" Lynn asked more urgently.

"Girl!" I said jerkily. "A girl!" I held the little thing as I had seen babies held in pictures and made plans to burn the rose pink nightgown.

"Well," said Lynn with a tiny smile, as pounding began on the front door, "damn if I'm going to name it after you."

It took some time to sort out the situation in Jane's little house, which seemed more crowded than ever with all the policemen in Lawrenceton.

Some of the policemen, seeing Arthur's former flame kneeling before his new wife, both bloody, assumed I was the person to arrest. They could hardly put cuffs on me or search me though, since I was holding the baby, who was still attached to Lynn. And when they all realized I was holding a newborn baby and not some piece I'd ripped from Lynn's insides, they went nuts. No one seemed to remember that there'd been a break-in, that consequently the burglar might be on the scene.

Arthur had been out on a robbery call, but when he arrived he was so scared he was ready to kill someone. He waved his gun around vaguely, and when he spotted Lynn and the blood, he began bellowing, "Ambulance! Ambulance!" Jack Burns himself pushed right by the Rideouts to use the phone in the bedroom.

Arthur was by me in a flash, babbling. "The baby!" he said. He didn't know what to do with his gun.

"Put the gun away and take this baby," I said rather sharply. "It's still attached to Lynn, and I don't know what to do about that."

"Lynn, how are you?" Arthur said in a daze.

"Honey, put a towel over your suit and take your daughter," Lynn said weakly.

"My—oh." He holstered his gun and reached down and took a towel off the stack I'd brought out. I wondered if Jane could ever have imagined her monogrammed white cotton towels being used for such a purpose. I handed the baby over with alacrity, and stood up, trembling from a cocktail of fear, pain, and shock. I was more than glad to vacate my position between Lynn's legs.

One of the ambulance attendants ran up to me then and said, "You the maternity? Or have you been injured?"

I pointed a shaky finger at Lynn. I didn't blame him for thinking I'd been seriously hurt; I was covered with smears of blood, some of it Lynn's, some of it Torrance's, a little of it mine.

"Are you all right?"

I looked to the source of the voice and found I was standing next to Torrance. This was so strange.

"I'll be okay," I said wearily.

"I'm sorry. I was never cut out to be a criminal."

I thought of the inept break-ins, Torrance not even taking anything to make them look like legitimate burglaries. I nodded.

"Why did you do it?" I asked him.

Suddenly his face hardened and tightened all over. "I just did," he said.

"So when Jane dug up the skull, you dug up the rest of the body and put the bones by the dead end sign?"

"I knew no one would clean up that brush for years," he said. "And I was right. I was too scared to carry the bones in my trunk, even for a little while. I waited till the next night when Macon went over to Carey's, and I carried the bones in a plastic bag through his backyard and up the far side of his house; then it was just a few feet to the brush . . . no one saw me *that* time. I was so sure whoever had taken the skull would call the police. I waited. Then I realized whoever had the skull just wanted . . . to have it. For me to squirm. I had almost forgotten that trouble about the tree. Jane was so ladylike. I never believed . . ."

"And he never told me about it," said Marcia, to his left. "He never let me worry, too." She looked at him fondly.

"So, what did you do it for?" I asked Torrance. "Did he make a pass at Marcia?"

"Well . . ." said Torrance hesitantly.

"Oh, honey," Marcia said, reproving. She leaned over to me, smiling a little at a man's silly gesture. "He didn't do it," she told me. "I did it."

"You killed Mark Kaplan and buried him out in the yard?"

"Oh, Torrance buried him when I told him what I'd done."

"Oh," I said inadequately, swallowed by her wide blue eyes. "You killed him because—?"

"He came over while Torrance was gone." She shook

her head sadly as she told me. "And I had thought he was such a nice person. But he *wasn't*. He was very dirty."

I nodded, just to be responding somehow.

"Mike Osland, too," Marcia ran on, still shaking her head at the perfidy of men.

I felt suddenly very, very cold. Torrance closed his eyes in profound weariness.

"Mike," I murmured interrogatively.

"He's under the sun deck, that's why Torrance built it, I think," Marcia said earnestly. "Jane didn't know about him."

"She's confessing," said an incredulous, hoarse voice.

I turned from Marcia's mesmerizing eyes to see that Jack Burns was sitting on his haunches in front of me.

"Did she just confess to a murder?" he asked me.

"Two," I said.

"Two murders," he repeated. He took his turn at head shaking. I would have to find someone at whom I could shake *my* head incredulously. "She just confessed two murders to you. How do you do it?"

Faced by his round, hot eyes, I became aware that I was in a torn and disheveled and rather skimpy-at-the-top nightgown that had become quite soiled in the course of the night. I was definitely reminded that I was not Jack Burns's favorite person. I wondered how much Lynn would remember of what she'd overheard while she was having the baby—was it possible she would remember my telling Torrance that I knew the whereabouts of the skull?

Lynn was being carried out on a stretcher now. I presumed that the afterbirth had been delivered and disposed of. I hoped I wouldn't find it on the bathroom floor or something.

"This man," I told Jack Burns, as I pointed to Torrance, "broke into my house tonight."

"Are you hurt?" asked Sergeant Burns, with reluctant professional solicitude.

I turned to look in Torrance Rideout's eyes. "No," I said clearly. "Not at all. And I have no idea why he broke in here or what he was looking for."

Torrance's eyes showed a slow recognition. And, to my amazement, he winked at me when Jack Burns turned away to call his cohorts over.

After an eternity, every single person was gone from Jane's house but me, its owner. What do you do after a night you've had a burglary, been battered, delivered a baby, and nearly been mown down by the entire detective force of Lawrenceton, Georgia? Also, I continued enumerating as I hauled the remains of the nightgown over my head, heard a confession of double murder and had your scarcely covered bosom ogled by the same detectives who had been about to mow you down minutes earlier?

Well. I was going to take a hot, hot bath to soak my bruises and strains. I was going to calm a nearly berserk Madeleine, who was crouching in a corner of the bedroom closet hoping she was concealed underneath a blanket I'd thrown in there. Madeleine, as it happened, did not react well to home invasion. Then, possibly, I could put my tired carcass back between the cool sheets and sleep a little.

There'd be hell to pay in the morning.
My mother would call.

B ut I only slept four hours. When I woke it was eight
o'clock, and I lay in bed and thought for a moment.
Then I was up and brushing my teeth, pulling back on
my shorts set from the night before. I managed to get a
brush through my hair, which had been damp from the
tub when I'd fallen asleep the night before. I let Madeleine
out and back in—she seemed calm again—and then it was
time to get to Wal-Mart.

I walked in as the doors were unlocked and found what
I was looking for after a talk with a salesperson.

I stopped in at the town house and got out my box of
gift wrap.

At Mother's house both cars were gone. I'd finally gotten a break. I used my key one last time; I never would
again now that John lived here, too. I sped up the stairs
and got the old blanket bag out of the closet and left the
gift-wrapped blanket bag on the kitchen table on my way
out. I left my key by it.

Quickly out to my car then, and speeding back to the
house on Honor.

Another stroke of luck; no police cars at the Rideouts' yet.

I went out the back kitchen door and looked around as
carefully as Torrance Rideout must have the night he buried Mark Kaplan, the night he buried Mike Osland. But

this was daylight, far more dangerous. I'd counted cars as I pulled into my own driveway: Lynn's car was at the house across the street, Arthur's was gone. That figured; he was at the hospital with his wife and his baby.

I did falter then. But I reached up and slapped myself on the cheek. This was no time to get weepy.

The elderly Inces were not a consideration. I peered over to Carey Osland's house. Her car was home. She must have been told of the confession by Marcia Rideout that Mike Osland was in the Rideouts' backyard. I could only hope that Carey didn't decide to come look personally.

As I started across my backyard, I had to smother an impulse to crouch and run, or slither on my belly. The pink blanket bag seemed so conspicuous. But I just couldn't bring myself to open it and carry the bare skull in my hands. Besides, I'd already rubbed my prints off. I got to the sun deck with no one shouting, "Hey! What are you doing?" and took a few deep breaths. Now hurry, I told myself, and unzipped the bag, grabbed the thing inside by hooking a finger through the jaw, and, trying not to look at it, I rolled it as far as I could under the deck. I was tempted to climb the steps to the deck, look between the boards, and see if the skull showed from on top. But instead I turned and walked quickly back to my own yard, praying that no one had noticed my strange behavior. I was still clutching the zip bag. Once inside, I glanced in the bag to check that no traces were left of the skull's presence, and folded one of Jane's blankets, zipped it inside, and shoved the bag to the back of the shelf in one of the guest bedroom closets. Then I sat at the little table in the kitchen, and out the window toward the Rideouts' I saw men starting to take apart the sun deck.

I had just made it.

I shook all over. I put my head in my hands and cried.

After a while, that seemed to dry up, and I felt limp and tired. I made a pot of coffee and sat at the table and drank it while I watched the men demolish the deck and find the skull. After the hubbub that caused was over and after the skull had been placed carefully in a special bag of some kind (which actually made me smile a little), the men began digging. It was hot, and they all sweated, and I saw Sergeant Burns glance over to my house as though he'd like to come ask me a few questions, but I'd answered them all the night before. All I was ever going to answer.

Then one of the men gave a shout, and the others gathered round, and I decided maybe I wouldn't watch anymore. At noon the phone rang, and it was my mother, thanking me crisply for the lovely new blanket storage bag and reminding me that we were going to eat dinner together and have a long talk.

"Sure, Mom," I said, and sighed. I was sore and stiff; maybe she would cut it short. "Mom, tomorrow I'm going to come in and list this house."

Well, that was business. That was different. Or maybe not. "I'll list it myself," she promised meaningfully, and hung up.

The phone was on the wall by the letter rack and the calendar, a sensible and convenient arrangement. I stood staring blankly at the letter rack for a few seconds, finally taking down a charity appeal, pulling out the begging letter, looking it over, throwing it away. I took out another letter, which should have been a bill from the bug-spray people by the envelope . . . why didn't Bubba Sewell have it? He should have all the bills. But the stamp had been canceled months before.

Suddenly I knew what this was, knew even as I shook the paper out of the slit that it was not going to be a bill from Orkin.

Of course: "The Purloined Letter." Jane liked *classics*.

"On a Wednesday night in the summer, four years ago," the letter began abruptly,

I, Jane Engle, was sitting in my backyard. It was very late because I had insomnia, and I often sit in the garden in the dark when I have insomnia. It was about midnight, when I saw Mark Kaplan, the Rideouts' boarder, go to Marcia's back door and knock. I could see him clearly in the floodlight the Rideouts have at their back door. Marcia always leaves it on all night when Torrance is out of town. Marcia came to the door, and Mark Kaplan, right away, attacked her. I believe he had been drinking, that he had a bottle in his hand, but I am not sure. Before I could go to her help, she somehow knocked him down, and I saw her grab something from her kitchen counter and hit Mark Kaplan on the back of the head with it. I am not sure what she picked up, but I think it was a hammer. Then I became aware another car had pulled up into the Rideouts' carport, and I realized that Torrance had come home.

I went inside, thinking that soon I would hear police cars and I would have to talk to the police about what I'd seen. So I changed into my regular clothes—I'd had my nightgown on—and sat in the kitchen and waited in the dark for something to happen.

Instead of police cars, sirens, and whatnot, I saw Torrance come out in a few minutes with a tablecloth. Clearly something body size was wrapped in it, and I was sure it was Mark Kaplan. Torrance proceeded over to their old garden plot, and began to dig. I stayed awake the rest of the night, watching him. I didn't call the police, though I gave it some thought. I knew what testifying in court would do to Marcia Rideout, who has never been any too stable. Also, Mark Kaplan did attack her, and I knew it.

So I said nothing.

But a little over a year and a half later, I got into a dispute with Torrance over my tree, from which he arrogantly trimmed some branches. Every time I looked out my kitchen window, the tree looked worse. So I did something I'm not proud of. I waited till the Rideouts were both out of town, and I went over in the night and dug where I'd seen Torrance dig many months before. It took me three nights, since I am an old woman, but I reached the skull. I removed it and brought it home with me. And I left the hole open, to be sure Torrance knew someone had the head, someone knew.

I am truly not proud of this. Now I am too sick to put the skull back, and I am too afraid of Torrance to just give it to him. And I have been thinking of Mike

Osland; he disappeared before Mark Kaplan was killed, and I remember seeing him look at Marcia at parties. I think now that Marcia, just a little eccentric on the surface, is actually quite disturbed, and I think Torrance knows this; and yet he goes on with his life as though by denying she needs special care, she will get better.

I am too close to my own death to worry about this anymore. If my lawyer finds this, he must do as he thinks best; I don't care what people say about me when I am gone. If Roe finds this, she must do as pleases her. The skull is in the window seat.

Jane Engle

I looked down at the paper in my hands, then refolded it. Without really considering it, I began shredding the letter, first in halves, then quarters, then thirds, until finally I had a little pile of confetti on the counter. I gathered it all up and dropped it down the sink, running the water and starting the disposal. After it had rumbled for a moment, I turned off the water and carefully checked all the other letters in the rack. They were exactly what they seemed.

I looked at Jane's calendar, still turned to two months before. I took it down and flipped it to the right page and hung it back up. It was perfectly blank. The strangest thing about not having a job was that it made the whole week so shapeless. I wasn't even taking a day off from anything. Suddenly emptiness spread out in front of me like a slippery ramp. Surely there was something I had to do?

Sure there was. I shook my head in horror. I'd almost

forgotten that today was the day I was supposed to pick up my altered bridesmaid's dress.

Miss Joe Nell would have had a fit if I'd forgotten.

And then I knew what I'd do tomorrow.

I'd start looking for my own house.

I detoured by the cemetery on my way to Great Day. I walked up the little hill to Jane's headstone, already in place. If Bubba Sewell could get things done that fast, perhaps he was worth voting for. Feeling stupid and sentimental, I stared at the headstone for a few seconds. This had been a dumb idea. Finally, I said, "Okay, I'm going to enjoy it."

I hadn't needed to come out to the cemetery to do this. I could've talked to Jane from anywhere. A trickle of sweat tickled my spine. "Thanks a lot," I said, hoping I didn't sound sarcastic. "But don't do me any more favors," I told the stone, and began laughing.

I got back in my car and went to pick up the bridesmaid's dress.